T0405952

CHASING
ETERNITY

ALSO BY ALYSON NOËL

Stealing Infinity
Ruling Destiny

THE BEAUTIFUL IDOLS SERIES
Unrivaled
Blacklist
Infamous

THE IMMORTALS SERIES
Evermore
Blue Moon
Shadowland
Dark Flame
Night Star
Everlasting

THE SOUL SEEKERS SERIES
Fated
Echo
Mystic
Horizon

THE RILEY BLOOM SERIES
Radiance
Shimmer
Dreamland
Whisper

STANDALONE NOVELS
Keeping Secrets

Forever Summer

Cruel Summer

Saving Zoë

Kiss & Blog

Laguna Cove

Art Geeks and Prom Queens

Faking 19

Fly Me to the Moon

ALYSON NOËL

CHASING
ETERNITY

Entangled Publishing, LLC
644 Shrewsbury Commons Ave., STE 181
Shrewsbury, PA 17361
rights@entangledpublishing.com

Entangled Teen is an imprint of Entangled Publishing, LLC.

Visit our website at www.entangledpublishing.com.

Edited by Alice Jerman and Stacy Abrams
Cover design by Bree Archer
Stock images by EduardHarkonen/GettyImages,
remuhin/Shutterstock, and paulfleet/DepositPhotos
Interior design by Britt Marczak

ISBN: 978-1-64937-193-5
Ebook ISBN: 978-1-64937-436-3

Manufactured in the United States of America

First Edition December 2024

10 9 8 7 6 5 4 3 2 1

an imprint of Entangled Publishing LLC

For Ella, Finley, Sabine, and Avalon—

May your hearts always be filled with wonder.

Time is my greatest enemy.
-Eva Peron

Fact:

All of the artwork and ancient artifacts
mentioned in this novel are real.

PROLOGUE

Braxton

GRAY WOLF ACADEMY
PRESENT DAY

I wake with a start.

Skin slick with sweat, legs caught in a tangle of sheets, the strangled cry of her name yanks me out of my dream and into the bleakness of my current reality.

Tasha—Tasha, no!

My body jolts upright, chest heaving, gasping for breath. *It was just a dream.* I try to convince myself. *Only a dream.* But the words are a lie. Because the truth is, I watched as gravity failed. Watched as Elodie leaped onto the launchpad, grabbed Tasha's hand, and a rush of wind swept them away.

And I have no idea when—or even if—they'll return.

Outside, bright bursts of lightning blister the sky, as a hard-driving rain batters my windows so violently they quake in their frames.

Tasha is gone. And none of this—nothing—has gone as planned.

I sweep a hand across the barren stretch of sheets at my side, so desperate for a piece of her, I grab the pillow she used just a few hours before and shamelessly press it to my face, trying to capture whatever whisper of scent and warmth might remain.

Fuck. Tasha—why?

Oh, but you know why, my mind taunts. *Tasha did the one thing you should've done long ago. Only you grew too comfortable. Too weak. You traded your destiny for a life of soft luxury, leaving her no choice but to act in your place.*

I silence the thought, toss the pillow aside, and close my eyes tight, allowing an image of Tasha to bloom in my mind. The way she looked on that launchpad—so beautiful, heartbreakingly so. But it was the steely determination glinting in her green eyes that shook me to my core.

And me? I was so caught up in my own indignation, my own shock and hurt, I failed to tell her how immensely proud I am to call her my girl.

Failed to tell her that she's the most courageous person I've ever known.

On my nightstand I find the letter she left me, and my gaze darts straight to the bottom of the page where she wrote those four life-changing words: *I love you, Braxton.*

Even after all that I've done, even after confessing I was there when Killian murdered her father, Natasha Antoinette Clarke. Loves. Me. Whatever fate has in store from this point on, at least I have that.

I trace a finger over the *xoxo* that precedes her name, conjuring a memory of her kiss so vivid, damn if my body doesn't immediately respond.

Tasha.

In my mind, I see her beautiful face angling toward me.

My darling Tasha.

I watch as her eyelids fall heavily, her lips softly part.

Instinctively, my hand reaches down, recalling the contour of her waist, the swell of her breasts, the heat of her legs wrapped tightly around me.

Fuck. Tasha. Where the hell did you go?

My hand begins to move. Just the mere thought of her has me so far gone, it won't take long.

But no.

My hand stills.

No. There's no time for an indulgence like this.

I grip the edge of the mattress, push away from the bed, and restlessly set about pacing my room.

According to Elodie, Arthur is away, but he'll be back in two days.

As for Killian… All I know for sure is he won't remain stuck in Renaissance Florence for long. Sooner or later he'll find his way back, and then what?

Will he rush to tell Arthur how we purposely left him behind?

Or, like Tasha believes, will he make up some kind of excuse so as not to look weak?

With Killian, it's anyone's guess.

I collapse onto my worn leather couch, grab the old boot I unearthed from my closet last night, and retrieve the small silver ball Tasha left for me to find.

The Moon.

The storm outside continues to rage, a tempest echoing the chaos inside me as I roll the ball between my forefinger and thumb. This moon, so cold and unyielding in my hand, is a stark reminder of the choices I've made, the paths I've yet to tread.

To the untrained eye, it doesn't appear to be anything special. In fact, it's exactly the sort of thing you'd expect to find at the bottom of a junk drawer.

But for Arthur, this tiny treasure represents yet another triumph in his biggest quest yet—to restore the Antikythera Mechanism, take command over time, and ultimately achieve his one true dream of remaking the world.

I huff a frustrated sigh and return the Moon to the boot. What I need is an ally. Someone I can count on.

As an opponent, Arthur is a formidable force. Not only has he created a culture where we're made to compete for his favor, but he's fostered an environment of such deep paranoia it's impossible to know whom to trust.

And while I won't claim to know the full extent of it—I'm not sure anyone does—I do know that between the slabs Arthur insists we carry around, and the surveillance equipment he's rigged everywhere, there's not much that gets past him.

Not much…and yet, some things still do.

Like the Gray Wolf witches who use the book of magick to travel back and forth between timelines.

Not to mention how, according to rumor, both Song and Anjou used the book, too.

But did they really fly under Arthur's radar?

Or did he simply not care enough to stop them?

I rake a restless hand through my hair, rise from the couch, and take another lap around my luxurious room. When I arrive at Caravaggio's portrait of Narcissus, my mind reels in reverse, remembering the day I chose it from Arthur's Vault, hoping it would serve as a reminder to stay awake, to not allow myself to be hypnotized by Arthur's world.

For a while it worked. On the outside, I appeared to play by his rules. But inside, I stayed diligent, on high alert. And yet, somewhere along the way, I let my guard down and lost sight of myself. It was only when I met Tasha that I realized I'd let the pursuit of trophies like this take precedence over everything I once cared about.

Turns out Fade doesn't just happen while Tripping. It happens here too.

Still the question remains: Where and how to begin?

I turn my focus to the items Tasha left alongside her note—a red chalk portrait sketched by the great Leonardo da Vinci himself, and the small gold pocket watch that once belonged to my father.

The same pocket watch I'd spent countless hours playing with as a kid.

I trace a finger over the crystal, then gently flip it over to study the engraving on the back. The Flower of Life — an ancient symbol that's said to contain the secrets of the universe, the workings of time and space — and a record of all living things.

The same symbol I have inked on the crook of my arm. Though much like my training, the tattoo is unfinished.

I close my fingers over the circles and bury the watch in my fist. The fact that I'm even holding this, after it's been lost for two centuries, feels like a miracle of sorts.

The watch begins to vibrate, but I'm quick to dismiss it as my mind playing tricks. The pain pills I took before bed have worn off, leaving me lightheaded and woozy.

I make for the sink, thinking I could do with a glass of water and something to eat, when the timepiece begins to shake with such force, it threatens to rocket right off my palm.

Well, bloody hell, would you look at that?

I stand in my kitchen, staring in wonder as the watch continues to judder and jolt.

Is it possible Tasha unknowingly brought me the ally I seek?

Considering how I've spent the last several years suppressing my gifts, it's no surprise that when I first shutter my eyes and squeeze the watch tight, trying to immerse myself into whatever energetic imprint my father might've left behind, not a single message arrives.

But recalling what my father used to say: *Patience, my son. Remember, the enemy of your power is haste*, I keep at it until, finally, there's a discernible rocking under the soles of my feet as the ground beneath me begins to give way.

That's it, I hear him say, as though the voice is coming from somewhere nearby and not the nineteenth century. *Remain steady, focused, calm…*

The ground continues to disintegrate, forcing me back on my heels as my stomach clenches and rolls. Still, I stay with it, dutifully following my father's instructions: *Don't look—not until you've been called.*

My eyes remain shut, steadfastly ignoring the roar of crumbling walls, the splinter of shattering windows. Even after the roof is blown off and an explosive wind swirls through my room, making my hair stand on end, I continue to wait for the sound of my name.

When it does finally come, the elation of being reunited with my father has me so choked up, I need a moment to compose myself.

It's only when the voice sounds again—calling me by my true name, the one I went by before both my parents were reduced to a memory—that I finally blink my eyes open to take in the large, cloaked figure standing before me.

My eyes search for a mane of dark wavy hair, a hard angled jaw, an intense blue gaze the same shade of navy as mine. But this man—this dark faceless *thing*—bears none of those attributes.

"Hello, James." The shadowy figure speaks in a voice that echoes resonate and deep.

Though my first instinct is to flee, I soon find my feet refuse to cooperate.

I am frozen.

Held captive in place.

Left only to stare in dismay as this shadowy being makes its way toward me.

Last thing I remember is the press of crushing dread squeezing the air from my lungs as a horrifying question blares through my head: *My God—what the hell have I summoned?*

1

Natasha
NEW YORK CITY
1998

T ripping is risky.

It's the warning that's been drilled into me from the start. A fact I've learned to accept every time I travel into the past.

Technology can fail.

Glitches happen.

Portals can close, leaving a Tripper stranded in a time and place where they do not belong.

And God forbid you inadvertently cross your own timeline, since the duality of existence results in nonexistence. It's a theory I'd never willingly put to the test.

Yet, while I've had some close calls with all those things, no Trip to the past ever had so much riding on it, or felt quite as risky, as the Trip I'm currently on.

Then again, this is no ordinary Trip.

There's much more at stake than the fear of being caught nicking jewels from drunken aristocrats, or piecing together the clues found in numerology, Christopher Columbus's map, and a handful of tarot cards to uncover some long-hidden artifact.

Aside from what Arthur might do should he discover I'm

gone—never mind the very real possibility that, after this stunt, Braxton will have good reason to never trust me again—I don't think I'm being overdramatic when I say that if this Trip doesn't go as I hope, then the state of the world—hell, the state of time itself—may never recover.

"Welcome to nineteen ninety-eight," Elodie says, the sound of her voice snapping me out of my reverie. "A time when Google is still in its infancy, *Sex and the City* premiers on cable TV, and cell phones are basically the size of bricks."

She gestures toward a guy in a suit shouting into a phone that's nearly the size of his forearm. I guess I don't respond quickly enough, because she places her hand on my shoulder, and says, "Hey there, you okay?"

Inhaling deeply, I nod. "I'm just…" I pause, collecting my thoughts. "Just trying to get my bearings." I take a quick look around, my gaze skipping along a collection of skyscrapers so tall they seem to merge with the clouds. "The city is so much bigger in person. It's a bit overwhelming," I say.

"There's a bar up ahead." Elodie points toward a red awning where a bunch of people are lingering. "What do you say we start there?"

I turn to her in disbelief. A bar? Is she serious? "I didn't come here for a pub crawl, El." I shake my head, start to head down the crowded avenue, acting like I know exactly where I'm going, when we both know I don't.

Still, what is she even doing here when she knew from the start I'd planned to Trip on my own?

All I know is one minute I was standing on the launchpad, fully convinced she was about to blast me into the past without the necessary clicker I'd need to find my way back. Then, before I can so much as blink, she's right there beside me, eyes gleaming, lips stretched into a teeth-flashing grin as though it was all just some big, grand adventure.

As though Braxton wasn't looking on, wearing an expression of shock and betrayal so deep, the image still haunts me.

"C'mon." She trots up alongside me. "It looks decent enough."

I can't help but roll my eyes as I silently fume. It's a classic Elodie move, always so eager to turn every mundane task into a party. Usually, it's harmless enough, maybe even admirable. But in this instance, it's a definite pass.

"This isn't like ditching school, El." I huff out a breath, not even trying to hide my annoyance. "This is serious. Probably the most serious thing I've ever done. I need to find my dad and, since I don't exactly need you for that, then fine. Cheers! Salut! Bottoms up! Have your drink. Whatever. All I'm asking is that you leave me to do what I need to."

Elodie's fingers circle my wrist, stopping me cold. Lashes fluttering, blue eyes widening, she says, "Are you done?" She quirks a brow, but otherwise waits like we have all the time in the world.

I roll my eyes, try to free myself from her grip, but Elodie is stronger than she looks, and she locks me in place.

"Why are you always so determined to think the worst of me?" she asks. "Less than two hours ago you promised to put the past behind us and wipe the slate clean."

I stare down at my feet, knowing she's right. And yet, ever since she pulled that stunt on the launchpad, it's like we're right back where we started—with Elodie working an agenda known only to her, and me frantically trying to second-guess the true motivation behind her every move.

"Look, El," I say, my voice competing with the New York City soundtrack of honking, shouting, and blaring police sirens. "Two days isn't as long as you think, and—"

"Just do me a favor and kindly read the date, please." Elodie plucks a copy of *The New York Times* from the kiosk beside us and waves the newspaper before me.

Is she for real? With a determined jerk of my arm, I yank myself free. "Elodie, I don't—"

"Pretty sure I said *please.*" She jiggles the paper impatiently.

I blow out a frustrated breath and squint at the small print. "Wednesday, June 3, 1998." I shrug. "Okay, so, you got the year right. Well done. Now can I please just—"

"June third." Elodie returns the newspaper to the stand and makes a theatrical display of tilting her head and tapping her chin. "Hmmm…I wonder why that date is *so* familiar?" She trains her gaze directly on mine, having already grasped what I'm just now remembering.

June third is my dad's birthday!

"How did you—" I start, but the words quickly fade. "Of course." I tilt my head to the side and study her face. "You read my file." My gaze holds hers. "Which means that first day, when you approached me at school, you already knew everything about me."

She shrugs like it's no big thing.

But it is a big thing. It gave her a massive advantage over me. Elodie had studied me, my interests, my family history. She knew exactly how to approach me, how to befriend me, how to manipulate me…and the worst part is, the same could be said of Braxton.

But like Braxton, does Elodie know the *full history* of my ancestral lineage?

Does she know that I'm a Timekeeper—the first female Timekeeper ever—and that my destiny is to stop Arthur from achieving his dream of controlling time and remaking the world?

And if so, does she also know that Braxton's a Timekeeper, too?

And, more importantly, does she realize the entire purpose of this Trip isn't just so I can reconnect with the dad who disappeared when I was eight, but so that I can convince him that I'm his future daughter—the one he won't actually father for another seven years with a woman who, at this point, he hasn't actually met—in hopes that he'll teach me the tricks of the Timekeepers' trade?

And if she is clued into all that, then what does it mean that she's insisted on tagging along?

I study Elodie's beautiful face, searching her expression for some sort of clue as to what she might be thinking beneath her flawless facade. But Elodie's a master at disguising her true feelings, so I don't get very far.

"Okay," I finally say. "It's his birthday. Not sure how that helps, but—"

Elodie smirks. "Do the math, Nat. I'll wait."

Quickly, I run the numbers in my head. "Oh. Okay, yeah," I mumble. "I get it. Today's his twenty-first birthday."

The grin she grants me is decidedly smug. "And how exactly do you think a young, single, future accountant might choose to celebrate such a milestone?"

I glance between her and the bar she's now heading toward. "But there's got to be, like, hundreds of bars in this city," I say, as the two of us weave our way through a throng of rush hour commuters. "So, how can we possibly know this is the one?"

I shoot Elodie a sideways glance, reluctant to give up my original plan to head to Columbia University, where my dad is currently an undergrad, then scour the campus until I find him. Which, I realize, is probably about as unlikely a success as hopping from bar to bar in search of a green-eyed, shaggy-haired Timekeeper, celebrating his twenty-first trip around the sun by drinking his first legal beer.

As for Elodie, she remains undeterred. She just leans closer and whispers in my ear, "Now's the part where I really need you to have a little faith for a change. After all, I did get you this far, no?"

I watch as she slides the serpent charm across the gold chain that hangs from her neck, and despite the heat and humidity of a New York City summer day, my skin is suddenly swarming with chills.

"El—" I start, but my voice quickly falters, forcing me to clear my throat and try again. "El, did—did you use magick? I mean, in addition to Arthur's technology?"

Elodie shoots me a sidelong glance. "What I used is *intent*," she says. "So, now's our chance to see if it worked."

I watch as she tilts her chin high, tosses her long blond hair over her shoulder, and strides inside the bar, much like she did the day she took me to Arcana, the underground club that turned out just to be another of Arthur's holograms.

The club that started the whole chain of events that eventually led me to Gray Wolf.

I pause before the threshold, unsure what to do. But, since we're already here, I repeat what I did back then: I bury my doubt and trail right behind her, all the while whispering to myself, "I really hope I don't live to regret this."

2

I pause in the threshold, the opening strains of "Bittersweet Symphony" blaring in the background as I pull at the hem of my T-shirt and tug up the waistband of my low-rise jeans, determined to make the two meet.

Why did I agree to wear this? Why didn't I insist on swapping outfits with Elodie? Clearly her black slip dress, white baby tee, and chunky black boots would make a much better impression on my dad than this belly-baring catastrophe.

"Quit fidgeting," Elodie snaps, shaking her head. "Sheesh, you should be grateful you're not stuck in some awful corset or one of those dreadful panniers. Besides, it's not a crime to look hot, you know."

"Looking hot was never the goal," I grumble, following her lead as she presses through the crowd, navigating this late nineties version of a Manhattan bar as easily as she navigated 1745 Versailles, 1813 London, and present day Gray Wolf Academy. Elodie is a born chameleon; she can easily blend into any environment. And I find myself wishing, once again, that I could trade all my social awkwardness for just an ounce of her confidence.

"And now..." She turns to me and winks as she sidles up to the bar, shouldering ahead of two young Wall Street types dressed in sharp navy suits, crisp white shirts, and expensive red silk ties, both vying for the bartender's notice.

At first, they're annoyed by her cutting in front of them. But when she flashes them one of her dazzling grins, they're practically begging for the chance to buy her a drink.

"Has anyone ever told you you look like a young Carolyn Bessette-Kennedy?" says the one with slick dark hair, his squinty brown eyes roving over her like a dog eyeballing a particularly juicy lamb chop.

"Never," Elodie tells him. "Although Carolyn once told me she's often mistaken for an older version of me."

And…we're off. I frown, watching as Elodie transitions into full-blown flirtation mode. This is exactly the sort of situation I'd hoped to avoid. Clearly, we both know this isn't my father. But Elodie never misses a chance to revel in being desired.

"I'm Brooks." Mr. Tall, Dark, and Smarmy grins.

Elodie extends a hand and dips her chin like we've Tripped to Regency England again. "And I'm Elodie," she says, literally batting her eyes.

"Beautiful name for a beautiful girl." When he presses his lips to the back of her hand, I have to clench my teeth to stifle a groan.

"Please, let me buy you a drink." He pulls a platinum card from his wallet and waves it in the air with a flourish, as Elodie shoots him a considering look.

"On one condition," she says, her fingers toying with her gold serpent charm.

Brooks leans in, eyes glinting, lips parting with anticipation.

"I'm going to ask you a question, but you must answer truthfully." She raises her brow. "I'll know if you're lying."

"Ah." He nods. "I know what this is about." Clearing his throat, he assumes an expression of false humility, and says, "Yes, as it turns out, I am often mistaken for JFK junior, which is why I think we go so perfectly together." He lifts his chin, rears his head back, and waits for a laugh that never arrives.

"Interesting," Elodie says, her flat expression suggesting otherwise. "But what I really need to know is what day you were born."

Brooks squints, takes a quick look at his friend, then, returning to Elodie, he says, "Is this some kind of astrology thing? Because I'm a Leo. And you know what they say about lions—they're king of the fucking jun—"

Before he can finish, Elodie's already turning away.

"Hey, what—what just happened?" Brooks glances between the back of Elodie's head and me. "What'd I do wrong?"

"She's looking for a Gemini," I say, then giving him a view of my own back, I take a quick but thorough survey of the room.

The place is packed with a young and fashionable after-work crowd, and though I sift through the sea of faces, searching for one that matches the memory I hold of my dad, so far, no one comes close.

A few moments later, Elodie reappears and hands me a martini glass filled with a bright pink liquid with a candied lime peel clinging to its side.

"A cosmo?" I blink at her. "Seriously?"

"I will not be denied my Carrie Bradshaw moment." She grins, happily clinking her own glass to mine.

"I can't believe you spent what little money we have on cocktails," I grumble.

Elodie rolls her eyes. "Why would we need money when we have the most powerful currency—our youth, good looks, and charm?"

I shake my head. "You've made way too many Trips to Regency England," I say, laughing in spite of myself. "Also, you're way more of a Samantha. Also-also—I'm not drinking this. I need a clear head when I do finally meet him. Or should I say, *if* I meet him?"

"No *ifs*." Elodie wags a scolding finger. "Seriously, Nat, it's going to happen. You just need to trust. So please, take a damn sip already. And, by the way, I can't believe I have to beg you. Do you even remember how fun you used to be?"

My body goes rigid, my fingers tense against the stem of my glass. *Do I remember?* Like I could ever forget the impulsive, reckless, earlier version of me. The girl who loved nothing more than ditching school, going to clubs, and making out with random boys. Sure, we had fun, but look where it got me.

Knowing better than to take her bait, I skate past it and say, "Look around, El—he's not here. This whole intention thing isn't working, and I'm starting to think I've made a huge mistake by taking this Trip. It was impulsive, and stupid, and…" I shake my head, knowing I'm getting worked up but unable to stop.

I mean, why did I ever think I could show up in a timeline that isn't mine, and just stumble upon my dad in a city that's said to be over six million strong? It's the worst kind of magical thinking. And what happens if we never find him, and Arthur returns early and discovers we're gone? I can't even imagine how he'll react. But one thing's for sure, it won't be good.

The thought alone is enough to set my mind reeling with all the possible repercussions and punishments Arthur could likely bestow.

He could stop all payments to my mom.

Or worse, he could send me right back to juvenile hall.

Considering how it wasn't all that long ago when I wanted nothing more than to return to my old life no matter the cost, it's funny to realize I now view it as the worst possible outcome.

The difference is, now that I know what's at stake, it's imperative I remain at Gray Wolf long enough to find a way to crush Arthur's dream.

And yet, because of this one incredibly rash decision, I've single-handedly put the fate of the entire world at ris—

Suddenly, an elbow jams into my side—a sharp, brutal blow

that instantly knocks me off balance.

My arms flail, frantically trying to regain my footing, but it's no use. My glass slips from my grasp, sending a shower of sticky, pink liquid splashing down the front of my top, before it crashes to the floor, shattering with a loud piercing sound.

"Watch it!" Elodie's voice cuts through the noise as she pushes the drunk guy out of the way and rushes to my aid.

But she's too late. My foot skids on a slick patch, and in a moment that stretches out for eternity, I find myself plummeting straight toward the floor.

"Shit!" Abandoning her own drink, Elodie drops down beside me where I've landed in a puddle of liquor. "Nat, you okay?" Her voice is laced with worry as her eyes search my face.

My gaze bleary, I shift my focus to the crowd of onlookers, their expressions a mix of derision and pity. *Great. Just. Fucking. Splendid.*

"Can you get up?" Elodie asks. "Do you need help?"

I shake my head, attempting to stand only to be met by a sharp jolt of pain as a glass shard embeds itself in my palm.

Fuck. I squeeze my eyes shut, wishing I could disappear. I mean, seriously, I'm on the floor, covered in sticky pink cocktail, with blood oozing from my palm—*could this get any worse?*

"C'mon." Elodie grabs hold of my arm, hauls me back to my feet, and presses a cocktail napkin to the small wound, trying to sop up the mess.

It's only then that I notice just how badly my hands are shaking.

"I'm okay," I say, quickly pulling away. "I'm fine. Really," I insist, all too aware that I'm anything but.

My body is trembling.

My ears are vibrating with the erratic rush of my pulse, as the furious beat of my heart threatens to jackhammer a hole through my ribs.

And when my lungs freeze up, depriving me of breath, I instinctively squeeze my eyes shut, desperately hoping to fend off a full-blown panic attack, even though all the signs tell me I'm already there.

Oh no. Oh please, not here. Not now. This can't be happening.

Oh, but it is. Despite my resistance, I'm spiraling so fast there's no way to slam the brakes on this thing.

"Nat?" Elodie says. "Just hang on, okay? I'm going to get us out of here."

"Yeah, okay," I manage to mumble. But beneath the surface, all I can hear is the relentless chant: *I'm not okay. I'm not okay. I'm not…*

My body bumps against hers as she slips an arm around my waist, guiding me through the crowded space. "Would you look at that," I hear her say, though her words are distant, like echoes from a faraway place. "We finally Trip to a time with flushing toilets, only to find the line for the bathroom so long, I miss the days of chamber pots."

When she laughs, the sound is bright and melodic. And though I appreciate the gesture, knowing she's only trying to lighten the moment, I'm afraid any attempt to join in will only further set this thing off.

This has nothing to do with your dad or this Trip, I remind myself as I shuffle along. *This is about the duke and what happened in Versailles. But you survived. No, even better, you thrived. And the duke is stuck in a long-ago past you will never revisit. You are safe. You are strong. You can—*

"Nat—" Elodie's hand rubs a soothing circle over my back. "Try to breathe. Nice and easy, can you do that?"

I nod, struggling to fill my lungs with air and holding it for a moment before letting it out. After the fourth round, I'm starting to feel almost centered again.

"I'm—I'll be okay," I say, keeping my head bowed, so Elodie

can't see the way my cheeks burn with shame. "I just need a minute," I lie, well aware that it'll take a lot more than that. Ever since my encounter with the duke, panic attacks have become a semi-regular occurrence, whenever I feel threatened, confined, overwhelmed, or unsafe.

"Take your time," Elodie says. "There's no rush."

When my breath finally returns to a more regular rhythm, I lift my chin, tuck my hair behind my ears, and take a sweeping look around this new space. Surprisingly, Elodie hasn't led me back onto the busy street like I initially thought. Instead, we're on a small patio tucked away from the chaos of the crowded bar.

"Thanks," I say, tentatively meeting her gaze. "It's just, sometimes I—"

"No need to explain." Elodie holds up a hand, stopping my words. "I recognize the signs. And just so you know, you're hardly alone. I don't know a single Blue who hasn't experienced a dicey situation that continues to haunt them from time to time. Believe me, I've had my share."

I stare at her in astonishment. Elodie isn't usually one for showing weakness or sharing stories that place her in a less-than-confident light. "But you're always so sure of yourself. Always in full control of every room you walk into."

"Well...clearly not *every* room." Her shoulders lift in a nonchalant shrug, but she offers no more. And though my curiosity is piqued, I know better than to push.

A moment of silence wedges between us, with Elodie gazing down at her chunky black boots, as though weighing just how much to reveal.

"There's a reason we Blues call it Tripping," she finally says, her bright blue gaze fixing on mine. "Because it can truly mess with your head."

"So how'd you get past it?" I ask, eager for any tips she might offer.

"Time." She nervously scratches her arm. "And lots of visits to Dr. Lucy."

My eyes graze over this gorgeous, poised girl as though I'm seeing her through a new lens. With her tall, willowy frame, shiny blond hair, and heartbreaker face, at first glance, she appears to have everything going for her. And in a way, that's still true. But, for the first time ever, I detect a shadow of sadness lurking within.

Knowing a window's been cracked, and that it probably won't stay open for long, I summon the courage to ask, "El, don't you ever…" I pause, gnawing the inside of my cheek as I search for just the right word. "Well, I guess what I want to know is, don't you ever get mad or resentful toward Arthur for putting us in these dangerous situations just so he can add to his collection of fine art and jewels?"

I freeze as I wait for her reply, worried I might have crossed a line. Elodie's fiercely devoted to Arthur, and she's told me multiple times that she thinks of him as a father.

Surprisingly, she just shrugs. "I guess I always figured it's a small price to pay after everything he's done for me," she says, her voice quiet, face pensive.

"You mean like, saving you from the children's home?" I ask, holding my breath as I wait for her to respond.

Elodie sighs. "You say that like it's nothing, but you have no idea how truly Dickensian it was. If Arthur hadn't stepped in when he did, I wouldn't be standing here today. And I don't mean here, with you, in New York City. I mean I never would've made it past my tenth birthday."

As I continue to study her, I can't help but wonder if, like Braxton and Killian, Elodie is also not from my timeline.

Before I can ask, she says, "Now, my turn to ask you a question."

I give a tentative nod, braced for just about anything,

as I watch her long lashes flutter and her lips curve into a mischievous grin.

Glancing past my shoulder, she says, "How come you never mentioned that your dad is so smokin'?"

I squint, trying to decipher her words.

"Between the tousled hair you just want to run your fingers through, that piercing green gaze, and the sexy, intellectual vibe, not to mention the way he fills out those jeans...I could easily forget about Jago. Nash too, for that matter."

I follow her gaze to the back wall, over to where a man with wavy brown hair, wearing faded jeans and a light blue button-down shirt, is surrounded by friends, casually sipping a beer.

In an instant, my jaw falls slack, my tongue sticks to the roof of my mouth, as a kaleidoscope of butterflies takes flight in my chest.

It's him. Ohmigod-Ohmigod-Ohmigod—it's really, truly him!

I gape at the sight, aware that I'm staring, but unable to stop. He's a lot younger than I remember. His hair is darker, devoid of a single hint of gray, and the fine lines that will later spread like wings around his eyes have yet to appear. Yet, all the familiar mannerisms are there.

The way he stands with one hand hooked into his pocket as he rocks on his heels.

The way he tosses his head back when he breaks into a belly laugh.

The way he pinches his lips together in the same way I do.

The dad I haven't seen in a decade—the man who was murdered by Killian's hand—is now here, in the back patio of this random New York City bar, celebrating his twenty-first birthday, just a handful of steps from where I now stand.

This is exactly the moment I'd hoped for.

The very reason I put everything at risk by choosing to embark on this Trip.

And yet, now that the moment has come—now that he's well within reach—I find that I'm frozen, numb, completely immobilized, unable to do anything more than gawk at the sight.

"I mean, it is him, right?" Elodie shoots me a tentative look, but all I can do is silently nod in return.

I should've come up with a plan. I mean, even if I could manage to make it across the room, even if I could get my tongue unstuck enough to form actual words, what the hell would I even say?

What's the correct way to approach the parent you once shared such a strong bond with, but who doesn't even know you exist because your conception is still seven years away?

"Honestly, Nat..." Elodie goes on, but her voice is like white noise in my ear.

My dad is here. I found him. Well, to be fair, Elodie found him. But still—he's right over there!

"...acting weird, and if you're not going to carpe diem, then I guess you leave me no choice but to—"

Wait—what?

I tear my eyes away from my dad just in time to see Elodie fluffing her hair and running her tongue across her front teeth. "Just think." She grins brightly. "If I play this right, then maybe I'll end up being your mommy."

Then, before I can stop her, she's headed straight for my dad, leaving me stunned in her wake.

3

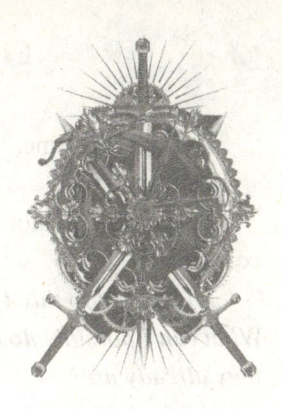

O h, no.
No-no-no-no-no-no-no!

I race to stop her, but Elodie got a head start, so I'm literally three steps away from my dad when she's already standing before him.

"I don't mean to bother you," she says. "But I wanted to wish you a happy birthday."

I grind to a stop just beside her, holding my breath as I watch Elodie shoot my dad the sort of smoldering look that could easily set the whole city on fire.

I should've known she wasn't joking about being my mom. If he flirts back, I honestly don't know how I'll react.

My dad squints, shifts his weight between his feet. "You sure you're old enough to be here?" he asks, causing me to exhale with relief as one of his friends barks out a laugh.

"Sure looks that way." Elodie grins. "I mean, seeing as how I'm standing here with you, holding a drink in my hand."

At first, I'm confused. Having abandoned her drink back in the bar, both her hands are currently empty. But then I watch in shock as she seizes my dad's beer from his grasp, tilts it to her lips, and takes a long, thirsty swig, all the while her eyes never once leaving his.

In any other time, on any other Trip, I might admire how brazen she is.

But not this time.

Not this Trip.

And definitely not when she's targeted my dad as her next conquest.

I have to stop this. I have to intervene in some way. But how? What can I possibly do or say that won't make things worse than they already are?

"And what about you?" Elodie asks. "Twenty-one for less than a day, and you're already here." She lifts the bottle of beer, about to take another sip, when my dad gently takes it from her and sets it on a table that's noticeably out of her reach.

"How'd you know it's his birthday?" asks one of his friends, a guy with red hair and a spattering of freckles across his nose and cheeks.

Elodie turns to him, grinning as though she's delighted by the question. As for me, my belly is churning with anxiety. There's no telling what she might say.

"And you are?" she asks, squinting at him.

"I'm Mark," he says.

Elodie nods. "Well, Mark, my name's Elodie," she says, "Elodie Blue, and, as it turns out, I'm psychic."

Mark laughs, and my dad looks on with a healthy dose of skepticism, as though he's not quite sure what to make of the Elodie Blue Show.

"Psychic?" Mark repeats, his eyes narrowing with disbelief.

Elodie nods, like it's no big thing.

"So, psychic," another friend says, this one with wavy black hair and suntanned skin, "can you tell us what the future holds for the birthday boy, here?"

It's all the encouragement she needs. But while Elodie is completely lit up, there's no way I can let her go through with this.

"Elodie—" I start, desperate to stop this before it turns into a full-blown derailment. But Elodie is on a roll, the spotlight is hers, and she will not be deterred.

"May I?" Ignoring me, she gestures toward my dad's hand, and with notable, if not reassuring reluctance, he agrees to play along. "Now, let's see…" She traces a light finger over the lines of his palm. "You're a student at Columbia University, am I right?"

Mark slaps my dad on the back, but my dad merely nods in return.

"And you have a real aptitude for numbers." She presses her index finger against a soft, curving line, as though she gleaned the information from there, as opposed to the file of my family history that she pretty much memorized. "You're considering a career as an accountant, mainly because it seems stable enough. But you're also a bit of an adventurer at heart, so you worry about getting stuck in one place for too long."

She looks to him for confirmation, only to find my dad's brow is furrowed, his lips pressing into a thin, grim line.

Elodie goes on about a possible move to California, followed by marriage, and kids, or rather, *a kid*. "Just the one, and most likely, a girl." She draws a finger over a short line at the side of his hand. Then finally, mercifully, releasing him, she adds, "You know what's weird, though? You look like you could be related to my friend Natasha, here. Your eyes are the same shade of green. Same shape, too. Is it possible you're family? Distant cousins, long-lost siblings separated at birth?"

All eyes pivot my way, as if they've just now become aware of my existence. And though I'm used to being eclipsed by Elodie, when my dad shifts his focus to me, and his gaze locks onto mine, it's like all the oxygen is sucked out of the room, and I find myself longing for the comfort of being invisible again.

But that's only because I'm afraid of what happens next. There's so much riding on this moment—not just for me, but for time itself. And though I've rehearsed this reunion in my head a thousand times since I first dreamed up the plan, I guess I always fast-forwarded to the part where we we're both hugging and crying, so overcome with emotion for all that we've lost, and all that we still stand to gain, in the brief time we have left.

What I failed to imagine was everything that would happen leading up to that point. Especially the most important part when I break the news—*Surprise! I'm your daughter from the future!*—which I know I can't exactly say, but I'm so nervous, there's no telling what might pop out of my mouth.

From some distant place, I vaguely register one of my dad's friends saying, "Wow. The resemblance truly is…uncanny."

But in the liminal space I currently occupy, it feels like the world around me has gone dark, leaving only a single point of light that encompasses both me and my dad.

Tell him. Seize the moment, and do it, already. There is literally no time to waste!

I continue to gaze at my dad, wishing there was some way to convey it all with a look, since I've failed to come up with the appropriate words.

The silence is broken by the sound of Elodie clearing her throat, making me realize just how weirdly uncomfortable this probably is for everyone else.

Though I also know that, in her own, also weirdly uncomfortable way, Elodie has unlocked the door, and now it's on me to kick it wide open and get what I came for.

And yet, I can't exactly tell him with everyone watching. I need to find a way to get him alone, go someplace quiet where the two of us can talk. And then I'll—

"Natasha?"

The sound of my dad saying my name is enough to send a ripple of shivers skipping like stones down the length of my spine.

It's been ten long years since I heard his voice.

Ten long years since he was the single most important person in my world.

"You're bleeding." He gestures toward the arm I'd been unconsciously rubbing that's now streaked with red.

Between that, the pink stain trailing down the front of my shirt, and my belly button and hip bones on full display, what a stellar first impression I must make.

"Oh, um…" I swallow hard, forcing myself to play it cool. "It's nothing. Just…not a big deal."

"May I take a look?" he asks.

With my heart hammering wildly, I bite down on my lip and offer my hand, half expecting him to distract me with a song or a story as he tends to the wound, just like he did when I was a kid.

"You should get this cleaned up," he says, eyes narrowed as though weighing this strange situation he finds himself in. "You don't want it to get infected."

I swallow hard, sneak a quick peek at Elodie who's now reading Mark's palm, advising him to buy stock in Google, Apple, and a little start-up called Netflix, then I return to my dad.

"Um, yeah." I shrug. "We don't want that." I try to laugh, but my throat is so raw, it comes out sounding like a record scratch.

"It really is remarkable." His gaze lingers on me, contemplative and intense. "There's something so familiar about you. Something that goes beyond the eyes."

I bite my bottom lip so hard I wouldn't be surprised if I start bleeding there, too.

"Maybe we are related." He laughs nervously. "What's your last name?"

I take a deep breath, and with my voice lowered to nearly a whisper, I say, "Clarke. My name is Natasha Antoinette Clarke."

Then I wait, taking note of the sharp intake of breath, the way his eyes widen and his jaw slackens. This is my chance, the only one I may get, so I clear my throat and continue. "And, I hope this doesn't seem weird, but if we could go someplace more…" I take a quick look around. "Well, someplace more private, there's something important I need to tell you."

I pause, anxious to hear what he'll say. Only my dad doesn't immediately respond like I hoped. He doesn't spring into action and whisk me away.

Instead, he remains frozen in place, staring at me like he's just seen a ghost. Which I totally get, because I feel the same way.

"What's this about?" he finally says, his voice a mix of the same sort of anticipation and dread I currently feel.

"It's about…" I hesitate, aware of the weight of everything still unsaid pressing against me, urging me to share the truth before it's too late and the moment has passed.

It's about dropping a bombshell—a startling revelation that transcends time itself.

It's about the Antikythera Mechanism getting dangerously close to being restored.

It's about Arthur Blackstone's plans to control time and remake the world.

It's about your premature death, and how I need you to teach me everything you never had a chance to…

"Natasha," my dad breathes, his voice slicing through the charged air like a finely tuned blade.

I take another look at Elodie to see she's now predicting the other guy's future. Still, knowing I can't risk being overheard, I press a finger to the wound on my palm. Then, using my own blood and the tip of my fingernail, I set about drawing a series of crude, interlocking circles meant to represent the flower of life, on the crook of my forearm.

As I complete the final arc, I chance a look at my dad just in time to see him blink, once, twice. When his eyes reconnect with mine, there's a shared understanding that goes beyond spoken words.

"It's about…" I stall, aware of the world, once again, whittling down to just him and me. Then, sensing it's now or never, I lean closer and whisper, "It's about…a family lineage thing."

The words pulse between us. The air tightens with the weight of my words.

"My God," he breathes, his gaze drinking me in as though he's not sure if I'm real. "Are you—" He shakes his head. "Is this—"

My eyes fill with tears. "It's real," I say, choking down a sob that leaves my throat tender and burning. "It's really happening. It's not an Unraveling."

He nods quickly, but the uncertain glint in his eyes reveals he's still trying to process, wrap his head around it, make sense of the completely inexplicable situation I've put us both in.

If I weren't the one who traveled back nearly three decades in time, I'm sure I'd feel the same way.

"And the thing is," I continue, voice steady but urgent, knowing that this, most of all, is what needs to be said. "I'm here because…" I inhale a breath, and on the exhale, I say, "Well, Dad, I'm in desperate need of your help."

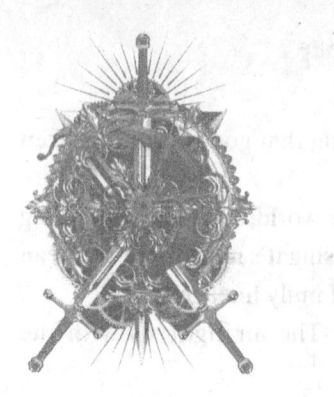

4

"*D*ad."

I actually called him Dad.

I mean, of course that's who he is. But still, considering how I won't be born for another seven years, it must have been pretty shocking to hear.

And yet, it's out there now, and there's no reeling it back. So all that's left is to wait. Wait for my dad to respond. To say something. Do something. Anything that might give me some clue as to what he might be thinking about me and the startling truth I revealed.

But he just stands there, his jaw locked tight, a flicker of something unreadable crossing his eyes — confusion, fear, maybe a reluctant spark of recognition? All I know for sure is he's taking me in, scrutinizing every inch, and with each passing second, the wall of silence between us continues to build.

I never should've pushed the reveal. I should've waited until I could get him alone before I dropped that bombshell.

The quiet is unbearable. Just when I'm sure I can't take another second, my dad shakes his head as though awakening from a trance. Sliding an arm around my shoulders, he announces to his friends, "Natasha injured her hand. We're going to swing by my apartment to get her cleaned up."

His friends turn in surprise, shooting me an appraising look that makes me feel so gross, I have to fight every impulse to explain how this is not at all what they think.

"You'll be okay?" I ask Elodie, feeling weird, and a little guilty, about leaving her alone with the two guys we just met.

"Please." She rolls her eyes with her usual bravado. "When am I not okay?" And just like that, she returns to her admiring audience again.

The journey to my dad's apartment is a blur of bumper-to-bumper traffic and bustling city streets—a world that's seamlessly, obliviously, transitioning from day to night, as though nothing out of the ordinary has happened. As though two girls haven't just landed here from nearly thirty years in the future.

When we finally arrive, and are tucked away safely inside, my dad nervously rubs his hands together and says, "Okay, first things first. Let's have a look at that wound."

I follow him into a small, tidy bathroom, where he cleanses and bandages my hand the same way he did back when I was a kid, minus the storytelling and song, of course. Once he's finished, he reaches for the cabinet to return the roll of gauze and antiseptic spray, but the bottle slips from his grasp and clatters to the floor, and we instinctively stoop to retrieve it.

"I got it!" we both say, our heads colliding with the sort of cartoonish thud that makes me burst out laughing. When my gaze meets his, I catch a glimmer of surprise in his eyes before he joins in.

It's been ages since the two of us laughed. And though I know he has no memory of any of the fun times we once shared, I can't help but wonder if he can sense how layered this is—a burst of amusement floating on the surface, while just beneath lies a tremor of sadness born of a thousand what-ifs.

This is exactly the sort of clumsy, awkward, ordinary moment I've missed.

As my laughter fades into a sigh, the absurdity of it all settles on my shoulders like a bittersweet cloak. Still, as hard as this is for me, I imagine it's even more heightened for him.

"I promise to explain everything," I say. "Or at least, I'll try. But first, can I borrow a T-shirt? I don't normally dress like this, and..." My voice fades when I realize how ridiculous this must seem. He's an undergrad student with zero paternal instincts. It's not like he's going to give me a time-out for wearing a midriff top and low-rise jeans.

Still, he nods, roots around in a drawer, then tosses me a gray Columbia University T-shirt that's far too big for my frame, but I instantly love it anyway.

After I'm changed, he pours us each a tall glass of water and we settle onto an old slip-covered couch, where, without further delay, he says, "Look, for the record, I believe you. Which is probably the biggest hurdle of all."

Well, that's a relief. I take a grateful sip of my water and sink deeper into the cushions.

"And yet—" He scrunches his nose, props his foot on one knee, and fidgets with the frayed hem of his jeans. "Well, I guess the part I'm struggling with is *how*? How did this happen? How is this possible? What year did you say you traveled from?"

I place my glass on the coffee table before me. "The year twenty twenty-four," I say.

My dad balks at the news.

"And, just so you know, there are no flying cars." My face curves into a grin, trying to insert a little levity into this strange situation we find ourselves in. "Though that's not to say there aren't people who are actively working on it."

"And time travel?" he says. "Is this part of the future?"

I shake my head. "Only those of us at Gray Wolf Academy know that it's possible."

"Gray Wolf," my dad repeats. "As in antimony, or Lupus Mettallorum—the wolf of metals that purifies gold?"

I shrug. "So I'm told."

"The gray wolf is the penultimate stage in the making of the philosopher's stone." He speaks with a sort of hushed wonder. "So, is this an academy for alchemists?" His eyes narrow.

"In a way," I say, aware that I'm being ridiculously vague. Then again, this is not what I came for. I need answers. I need help. And yet, I also know that at the very least, I owe him some of the basics for how this all came to be.

"I'm a student there," I press on, swallowing the knot of frustration building deep in my throat. "Though, to be clear, it's not the usual curriculum. And while I have every intention of answering all your questions, or at least I'll try, first, I want you to know this is weird for me, too. I guess the difference is I already know you. I spent the first eight years of my life with you. I was your favorite girl, and you were my hero dad, and yet, even though we're together now, I realize I'm a total stranger in your eyes."

"But that's just it." He swipes a hand through his hair and casts a nervous glance around the small space.

I follow his gaze from the Formica-topped table and its four random chairs, the short hallway with a door on either side that I assume leads to bedrooms, the worn, braided rug stretched across the scuffed wood floor, and the towering piles of books that, along with the massive CD collection, cover nearly every flat surface.

"That's what makes this so strange." He returns his focus to me. "There's an undeniable familiarity. Maybe it's because I can see Natasha in you." His expression softens as he releases a long, wistful sigh.

"My great-grandmother." I nod. "You told me you were her favorite," I add, feeling the need to prove that I really am legit, that I remember most, if not all, of his stories.

"I always thought that if I did have a daughter, I'd give her that name." His mouth tugs up at the corners, though there's an undeniable sadness that shadows his gaze. "And apparently, I did."

"And yet, you didn't actually want kids," I say, then proceed to tell him about a particularly painful Unraveling where I stood on the sidelines, playing witness to my dad's look of distress after my mom showed him her positive pregnancy test.

I'm not entirely sure why I tell him that. I mean, out of all the things I could've shared, it seems like the absolute worst choice I could possibly make.

Then again, it was only yesterday when I saw the energetic message he left for me in the Sun. And now that he's sitting right here beside me, I really need his assurance that it wasn't at all like I thought.

Briefly, he shutters his eyes. When he opens them, he says, "Since that moment is still several years away, I can't exactly defend myself. But whatever you saw, I'm sure it had nothing to do with you not being wanted, and everything to do with my anguish over the burden I'd unwittingly pass on to you."

"And by burden, you mean the whole Timekeeper thing?"

He frowns, pinches the bridge of his nose. "It's this damned lineage and all that comes with it." He shakes his head. "Look, I admit, I've probably had it easier than most. Still, between the Unravelings, the training, the responsibility, and the secrets—it's a lot." His shoulders slump with the weight of all that's been required of him—all that's now required of me. "People like us don't get to move through the world with the same blissful ignorance as everyone else." His gaze lands on mine. "A normal life is off the menu for us. Still, I guess I thought…" He pauses, takes a quick breath, then goes on. "Well, I thought that by refusing to have kids I could spare future generations from living like I do."

"And exactly how do you live?" I gesture around the small, neat space. "It looks pretty normal to me."

He smiles at that. But it's not the sort of carefree grin you might expect. Instead, it's a smile weighted by melancholy, causing the corners of his mouth to turn up in a reluctant arc, his eyes flickering with a silent acknowledgment of the complex situation we find ourselves in.

"A lot of work goes into making it seem that way," he says. "But tell me, Natasha, while we're on the subject — are you happy?"

The question takes me aback, and I'm not entirely sure how to reply.

Am I happy?

One year ago, I would've answered with an unequivocal *no*. But so much has changed since then. My circumstances for one, obviously. But, more importantly, I've grown in ways I never could've imagined.

My dad is watching, waiting for me to respond.

"Am I happy?" I say, buying another moment to think. I'm about to say something vague like: *Sometimes, or at least, most the time, yes.*

Or: *Is anyone really happy?*

Or even: *Well, I'm happy right now, sitting here with you.*

But then I remember something Arthur once said, something important I still can't shake. So, I offer that up instead.

"Someone recently told me that we're always writing our own stories — all day, every day. That it's the ones we play on repeat that determine our destiny." I sneak a peek at my dad, seeing his gaze narrow with interest. "He also said that we alone are the alchemist of the reality we create. So, I guess that means whatever state of happiness, or unhappiness, I might claim, it all depends on whatever story I've decided to tell myself, about myself."

"Sounds a lot like Amor Fati," my dad says, his gaze locked on mine.

"That's exactly what I said to him." I grin.

"And who is it who told you this?" my dad asks, brow creased with interest.

My fingers nervously pick at a small tear near the hem of the borrowed T-shirt. "Arthur Blackstone," I say, then I wait. Wait and watch. Looking for some sort of sign, a glimmer of recognition in my dad's eyes.

But it seems the name means nothing to him. My dad merely says, "Well, this Arthur Blackstone sounds like a very wise man."

"He is," I agree, an unmistakable gravity creeping into my voice. "And he's much more than that. He's also extremely rich, incredibly powerful, a curator of sorts—"

"Is he a mentor of yours?"

I give a thoughtful nod. "He's taught me a lot. Saved me from my worst instincts. And…yeah, he's helped me in innumerable ways. But, as it turns out, he's also my worst enemy."

I lean deeper into the cushions, noting the array of complex emotions that play across my dad's face.

"So, I take it he's not a Timekeeper?" My dad's eyes stay fixed on mine.

I let out a heavy sigh, my head slowly shaking as I grapple with the urgency of the words still to come. "He's pretty much the antithesis of everything we stand for. And that's why I'm here," I say, voice tinged with determination. "I need you to teach me all that you can, arm me with all the necessary skills, whatever it takes to stop Arthur from seizing control of time and remaking the world."

Once again, we find ourselves enveloped in a weighted silence, my words lingering heavily between us. My dad, lost in contemplation, turns the glass in his hand, its contents catching the light in a dance of reflections.

Beside him, I sit, silently urging him to understand the gravity of everything I just said, my hope hanging in the balance as I await his response.

Finally, with a notable shake in his voice, he says, "So, the fact that you've traveled all this way must mean that I..." His voice trails off, but his gaze remains fixed on mine, as though asking me to confirm the very worst.

But how can I?

How am I supposed to tell him about the day he left home and never returned?

How am I supposed to tell him how, because of it, my once vibrant mother, strained by her new role as a single mom trying to make ends meet on a meager income, slowly faded away like a photograph left out in the sun?

How am I supposed to explain that I spent the following years filled with such anger and resentment toward him, I devoted myself to scrubbing my mind of his memory, only to have it all come flooding right back the moment I entered Arcana?

What are the right words to explain to someone—on their twenty-first birthday, no less—that in fewer than two decades from now they'll be murdered in an ancient necropolis in 1741 France?

Though I should've expected a conversation like this, chalk it up to yet one more thing I failed to rehearse.

My dad must read the distress on my face because he's quick to lift a hand and wave it away. "It's okay. Really," he says, his expression grave, but his voice is resigned to a fate that was never his to control. And I'm stunned by his effort to comfort me when it's me who should be comforting him. "Now," he goes on, scrubbing a hand over his face and leaning closer to me. "Why don't you tell me more about this Arthur Black—"

At the sound of muffled voices coming from the other side of the door, and the soft, mechanical whisper of a key sliding into a lock, my dad's voice fades as his gaze darts past me and zeroes in on the entry.

"It's my roommate, Mark," he says, his expression morphing into one of concern. "We can't talk here. I need you to come with me—quickly!"

The definitive clunk of the dead bolt retreating seems to echo through the small space, and before I can ask, my dad's already leaping from the couch, grabbing hold of my hand, and pulling me out of the small living space and down the short hall.

"In here," he whispers, ushering me inside the room just as the front door bangs open and Mark calls out, "Honey, we're home!" followed by the unmistakable sound of Elodie's laugh.

I look at my dad, eyes wide with alarm. But he just moves toward the overflowing bookshelf that sits against the far wall.

Then, with a deliberate tweak of one of the books, the entire unit swings open, revealing a dim, narrow passageway that beckons from beyond.

"What is this place?" I whisper, watching as a complex tapestry of emotions flits across my dad's face.

"Come," he says quietly, urging me to follow.

With my pulse quickening and my heart pounding with anticipation, I shadow him into the dark.

Do you believe then that the sciences would have arisen and grown if the sorcerers, alchemists, astrologers, and witches had not been their forerunners?
-Nietzsche

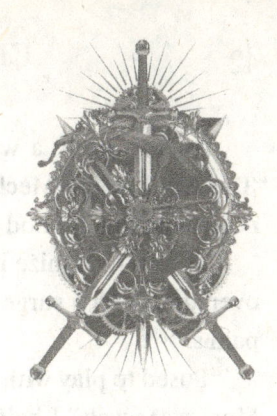

5

My heart races as we plunge into the shadowy corridor, the comforting light from the room fading behind us as the sounds of Elodie and Mark calling to us from the apartment recede into silence.

"Where are we?" I ask, my voice shaky as I squint into the dark, rubbing my hands briskly over my arms. The chill in the air is seeping straight into my bones. "What exactly is this place?"

"Think of it as a sort of sanctuary where we won't be disturbed."

My dad strikes a match, releasing a sharp tang of sulfur that pierces the stale, musty air. When he goes about lighting a series of candles, I can't help but notice the way the flickering flames cast eerie, dancing shadows across the room.

From a basket, he retrieves a soft wool throw and tosses it to me. As I wrap it around my shoulders, he says, "This place is safe, known only to me, a handful of other Timekeepers"—his eyes latch onto mine—"and now you."

My curiosity piqued, my eyes drink in the sight of exposed brick walls and floor to ceiling shelves overflowing with arcane tomes, aged scrolls, and a myriad of mystical artifacts that practically hum with ancient secrets.

My dad turns his attention to an ornate chest. His hands, I notice, tremble slightly as he opens it to retrieve a complex ancient relic.

In an instant, a wave of recognition floods through me. "The Antikythera Mechanism," I whisper, voice thick with the nostalgia of childhood memories.

"So you recognize it?" He hands it to me, and I'm instantly overcome with a surge of emotion as I cradle the object in my palms.

"I used to play with this as a kid," I tell him. "But only when Mom was away." I half grin at the memory, though honestly, I could just as easily cry. As I steal a glance his way, I'm struck by the surreal nature of this entire situation, and I know I need to acknowledge how weird this must make him feel. "What's it like," I venture, my voice tentative, "to hear me talk about shared memories that are still in the future for you?"

He smiles wryly, rubbing a nervous hand along his jawline. "Strange," he says. "Though the very fact that you're here tells me how badly I must've failed." The grin slips away, instantly eclipsed by a long, dark shadow that crosses his face.

"Failed?" I squint, wondering what it is that he's getting at.

He shifts uncomfortably. "You mentioned something earlier about me being part of your first eight years. Which leads me to assume I wasn't around after that."

I inhale a quick breath. "Oh. Yeah," I mumble, pretending to inspect the ancient reproduction, turning it around and around in my hands to avoid looking directly at him. This is the part I was dreading the most.

"It's okay," my dad says. "Really. Life as a Timekeeper prepares you for this sort of thing."

I glance up to see him nodding, trying to convince me. Still, I hesitate. What happened to him is far from okay. I don't think I'll ever make peace with it, so how could he?

"How much do you want to know?" I ask, deciding it's better to let him set the limits.

"Whatever you're comfortable sharing." His shoulders

lift in an obvious effort to appear nonchalant, when I get the impression that, like me, he's feeling anything but.

"Okay…" I start, hesitant to go on, "here's the thing—while it's true that our time together was brief, the thing is, Dad—" I freeze, aware of what I just said. "Um, is it all right if I call you that?"

His lips curve into a grin. "I'm getting used to the idea," he says, as I fight with all my might to hold back the sudden threat of tears.

"So," I continue, "if you really want to know what happened, or rather, what will happen, I'll tell you. But I am on a bit of a time crunch. If I'm not back in two days when Arthur returns, I'm pretty sure there'll be hell to pay."

My dad pauses for a handful of beats. Coming to a decision, he says, "Give me the short version."

Taking the Antikythera from me, he sets it on a nearby table, then directs me to an overstuffed chair while he drops onto a velvet floor cushion. Once we're settled, I pull the wool throw tighter around me and proceed to catch him up on everything that happened over the last ten years.

Through it all, my dad doesn't breathe a word. He just listens intently, his expression veering from stricken, to heartbroken, to angry, only to circle right back again.

When I finish, he says, "He who controls time, controls the world. This is what Arthur Blackstone has planned?"

"Yes," I say. "But exactly how he plans to control the world— what that might look like—is a mystery."

My dad leans back, pondering. "From what you've told me, Arthur sees himself as a curator of beauty and art. And he despises the results of the very technology that built his fortune."

I nod. It's all true. "He claims that, unlike the Timekeepers, he believes humanity has a right to know the true workings of time. But everything he does contradicts that. He steals great works of art because he thinks people have lost the right to appreciate them. He's a control freak like you've never seen. On the surface, Gray Wolf is an amazing place, but he runs it with an iron fist—constant surveillance, strict rules. Oh, and we're not allowed to leave unless he sends us out on a Trip."

My dad's eyes narrow, the tension in the room thickening. "Sounds like he's building a prison under the guise of a sanctuary."

"Exactly," I say, my voice trembling with the weight of the truth. "And if the way he runs Gray Wolf is any indication, it's a glimpse into how he plans to reshape the world."

"The name alone says it all." My dad stares into the distance.

"What do you mean?" I ask.

"Well, like I said, it's the penultimate stage in making the philosopher's stone. It makes me think Arthur views this academy as the final step to achieving his ultimate goal."

I nod. "By restoring the Antikythera Mechanism, yes."

"But to what end? Aside from controlling time, what else does he want? Is it immortality he's after, by inserting himself and his influence into a vast selection of timelines?"

I shrug, wishing I had an answer.

"Tell me," my dad says, "how many more pieces are left to find?"

"So far, I've brought him the Sun and the Moon, which means there's still quite a long way to go."

"Well, that's a relief," my dad says. "At least it gives you time to hone your skills and stop him before it's too late."

My fingers instinctively reach for my talisman, swinging the small golden charm back and forth on its chain.

My dad immediately takes notice. Narrowing his eyes, he asks, "What is that?"

I gaze down at the tiny lapis moon, and the diamond-encrusted star nestled inside the small gold cage. "Braxton gave it to me. All of us Trippers carry some kind of talisman," I say, going on to explain about the dangers of Fade and how wearing this reminder keeps me grounded, centered, never losing sight of my real identity, my true time and place.

My dad's eyes light up, a flicker of a new idea taking shape. "And if I were to ask you to remove it?"

"No," I say, slowly shaking my head as my belly clenches with dread. "I can't do that."

My dad's gaze deepens, and though I try to read his expression, his emotions are locked into neutral. "Then let me ask you this," he says. "You came here to learn, right?"

I squirm, a restless energy coursing through me as I nervously shift in my seat, crossing and uncrossing my legs, as the repeated warnings about never removing my talisman ricochet in my brain.

"Last time I was without it, things got pretty…dark." I cringe as an image of the duke's hateful, leering face blooms large in my head. The idea of deliberately making myself that vulnerable again is totally nonnegotiable.

"I understand," my dad says, pulling me away from my thoughts. "But let me ask you this: what matters more—who you are now, or who you'll be when you return to Gray Wolf?"

I'm struck silent. The answer is obvious. Yet I find myself reluctant to cross that particular line.

"If you truly want to claim complete mastery over your skills and your fears, you can't rely on things like talismans and charms. You need to learn to rely solely on yourself."

It makes sense, but that doesn't stop me from shaking my head even more firmly this time.

"You said the last time you were without it, things got dark." He waits for me to reply, but I just give a slight nod, nervous about where this is going. "And what if that happens again and you're not—"

"It won't," I cut in, unwilling to discuss it. "There's no way

I'll ever let that happen again."

His eyes narrow on mine. "Does that mean you let it happen last time?"

I close my eyes, reminding myself that I came here to learn, even if it means being pushed well outside my comfort zone. When I open them again, I set my focus on him. "No," I admit. "Last time, I lost it, and…" My voice trails off, I give a brisk wave of my hand. The details are hardly important.

"Natasha," he starts, "I know this makes you uncomfortable. But if you're truly here to grow and learn, then you'll need to leave your past behind. Forget everything about who you once were—forgo all your assumptions about who you think you are— and start all over, begin anew."

"It's just…" I frown, feeling bad about my resistance, but this is not at all what I expected. "Before, our lessons were always focused on tarot, numerology"—I gesture toward the Antikythera—"and that."

My dad grants me a patient nod. "And the fact that Arthur relies on you tells me you've already mastered those skills. Besides, you weren't ready back then. No eight-year-old is. But you're older now, and the stakes have never been higher. Every metamorphosis is always preceded by a mental one as well as a physical one. It's like Shunryu Suzuki said: *If your mind is empty, it is open to everything.*"

My fingers nervously play with my charm, reluctant to let it out of my grasp. "Can't I just fast-forward to the tattoo?" I motion toward the flower of life inked on the crook of his forearm.

"This is not where you start." He taps a finger against the tattoo's center. "This is where you end."

I take a moment to process. After a moment, I say, "Is it really possible to start over?"

My dad rises and extends a hand. "It's not only possible,"

he says, "it's imperative. Your trauma has imprinted on your subconscious, causing you to mentally time travel to relive it repeatedly. I'm going to show you how to let go of this self-conception you've formed. But first, I need you to trust me."

I inhale a slow breath, reminding myself that, despite his looking like one of my peers, he really is my dad. And if he says this is what's required for me to transcend, then who am I to question him?

Hardening my resolve, I reach behind my neck and unfasten the clasp. When it falls onto my open hand, it seems weighted with more than just its physical form. It's like I'm holding a piece of myself—the only tangible link to who I really am.

This is real. Irrevocably, irretrievably real. But the moment I hand this over, everything I know, all that I've been taught, will fade until it's completely erased from my mind.

I swallow hard. Overcome by a dreaded sense of finality as my gaze meets my dad's. *Get a grip*, I silently warn, struggling to compose myself. Still, there's a rawness to my emotions—a quivering lip, a hectic flush on my cheeks—that I can't fully mask.

"Dad," I manage to whisper, my voice betraying me with an embarrassing crack, as I gather my courage to hand over the charm. "You will give it back, though, right?"

He nods, his hand open and steady. "But by then, you won't need it. After this, there's no going back to who you once were."

"And who do you think that is?" I ask, eager for a glimpse of his perception of me.

His face softens and, without hesitation, he says, "A smart, clever, resilient, courageous, beautiful young woman who's had a bit of a rough go. And, because of that, she's spent the last ten years living in survival mode."

He pauses, maybe to let his words sink in, or maybe to allow me a chance to respond. But I remain silent, sensing there's more to come.

"You've been taught that life happens to you, not for you," he says. "And because of that, you've been shadowboxing your way through each day—fighting an invisible opponent seen only by you."

"Invisible?" I balk. "You do remember what I shared about Arthur, and Killian, and even Elodie?" I shake my head, wondering how he could possibly say such a thing.

"I heard every word," he says, his voice resolute. "And while your concerns are valid, from what I can see, the only person standing in your way—is you."

The words float between us, mingling with the tiny dust motes dancing in the candlelight. In my discomfort, my fidgety hands and burning cheeks, I recognize the stark seed of truth.

I have one destiny.

One enormous task to complete.

Everything outside of that is just small dramas I use to distract myself.

"I—I do want to do this," I say, my voice steady, resolved. "I'm ready to change."

In my hand, the slick, cool metal of my charm is a reminder of a past I'm about to transcend. With a determined exhale, I uncurl my fingers, allowing the small golden cage and its chain to drop gently into my dad's waiting palm.

"At this moment," he says, securing the talisman in his pocket, "you're like the minotaur at the center of your own labyrinth. But by the time you leave here, you'll understand the most crucial truth of them all."

His intense gaze levels on mine. I lean forward, heart pounding with anticipation.

"Your true strength and power, Natasha, comes from within."

6

"I know what you're thinking," my dad says, a wry grin lifting the corners of his mouth. "It sounds cliché—like something you've heard, or seen, or read a million times before. But let me ask you this: Have you ever truly lived it? Can you imagine how it feels to be so deeply anchored in your own power that you're no longer swayed by external judgments or outside circumstances?"

The question is rhetorical. Obviously, I have no idea what it's like to live with that sort of conviction. Still, it sounds like the ultimate freedom. And as I watch him sort through stacks of dusty, old tomes, his fingers gently brushing over cracked spines and worn leather covers, I say, "And that bit about the minotaur?"

My dad looks over his shoulder, casting a thoughtful glance my way. "It's about delving deep into yourself. It's the process of confronting and conquering all the fears that have accumulated over the years. Once that's behind you, you'll begin again as a new, more powerful, version of yourself."

"Didn't realize it would be so easy," I joke. "Do I get a red string like Ariadne gave to Theseus in the myth?"

I watch as my dad sets a few selected books aside. When he looks up, his gaze levels on mine. "Let's start there." He frowns. "Your use of humor and sarcasm to shield your insecurities."

I shift uncomfortably, painfully aware that I've failed the

first test. "Don't most people do that?" I ask.

"Perhaps." He shrugs, peering at me like his eyes can strip through layers of flesh and bone, all the way down to my deepest, most shadowy, shameful self. "But you're not here to become ordinary. You're here to achieve the extraordinary, no?"

His voice resonates with a sobering truth, and I find myself nodding in place of words. My throat is tight with a mix of apprehension and the promise of liberation from the me I've come to know—the me I'm increasingly desperate to outgrow. And yet, I still have my doubts.

"I've learned a lot at Gray Wolf," I say, the words coming out in a rush, as though I might soon forget the proper use of language as well. "And a lot of it, most of it, is not the sort of stuff I can afford to forget if I have any hope of defeating Arthur."

My dad raises a hand to stop me. "Let me be clear," he says, "your memories and skills will return. It's the narrative you've woven around them that will evolve."

"So, like rewriting my story?" I ask, recalling Arthur's advice once more.

He nods. "Only this goes much deeper. It'll become second nature, an intrinsic part of who you are, requiring no conscious effort on your part. And this is where we begin."

He lays open a book before me, tapping his index finger to the center of the page where an enigmatic sketch is displayed. "Albrecht Dürer's *Melencolia I*." His finger hovers over the image.

I lean forward, making a closer study of the picture. It's so vivid, so intricate, centering on the figure of a melancholic angel surrounded by various objects—a scale, a geometric shape, tools, even an hourglass. And though I have no idea what any of it means, with all that symbolism, there's clearly a story to unravel.

"It depicts mankind's struggle to comprehend the ancient

mysteries. It's a puzzle scholars have been debating for centuries," my dad says.

"And what's your take?" I ask. "I mean, as a Timekeeper, what do you think it means?"

"Look closer." He edges the book nearer to me. "Do you see how every element symbolizes a different aspect of the human experience? Knowledge, measurement, time, and the limitations they impose on us all—it's all there."

I study the image, noting how the angel, despite being surrounded by symbols and tools, looks lost in thought, maybe even paralyzed with thought.

"She seems overwhelmed," I venture, biting my lower lip as I gaze up at my dad.

He nods. "She represents the mind's potential trapped by its own self-imposed barriers. And your journey, Natasha, much like hers, is about breaking free from the mental constraints you've forced upon yourself."

"And how do I do that?" I ask, feeling a sudden kinship with the angel's burden, the parallels between my journey and hers.

"You've already begun," he says, his gaze reflecting a blend of empathy and determination. "Each element in this image stands as a metaphor for the layers you need to peel away. The scale for balance, the geometric shape for perspective, the tools for skill."

I glance at the hourglass, its sands slipping from one chamber to another. "And time?"

He grins. "Time," he says, "is about the flow of life. So far, the Unravelings you've experienced have come suddenly, unexpectedly, seemingly from a place beyond your control."

"Seemingly?" I frown, wondering if he really meant what he said. "Just so you know, I've never asked for any of them. They just happen. And usually, at the most inopportune moments."

His expression shifts, his face becoming a canvas of regret.

"Only because I never got to teach you how to not just control an Unraveling, but to harness it, summon it, and bend it to your will." Though his expression still holds traces of sadness, his voice is strong, imbued with a deep sense of purpose. "But first, there's an exercise you must do. Come."

I leave the wool throw on the chair and follow him to a secluded part of the room, a long narrow hall where a large target with colorful rings stands on a sturdy frame at the end.

Confused, I turn to him, only to find him offering me a square of silky black fabric and what I instantly recognize as archery equipment.

"What is this?" I scrutinize the bow and arrow, my curiosity tinged with unease.

"Blindfold Archery," he says. Then, reacting to my wary expression, he goes on to explain, "It goes beyond merely hitting a target. It's a practice of mental discipline, sharpening focus, honing intuition. It's about seeing beyond the visible, as the eyes can grasp only what the mind is prepared to understand."

His words stir up a memory. "You sound like Arthur," I say, recalling what Arthur once told me about the difference between mere sight and true vision.

My dad studies me with a reflective pause. "He may have his flaws, but he's not entirely misguided. And that, I suspect, will make the choices ahead of you even more challenging." He lets the words hang between us, allowing the gravity of his statement to take root. "Ready to start?" he asks, shifting back to the task at hand.

With a hesitant nod, I let him secure the blindfold over my eyes, instantly plunging me into a world of darkness. After correcting my stance, he carefully guides my hands, steadying my grip on the bow.

"Focus on the bullseye," he says. "Even though you can't see it. Trust your instincts."

I grip the cool wood of the bow, its smooth curve nestling into my palm. Beneath my fingers the string feels taut, and as I nock the arrow, its feathered fletching whispers softly against my cheek.

In my mind's eye, I visualize the target, imagining its concentric circles, the gold center waiting for the punch of my arrow. Then, with a deep breath that fills my lungs and steadies my nerves, I draw the bow and release the string.

A rush of exhilaration surges through me. For those few seconds as the arrow cuts through the air with a faint, almost imperceptible hiss, there's a weightlessness to my being, a freedom found in the uncertainty of this moment.

I brace for the sound of impact, the telltale thud of the arrow striking its target. But just as I reach back to tear the blindfold away, a crushing wave of nausea violently overtakes me.

The bow slips from my fingers, clattering to the ground.

My head spins, the room tilts and swirls, as reality quickly dissolves, leaving a familiar sense of dread in its place.

This sensation, this feeling—I know it all too well. It's the terrifying onset of a full-blown Fade.

With desperate fingers, I claw at my neck, seeking the comforting touch of my charm. But it's not there. My lifeline is severed, sending me adrift, a solitary speck in a tumultuous sea.

"You're okay," someone says.

It's the voice of a man, and I have this unexplainable urge to call him *Dad*. But how can that be?

"Stay with me," he says. "Ground yourself in the present and breathe."

I nod, my face sheathed in sweat, struggling to obey. But my mind is too frantic, trying to capture a trove of fleeting memories, only to watch them slip away like grains of sand spiraling down an hourglass.

Eighteen years of my life, fragmenting into nothingness, leaving behind only a dark, hollow void.

Without these memories, these anchors to my past and the narrative of who I am, do I even exist?

"Natasha," the man says. "You can do this."

I cling to the words like a drowning person desperately flailing toward land, but the tide of oblivion continues to surge, gathering into a monstrous force that defies my attempts to withstand it.

Next thing I know, I'm swallowed whole, ripped away from reality's comforting shores and hurled into an unfathomable abyss.

7

My heart doesn't just race, it hammers against my ribcage—a frantic drummer echoing the loss of every cherished memory. Each breath is a battle of frantically dragging air through my lungs, as I desperately try to tether myself to an increasingly distant reality.

"I—I can't remember…" My voice breaks, a reflection of the chaos unraveling within me. "I can't remember anything good. It's only the darkness that's left."

"Focus on my voice," the man says, his words a lifeline thrown across the chasm of my splintering mind. "Let it be your guide."

His hand finds mine, but as I struggle to concentrate on the cadence of his speech and the assurance of his touch, it's elusive, futile—like trying to catch a curl of smoke in your fist.

"You're clinging to your trauma because you've woven it into the very fabric of your being," he says. "You've built your whole persona around abandonment, hardship, and betrayal. You've repeated these stories so many times, the idea of letting go feels like you're losing yourself. What you need to remember is that they're no more than threads that bind you to the past. Your only job now is to sever them."

It's true. I know it's true. And yet—

"I promise you this," he goes on, "you are so much more than the negative things that happened to you."

It's a promise I desperately cling to, while simultaneously

holding space for my worst, darkest moments to date.

The day my dad left doesn't just replay in my head, it reopens that wound, providing details so vivid and sharp I can see the front door close, hear the soft thud of his footsteps receding down the drive, and smell the scent of his cologne lingering in the empty hall.

The day I was sent to jail for a crime I didn't commit plays out exactly as it was back then—the harsh clang of the cell door, the cold iron grip of fear seizing my heart, the distant echo of voices crying out in anger and despair.

That rat-infested prison where I was assaulted by the duke doesn't just resurface, it invades all my senses—the cold, slick feel of the shiv in my hand, the revolting clamminess of the duke's fat, greasy fingers groping my flesh, the satisfying crunch as my foot jams into his knee, the bone snapping with a resounding crack.

Each memory, a specter from the past, tears at my consciousness, threatening to pull me back into the abyss.

Then suddenly, materializing out of the void, rises a terrible, faceless entity that towers above me. The top of its head nearly grazes the ceiling, its impossibly broad shoulders stretching the gap between walls.

At first glance, this strange, menacing figure is such a dead ringer for the duke, I instinctively recoil in fear. My muscles go rigid and tense, my heart pounding so quickly it thunders in my ears.

As this hideous being rears its ugly head, and those dark beady eyes fixate on mine, my jaw drops open and an involuntary, primal scream shreds through the silence.

"You must destroy it," a voice shouts, and a second later, a sword materializes in my hand.

Instinctively, every lesson, everything I've ever been taught about swordcraft, surges through my veins, priming me for the confrontation ahead. With my weapon raised, I face my adversary with unwavering resolve. As he lunges forward with unprecedented ferocity, my first instinct is to cower, hide, and shrink away from the fight. Retreat to my usual place of seeking refuge in self-blame, chastising myself for allowing this to happen again—for purposely putting myself in such a terrible situation.

And yet, deep down, I know the time has come for that fearful side of me to die. The weight of my old identity, a mosaic of darkness and pain, is locked in a battle with the core of my being that yearns to shed the shackles that have so far defined me.

With determined precision, I guide my sword, executing a sweeping arc that cleanly severs the head from the looming spectral form.

I stand rooted in horror as the figure stumbles, falters, then collapses in a heap on the floor, the duke's head rolling to a stop at my feet with a sickening thud.

But then, in the merest fraction of a second, it morphs into an entirely different entity. The hair on the severed head cascades in long, dark, softly flowing waves that are remarkably like my own. Those dead, piercing green eyes seem to latch onto mine, accusing me of this terrible crime.

A chill grips my heart. *My God, what have I done?*

My gaze drifts to the body, only to find its clothing—a cropped T-shirt and low-slung jeans, mirroring the outfit I arrived in. As I absorb this ghastly sight, a whispering realization dawns, echoing a truth in the deepest recesses of my mind: *the real monster I've been battling all along is none other than myself.*

Or rather my perception of myself and everything that's ever happened to me.

The monster I killed isn't the duke; it's the fear and anxiety I've been carrying. And I know in my heart the real truth: the assault by the duke was never my fault, and feeling bad about that was never a weakness—it was part of my healing.

"Do you understand now?" a voice asks.

I can only nod. My throat is so parched it's all I can manage.

"Good," the voice says. "Now that you've annihilated the old you, you've made space for the new one to flourish."

As I gaze upon the slain monster slowly disintegrating at my feet, a part of me is overcome by grief as I wonder: *and now who will I be without my sad stories?*

In the depths of my despair, amid the howling of old ghosts, I sense an unexplored path. It's obscured, daunting, yet it whispers of the metamorphosis I long to attain—a rebirth that awaits just beyond the veil of my fears.

"Release them," the man urges, as though reading my mind. "None of those events define you. Remember, an interesting experience on the path is *not* the path. The same goes for the terrible experiences. They're simply fragments of a larger sequence that led you to this moment. What matters isn't what happens, but what you make of what happens. The only way to become your best and brightest self is by transforming your experiences into opportunities, growth, and in your case, into seizing your destiny. Think of it as emotional alchemy. Your strength grows from your struggles. It's how you'll truly live amor fati."

As I grapple with his words, desperate to absorb them, let the truth of them seep through the cracks of my fractured identity, a startling new vision begins to emerge.

It's me, standing in this very space, encircled by a fiery blaze.

My breath catches in my throat as an overwhelming heat engulfs me. The sensation is so real, so visceral, it feels like actual flames are searing my skin, incinerating every trace of my former self. Yet it's in this inferno that I am reborn—a luminous new version of me rising from the ashes of the old—untouched by any of the negativity that once defined me.

A formidable strength courses through my veins, filling me with an awe-inspiring energy I've never known, never imagined I could claim. It's as though I've been resurrected into a dawn of possibilities beyond my wildest dreams.

"Describe what you see," the man says, sensing the shift in my energy.

I'm on the verge of sharing the profound metamorphosis I didn't just witness but vividly experienced when another vision disrupts my thoughts. It's only a fragment, barely more than a sliver of memory, yet its impact leaves me awestruck.

It's me.

Standing in this very room.

Doing the exact same thing I am now.

"It—it's perplexing," I say, finally finding my voice. "It doesn't make sense, but it feels incredibly real." I continue watching as the vision of me flickers as though threatened by an unseen wind. "It's like I'm retracing my steps on a path I've already walked. And there's this undeniable certainty in my heart that I've been here before, lived all of this. It's a truth that resonates deep in my core."

I cling to this fleeting scrap of memory, aware of how my breath steadies as all the panic and fear bottled up inside loosen their hold and recede into nothing. With the bonds of my past now broken, I am open, liberated, emancipated from the me who entered this room.

This brilliant white light now burning inside me has banished every shadow that once lurked in my psyche. In its wake stands a person with no attachment to her personal tragedies, reminding me of what Michelangelo said about creating the statue of David: *I saw the angel in the marble and carved until I set him free.*

A pair of hands fumble at the back of my head, removing my blindfold and leaving me gazing into a pair of deep green eyes, the same shade as mine.

"I am Natasha Antoinette Clarke," I hear myself say, my voice resonating with newfound conviction. "And you're my dad," I whisper, relief washing over me in waves as I gaze upon his encouraging face. "And I—" I shake my head, needing a moment to find the right way to explain. "I know who I am. Just as I know that I've lived this before. And yet…" I look to him, desperate for answers. "How is that even possible? Was it some sort of déjà vu?"

My dad studies me for a moment, his face a potent mix of relief and concern. "Sounds more like déjà vécu," he says, carefully enunciating the unfamiliar term. "Rather than the feeling that you've seen something before, it's the sense of having lived it already. As though your experiences are replaying with a familiarity that extends beyond mere visuals."

"But…it was more than just a feeling," I say, needing him to understand. "I actually saw myself experiencing this very thing— like a visual echo of something that's already occurred."

My dad's gaze remains fixed on mine, hanging on every word.

"And it reminds me of something Jago, a friend of mine at Gray Wolf, once said," I continue, my words hurried, voice rising in pitch. "That every moment has already been lived and continues to be lived."

"Sounds like the metaphysical explanation of Friedrich Nietzsche's eternal recurrence," my dad says. "*Life is a flat circle*—a philosophical theory suggesting our lives are caught in a continuous loop of existence. Everything that happens has happened before and will happen again, without end."

I squint, not sure that I follow. "I always thought it meant the past is a continuous echo, looping through time, which is what makes time travel possible."

"That's one way to look at it," he says. "There's also the idea of quantum jumping theory."

"Which is?"

"It follows the many-worlds idea," he says. "Suggesting that every possibility in our lives leads to the creation of a new universe where that possibility is realized. Or, if you've seen the movie *Groundhog Day*, you can also think of your vision like that. Only, in this case, instead of one day that plays on repeat, your entire life is lived again and again, caught in an endless cycle of cause and effect. Sort of like reincarnation, only instead of multiple lives, it's just the one, lived on repeat."

A continuous loop of existence. The idea is as comforting as it is daunting.

"So, if all this has happened before, doesn't it mean I must've failed the last time around?"

My dad shrugs. "It's possible. Not to mention, there are other, less metaphysical explanations for what Nietzsche was referring to. What I do know is that Einstein was right about the distinction between past, present, and future being a stubbornly persistent illusion. Though whether you've lived this before is of no real consequence. What matters is that you've freed yourself from the tyranny of the past. Freed yourself so successfully, it seems, you've forgotten to check your target."

With a hand on each of my shoulders, he turns me toward the archery target, revealing a shot so wildly off the mark, the arrow landed on the far left side of the wall.

"Shooting to the left indicates a reluctance to let go of the past," he explains, and I can't help but wince. I knew it was true, but it's kind of embarrassing to see the evidence presented so plainly before me.

"We'll revisit this," he assures me. "It's a good marker for the progress I expect we'll make. But for now, I think it's time I show you not just how to control an Unraveling, but how to summon one so you can use it to your advantage."

8

"You're serious," I say, unable to mask my skepticism. "I can actually learn to summon an Unraveling?"

"Sure." My dad shrugs. "Once you master it, you'll be able to peer into the past, present, and sometimes, the future, at will."

"The future?" I ask, surprise in my voice.

A wry grin plays at his lips. "You can view only a future that wants to be known. Still, I'm inclined to warn you against it. You run the risk of opening a whole Pandora's box of destiny versus free will."

I frown, needing more. "Meaning?"

"You and I are bound by our roles as Timekeepers," he explains. "Yet, we still exercise free will in how we choose to navigate that destiny."

I take a moment to consider. "It doesn't feel like much of a choice."

"Didn't you choose to come here?" he counters, lifting his brow.

I nod, albeit reluctantly. "But only because someone needs to stop Arthur. And, as a Timekeeper, that someone is me."

"But Braxton is also a Timekeeper. Why not leave it to him?"

Without hesitation, I shake my head. "Not an option," I say. "I wouldn't do that to him."

"It's still a choice," he points out. "You're framing it as moral imperative, but it's still yours to decide. Consider this…" He leans closer, voice dropping an octave. "Theoretically speaking, I could go outside now, hunt down Arthur Blackstone, and eliminate him. That would solve your problem, right?"

I freeze, unsure how to respond.

"Arthur would be dead, but I would likely end up in jail. Which means no meeting your mom, no marriage, no you. And if there's no you, then you wouldn't exist to come back to this moment, which in turn makes my action impossible. Or you could leave here and eliminate him instead. But what then? Even if you did manage to evade capture, where would you go? Without Arthur, the technology doesn't exist for you to return to the future. And, according to what you've told me, in less than a decade from now, you'd run the risk of crossing your own timeline."

"My head is spinning," I admit.

He laughs. "The point is, peering into the future isn't as helpful as you might think. It raises more questions about whether we're acting from free will, or merely fulfilling a self-made prophecy. Anyway..." He places a hand on my shoulder, instantly grounding me. "Ready to move on?"

I nod, pushing aside the whirlwind of *what-ifs* spinning through my mind.

"Seeing as how this is your first lesson, nothing wrong with having a bit of fun. So, consider this your journey. You choose the timeline. I'm here only as your guide. You'll start by choosing an object that links you to whatever time you wish to explore."

He gestures toward a small table where he's arranged an eclectic array of items: an ancient tome, its pages yellowed with age; today's issue of the *New York Times*, its crisp lines and modern typography making for a stark and modern contrast; and a small crystal ball that, according to my dad, once belonged to the sixteenth century seer, John Dee, an advisor to Queen Elizabeth I. Each item offering a sort of portal to view the past, present, or even the future.

My gaze wanders over these artifacts, pausing on the old, weathered book. Maybe by delving into history, I'll get some insight into Arthur's own obscure past. What drives him to do what he does? And, more importantly, what does he fear?

I start to reach toward it, then quickly change my mind. If this practice journey is for only me, then none of these objects will provide what I really want to see.

I lift my gaze to meet my father's. "Can I have my talisman?"

My dad hesitates, studying me for a moment before reaching into his pocket and returning the necklace to me. "Now," he instructs, "to prepare your mind to reach beyond its usual boundaries, close your eyes, take a few deep, cleansing breaths, and focus on your intention. What do you wish to perceive—a person, an event, a location? Whatever it is, center your focus, then visualize a door that will lead you from this reality to the one you seek. Can you see it—the doorway?"

I nod, enveloped by a sudden sense of familiarity. "So far, the ground isn't shaking," I say. "And the walls aren't crumbling. But otherwise, it seems a lot like psychometry."

"It is," my dad explains. "Think of this as a warm-up. While psychometry is the ability to obtain information about an object or its history by touching it, an Unraveling allows you to see through time and perceive information about a distant target without the need of physical contact. And, if you're very advanced, you can sometimes interact with that subject. Now, with the doorway clear in your mind and the charm in your hand, focus on merging your consciousness with the energy it holds."

Following his guidance, I center my focus, feeling the charm begin to pulsate with a warm, rhythmic hum.

It's happening—I'm actually doing it!

A surge of excitement shoots through me as Braxton's form begins to take shape, igniting a deep, aching longing within me.

The vision is so vivid, so potent, it feels like one of Arthur's holograms come to life.

"Now, once you're in, the trick is to let go of whatever it is you hope to see," my father says, his voice a faint echo in this surreal new landscape. "Let the vision unfold on its own."

I do as he says, relinquishing control and letting the vision steer me wherever it wants.

Before me, I see Braxton bent over his desk, pencil in hand; he concentrates on sketching the intricate design of my small golden charm.

Abruptly, the scene skips forward. I hear the quickening of his heart echoing in my ears, as he stands nervously before me on my eighteenth birthday, holding a small, beautifully wrapped gift.

When the scene shifts again, I'm acutely aware of the warmth of his touch, the faint tremble in his fingers as they gently brush against my skin, securing the clasp of the charm at my neck, and centering it just over my heart.

"Are you in?" My dad's voice intrudes.

I respond with a nod, not wanting to risk breaking the spell.

"Good," he says, his voice gradually fading with the soft echo of his departing footsteps. "I'll leave you to it."

A moment of hesitation grips me as I toy with the idea of peeking into the future. But heeding my dad's warning, and somewhat worried about what I might uncover, I decide instead to seek out Braxton's current whereabouts, which is also a bit of a risk.

Is he mad at me for leaving?

Did he read the note where I told him I loved him? And if so, what did he think?

In my palm, the charm starts giving off intense heat, and I watch as a fresh new vision of Braxton materializes before me.

My gaze sweeps over him, greedily absorbing every detail.

His hair, tousled from sleep, adds a touch of vulnerability. The bandages around his head and neck are stark reminders of the wounds I've caused, both seen and unseen. His stance, usually so confident and assured, now carries an unspoken burden.

But it's his eyes that get me the most—the deep, ocean blue reflects a tempest of emotions churning just beneath the surface, hinting at the inner turmoil he struggles to conceal.

"Braxton," I whisper, as though he can hear me. "I'm so sorry, I—" The words hang unfinished, choked off by an intense, creeping dread.

An icy shiver slithers down my spine as the atmosphere thickens, pulsing with an ominous, unseen danger.

Braxton is no longer alone.

The realization strikes hard, a silent alarm echoing in my thoughts, mere moments before it unfolds before my eyes.

From the dim, shadowy recesses of his room, a hooded figure emerges. Its face hidden, shrouded in darkness, radiating an aura of menace. While Braxton, lost in contemplation of his father's gold pocket watch, remains oblivious to the sinister presence now inching closer.

As the eerie figure draws near, Braxton's body stiffens, eyes widening in alarm.

Braxton—watch out! I struggle to shout, but my words evaporate before they can form. My heart pounds wildly as I try to rush toward him, desperately hoping to bridge the gaping chasm between our realities. But I'm not nearly advanced enough for that. I remain rooted in place, immobilized and powerless, left only to watch, as dread wraps its icy-cold fingers around me.

In the final moments, before I'm yanked from the vision and the world plunges into darkness, a haunting realization rings in my head: *we are not the hunters in this sick, twisted game; we are the prey.*

9

Braxton
GRAY WOLF ACADEMY
PRESENT DAY

Nothing is at all like I thought.

My perception has failed to such a degree I'm reminded of something Arthur once told me: *reality*, he said, *depends on an observer*.

If that's true, what does my initial observation say about me? The figure I mistook for a faceless, menacing monster is anything but.

The man who emerges from the shadows is imposing, broad-shouldered, and tall. When he lowers the hood of his frayed brown cloak and steps into the light, I see a rumpled mane of silvery-white hair, a long, straight nose, and a weathered jawline. But his eyes—kind and bright—shine with the same intense blue as mine.

"It seems my arrival has caught you unawares," he says, his voice clipped and genteel. "Yet I have anticipated this moment for centuries."

Before either of us can speak, he raises a hand, and in a blink, it's like we're transported to another world. Though I'm pretty sure it's the same world, only transformed.

The familiar confines of my room dissolve into an expansive chamber with towering stone walls that radiate a mysterious, golden glow. This must be some kind of temple. The air feels denser, humming with the charged energy of ancient times, as if history breathes within these walls.

"Where are we?" I glance around quickly. "And who are you?" I add, though I'm sure I already know.

"I am your grandfather," he says. "Your father's father—the one you are named after."

"My grandfather James—my—my namesake," I stammer, a mix of awe and disbelief coloring my words. "You look just like your portrait. The one that hung over the mantel in Father's private study."

"We have met once before." My grandfather nods. "Briefly, just after you were born."

"And then you vanished, and I never had the chance to know you." My gaze flickers with memories, a legacy lost and now found.

"As for where we are"—he dips his head—"we stand at the threshold of knowledge, a place of deep learning. We stand at the place where it all began."

"The Mystery Schools of Egypt?" I ask.

He responds with a grin. "This is where the secrets of the true nature of time, reality, and consciousness were imparted to the members of this ancient and secret society. The type of knowledge that was forbidden to ordinary people."

I open my mouth, about to ask him why he's showing me this now, but he cuts me off before I can speak.

"We must hurry," he says. "We have much to do, and time is a luxury we no longer possess."

I nod, feeling torn between playing along and struggling to comprehend just exactly what this is. I'm well-versed in psychometry, and no stranger to an Unraveling. But what's happening now is entirely new.

"I'm not sure I understand any of this," I say. "I was only trying to see if I could uncover a message left by my father. I never expected to release an actual being, like Aladdin from his lamp."

My grandfather studies me with a look of bemusement. "The reason you're seeing me now is because I knew this day would come."

I take a moment to consider his words. "So, you're saying none of this is happening in real time? That it's some sort of illusion—like one of Arthur's holograms?"

"I assure you, my boy," my grandfather says, "I am no hologram. Though I am well acquainted with Arthur."

His gaze burns with such intensity, I flinch as though I've been scorched from its heat. And I watch as he removes his cloak and lifts the hem of his worn muslin shirt, revealing a large circular wound that spans the entire width of his chest.

My eyes lock onto the startling sight. The margins are so surgical and precise, they stand in stark contrast to the scar's harsher landscape—a brutal crust of angry, red tissue stretched taut, like a distorted canvas over the hollow where flesh once was.

My first thought is one of amazement that anyone could survive such an attack. A moment later, I realize he didn't.

"This," my grandfather says, pressing a finger to the center of his chest, "is the result of my meeting with Arthur Blackstone."

The revelation strikes with the force of a tidal wave, relentless and unyielding. *How could Arthur, a man of the twentieth century, have orchestrated such a gruesome fate for someone from the early 1800s?*

Then I remember, and all the ominous pieces fall into place. It wasn't that long ago when Arthur made regular Trips to the past. Trips I now realize weren't just exploratory, but predatory.

It's how he found me, Killian, and possibly even Elodie, along with the rest of the support staff.

"Yes, Arthur appeared to be from another time," my grandfather says, pulling me back to the present. "Yet he hunted me down all the same."

The gravity of his words presses heavily upon me, leaving me immobilized, caught in a tempest of fury and grief.

"He's the reason you—" I pause, take a steadying breath. "Arthur is the reason you were absent from my life, isn't he?"

My grandfather's shirt falls back into place, veiling the brutal reminder of a violent end. "Arthur made many visits to our time." His voice is grave, loaded with insinuation, but I'm looking for fact—hard confirmation.

"Did Arthur—" My voice falters, and I force myself to continue. "Did he kill my father, too?" My whisper slices through the air, every word spiked with dread. My stomach twists as I wait for his answer.

The sorrow etched on my grandfather's face speaks volumes before he even utters a word. "My failure to warn you about Arthur is one of my greatest regrets," he says.

My God. I stare at my grandfather through unseeing eyes, the magnitude of the truth almost too great to bear. The man I've loyally served—the man who's steered my life for years—is responsible for the deaths of those I've loved most. Anger and betrayal churn within me.

How could I have been a pawn in such a cruel, twisted game?

How did I not see the architect of my own suffering for what he truly is?

"And yet," my grandfather says, "maybe it's a blessing."

"A blessing?" I balk. "How can you possibly say such a thing?"

"It put you right under his wing, brought you closer to him than any of us could have ever hoped to be." My grandfather's words are a cold comfort amid the swirling chaos of our joined emotions. "There's no point in regretting the past, my boy," my grandfather cautions. "Not when it places you exactly where you need to be."

"But how can I face Arthur now, knowing he's responsible for so much pain?"

"You will face him as you always do. Only now you will know that while I did not go without resistance, for the primal instinct to live cannot be denied, I foresaw the impending event when I peered into the future. What you are seeing and experiencing now is real. You stand here, in this juncture of time, by virtue of the path you elected to explore."

"You say that." I frown. "But it's starting to seem like we're all just actors on some grand stage, dutifully sticking to the script where everything—every dilemma, every choice—is already determined."

"You used your free will to pick up your father's pocket watch," my grandfather says. "If you'd made another choice, you never would've seen this, but the message contained would continue to exist as a possibility."

"Okay—" I raise a hand. "So, my being here, talking with you, was always one of many possible choices. Which means both you and my father were always possibly going to die at Arthur's hand, and I was always going to possibly end up at Gray Wolf, and not knowing any of this beforehand, I foolishly chose to walk this path like some mindless cog in the massive wheel of time that—"

"There exist many paths," my grandfather cuts in. "It was by your own volition that you embarked on this journey. Had you opted for an alternate course, our encounter may have manifested differently, or perchance not at all. The vagaries of fate are indeed inscrutable. Now, permit me to pose a question to you: would the role of a Timekeeper hold any significance were all our choices predetermined?"

He pauses, allowing time for me to consider his words.

"The tree of life has many branches," my grandfather continues. "And *time* — according to what your fellow Timekeeper and friend, Leonardo da Vinci, once said — *stays long enough for anyone who will use it.* So, tell me, my boy, are you ready to heed his advice and use what little time we have left?"

I inhale a deep breath and nod.

"Good." My grandfather grins. Then lifting his chin, his gaze locking onto mine, he says, "The Elders are eager to meet you. They have much to teach you about your origins, your duties, your gifts."

I nod, eager to begin when a sudden, jarring knock echoes through the space, violently jolting me out of our shared liminal space and back to the reality of my room at Gray Wolf.

My head snaps toward the door, eyes widening in alarm.

The knocking grows more insistent, accompanied by the sound of Arthur's unmistakable voice. "Braxton," he calls, a note of concern in his tone. "Are you okay? I hear you've been injured."

Arthur? How the hell did he get back so soon?

Elodie swore we had two more days until he returned. I should've known better than to trust her.

Shit. A surge of panic claws through me, and I glance back to where my grandfather stood, only to find an empty void in its place.

"Braxton?" Arthur's voice grows louder, followed by the electronic beep of the door unlocking.

In a blur of motion, the door swings open and Arthur bursts in.

10

Natasha
NEW YORK CITY
1998

When the vision ends, I find my father waiting for me, his eyes narrowed in scrutiny. "How was it?" he asks.

I'm too shaken to speak, lost in the tumultuous sea of emotions churning inside me. The relief of seeing Braxton is completely overshadowed by the dark presence I saw in his room.

"It—it felt like a dream," I say, my voice trembling. "Or, actually, more like a nightmare." I glance at my dad, seeking guidance and reassurance, like a little girl looking to him to help sort out my problems.

"What happened?" he asks, his voice steady, though his hand betrays his concern as he unconsciously rubs his chin.

I rake my fingers through my hair, trying to steady myself, and quickly relay what I saw. My dad frowns, clearly torn.

"You said he was holding his grandfather's pocket watch?"

I nod, my mind still caught up in the vision.

"Then perhaps you misunderstood what you saw."

I take a moment to consider. It's possible, and yet, the doubt clings to me like a shadow.

"Natasha," my dad says, grounding me in the present. "There's so much more I still need to teach you. I think it's best if you trust that Braxton can handle it. Count this as one of those tough choices you'll need to make as a Timekeeper. Our individual desires must take a back seat."

My shoulders slump, a weighted sigh escaping my lips. Despite the turmoil inside, I know he's right.

"Okay, so what's next?" I ask, trying to focus despite the whirlwind of thoughts.

My dad studies me for a beat. "So far," he says, "I've been training you much like my own father trained me. Granted, that was over the course of many years, which, unfortunately, we don't have. Not to mention…"

I stare at him, waiting, my heart pounding in the silence.

"You do know you're the first female Timekeeper in history?"

Chills prickle my skin as I remember Killian uttering those same words. But what does it mean, if anything?

Reading the question in my eyes, my dad says, "Honestly, I don't know what it means. Though if I had to guess, I'd say it signals some kind of evolutionary shift, indicating a significant change or rare cosmic event that necessitated your birth."

"It's Arthur," I say, surer than ever. "Arthur Blackstone, his technology, and his determination to restore the Antikythera Mechanism and control time are the event."

My dad gives me a considering look. "Maybe," he says. "And yet, with his ability to travel through time, Arthur has been at this for years—centuries really. Still, it strikes me as strange that he pulled Braxton out of his timeline and brought him to Gray Wolf, only to bring you there, too."

"I don't get it, either," I tell him. "Though, according to Killian, it wasn't until what…" I pause, unsure how to say it. "Well, it wasn't until what happened to you that Arthur realized he needed a Timekeeper to carry the pieces back to Gray Wolf.

And yet, he waited for me to come of age before he resumed his efforts."

We fall into a tense silence. My dad breaks it when he says, "While we may not know Arthur's motives, consider it a blessing. Life as a Timekeeper can be lonely. You're fortunate you have someone to share it with."

I nod, feeling the full weight of his words.

"At any rate," he continues, "I'm going to put you through that exercise again. Only this time, we're going to take it up a notch."

I nod, starting to reach for the talisman, but my dad shakes his head. "No objects. I told you I'd show you not only how to control an Unraveling, but also how to summon one. This is where we begin. Though I should warn you, only a rare few become any good at it, and even then, it's after rigorous training and practice."

After getting me comfortably settled in a chair, he leads me through a series of breathing exercises and meditations. Once I'm in a relaxed state, he tells me to choose a target to focus on—a specific location, object, person, or event.

If my heart was in charge, I'd choose Braxton. But it's not, so I focus on Arthur Blackstone instead, envisioning him as though he were standing right here before me.

"What do you see?" my dad asks.

"Arthur," I say. "But so far, it's only in my head, it's not—" Just then, the ground begins to shake, and I open my eyes to see the ceiling falling and the walls crumbling away. "The world is fading," I whisper.

"Good," my dad says. "Stay with the vision and expand your senses beyond these walls."

I do as he says, and soon, a hazy image begins to form, sharpening into focus as I direct my attention toward Arthur. In an instant, my father's secret room dissolves, replaced by a part of Gray Wolf I've never seen before—a vast, empty, all-white space, like a blank canvas ready to be painted.

But it's not a painter who stands before me. It's Arthur, his back to me in a confident stance. Like a conductor commanding an orchestra, he raises his hand and suddenly the room erupts with color, so bright and vibrant it takes a moment for my vision to adjust. When it does, I'm both mesmerized and repulsed by the twisted sight unfolding before me.

This isn't just a vision, it's a holographic manifestation of Arthur's insatiable desire for dominance and control. In this distorted future he imagines, he alone wields absolute power to rewrite history and reign over us all.

I watch in horror as entire populations of people who don't meet his standards—those he deems dull, boring, mundane, aesthetically challenged—are erased from existence.

With a mere flick of his wrist, timelines are manipulated, boundaries are redrawn, and the past is reshaped to create a present where conformity to Arthur's preferences is mandatory.

It's a world remade in his image—a world devoid of diversity, individuality, and freedom.

A world where we are nothing but mindless puppets, conforming to his narrow ideals, and forced to worship him as a god.

"Natasha," my dad calls, "can you describe what you're seeing?"

"It's Arthur," I whisper. "He—" I struggle to hold the connection, feeling the strain in every fiber of my being as the vision wavers, then sharpens again. My strength is waning, but I push myself to hold on to the nightmarish future Arthur seeks to impose on us all.

This new world he dreams of reminds me of Gray Wolf—beautiful, elegant, populated by people completely under his rule.

In other words, an aesthetically pleasing, totalitarian nightmare.

"My God," I say, "it's—"

A loud knock suddenly booms through the space, and with a quick swipe of Arthur's hand, the vision instantly fades, returning the room to white once again. When he turns, his dark eyes seem to pierce right into mine, as if he somehow knows I'm watching. Then he heads for the door and opens it to find Roxane waiting in the hall.

"Braxton's been injured," she tells him. "You should probably look in on him."

"Oh my God," I whisper, struggling to stay with the vision. But the connection is soon severed, and I'm pulled back to the room, only to find my father's concerned face just inches from mine.

"What did you see?" he asks urgently.

It's a moment before I can reply. When I do, I say, "I saw the end of freedom—autonomy. I saw the end of the world as we know it." My eyes meet my dad's and I watch his brow crease with worry as I add, "And I need to find Elodie and get back to Gray Wolf, because Arthur is back."

11

"I—I have to go," I stammer, my voice quivering with dread and determination, my eyes wide with fear and regret. "Now that Arthur's back, there's no time to finish my training. If he discovers we're gone…" I leave the thought unfinished, but the potential consequences swirl through my mind like a gathering storm.

My dad frowns, clearly torn. "There might be another way," he suggests, his tone resolute but his eyes uncertain. "It's not ideal. Hands-on experience is always best, but it might work."

"What is it?" I ask, scrutinizing his face. "I'll do anything. As long as it's quick."

"When my father trained me, what I didn't learn through him, I learned from the Mystery School elders."

I stare at him blankly, not comprehending.

"You won't actually go there. Rather, it's a form of mental time travel, like the Unraveling you just experienced with Arthur. Your physical body stays here, but your consciousness travels back in time to connect with and learn from the elders."

"Okay…" I say, seeing his hesitation. "What's the catch?"

He rakes a hand through his hair, his green eyes locking onto mine. "It took me years to master. I think it might help if we do it together, but are you sure you can't stay a bit longer?"

The thought of leaving my dad, knowing I'll never see him again, presses heavily on my heart. If circumstances were different, I'd stay without a second thought. Hell, I'd even risk crossing my own timeline to maximize whatever time we have left. But, as he said, a normal life is off the menu for people like us.

With great sadness, I say, "I can't. Braxton will cover for us, but Arthur's no fool. He'll realize we're missing soon enough." My voice carries the weight of regret.

"Then let us begin," my dad says, his tone firm, despite the sorrow in his eyes.

Extending his hands toward mine, our fingers touch, and our palms press together. "Close your eyes," he says. "Focus on your breathing and clear your thoughts. Let your mind be a blank canvas, receptive to whatever impressions may come."

A tingling emanates from his hands into mine, growing into a wave of energy that envelops my entire being like a comforting, tranquil embrace. The sensation is so peaceful, I yearn to linger here forever.

In this altered state, the world transforms, and I find myself in a room with stone walls bathed in the golden light of flickering candles. A man with long white hair and a matching beard sits at a desk, writing on parchment. Though I can't make out the words, I immediately recognize him. He's the same man I saw just after retrieving the Moon from its centuries-old hiding spot, during the Unraveling in the Baptistery of San Giovanni.

"What do you see?" my dad whispers.

I describe the scene unfolding before me.

"Good," he says, removing his hands from mine. "Now wait until you're called."

I do as he says, remembering how last time, the man peered at me through centuries of time, only for the vision to shatter when Braxton arrived.

This time, I watch as the quill drops to the table, the man lifts his head and raises a hand, calling me forward.

"Go to him," my dad instructs.

"But how?" I ask, unsure how to proceed.

"In your mind, see yourself walking to him. But whatever you do, don't lose the connection."

I envision myself moving toward the man. As I approach, he rises from his desk, his presence towering and commanding. Placing his hands on either side of my head, a rush of energy surges through me, elevating my frequency to a much higher vibration. It's as if a symphony of stars and the heartbeat of the earth are resonating within me, unlocking the wisdom in the deepest recesses of my soul.

Images, insights, and knowledge cascade into my mind, revealing centuries of arcane secrets in mere moments. I see ancient rituals, forgotten histories, and the delicate threads of time weaving the fabric of reality. When the flow subsides, the man steps back, his eyes holding a depth of understanding. Without a word, he returns to his desk and the vision snaps away, leaving me standing in my father's secret room, the echoes of that cosmic symphony still vibrating in my bones.

I open my eyes, feeling awakened, transformed, brimming with newfound insight. When I meet my father's gaze, suddenly, everything I've learned, all the knowledge I gained, slips away—except for one thing that continues to resonate in my mind like a whisper piercing through the haze.

"I know why I'm here," I say, the words tumbling out in a rush. "I know why I'm the first female Timekeeper."

My dad nods, encouraging me to go on.

"My birth coincided with Arthur taking possession of the Antikythera Mechanism. His actions were mostly harmless until he discovered its power. It's his ambition to control time and remake the world in his image that triggered my emergence. It's as if the universe recognized the potential for tyranny and imbalance. And after centuries of male-centric brute force used to keep the pieces hidden, my feminine energy and intuition are the counterbalance—the force sent to prevent Arthur from attaining his darkest ambitions."

My dad studies me for a long, silent beat. "It makes sense," he says. "Is there anything else?"

"Nothing that stuck," I say, my voice betraying my panic.

"The knowledge lives inside you now," my dad assures me. "It would be too overwhelming to move through the world with that sort of energy stirred up all the time. Trust. Have faith. I promise it'll be there when you most need it."

I want to believe him, but I still have my doubts. He must see the hesitation on my face because he quickly adds, "You need proof. Luckily, we can do that." He retrieves a blindfold and the archery bow. "Told you we'd revisit this." He grins.

Once the blindfold is securely fastened over my eyes, casting me into darkness, my dad positions me before the target and places the bow and arrow into my hands.

"Trust your skills," he says, "and the newly awakened wisdom within you."

As the world beyond the blindfold slips away, leaving only the steady rhythm of my heartbeat, the tension building in my shoulders and arms, and the target I envision in my mind, I draw in a deep breath, pull back on the bowstring, and with a measured exhale, I channel my intention and release the arrow toward a destination unseen.

As the arrow slices through the air, a mere whisper in the silence, time seems to stretch and pause, resuming once more with the telltale thunk of the arrow finding its mark.

A surge of anticipation rushes through me, a blend of hope and anxiety tingling in my veins, as I wait for the blindfold to be lifted from my face.

"Ready?" my dad says. A second later, the blindfold is gone, leaving me blinking, once, twice, just to make sure. "Looks like my work is done." He beams with pride, motioning toward the arrow now perfectly lodged into that tiny gold center. "In just a matter of hours you've achieved what took me over a decade to learn."

A mix of triumph and sorrow beats inside me. I'm as ready as I'll ever be, yet knowing I'll never see him again is making it impossible to leave.

"I don't want to do this," I say, voice breaking as I fight back tears. "I don't want to go."

"But you will," my dad says. "It's what you're meant to do. I believe in you, Natasha."

Tears stream down my cheeks, but I let them flow, making no attempt to wipe them away. Then, a new thought occurs to me. I look at my dad and say, "I can undo this, you know?"

My dad shoots me a wary look, as though he's already guessed what I'm about to propose.

"I threatened Killian with it, and while I was mostly just trying to scare him, I realize now that I can actually make it happen. I don't need Arthur or Elodie to Trip. I can just wait for the right moon cycle, then travel back to 1741 and stop Killian before he can—"

I don't even get to finish before my dad says, "I'm sure Arthur has warned you about the dangers of tampering with history, even personal history?"

I give a dismissive shrug. "But isn't that what he plans to do? So, what's the difference if I—"

"Natasha—" My dad reaches for my hand, his grasp gentle but firm. "Your only job is to stop Arthur. It's the single most important thing you can do. Everything else is secondary."

"But why can't I do both?" I counter, refusing to give in. "It's not like the two are mutually exclusive. I'm sure I can handle—" My voice falters as I take in his somber gaze, the way his head slowly shakes.

"You don't understand the gift you've already given me." His gaze brims with emotion, cheeks misted with tears. "By coming here, you've granted me something invaluable—a chance to make better choices, to live differently, and more fully. Knowing what's going to happen has given me a whole new perspective. And because of that—because of you and the courage it took to find me—I won't waste a single second of what's left of my existence."

Emotion wells up inside me, spilling over as silent tears trace a wet path to the neckline of my borrowed tee.

"Thanks to you, my life won't be one of unexamined passivity," he says. "Nor will I waste a single moment of the time I have left."

My throat burns, my shoulders shake, and I'm pretty sure my mascara is a soggy, black mess. "I still wish you'd reconsider," I manage to say.

"I know." He pulls me close, rubbing a soothing hand over my back. Then, in a voice so low I can just barely hear, he adds, "Just remember, time is like a river—everything flows, and nothing stands still."

A flicker of recognition sparks in my mind, and I pull back slightly and look into his eyes. *I've heard that before, but where?* Then I remember—it's a quote he taught me early on, one I'd pretty much forgotten until I entered Arthur Blackstone's world.

"Panta Rhei," I say, explaining how those ancient words are etched onto the plaque over the Gray Wolf Academy gate.

I guess I'm expecting more of a reaction, some sign of surprise. But my dad simply nods, a knowing look in his eyes.

"Everything is connected," he says, with a gentle finality. "The flower of life"—he taps a finger to his tattoo—"serves as a reminder of that. It's a powerful and ancient symbol that embodies the profound interconnectedness of the universe, the cycle of creation, of all living things."

Then, changing the subject, he adds, "Listen, there's something I want you to have." He motions for me to follow. "Come this way."

I expect him to exit through the same door we entered, but instead, he veers down a short, narrow hall and heads toward a painting that hangs on the opposite wall. Its surreal landscape and melting clocks serve as a stark reminder of the world I left behind.

"*The Persistence of Memory*," I gasp, my voice barely more than a whisper.

"You know it?" My dad glances between the painting and me.

"I own it," I tell him. Realizing how implausible that must sound—me claiming to own an original Salvador Dalí—I quickly add, "Well, it's on loan. It's the painting I chose on my first visit to Arthur's vault, and it's been hanging in my room ever since."

"Astonishing." My dad's eyes widen in wonder.

"I don't know about that." I shrug, feeling suddenly and strangely self-conscious. "Mostly, I chose it to remind myself that no matter how opulent and enchanting life at Gray Wolf is, it's not where I belong. It's not home. I know it probably sounds weird, but once you're entrenched in Arthur's world, it's easy to forget there's a whole other one that continues to exist outside those walls."

My dad's gaze remains fixed on me, clearly unconvinced by my attempt to brush it off. "And yet, any number of paintings could've done the same thing," he insists. "Take *The Birth of Venus*—it symbolizes the endless cycles of time: birth, life, renewal. The point is, there's no such thing as mere coincidence. Remember Natasha, everything truly is connected. It's not just a fluke. Everything that's happened on your path has led you right here."

I take a moment to consider his words. Honestly, it all

sounds a bit farfetched, and yet I'm definitely intrigued by the concept.

"So, you think the vision I had—where I saw myself here— might've actually happened?" My voice rises in pitch. "Like I'm caught in some kind of loop? And that, maybe subconsciously, I was drawn to Dalí's painting because it's what I always do?"

"It's possible." My dad shrugs, rubbing at his chin.

"But if it is true, then how do I break free?"

My dad sighs, heavy and deep. "By using your free will," he says. "And never losing sight of your destiny. Those are two things Arthur can never take from you." His words float between us. Then, abruptly shifting gears, he gestures toward the painting and says, "Why don't you take the lead?"

He guides my hand to the frame's bottom left corner, gently nudging it upward. My eyes widen in astonishment as a soft, almost inaudible click sounds, and the wall swings open, revealing yet another one of his secrets.

12

"So, let me guess—you secretly occupy the whole building?" I peer beyond the hidden doorway that leads into yet another apartment.

"Just this floor," my dad says, swiping a hand across his jaw. "It's been in the family for ages."

Our footsteps softly echo as I take a look around. The entertainment system is state-of-the-art for its time, and there's not a single piece of second-hand furniture to be found. This apartment is so much nicer than the one he shares with Mark, it's like stepping into a whole other world.

"Well, it's definitely an upgrade." My gaze lingers on a fridge that would definitely look dated in the twenty-first century, but in 1998, it's top of the line. "It's like the other side is staged to look like a typical undergrad's apartment, while this side is more…" I pause, searching for the right words. "Bougie and aspirational," I say, settling on two.

His lips pull into a half grin. "It's like I said earlier, a lot of work goes into appearing normal."

"I wonder what's happened to it now?" I glance over my shoulder to gauge his expression. "And, by that I mean, the 2024 version of now."

My dad shifts uneasily. "Considering everything you've told me about my disappearance, I suppose it's left vacant. Which is something I can't quite wrap my head around. I would've hoped I'd arranged for it to pass down to you, along with a considerable sum when you turned eighteen—same way it was handed to me." He stops briefly at the doorway, lines of concern etching his brow. "I can't believe I would've been so negligent," he says, truly perplexed.

A hollow feeling creeps into my chest. *Money. A potential inheritance that could've changed everything.* The revelation of unclaimed wealth hangs heavily between us.

"Just because there was no inheritance," I say, my voice flat, "doesn't mean you're to blame."

"Arthur?" my dad says, as though reading my mind.

"Who else?" The words leave my lips with a bitter tang.

Just how long has he been watching me, manipulating me, steering my life straight into his trap, while I unknowingly played right into his hands?

"Well, there's one thing I can change." He reaches into his pocket and retrieves a set of keys. My eyes follow his movements as he slides one free of the ring and extends it toward me. "It's the key to this apartment," he says.

I take it, feeling its slick, cool weight in my palm. I'm so overcome with emotion—gratitude and sorrow, such unlikely companions—that it steals my words along with my breath.

"When you've done what you need to, you'll always have a place to call home. I'll also arrange for an inheritance for you and your mom that Arthur won't discover, so you'll never be forced to rely on him again."

Torn between desperately wanting the easier life that sort of inheritance will provide, and the fear of disrupting the already established events of my timeline, I say, "But isn't that messing with personal history?"

My dad pauses, a bittersweet curl tugging at the sides of his lips.

"And besides," I continue, "as hard as it was, that struggle is partly responsible for who I am now."

"And who's that?" my dad asks, eyes glinting with pride.

"Strong. Independent. And, thanks to you, ready to confront Arthur Blackstone, once and for all."

My dad studies me for a long, silent moment. "Fine," he says. "I'll make you a deal. While I won't mess with what's passed, I will make provisions for your future. Behind *The Persistence of Memory* is a safe. I'll change the combination to your birthday. Sound good?"

I nod, feeling so choked up, it's difficult to speak.

"Oh, and one more thing," he says. "Do you mind telling me my future wife's name?"

I hesitate. "Are you sure?" I ask. "I mean, knowing how it ends might spoil the romance, change the way you live that story."

My dad shrugs. "I'm less interested in the surprise factor, and more interested in living a story worth telling."

I'm about to tell him when I remember something I dragged all the way here—something I've had for a while but couldn't bring myself to confront.

Am I ready now? Can I face what she wrote? And should I really share it with him?

My gaze shifts to my dad, as I reach into my tiny backpack, surprised to find his copy of the Antikythera Mechanism stashed inside.

"What's this for?" I say, brow furrowing in confusion.

He shrugs. "I had a sense you might need it."

Reaching past it, my fingers find the letter my mom wrote to Mason that was really intended for me. "I need you to read it," I tell him, placing the envelope into his hand. "Out loud, so I can hear."

He studies me for a moment, an unspoken understanding passing between us. With careful fingers, he opens the envelope and unfolds the letter. Clearing his throat, he begins to read.

"*Dear Mason, I know you probably miss her. I miss her, too. I also know you're probably confused, wondering what might've happened to her. My hope is this letter will help ease your mind. And perhaps my mind as well.*"

My dad pauses, casting a questioning glance my way. I nod slightly, encouraging him to continue. I've already read this part. It's what comes next that I most need to hear.

"*By now you've likely realized Natasha is gone and she won't be returning anytime soon. It's a reality that weighs on my heart every day.*

"*After her arrest, I felt broken. Not only did I fail her as a mother, but the thought of losing my precious daughter to a system that would swallow her whole was unbearable. So, when Arthur Blackstone offered an alternative—a choice between a juvenile detention center and a private academy where she could thrive in the way she deserved—well, it seemed like a lifeline, a chance to restore all the hope that was lost in the wake of her father's absence.*"

As my dad reads, he's so overcome by the words, his voice wavers. Choked with emotion, he's forced to stop and take a steadying breath before continuing.

"*Still, the decision didn't come easily. In fact, sending Natasha away was the hardest choice I've ever made. And though I managed to convince myself it was the only viable path out of the bleakness of our lives, I'm now left to grapple with the guilt and doubt that have become a regular part of my day.*

"*If you've passed by our house recently, you may have noticed that I benefitted as well. Arthur has provided a generous monthly stipend, which has freed me from the financial burdens that have long plagued our family.*

"*At the time, the cost seemed minimal—no contact with Natasha in exchange for a brighter future for her. What I didn't* anticipate was the profound sense of loss, the deep relentless ache that her absence has made. And I'm often reminded of the quote from Matthew, 16:26:

"What will it profit a man if he gains the whole world, yet forfeits his soul?

"I pray every day I haven't made that mistake.

"And in my darkest moments, when I'm wrestling with all that I've done, I find myself thinking of you, the bond you and Natasha shared, and how positively you influenced each other.

"My greatest hope now is that, once this chapter of our lives comes to a close, Natasha will be well on her way to a life far better than anything I ever could've provided alone.

"I hope she'll understand that my choice stemmed not from greed, but from the depths of a mother's love for her daughter.

"I hope, too, that she can find it in her heart to forgive me. Maybe then, I can begin the journey of forgiving myself.

"And I hope that you, Mason, can forgive me as well.

"Wishing you only the best, today and always.

"Amanda Clarke."

When my father finishes reading, he gazes at me, his voice clogged with emotion. "Amanda?"

With tears streaming down my face, I give a tentative nod.

"There are a lot of Amandas out there," he says, carefully refolding the letter with trembling fingers, before handing it to me. "Maybe you can help narrow it down and tell me her maiden name, at least?"

I'm on the verge of telling him, but then I pause. "I think it'll be a lot more fun for you to discover that on your own," I say, a small smile breaking through the thick haze of tears.

My dad laughs in response, a warm, rich, infectious sound. I find myself clinging to it, engraving it onto my memory as a treasure to carry with me into whatever comes next.

As we approach the door, the finality of the moment hits me.

This is it. I'm never going to see him again. Whatever's left to do or say needs to happen quickly.

"Dad—" My voice falters, and I force myself to summon the strength to speak the words that have been pressing persistently against my heart. "Just so you know—you were a really amazing dad. The best any daughter could ever hope for."

Tears flow freely down his cheeks as he pulls me into a tight embrace. I absorb the warmth of his arms, the steady beat of his heart, determined to imprint the comfort of his presence directly onto my soul. Then, with great reluctance, I pull away.

"Ready?" he asks, wiping the tears with the back of his hand.

Part of me wants to say *no*, dig in my heels, and demand to stay here. But strangely, the word just won't come. Because the truth is, I am ready—or, at least, as ready as I'll ever be. Just as he's about to open the door, a sudden thought stops me.

"What about the tattoo?" I bite down on my lip, fearing that not only has time run out, but also that it'll be impossible to hide, much less explain, should Arthur ever catch sight of it.

My dad looks at me, a deep, understanding flickering in his gaze. Then, leaning down to place a tender kiss onto my forehead, he says, "I have a feeling the mark will find you." He speaks with the sort of quiet certainty I find myself cleaving to.

Then, taking my hand in his, he says, "And Natasha"—his tone grows more solemn—"I meant what I said about not trying to save me. I've found my peace with it, and now it's time for you to find yours."

I avert my eyes, staring down at my shoes in a silent rebellion against his acceptance of fate.

"You know," he says, gently lifting my chin, guiding my gaze back to his, "there's a Zen proverb that says: *When the student is ready, the teacher will appear. When the student is truly ready, the teacher will disappear.*"

A wave of uncertainty washes over me. "I feel ready," I say, "but what if that's just wishful thinking?" The question slips out, tinged with vulnerability.

"It's not," he assures me. "And someday soon, you'll know that for yourself. But I'd be remiss not to urge you to try to determine exactly what drives Arthur to do what he does. Something tells me it goes far beyond a simple love of beauty and art. And it may provide just the clue you need to figure out how to stop him."

I nod, a mix of hope and apprehension swirling within me. Knowing these are my final moments with him, and wanting to end on a lighter note, I playfully tug at the frayed hem of the borrowed T-shirt. "Is it okay if I keep this?"

My dad laughs, a rich, warm sound that's so infectious, I can't help but join in.

The laughter continues as we exit the apartment and head down the hall, connected in an unspoken understanding, we make our way to where Elodie waits.

13

"I still don't get how you know Arthur's back," Elodie says, her voice rising above the cacophony of city sounds as we leave my dad's building and step onto the bustling street.

"I just need you to trust me," I say, my voice firm despite the gnawing hunger that seizes my belly the second I catch a whiff of grilled burgers and fries wafting from a nearby restaurant. Its welcoming lights seem to beckon as I stare longingly into the window.

No time, I remind myself, as I summon the strength to rush past. *We'll eat when we get back to Gray Wolf. If Arthur's still willing to feed us, that is.*

Elodie casts a skeptical glance my way. "Fine. Whatever," she says. "But before we go, there's something I need you to see—"

Before I can react, she's latched onto my arm and is pulling me into the middle of traffic. Joined in a frenzied dance of blaring horns and shouting drivers, we dart through buses and cars, racing toward the other side of the street.

"I'd really prefer not to die in these ridiculous jeans," I grumble under my breath, only half joking. When she stops before a storefront with a flashing neon eye in the window, I glance between her and the sign. "Elodie, what the—"

She's just about to press the buzzer when the door swings open, an older woman steps out, and Elodie swoops in. "Here, let me get that for you," she says, acting as though she's only trying to help instead of her real mission of gaining entry without taking the risk of announcing herself.

The woman narrows her eyes, casting a suspicious glance in our direction. Then, deciding it's not her problem, she rushes onto the sidewalk without a second glance.

"After you," Elodie says, her voice tinged with an unspoken secret.

Reluctantly, I step inside the psychic's lair, a room that reminds me a bit of my dad's secret den. The walls are draped in rich purple tapestries adorned with celestial patterns that seem to dance in the dim light. Shelves overflow with an eclectic mix of mystical artifacts: crystal balls, tarot decks, and astrology books. The pungent scent of burning incense fills the air.

I'm about to question the logic of visiting a psychic when Elodie already knows the future—or at least everything that's going to happen over the course of the next twenty-six years—but the words quickly die on my lips as another voice cuts through the silence.

"Please, have a seat," a female voice calls. "I'll be with you shortly."

I whirl toward Elodie, confusion pinching my brow. A moment later, the purple velvet curtain is swept aside, and a girl with long dark hair and brown eyes peers out. "Do you have an appointment?" she asks, her tone professional with a dash of caution.

Elodie confidently steps forward, flashing a feigned apologetic grin. "Sorry, no," she says. "I'm afraid this was all a bit spur of the moment."

I study the girl, noting the way her eyes widen, the way the flush instantly drains from her cheeks.

No, it can't be. Not here, and certainly not now. I'm exhausted. It's been a long day. My mind must be playing tricks on me...

And yet, I continue to gape, only to find the girl frozen in place, her wary gaze darting between Elodie and me.

Even without the designer clothes and priceless jewels, even though she's dressed casually in a pair of faded jeans, a simple white tee, and a silk blue shawl draped around her shoulders, she carries herself with such elegance and grace there's no doubt in my mind she's one of Arthur's protégés. When I see the crystal charm hanging from her neck, my suspicion is confirmed.

Somehow Elodie knew. This is why she joined me on this Trip.

"Magick has always been the currency of the oppressed," I say, repeating something she once said to me. "Which, I guess, explains this place." I gesture around the small psychic's den. "Only question is"—my gaze fixes on hers—"what the hell are you doing here, Song?"

14

Panic flares in Song's eyes, soon followed by a tempest of emotions—surprise, fear, and a sharp edge of suspicion.

"Did Arthur send you?" Her gaze frantically darts between Elodie and me.

I shake my head, quick to assure her. But from the pinch of her lips and the wary glint in her gaze, she remains unconvinced.

"You need to leave." Her arm is outstretched, finger jabbing toward the door. "Both of you, now! Or I swear I'll call for help."

Elodie is unfazed. With her usual brand of confidence and grace, she breezes past Song and the purple velvet curtain that divides the waiting room from the inner sanctum.

"Yeah…about that…" Elodie slips behind the desk with an air of ownership, sinking into Song's chair as though it were her rightful throne. "We could leave," she muses, her fingers dancing over a deck of tarot cards, shuffling them with practiced ease. "And we definitely will. When we're ready, that is. But not just yet." Her voice is casual, nonchalant, as she fans the cards into an arc. With a deft movement, she plucks one from the middle and lays it facedown before her. "But let's skip the theatrics, shall we? We all know your options for backup are limited to… what, Anjou?"

Her eyes gleam with unspoken meaning as she flips the card to reveal the High Priestess—the card of secrets, intuition, and psychic wisdom—the card I most associate with her.

Elodie's gaze briefly meets mine. Then, leaning back in her seat, she props her chunky black boots onto the desk. Her movements are languid yet full of intent as she glides the serpent pendant back and forth on its chain, her sharp and unwavering gaze fixed on Song.

Song stands with her arms firmly crossed, her brow furrowed into a frown. "Fine," she concedes, locking eyes with Elodie. "Just spit it out—tell me what you want from me."

Elodie tilts her head to the side. "Me?" She presses a hand to her chest, her voice pitching artificially high. "I don't want anything from you. Never have, never will." She laughs, a light, artificial sound completely devoid of amusement. "I'm just trying to set Nat's mind at ease. She's been tied up in knots over you. Pointing fingers at Arthur, even me, all because you decided to vanish without a trace. So, seeing as how we're both here, I figured it was the least I could do to prove to her, once and for all, that the only person responsible for your sudden disappearance is you."

Song's eyes shift toward me, her face clouded, impossible to read. "I left you a note," she says, her expression softening slightly, though her voice still holds an edge of defiance.

"I know," I say, the words tumbling out in a rush. "But you didn't really explain anything. And by the time I got to your room, you were gone."

"It couldn't wait," Song insists, lifting her shoulders and dismissing the gravity of her actions with a casual wave of her hand. "The moon was in place, and..." Her voice trails off. Then, with a sudden sharpness, she looks at us both. "So, what is this? You two on a Trip?"

I hesitate, unsure of just how truthful I should be. "I guess you could say it's an unauthorized Trip," I admit, biting the inside of my cheek, worried I may have revealed too much. Then, throwing caution to the wind, I add, "Arthur doesn't know about this."

Elodie, ever the instigator, leans in with a smirk. "Not yet anyway."

Song's gaze shuttles between us, apprehension reddening her cheeks and tightening her features. "Fine," she finally says, "you found me. Congratulations. But just so you know, I'm not going back to Gray Wolf. Not now, not ever."

"So you prefer this charade?" Elodie's tone drips with derision as she casts a scornful glance around the small room. "Fooling people into believing you're psychic?" She scoffs. "Like, this little dog and pony show you've created is somehow better than your life on the rock?"

Song shifts uncomfortably, her resolve wavering under Elodie's piercing stare. "At least here, I'm not part of some big con," she says. "Stealing from unsuspecting—"

"You can't be serious!" Elodie balks. "Last I checked, pretending to be psychic and taking money from vulnerable strangers who pay you for insights you don't actually possess is one of the worst kinds of scams."

Song bristles, her shoulders stiffening, fingers curling into fists, but there's a flash of doubt in her eyes that's impossible to miss.

"According to my clients," Song speaks through gritted teeth, "most of whom are repeat customers, my predictions are 'eerily accurate.'" She lifts her hands and wiggles her fingers, forming air quotes around the words. "When it comes to predicting the future, I have an eight-month waiting list."

Elodie nods, casually studying her cuticles. "Tell me, Song," she says, "how often are you and Anjou Tripping these days?"

Song's reaction is instant—her body stiffens, her eyes flicking wildly between Elodie and me.

"I mean, that is how you do it, right? According to the sign on the door, your little business here is by appointment only.

And I'm guessing that's because you first need to travel into the future, get whatever details you can about your client, and then impress them with your dazzling gift on the appointed day and time."

"Anjou travels," Song admits, a measure of defeat in her voice. "I stay here to handle the readings."

"And how much longer do you think you can go on like this?" Elodie arches a brow.

Song shrugs. "Not that it's any of your business, but long enough to get sufficient money to ultimately disappear into the timeline and the lifestyle we want."

"And you do realize you have Arthur and Gray Wolf to thank for that?" Elodie snaps.

Song grows quiet. Then she does something surprising, she sinks onto the chair opposite Elodie and drops her head into her hands.

"Magick may be the currency of the oppressed," Elodie says, her voice softening in a way I didn't expect. "But it also comes with a price. And I'm pretty sure you already know that, don't you?"

Song's gaze meets Elodie's, and in a quiet voice, she says, "But we're so close, we can't stop now."

Confused, I watch the scene unfold. Song is visibly distressed, and I'm curious about where this is going—what it is they're referring to. *What price is Song paying?*

Elodie turns to me then, as if reading my thoughts. "Tripping via the book can be really unstable. And it affects different people in different ways."

"Not everyone's affected," Song insists. "Freya and Maisie do it all the time and they're both fine."

"But I'm guessing Anjou's not one of the lucky ones, is she? Which is it—hair loss, bleeding gums, extreme fatigue, open sores…all the above?" Elodie directs a pointed look between

Song and me.

Song waves a dismissive hand, refusing to confirm or deny.

"Well, it's not like I didn't warn you against getting involved in the Way of the Rose."

"Way of the rose?" I look between them. "What is that?"

"It's their little secret society," Elodie says, voice filled with disdain. "Their time-traveling witchy cult." She shakes her head and rolls her eyes. "It begins with an invitation that comes in the form of a hard-to-find bottle of Niki de Saint Phalle perfume that mysteriously appears in your room. Then, once you open the box, looking for clues as to what it might mean, you'll find a little note tucked inside that reads—"

"*O follower of fools*," I begin, reciting from memory. "*You stand afore the oracle, serpent girdle at your waist, red roses spread above and below you, it's folly that binds you to this place.*"

I meet Elodie's gaze, catching the sly smile that spreads across her face. But when I glance toward Song, I see she's having the opposite reaction. She looks deeply concerned.

"How do you even know about that?" she asks, an edge of dread flattening her tone. "Because I know for a fact no one ever sent that to you. No one ever asked you to join. You were on the blacklist."

There's a glimmer of triumph in Song's eyes, but Elodie just laughs in response, a deeply disconcerting sound. Finally, settling deeper into her seat, she looks at each of us and says, "Well, as it turns out, Song, I'm the one who started it all."

15

"I don't believe you," Song says, her words as sharp as daggers.

Elodie meets her defiance with a cool, unwavering shrug. "I'm not sure that matters," she counters, her voice steady and unflinching. "You know the funny thing about belief? It's not a prerequisite for truth."

"You're so full of shit." Song shakes her head, refusing to give in, but the quiver of her bottom lip betrays her uncertainty. "You wouldn't do that," she says. "You'd never betray Arthur. You're like his fucking devoted little puppet." Her words are laced with bitterness, but the insult glides right off Elodie, leaving no mark.

"Did you ever consider that maybe, just maybe, I did it *for* Arthur?" Elodie quirks a brow, looking quite pleased with herself.

Song falls quiet. I join her in that silence.

Elodie leans back, her imperious gaze sweeping over us. "For too many years I've watched him collect these lost souls, showering them with every luxury, every opportunity a person could want. And yet, time and again, instead of appreciating the amazing gift they've been given, they yearn for their old, mundane, miserable lives. Or at least most of them, anyway. And you two"—she points an accusatory finger—"are no different. Honestly, I got so tired of watching this tedious cycle that one day, I just thought: Fuck 'em. Fuck all y'all."

The laughter that follows is mocking and bitter. "I mean,

you really want to crawl back to your dreary life as a loser? Fine. Here's a grand adventure I arranged especially for you. A little trail of scattered breadcrumbs that'll make you feel special, important, like you were specifically chosen for your big secret mission. Oh, and here's an enigmatic leather-bound book for you to decipher." She shakes her head, a scornful expression pinching her features, like she can hardly believe how naive we are. "Of course, some of them surprised me by using it only to go back and forth, visiting their family and friends or whatever they do on their silly sentimental little journeys into the past—"

I'm struck by the way she says *family and friends*. There's so much contempt in her tone, but I know where it comes from. To her, Arthur and Gray Wolf are the only real family and friends she's ever known, and her abandonment issues run so deep that every time one of us manages to leave, she takes it as a personal affront, a rejection of her. Despite everything we've been through—or maybe even because of it—my heart aches with empathy for her. I tuck this new insight away, refocusing as she continues.

"While I don't necessarily approve of that," she goes on, her voice gaining intensity, "at least they're smart enough to want to stay in Arthur's world. But for the rest of them—the ones like you and Anjou—" Her eyes narrow, shooting a glare at Song that seems like it could singe the very air between them. "Well, y'all can stay gone for all I care. Gray Wolf doesn't miss you— doesn't need you. There's plenty more where y'all came from."

Elodie's face, usually the epitome of poise and control, is now a canvas of someone becoming increasingly unstrung. An angry red splotch creeps up her neck, staining her cheeks, and a small speck of spit glistens at the corner of her mouth. When her flashing blue eyes find mine, they're churning with an intensity that's equally unsettling and mesmerizing.

It's rare to see her perfect facade cracked wide open like

this. To witness such raw, unfiltered emotion is a jarring and unexpected glimpse into a part of her she rarely, if ever, allows anyone to see. But it's her startling admission about being the mastermind behind the Way of the Rose that sends a shockwave crashing through me.

My heart pounds a furious drumbeat that echoes the turmoil in her eyes. It's like the ground beneath me has shifted, calling into question everything I once thought I knew about our lives at Gray Wolf.

Turning her fierce gaze on me, Elodie says, "And didn't I try to warn you at your farewell party? When I pulled you aside and urged you to stay out of this mess? To your credit, you mostly listened, which, honestly, I didn't expect."

"Elodie," I begin, my voice calmer than I currently feel, "does Arthur know you're the mastermind behind all this?"

Elodie dismisses my concern with a nonchalant flick of her wrist, as if swatting away an invisible fly. "Probably." She shrugs. "Not much gets past him, you know. But all I can say for sure is, he never asked, and I never volunteered the information."

"But if he did know," I press on, "don't you think he'd be furious? I mean, after all the effort and resources he pours into the new recruits, and—"

Her voice sharpens, cutting me off. "Are *you* planning to tell him?" There's an edge in her gaze, a hint of challenge I'm not quite willing to meet.

I shift my focus to Song, who returns the look with one of alarm. Switching back to Elodie, I say, "What would be the point? Though I am curious about the book's origins." I study her, seeking any flicker of emotion, no matter how small. "I mean, clearly the book works, so we know you didn't create it on a whim."

What I don't say is that I saw the book during an Unraveling on my first day at Gray Wolf, when I stood before my window and watched a girl in a red cape dashing through a long-gone maze, carrying that same small leather book that now sits inside my backpack.

Elodie's eyes flash with a rare hint of uncertainty. After a considerable pause, she admits, "I didn't make the book. I—I found it," she stammers, her usual confidence faltering for a moment, another anomaly I silently note.

"Anyway..." Elodie circles the desk, her movements smooth yet purposeful, and she comes to stand beside Song. "Now that it's all out in the open, I have two bits of advice. First, be careful with using magick to Trip. It won't end as well as you think. Second, no one's going to tell Arthur about you, so just relax already."

Song's eyes narrow, her gaze fixed on the serpentine pendant at Elodie's throat. "And I'm supposed to just trust you—take you at your word?"

"Trust me, don't trust me." Elodie shrugs, her indifference swirling around her like dust in an abandoned room. "It's all the same to me. This is not my circus, and these are not my monkeys. I'm merely a tourist here. And I'm pretty sure the second I'm gone, this will get filed away with all the other insignificant events that have passed through my life."

Song gives a small, tentative nod, a flash of relief crossing her face. Her brown eyes seek mine, searching for answers. "And Oliver and Finn? Do they hate me for leaving?"

I shake my head. "Finn thinks you left by choice, but Oliver's convinced you were lost in time, and he's frustrated that Arthur's not making a better effort, or even any effort, to find you."

A shadow of sadness darkens her gaze, her shoulders drooping under an invisible weight. She looks conflicted, torn, caught between two worlds.

"If it helps, I can pass along a message to them. Let them

know that you're safe?"

Her eyes widen. "You're going back?" she asks, clearly not expecting that.

I nod. "It's not like I can stay here and risk crossing my own timeline."

Song's brow furrows. "But do we even know if that's true?" She glances between Elodie and me.

I look to Elodie, but she just shrugs. Turning back to Song, I say, "Are you really willing to take that chance?"

A tense hush descends upon the room, laden with unspoken questions and fears. The silence shatters when Elodie clears her throat, and says, "Now, if you could just tell us where you and Anjou Trip from, we'll be on our way."

I whirl toward Elodie, alarmed by her question. "Why don't we just use the portal where we—" The words quickly fade, as the harsh light of reality smacks me hard in the face. Our portal stayed open for only two hours, an amount of time we've long surpassed. The next one won't appear until tomorrow...unless Arthur has somehow managed to intervene and undo that.

Song shoots a glance between us. "You're lucky," she says, then pauses as a new thought dawns. "Or maybe you planned it this way. But, as it just so happens, the moon is in its waxing phase, which means there are three portals now open—the Rose Reading Room at the New York Public Library, the Temple of Dendur at the Metropolitan Museum of Art, and a little scenic spot in Central Park, which, at this late hour, is probably the only one you can access."

Once outside, the air between Elodie and me crackles with unspoken urgency.

"Are you sure we should go through with this?" I ask, the

worry evident in my voice. "I mean, if it's as risky as you say?"

Elodie dismisses my concern with an exaggerated roll of her eyes. "Nothing's going to happen the first time," she says. "And probably not even the second or third time. It's the repeat offenders who risk getting burned." She gives me a sidelong glance, adding, "Or at least I think that's the case. I can't say for sure."

My alarm must be visible because Elodie laughs. "So, tell me, Nat—was it worth it?"

I stare at her blankly, unsure what she's getting at.

"Did you get what you needed?" Her probing gaze searches my face. "Reuniting with your dad"—she tugs on the sleeve of the gray Columbia University T-shirt he gave me—"and collecting souvenirs."

A flood of memories rushes through me. That time spent with my dad will forever be one of the highlights of my life.

"Yeah," I whisper, the word choked with emotion. "At least, I think so. Only time will tell. And you?"

"What about me?" she asks.

"You knew Song was here, didn't you? It's why you insisted on coming along."

Elodie shrugs, a flicker of something unreadable in her eyes. "It was a lucky guess, nothing more."

Our eyes lock, and though I sense there's more she's not sharing, Elodie leaves it at that.

"And if Arthur is really there when we return—" she starts, but I cut her off.

"He is," I say, my annoyance flaring. "I know it for a fact."

She lifts a hand, her expression softening. "Sorry, let me rephrase that. If Arthur is actually waiting for us, then you need to let me handle it, okay?"

"Why, because you're his favorite?" I snap, instantly regretting my words when I see the hurt look on her face. "Oh…"

I say, voice small and contrite. "You're actually trying to cover for me, protect me."

Elodie tosses her head, tilting her face toward the sky, her long blond hair glinting silver under the glow of city lights. "Sheesh, Nat," she says, shaking her head with an exasperated sigh. "Don't go getting all maudlin on me."

I smile to myself. This is possibly the strangest, most complicated friendship I've ever had, and yet, it's a friendship all the same.

"Thanks," I say, watching her give a quick lift of her shoulders and quickly avert her gaze.

As we approach Belvedere Castle, its silhouette looms starkly against the night sky. I'm reminded of my arrival at Gray Wolf and how massive, unwelcoming, and foreboding it seemed that first night.

After we've made our way to the top, I dip a hand in my backpack in search of the book. My fingers graze the cool metal of the key my dad gave me, the counterfeit Antikythera Mechanism, and a mysterious slip of folded paper that I don't immediately recognize but plan to examine later.

When I find the small, leather-bound book, I pass it to Elodie. She flips through its time-worn pages with practiced ease. Finding the marked passage, I lean closer, and together, we recite:

"By the waxing moon's guiding light,
We wade into the river of time tonight.
Through unseen veils where eras intertwine,
Grant us passage through the flowing stream of time."

When it's done, Elodie decisively snaps the book shut, and our gazes lock in a profound silence that's charged with a shared understanding. Whatever happens next, we are in this together.

All around us, the atmosphere pulsates with an ancient energy—its invisible power a closely guarded secret, whispered among only the select few who know its full truth. Closing our eyes and clasping hands, a tangible electricity sparks between our fingers as we draw in a deep, unifying breath.

"To Gray Wolf?" Elodie says, her voice trailing into the night.

"To Gray Wolf," I echo, acutely aware of the gravity of our choice, the wrath we both risk should Arthur be waiting for us.

The next thing I know, we're lifted onto our toes, gliding effortlessly across a vast cosmic sea like sailors venturing into uncharted waters, trusting they'll carry us to our intended destinies.

There are more things in heaven and earth, Horatio,
than are dreamt of in your philosophy.
-Shakespeare, *Hamlet* Act I Scene 5

There are more Things in Heaven and Earth, Horatio,
than are dreamt of in your philosophy.
—Shakespeare, *Hamlet*, Act I Scene 5

16

We land inside the dimly lit lighthouse, its walls humming with the distant roar of the sea—a sound that mirrors my own erratic heartbeat.

"You expected the launchpad?" Elodie's voice, tinged with amusement, slices through the dim interior.

I look around, memories of the last time I was here flooding my mind—the night Elodie, Jago, Song, Oliver, and Finn basically abducted me, hypnotized me, and tested my loyalties by making me choose between my old life and Gray Wolf. To my surprise, I chose to stay on the Rock, and now I know why—this is where my destiny lies.

"If we'd used the portal made from the launchpad," she says, "we would've returned to the launchpad. But because we used the book, we ended up here."

As we make our way through the ancient structure, I can't help but think about all the lighthouse keepers who went missing through the years, whisked away from the life they knew, never to be seen again. The thought sends a chill straight through my bones.

"We're lucky," Elodie continues. "It could've just as easily been the tarot garden, which is tricky, you know? It's so visible, you run the risk of someone seeing. But here, it makes it easier to sneak back inside. Especially since I'm pretty much the only one who still uses this place."

The chill that pervades the lighthouse isn't just a physical sensation. It's seeped into my thoughts. As my eyes sweep the room, taking in the lush decor—the pile of velvet cushions, the casual drape of the soft faux-fur blankets, the towering candelabras scattered about—a sharp pang of jealousy gnaws at my insides.

I thought I'd moved past this.

Thought I'd made peace with the fact that Elodie slept with my boyfriend when I still haven't managed to cross that particular threshold.

But here, in this lavishly adorned space, those old insecurities are fully awake.

Then another thought occurs to me, this one far more unsettling.

If I'm still prone to these petty jealousies, if they're able to find a foothold in my heart, then what does it say about all that progress I was so sure I'd made?

Did anything I learned at my dad's actually manage to stick?

Shaking the thought away, I train my focus on Elodie. "How are we supposed to get back? I mean, it must be edging toward dawn. And with this weather, we'll be icicles before we even make it halfway."

Elodie rolls her eyes. "Please," she groans. "A little credit for once. Follow me."

Together we descend the spiral staircase, the steps groaning loudly under our weight. When we reach the bottom floor, Elodie retrieves a pair of heavy coats from a hook by the door. She's about to toss one to me when she cocks her head and says, "What the hell is that?" She gestures toward my arm. "Did you and your dad get matching tattoos?"

I follow her gaze to find a single luminous golden circle marking the pale white skin of my inner arm, as my dad's words replay in my head: *I have a feeling the mark will find you.*

Apparently, it did.

With Elodie still staring, waiting for an explanation, I clear my throat and say, "It's not a tattoo." I sneak a glance her way. She looks unconvinced. "Or at least not a real one."

"Well, whatever it is, you better not let Arthur see it." Her lips pinch. "He has a real double standard when it comes to those things."

An icy shiver slinks down my spine. *Double standard? Does that mean what I think it does?*

Casually, I say, "Arthur has a tattoo?"

Elodie regards me for a long, tense moment. Then, with a shake of her head, she tosses me the jacket and slips into her own.

As we tug the hoods over our heads and duck outside into the bitter cold night, I can't stop thinking about what she just implied.

Does Arthur bear the mark of the flower of life?

Outside, the wind is a living, howling thing. Fierce and unforgiving, it bites into every exposed bit of skin. I huddle deeper into my coat and look all around, noting how the moon casts a ghostly glow over the rugged terrain, turning the continuous onslaught of waves into an infinite array of silver cascades.

"Don't tell me we're walking." I squint into the distance at the fortress that is Gray Wolf, which, from this point, seems as unlikely a destination as an evening stroll to the moon. "Because even with—"

"Who said anything about walking?" Elodie laughs, the sound swallowed by a loud shriek of wind. "Do you honestly think this is the first time I've done this?"

I shoot her a sidelong glance. "Last time you dragged me along, you used a car. But I don't see one now."

"That's because I have something even better."

I follow her as she circles to the back of the lighthouse. Opening a small shed that blends so well into the landscape I never noticed it until now, she swings the door open to reveal a vintage pink Vespa.

"You've got to be joking," I say, pretty sure that thing will barely make it out of the shed, much less tackle such a steep climb.

"Do you have a better suggestion?" She swings a leg over and settles onto the seat. When she turns the key and revs it to life, despite the sound of its engine purring defiantly into the night, I still have my doubts.

And yet, unable to come up with a better plan, I climb on behind her. Circling my arms around her waist, I say, "You sure this thing can actually make it all the way up that hill?"

Elodie laughs. "Hold on," she says, veering the Vespa onto the narrow road, its single headlight piercing the darkness. "And get ready for the ride of your life."

Miraculously, we survive the journey. There were times when I wasn't so sure.

I wait as Elodie stashes the Vespa, then we head for the large iron door. She presses her thumb against the electronic keypad, and with a soft whir, it swings open.

I pause for a moment at the threshold, my eyes catching the inscription on the plaque overhead: PANTA RHEI. Instantly, I'm transported back to just a few hours earlier when I was in another time, in another place.

Time is like a river—everything flows, and nothing stands still, the echo of my father's voice now imprinted on my soul.

"I'm guessing you're headed for Braxton's room?" Elodie glances over her shoulder, her voice light and teasing. But is there something else, maybe her own pang of jealousy, floating beneath the surface? Or is she just a mirror for me, reflecting my own insecurities?

Abandoning that thread, I look at Elodie, shaking my head. As much as I want to see him and make sure he's okay, I'm not sure it's safe, considering Arthur is back.

"Seriously?" Elodie raises an eyebrow. "You're not even going to check on him—you know, because of the head wound and all? You do remember the state he was in when we left?"

I hold her gaze but remain tight-lipped. *Is Elodie accusing me of being a bad girlfriend?*

Part of me wants to stand up for myself, but the moment stretches too long, and anything I say now will only come off as defensive.

"Suit yourself." She shrugs, our footsteps echoing softly as we make our way through the tunnel. When we emerge into the tarot garden, the mosaic-tiled statues, bathed in moonlight, cast long, eerie shadows. "I'm going to swing by Jago's," she says. "Tripping always makes me ridiculously"—she shoots me a sly look—"thirsty." A light, melodic laugh follows, swirling through the night.

"But shouldn't we come up with some kind of story?" I whisper, pausing before the main door. "You know, just in case—"

"No need." Elodie ushers me inside the spacious entry with its upside-down theme. As we move past the velvet chaise that hangs from the ceiling and the crystal chandelier that sits in the center of the white marble floor, she adds, "Arthur's probably asleep, along with everyone else."

"And if he's not?" I ask, a tinge of panic flaring in my voice.

"Then we'll deal with it," she replies, her tone so casual it sets me on edge. *Does she have any idea how serious this is?*

When we finally reach my door, I turn to face her. "El,

thanks." I say. "That was really kind of you to—"

She silences me with a swift, dismissive gesture. Elodie's that odd blend of a person who craves recognition yet skittishly avoids anything that reeks of sentimentality, unless it's initiated by her.

"I had fun." She nods, a wry smile playing at the corners of her lips. "It was nice meeting your dad and his friends. And I'm glad you got what you needed." Her eyes follow me as I press my thumb to the keypad.

When the door opens and I'm about to step in, Elodie's voice stops me cold in my tracks. "Oh, but Nat—"

I turn to face her, only to find her expression has gone suddenly, alarmingly serious.

"Now that you got what you wanted, I feel I should warn you—" Her gaze pierces mine, and in the ominous hush that follows, my heartbeat quickens, its thunderous rhythm pounding in my ears, as my belly clenches with a cold, hard knot of dread. "If you try to harm Arthur or Gray Wolf in any way…" Her fingers idly slide the serpent charm back and forth on its chain, the motion as hypnotic as it is menacing. "Then you'll leave me no choice but to destroy you."

17

I watch, frozen in place, as Elodie retreats down the hall, her nonchalance a stark contrast to the lingering unease thrumming inside me.

You'll leave me no choice but to destroy you.

The echo of her words sends an icy shiver spiraling through me. It's only when I'm safely ensconced in my room that I finally breathe.

I don't think I've ever been so grateful to return to this space. These walls, the plush canopy bed, the classic works of art I've chosen, offer a much-needed respite, a semblance of normalcy on a day that's been anything but.

I lean against the door, caught in a swirl of emotions—a gnawing hunger jabbing at my belly, a heavy exhaustion weighing down my limbs, and a budding panic brought on by Elodie's threat—when the unexpected sound of Braxton's voice pierces the silence, snapping me back to the present.

"Tasha?"

My heart leaps. I whirl around. And there he stands, eyes brimming with a potent mix of relief and longing that mirrors my own.

In an instant, the distance between us vanishes, as his arms wrap around me, pulling me into a strong yet gentle embrace.

"Braxton..." My voice, barely more than a breath, quivers against the curve of his neck. I draw him closer, clinging to him like a lifeline and filling my lungs with his scent—a soothing blend of comfort and home, uniquely his. "Braxton, I—"

Gently, he cradles my face in his hands, pulling back just enough for our eyes to meet. There's so much I need to tell him, so much I need him to tell me, but first, I owe him a massive apology.

"I'm sorry," I whisper, my voice trembling. His eyes search mine, and I recall the heartbreak in them when he found me on the launchpad not long after I'd promised complete honesty and transparency. "I shouldn't have lied," I continue. "And while I could give you a list of reasons, there's no point. What matters is that I hurt you and gave you a reason to never trust me again. If you can't forgive me, I understand. I'm not sure I can forgive myself, either."

"Tasha…" His voice is barely a whisper as his gaze rests on mine. "It was awful watching you go. And yes, I was hurt that you didn't trust me enough to tell me the truth. But mostly, I'm just so glad you're back and that you're okay." His words vibrate with relief and a deep-seated yearning. "Did you get what you needed?" he asks.

Instead of answering, I pull away and lift my arm, revealing the luminous gold circle now marking my flesh.

He inhales sharply, his eyes widening as he traces the curving line with a gentle finger. But there's a flicker of unease in his gaze, like a storm cloud passing over the sun.

"It should've been me," he says, his voice loaded with regret. "I should've gone back, found my dad, completed my training, and come up with a plan. Instead, I let myself get seduced by this place, by the ease and comfort we have here. I feel like I should be apologizing to you."

"But you did seek help, didn't you?" I say, then tell him about the vision I saw of him holding the pocket watch.

At first, I worry he'll find it intrusive. I mean, I'm basically admitting to spying on him. But his expression softens, and he says, "I spoke with my grandfather. Unfortunately, we didn't get very far before Arthur showed up. Do you think Elodie knew and tricked us into thinking he'd be away longer?"

I shake my head. "She seemed genuinely surprised when I told her."

Our eyes meet again, and though there's still so much more to say, more to share, the need to remain close, to preserve this intimate connection, overpowers everything.

As though reading my mind, he pulls me to him and presses a soft kiss to my forehead, my eyelids, and finally the tip of my nose—the gestures both tender and fierce.

I melt against his chest, feeling his embrace tighten, enveloping me in a cocoon of protection and reassurance. In this moment of stillness, we stand locked in each other's arms, the chaos and uncertainty of the world beyond these walls fading away, leaving me cloaked in a sense of peace so profound, I vow to reclaim every moment we've lost, starting now.

"Braxton," I say, just as he whispers my name. "You first," I laugh softly, my gaze searching the depths of his.

"I read your note." His eyes hold mine, those deep ocean depths revealing a world of emotions.

A warm blush creeps up my cheeks, recalling the raw honesty of the words I wrote.

"And I love you, too," he confesses, his voice steady, resonant. "I always have and suspect I always will."

His words instantly dissolve as he captures my lips in a kiss so fervent and deep, it resonates through every fiber of my being. Our tongues swirl, our bodies press and meld; the promise of a perfect fit is so tantalizingly close, yet still thwarted by too many stubborn layers between us.

"I don't want to wait any longer," I whisper feverishly against his lips. "I don't want to wait for someplace more special. This moment is all we truly have, and it's more than enough."

Braxton pulls back slightly, his dark blue gaze searching mine. "Are you sure?" he asks, the tenderness in his voice contrasting with the heated need smoldering in his eyes.

I trace a finger lightly along the slight bend of his nose, a charming imperfection in a face so flawless it looks as though it were sketched by Leonardo da Vinci himself.

"I've never been more certain of anything," I say, my voice thick with emotion and an unquenched desire to finally be with him, to truly know him in the way that I've dreamed of.

In an instant, my wind-and-rain-soaked jacket falls to my feet. My borrowed T-shirt is next, swiftly followed by the whispering slide of my jeans. The room crackles with an electric charge, as Braxton's gaze roams the length of me, awe and desire intermingling in his eyes.

"My God," he says, his voice thick with wonder. "How did I ever get so lucky?"

Gently lifting his T-shirt over his head, I silence his words. When his jeans join mine on the floor, I reach out to him, pulling him so close, a shared shiver runs through us.

"Tasha," he exhales, his voice threaded with longing and a tinge of disbelief. Finally, we find ourselves here, in a moment that feels like we've waited several lifetimes for.

Together, we move toward the bed where he gently lays me onto the sheets and settles his body over mine. Our kisses deepen, growing more fervent—a dance of longing and need, of dreams deferred but never forgotten.

He unhooks my bra and flings it to the floor. Then lowering his head, he draws me into his mouth, eliciting a feeling so sweet, so intense, I'm sure I'm about to rocket right off the bed.

I reach down to find him, confirming he's more than ready for this. "There's a condom in the drawer," I say, watching as he retrieves it, rips into the package, and fits it onto himself.

"Tasha," he groans, his fingers curling around the lace band of my underwear. "You have no idea how much I want this—how much I want you."

I respond with an arch of my back, a roll of my hips, and a kiss so deep it leaves no doubt that we're finally about to cross this invisible threshold into a new realm of intimacy.

With my underwear discarded, Braxton centers his hips over mine. I draw a sharp, anticipatory breath, bracing for this long-awaited moment of connection, when a sudden series of loud, insistent dings shatters the silence.

Braxton freezes, his glazed eyes meeting mine in a shared moment of confusion. The spell that bound us just a moment before is now broken by the all-too-familiar intrusion of the reality of living at Gray Wolf—a harsh reminder that even here, in our most private moments, we are never truly alone.

"Ignore it," I plead, desperately trying to pull him back to me and reclaim the moment when we were so frustratingly close.

"Would if I could," he mutters, a weighted note of regret in his tone. With a reluctant sigh, he rolls away as the ding sounds once more, an insistent electronic chorus that refuses to be silenced.

As he reaches for the slab on my nightstand, I sink back against the headboard, my gaze tracing the contours of his form, pausing on the stark white strip of bandages that mark the back of his head and the side of his neck.

A swell of guilt and shame surges within me, tightening its iron grip around my heart. Those bandages serve as a glaring reminder of a suffering I'm responsible for, and I still can't believe how misguided I was to be swayed by Killian's lies over Braxton's truths.

"What does he want?" I ask, voice heavy with apprehension, already dreading the answer.

Braxton, his expression fraught with tension, hands me

the slab. With a deep breath, I brace myself as I read Arthur's inspirational quote of the day. The selection sends a cold wave of foreboding rippling through me:

He who controls the past controls the future.
He who controls the present controls the past.
– George Orwell, *1984*

The words linger in the air, heavy with implication. Arthur's choice of Orwell's quote—a novel depicting a world of absolute totalitarian control, where even thoughts aren't free—feels like a veiled warning. A not-so-subtle hint that he knows far more than he's letting on. His awareness of our actions, perhaps even our intentions, looms over us like a silent observer lurking in the background.

"Anything else?" I ask, returning the slab.

Braxton shakes his head and places the tablet back on the nightstand. "Just that," he says, his voice grim.

I let out a slow breath, determined to steady myself. "What are we going to do?" I ask, my voice edged with worry. Arthur's omnipresence in our lives feels like a shackle, binding us to a reality we both long to escape. I have no idea of how we'll ever manage to stop him, much less break free.

Braxton looks at me, his eyes reflecting an uncertainty that mirrors my own. "We'll figure it out," he says firmly. "Together."

This time, when he reaches for me, I fold into his arms, seeking his comfort. He kisses me again, starting at my forehead and working his way down. When his mouth finds mine, I start to slide down the bed, taking him with me, when my phone begins to ring.

"Noooo!" I fling my head back against the pillows. "What now? What could he possibly—"

The ring sounds again, seemingly louder this time. Braxton

reaches over, lifts the receiver from the cradle, and hands it to me.

Arthur's voice barks in my ear, "Natasha. Good, you're there. I've had breakfast sent to your room. Meet me in my office as soon as you're finished. There will be an escort waiting for you at the bottom of the stairs."

No sooner does the call end than a knock sounds at the door, and a male voice calls out, "Natasha Antoinette Clarke, your breakfast is here."

18

I stand outside the door of Arthur's office, the cool, hard metal of the Moon pressing into my palm, while a mix of cappuccino, fresh organic berries, and almond croissants churn uneasily in my belly.

Give him this, but don't offer up anything else, Braxton had said, handing over the Moon I'd left hidden for him. *Let Arthur take the lead. He'll probably try to trap you into revealing something, but don't let him. Do whatever it takes to stay one step ahead of his game.*

I take a steadying breath, trying to stifle the knot of apprehension wedging high in my throat, as I muster the courage to knock. But just as I lift a hand, the electronic click sounds, the door springs open, and Killian steps out just as I step in.

My jaw drops, my eyes widen, and I freeze in my tracks, totally and completely stunned.

Killian.

Killian Fucking de Luce is standing directly before me.

Last time I saw him was in Renaissance Italy, where Braxton and I purposely left him behind with no clicker and no immediate way to return. While I figured he'd eventually find his way back, I certainly wasn't expecting him to do so this quickly. I thought for sure I had more time before I'd be forced to face him.

Killian remains rooted in place, his towering, nearly six-foot frame easily overshadowing mine. The muscles in his arms visibly flex as he lazily sweeps a hand through his tumble of sunshine blond curls. Those lips—the same full lips that once pressed against mine, devouring me in a kiss—now pinch into a faint, knowing smirk.

On the surface, he's as resplendent as the first night we met at the Yew Ball in 1745 Versailles. Yet after all that's unfolded since then, I've come to see his natural good looks and charm as nothing more than a flimsy facade, masking a deep-seated bent toward deceit.

This slick, golden boy with his superficial allure murdered my father. And despite my dad warning me against seeking revenge, or even going back in time to reverse that tragic event, I've never been more determined to make Killian de Luce pay for his actions.

"Well, hello, Shiv," he says, his voice low and flirtatious as his eyes lock onto mine, twin blue flames blazing dangerously bright. "You're looking rather…" He lets his gaze wander leisurely down my body, tracing every contour and curve as if it's a meandering trail meant for him to explore. "Well, I'm just glad to see you're on the mend."

On the mend?

My gaze sharpens, then shifts beyond his shoulder to where Arthur sits behind his large, intricately carved wooden desk. Stretching across the ceiling above him is Michelangelo's iconic work, *The Creation of Adam*, a masterpiece depicting the biblical tale of the divine breath of life God bestowed upon man.

Of course, in the Gray Wolf Academy version, God is painted wearing a gold ring that's identical to the one Arthur wears—a modification that strikes me as a glaringly obvious symbol of his own outsized ego and arrogant sense of omnipotence.

"Let me know when you're back to one hundred percent," Killian says. "We'll meet for a drink, or even a meal if you're up for it. Seems you and I have a lot of catching up to do." His cheeks spread into a wide, Cheshire Cat grin. "Maybe the Hideaway Tavern?" He cocks his head to the side, his shallow swimming-pool eyes exploring the depths of mine. "I remember how much you enjoyed the shepherd's pie when I took you there last time. Besides, I'm curious to hear what you've been up to since you ditched me in Renaissance Florence. But for now, best not to keep Arthur waiting."

He pulls the door wider and ushers me inside. As I pass, he leans in, placing a hand on my arm, his lips lightly brushing the curve of my ear. "And by the way," he whispers, so only I can hear, "I didn't breathe a word of it to Arthur. I figure it can be our little secret." He pulls away, his gaze searing into mine. "Or at least for now. Guess we'll see what transpires from here."

Even after he releases me and goes his own way, his words linger, sending involuntary shivers through me.

That's two threats in one day. Well, at least I know who my enemies are.

With my heart slamming in my chest and my breath coming short and fast, I force my legs forward, my rubber-soled sneakers echoing softly against the mother-of-pearl mosaic floor.

"Natasha—splendid. You're here." Arthur looks up from his desk, and I'm struck once again by how his actual appearance never corresponds to the picture I carry in my head.

My earliest impression of him, formed by glossy magazine covers, created a larger-than-life image in my mind that reality quickly corrects. In person, he's average in height, with the slim, athletic build of a long-distance runner. His hair is dark; his features strike a delicate balance between blunt and refined. His clothes skew toward the understated luxury of high-end cashmere sweaters, dark tailored jeans, and a recent fondness for Gucci loafers.

To the casual observer, he easily blends into the backdrop

of affluent anonymity—just another wealthy white male who's carefully curated himself to personify the look of success.

Yet his eyes quickly disrupt that illusion—they're deep, fathomless, and as complex as a shard of fractured obsidian.

Pushing a pile of papers aside, he motions for me to take the seat opposite him. "Killian tells me you had quite an eventful Trip." He pauses, scrutinizing my expression.

Remembering Braxton's advice, I give only the slightest of nods in response.

"Though I must say," Arthur goes on, "Killian was right, you don't quite look like yourself—are you still feeling unwell?"

I hesitate. *Did Killian actually cover for me by telling Arthur I'm sick? And does that mean I'm now indebted to him?*

"I'm, uh…pretty exhausted," I say, knowing it's better to stick with some semblance of the truth than to make up an outright lie. "Nothing serious, though," I add, hoping he won't insist on a visit to Medical. "I think I'm just a little run-down."

Arthur's penetrating gaze conducts a thorough study of my face. "Well, make sure you get plenty of rest this afternoon," he says. "I have another Trip planned for you soon."

I nod politely, though the truth is, I'm not exactly thrilled by the news. Every Trip he sends me on brings him closer to achieving his dream of restoring the Antikythera Mechanism and controlling time so he can remake the world.

And while I could purposely fail to bring him the Get, I'm not sure how long he'd allow me to get away with that. I desperately need to come up with a plan to stop him, but right now, I'm fresh out of ideas. Luckily, time is on my side. There's still plenty more pieces left for me to collect before he can come close to meeting his goal.

"But before we get into all that," he continues, "I hear you have something for me?"

He shifts forward in his seat, elbows gliding across the

polished surface of his desk. As I place the small silver sphere before him, he draws in a quick breath, eyes sparking with intensity.

"The Moon," he says, almost to himself. Fingers deftly rotating the shimmering orb, he seems captivated, lost in its allure. I use the moment to survey the room, which Arthur once referred to as the *inner sanctum*.

Like the rest of Gray Wolf, there's an undeniable opulence to this space. From the roaring fire crackling in the massive marble fireplace to the cabinet displaying a timeworn manuscript of Marcus Aurelius's *Meditations*, Arthur's favorite collection of essays. My attention then drifts to the majestic tapestry adorning the far wall—a piece I'm pretty sure once belonged to King Henry the Eighth.

"And where exactly did you find it?" Arthur asks, his gaze returning to me.

"Well..." I begin, then briefly relay how I deciphered the hidden clues in Leonardo da Vinci's *Salvator Mundi*, which ultimately guided me to the Baptistery, where I found it tucked inside an ancient reliquary of Saint John the Baptist's index finger.

"Extraordinary," Arthur says, his unreadable gaze taking me in.

I offer a humble shrug, though inwardly, I'm swelling with pride. Locating that piece was no easy feat. Especially since one of the clues he'd given me was completely misleading, forcing me to come up with an entirely new approach on the fly.

Yet despite the satisfaction of my achievement, I can't help but wish it served a more useful purpose, rather than steering us toward the end of time as we know it.

"I think this calls for another visit to the Vault. What do you say?"

There's a measure of expectation in his tone, likely stemming from the thrill that usually corresponds to selecting a piece from Arthur's seemingly endless collection of treasures. But torn between utter exhaustion and my concerns over Killian's sudden return, I can muster only a modest enthusiasm.

"Later then," Arthur says, his voice so brusque I worry my lukewarm response might've offended him. "When you're feeling up to it."

I nod, about to rise from my seat, thankful to have gotten off so easily, when Arthur adds, "Oh, and by the way, have you seen Braxton?"

My body goes rigid, fingers clenching the armrests with a tension that speaks volumes. "Yes, I have," I admit, my voice betraying me by sounding like a small, nervous child.

Arthur contemplates me with a long, considering look. "Such a strange series of misfortunes," he muses, his voice cool and detached. He scans my face with an almost surgical precision. "First Braxton suffers a serious mishap that requires stitches. Then Killian sends you back earlier, accidentally leaving himself without a clicker. And now you've fallen under the weather."

His gaze pins me in place, and it's everything I can do not to visibly recoil.

"Not ill," I'm quick to amend, the laugh that follows sounding forced, if not feeble. "Just a bit sleep-deprived."

He regards me with an inscrutable look, making it impossible to guess what he might be thinking beneath that impenetrable facade. "Well then," he finally says, "I trust you and Braxton will recover soon. I've grown rather accustomed to relying on you both."

My lips press into a thin, grim line. Determined not to fidget, I respond with a simple nod.

"However, before I let you go," he continues, "I would appreciate your insights on a matter."

I watch as Arthur stands and gracefully circles his desk,

motioning for me to follow him to an easel shrouded by a plain white cloth.

"It's an enigmatic piece," he says. "One that scholars have debated for centuries."

"And you think I have something to contribute?" A hint of incredulity creeps into my voice.

"I wouldn't ask if I weren't confident," he replies. "I believe there's value to be had in an open and eager mind, one free of all preconceptions or expectations. It's akin to what Shunryu Suzuki said, *In the beginner's mind there are many possibilities, but in the expert's there are few*."

Shunryu Suzuki? My jaw practically drops to the floor. *Isn't that the same Zen master my dad quoted to me?*

"If your mind is empty," I say, repeating what my dad recently said, "it is open to everything."

I stare at Arthur, a strange sense of déjà vu, or even déjà vécu, swirling within, leaving me feeling lightheaded, woozy, unsteady on my feet.

"Yes," Arthur says, studying me with an inscrutable gaze. "It seems you're familiar with the concept and its author."

I give an uneasy shrug. At this moment, it's all I can manage. Then, with a fluid gesture, Arthur unveils the artwork, leaving me gaping at the sight.

"*Melencolia 1*," I whisper, not realizing I've spoken aloud until Arthur's attention sharpens on me.

"So, you know it?" His gaze penetrates so deeply into my flesh, it feels like an anchor dragging me into depths I'll never escape.

"Yeah, um…I mean, yes," I manage to say. "I'm…familiar with it."

What I don't say is how I came to be familiar with it— because my dad showed it to me on my illicit visit to 1998.

Everything is connected, my dad explained. *There's no such thing as mere coincidence. Everything that's happened on your path has led you right here.*

A swarm of chills blankets my skin, and as I dare to meet Arthur's gaze, I'm struck by the unsettling realization that he not only knows where I've been, but also what I intend to do next.

19

"So, first impressions," Arthur prompts, leaning slightly forward, an air of genuine curiosity shaping his tone. He gestures toward the mysterious engraving on the easel before me.

Feeling a lump beginning to form in my throat, I take a moment to gather my thoughts. "Well, the first thing that strikes me is the angel," I say, my voice steadier than I currently feel. Casually, I tuck my hands into the front pockets of my jeans, hoping to hide any signs of shaking or nervousness.

"Care to elaborate?" Arthur's scrutiny intensifies, a careful balance of skepticism and intrigue as his eyes lift from the artwork to me.

"She's placed in a crowded, bustling, disorderly scene. And yet, she remains wholly detached, immune to the chaos surrounding her. Her gaze is fixed on something beyond the visible—beyond anything we, the viewer, can see." Catching Arthur's slight nod, an unspoken cue to continue, I go on. "Some claim it's a sort of spiritual self-portrait of the artist himself—representing the solitude and melancholy involved in creative endeavors."

"And you," Arthur probes, his interest clearly piqued. "What do you think?"

Releasing a breath, I say, "To me, it speaks of elevation, ascension, or maybe even transcending the immediate in the hope of grasping something profound."

Arthur's piercing gaze holds mine, igniting a spark of resolve that instantly dispels any lingering sense of fatigue. "And what might that be?" he asks. "This profound thing that you hint at?"

"For one thing"—I slip a hand from my pocket and gesture toward the engraving—"notice the caliper in her hand." I point toward the object in the angel's grasp. "Traditionally, they're used for measuring the gap or scope between two points. Which makes me wonder if it might symbolize her attempt to approximate the distance between her current existence in this worldly domain and a higher celestial realm from which she may originate."

Arthur nods, urging me to continue.

"And see this ladder?" I motion toward the ladder that leans against a windowless structure. "It has no visible beginning or end, and yet seven rungs are distinctly displayed. In numerology, the number seven pertains to matters of spiritual inquiry and introspection. It symbolizes the thinkers, the seekers, those committed to delving beyond the surface to unearth deeper truths."

As I speak, my confidence surges. Though I'm not entirely sure where any of this originates from, I can't help but wonder if this is some of the knowledge the Mystery School Elder imparted.

"Sevens are the investigators, the analysts," I continue, the words practically leaping off my tongue. "Those who know that the details are the key to true understanding. And to me, that's what this picture is truly about. This artwork mirrors a profound journey—a quest not just for knowledge, but for deeper comprehension. All these tools that surround her, they're not just some random assortment of objects, but rather symbolic tools to aid in her exploration of life's intricacies, of her own existence, of the process of creation, and perhaps most ambitiously…" I pause for a breath, locking eyes with Arthur once more. "…of the elusive nature of time itself."

After a brief silence, I point to another detail on the engraving. "Also, see this?" My finger rests above a square divided into sixteen smaller squares, each with a different number etched inside. "It's a magic box. No matter which way you add the numbers—vertically, horizontally, or diagonal—the total always equals thirty-four."

I glance at Arthur, checking to see if he's still following, and he nods for me to continue.

"If we look at this from a numerology standpoint—apart from the master numbers eleven, twenty-two, and thirty-three, of course—you always calculate down to a single digit. So in this case, when you add the three with the four, you get seven. Which just so happens to match the number of rungs on the ladder."

Arthur regards me with a look of deep contemplation. "I see," he finally says, his expression flat, giving nothing away. "Anything else?"

"There's a body of water in the distance," I continue. "Which often symbolizes time, and beyond that is a rainbow. But, since the sky is darkened, lit only by a comet, a star, or as some suggest, Saturn, my guess is this scene is unfolding under the cover of darkness. Which would imply the rainbow is a lunar rainbow—the kind visible only at night, manifesting in ethereal shades of black, white, and gray—a sort of ghostly mirror to the moon's luminescence."

I pause to catch my breath, astonished by my own words. *Did I really just say all that? And did Arthur notice how that last bit didn't even sound like me?*

And yet there's more, so much more. The words crowd at the edge of my mind, practically begging to be spoken. "That sort of rare and elusive phenomenon," I say, "hints at the extraordinary—at the thresholds of perception where the edges of light and shadow merge and blend into one. It's as if the engraving whispers of those moments when the veil between the worlds thins, offering a glimpse into the profound mysteries of being."

Um, okay...

My heart slams hard against my ribs as I sneak a glance at Arthur, worried I've said too much, or perhaps not enough, or simply come across as having just had a serious break from reality.

"And the hourglass?" He gestures toward the object that's positioned to the left of the magic square.

"It represents time," I say, stating the obvious. "But not merely the passage of time, rather its poignancy—the transient, fleeting nature of existence, the boundaries of human knowledge and achievement, and"—my eyes lock with Arthur's, a silent challenge in my gaze—"the inevitability of death."

Like my father's death.

And Braxton's father's death and his grandfather's death, too.

And all the other deaths that were either directly, or indirectly, caused by you.

If Arthur reads the challenge, he gives no indication. Instead, he says, "Once again, your insights are impressive." With a practiced gesture, he drapes the cloth back over the engraving. "I'll have this piece sent to your room, so you'll have time to study it in more depth."

"Any particular reason?" I ask, my belly tightening with trepidation, not sure I want to hear the explanation.

Arthur fixes me with a probing look. "My hope is that it will lead you to the next Get."

I pause, curious to hear what that might be.

"I want you to bring me the Star," he says.

First the Sun, then the Moon, and now the Star. Despite the many pieces still left to find, I need to figure out what's driving his obsession so I can put an end to it soon.

"You all right?" he asks, his attention drawn to my arm where my fingers absently scratch at the stretch of blue fleece that covers the spot where my new mark resides.

"Yes," I say, immediately dropping my hand back to my side.

Arthur studies me for a long, tense beat. "We're finished for now, Natasha," he finally says. "You are free to go. Though I advise you to use your time to rest and recuperate. And don't forget to study the engraving and whatever else I send your way. I'll need you in peak condition for your forthcoming Trip."

"My forthcoming Trip to locate the Star?" I ask, knowing that's exactly what he meant, but needing him to confirm.

He gives a sharp nod.

I'm almost at the door when he calls, "Oh, and Natasha. You won't be traveling alone. I'm still debating between sending either Killian or Elodie along. I'll let you know what I decide."

20

By the time I make it back to my room, Braxton is nowhere to be found. And as much as I ache to have him by my side, tell him about my meeting with Arthur, it's probably for the best that he's gone. Exhaustion clings to me like a second skin, demanding sleep more than anything else.

After kicking off my sneakers and shedding my jeans, I slide beneath the covers, still wearing my blue Gray Wolf Academy sweatshirt. Within seconds, I'm out, claimed by a deep, dreamless sleep that lasts for the next eight hours.

When I wake, the soft, waning light that filters through my window tells me I probably have just enough time to dress for dinner downstairs. As I step inside my expansive walk-in closet and rid myself of my sweatshirt, I notice an additional golden circle has appeared on my arm.

I trace a finger over the delicate curving lines, staring in wonder at the sight. Taking it as a good omen that the knowledge I gained in New York really did manage to stick, my gaze drifts to the overflowing racks of designer dresses and gowns. I'm struck by how much I've changed since I first arrived on this rock to find all this waiting for me.

Before I came to this place, I used to fantasize about having a closet like this. The girl I used to be was sure that unlimited access to beautiful things would fill the emptiness in my life. I truly believed that surrounding myself with elegance and beauty could somehow compensate for my lack of identity, purpose, direction, and, most importantly, someone who genuinely loved me.

But now, as I stand among all this luxury, I can't help but view it as an extravagant waste. Of course, I still recognize the inherent beauty of these fabrics, the suppleness of the leathers, the thick, soft weaves of the cashmeres and silks, the artistic expression behind the designs, and the meticulousness of the handsewn buttons and seams, but they're no longer placeholders for what truly matters to me.

The essence of who I am, and the love Braxton and I share, can't be enhanced or changed by wearing fine clothes and jewels. Real fulfillment lies beyond designer labels. This fact seems so obvious now that I can't believe I didn't see it before.

None of these beautiful, aspirational things can ever fill the voids in my soul or prop up a weakened sense of identity. These things are fleeting, bound to lose their luster as seasons inevitably shift. The endless cycle of wanting, chasing, acquiring, and discarding stems from an unconscious quest to feed a need that no material thing ever can.

And yet, even after knowing all that, there's no denying the power of fashion when it comes to sending an unspoken message.

As I sift through my wardrobe, I find a dress that I hope will project my newfound strength and purpose. It's a vintage piece with long sleeves, a high neckline, and a bodice that cinches tightly at the waist before flaring out into a dramatic, asymmetrical hem that falls to mid-thigh. The fabric, a luxurious silk blend, shimmers in a rich emerald hue that catches the light.

For shoes, I choose a pair of black ankle boots. Their pointed toes, sleek leather finish, and slim heels add just the right touch of boldness to the sophistication of the dress.

And of course, no look is complete without the right

accessories. Along with my gold signet ring, I adorn my fingers with stacks of jeweled rings, each embellished with emerald details that tie in with the dress. I complete the ensemble with the beautiful emerald-and-pearl earrings Braxton brought back from Renaissance Italy, and the talisman he had made especially for me.

Slipping my slab into an elegant black clutch, accented with gold hardware, I turn my attention to makeup and hair, aiming for a look that's both striking and refined. I focus on my eyes, creating a dark, smoky look while leaving my hair to fall in long, loose waves that soften the sharp silhouette of the dress.

As I take in the result, I'm met with an image of a young woman who's stepped into her power, one who's ready for whatever challenges Gray Wolf, Arthur, Killian, and even Elodie, might throw her way—leaving no uncertainty in their minds that I'm no longer the girl they've mistaken me for.

Yet, beneath the surface, amid all that strength and resolve, a whisper of doubt continues to linger—an internal battle that bridges the gap between who I've become and the insecurities that still shadow my mind—throwing into question everything I felt so certain of just a few moments before.

Despite all the progress I made with my dad, am I truly ready to take on someone as powerful as Arthur Blackstone?

Ready or not, I have no choice but to keep moving forward. Still, before I go, I take a moment to pause before Salvador Dalí's *The Persistence of Memory*. Back when I chose it, I was hoping it would remind me that there's a whole other world outside these walls—a world where I truly belong.

But now, after seeing a print of the Dalí panting hanging on my dad's wall, I'm no longer sure which came first.

Could Nietzsche's notion of time being a flat circle really hold truth?

Are we all just caught in an eternal recurrence—an endless

loop of reliving the same experience—where every now and then a memory of that experience breaks through, and we unknowingly interpret it as déjà vu?

Or is this something of Arthur's making?

I'm halfway to the door when my slab dings and I check the screen to find a message from Braxton.

Braxton: Miss you.

My heart swells as I read those two simple words, and I don't hesitate to write back.

Me: Miss you more.

Braxton: Dinner in the Moon Garden?

I take a moment to consider. The Moon Garden is one of my favorite spots on this rock—a place I think of as uniquely ours. But as tempting as his offer is, it's better for us to eat with the rest of the Blues—to at least give the appearance of playing by Arthur's rules.

Me: Maybe after. See you downstairs?

Braxton: I'll save you a spot.

Moments before I'm about to enter the Winter Room, I pause just outside the doorway, captivated by the haunting cadence of the opening strains of one of the most beloved and recognizable pieces in classical piano—Beethoven's *Moonlight Sonata.*

It's funny to think how, before I came to Gray Wolf, I didn't know or care about classical music. Yet, standing here now, with the sonata's gently rolling notes washing over me, I'm so ensnared by the music's spell I barely register the warmth of an arm encircling my waist.

"You are breathtaking," Braxton says, and I turn to find his deep blue eyes brimming with such intense admiration, it ignites a surge of happiness within me.

"And you're as handsome as ever," I reply, noting how the bandages that once wrapped his head and neck are replaced by bandages that are far more discreet.

My eyes trace the sharp lines of his charcoal gray suit, surprised to see he's paired it with an emerald silk pocket square that perfectly matches my dress.

"Shall we?" He grins, clasping my hand. As we step inside the room, my eyes widen with wonder at the spectacle unfolding before us.

"Wow," I say, "Arthur has truly outdone himself."

Gone are the quaint, Disney-esque scenes Arthur usually favors for our dinners—like the hologram fawn teetering across ice, under the watchful eye of its mother as a light holographic snow falls from the sky. Instead, we're immersed in an environment that transcends mere decoration or theme.

Tonight, I'm actually walking the swirling landscape of Vincent Van Gogh's *Starry Night*.

This painting, a staple of college dorm rooms and a muse to countless artists, now surrounds us in stunningly real holographic form. Its iconic imagery brought to life in a way that's both breathtaking and surreal.

Yet, amid the awe, a deeper, more unsettling feeling begins to take root. As I watch the holographic night sky pulse with Van Gogh's vibrant collection of stars, the true message behind this choice seems to crystallize before me.

This isn't just a dinner.

It's a declaration, a signal of Arthur's intentions laid bare in the guise of artistic tribute.

Arthur is dead set on securing his Star, and he won't let up until I bring it to him.

21

Braxton and I navigate our way through *Starry Night*, surrounded by an immersive 360-degree panorama of Van Gogh's swirling cosmos brought to life. The haunting melody of *Moonlight Sonata* plays in the background, amplifying the palpable tension in the air. A flicker of deep apprehension simmers within, and the moment I see him, I know why.

Arthur has positioned himself at the head of the table where the Blues usually eat.

It's rare for Arthur to join us for dinner. Then again, this is no ordinary meal. Arthur has raised the stakes, and tonight, every gesture, every word, holds an unspoken weight.

Braxton, ever attuned to my moods, leans in, his breath a gentle whisper against my ear. "Tasha, you all right?"

I breathe in the scent of lavender and freshly cut grass, listening to the soft rustling Provence wind and the distant hoot of an owl weaving through Beethoven's opus. Masking my tension with forced cheer, I say, "Later. For now, we both play our parts."

I pause at the edge of my chair, anticipating Braxton's usual display of good manners. But Arthur stands quickly, and with an unexpected gallantry, he pulls my seat back.

"Impressive," he says, his voice carrying a note of genuine admiration as his eyes sweep over my attire, a mixture of approval and something deeper that I can't quite grasp.

Jago seizes the moment, echoing, "Stunning," sparking an immediate eye roll from Elodie.

Finn and Oliver offer warm smiles and nods, but my attention drifts past them to Mason at the far end of the table. He's dressed in a brilliant cobalt suit—a perfect match for Van Gogh's skies.

Our eyes meet. I shoot him a questioning look, surprised to see he's already advanced to Blue. Instead of explaining, he offers a quick, reassuring wave. The gold crown ring I gave him glints under the light, a subtle message of solidarity and a comforting reminder that he forgives me for the role I inadvertently played in bringing him here. He's still my best friend—someone I can rely on.

As I settle into my seat, a jolt of surprise roots me in place. Killian is here, seated at Arthur's right, and the look he gives me teems with an undeclared challenge.

"What's the occasion, Shiv?" His voice falls somewhere between an innocuous greeting and a sneer, as he darts a glance between Braxton and me.

Braxton's hand reaches under the table, grasping mine, giving it a reassuring squeeze. Ignoring my quickening pulse, I grip the stem of my glass and raise my champagne in a toast.

"Just happy to be celebrating with friends," I say. Casting a glance down the table, I add, "To Gray Wolf!"

The room fills with the sound of clinking glasses and hearty cheers. As I savor the chill of the bubbly champagne, Arthur's contemplative stare catches my attention, fixed on a singular star that shines brighter than all the others in this holographic night sky.

Our gazes lock, and a profound sense of unease washes over me, whispering a silent, daunting challenge: *how will I ever find a way to stop him?*

As the first course arrives, Arthur leans in, a playful curiosity sparking in his eyes. Addressing the table, he says, "Tell me, what do you know about Vincent Van Gogh's *Starry Night*?"

Instinctively, I glance toward Elodie. In the past, we were always so competitive about art, eager to show off our limited knowledge. Yet, this time, I'm content to sit back and let her claim the spotlight.

"It represents the view from the east-facing window of his asylum room at Saint-Remy-de-Provence, captured just before dawn," she says, casting a quick glance my way, as though expecting me to chime in with additional insights. But I no longer care about winning this game. Instead, I focus on the delicate flavors of the amuse-bouche, savoring how well it pairs with the effervescence of my champagne.

"Despite his illness," she continues, "his time at the asylum was marked by an intense burst of creativity, giving rise to many works now hailed as masterpieces…"

Elodie's voice fades into the background as I lose myself in the sparkling holographic stars, weaving a ballet of light across the white tablecloth. This immersive scene, this vivid display of emotion and color, ignites a profound appreciation deep within me.

You have been here before, a knowing voice whispers. *Done this before.*

The thought storms through my head, jolting me back to the moment. Suddenly, I find myself saying, "I've always been intrigued by the way he segments the canvas into the night sky, the village below, and the towering cypress tree."

Wait-what?

I pause, breath catching, uncertain where these words are coming from, or if I even believe them.

Have I always been intrigued by that? Really?

I'm no longer sure, and yet, now that I've started, I can't seem to stop.

"It's often seen as a representation of the connection between heaven and earth," I continue, feeling the layers of the painting unravel in my mind. "To many, it speaks to Van Gogh's inner turmoil, his search for solace amid all his struggles. The stars and swirling sky symbolize hope and eternity. The cypress, stretching from the earth to the heavens, might represent Van Gogh's feelings of loneliness or his aspiration to transcend the ordinary. But to me, this painting exemplifies the power of art to express and evoke intense emotions solely through color and brushstrokes."

I let my gaze drift along the table, adding, "It's said to hang in the Museum of Modern Art in New York. However..." I pause, scanning the faces around me. "I think we all know the true masterpiece resides in Arthur's vault."

Arthur grins, and as a team of servers steps in to remove our plates before introducing the next course, I sink deeper into my seat, taking in the opulent surroundings. When all this is over, when I've defeated Arthur and left Gray Wolf behind, it's moments like this that I'll miss.

Not everything here is bad. Arthur's obsession with beauty is something I can easily understand. I wish he could be satisfied with hoarding art and offering us extraordinary experiences — traveling the world, touring history in a way others can only dream about. But Arthur will never be content with what he already has. He will always crave more. That's why he must be stopped. No question about it.

For now, there is still plenty of time, so I let myself enjoy this moment, knowing it will one day become yet another beautiful memory that I'll take with me.

"I've noticed," Arthur says, "not a single one of you has dared to reach for the stars." He laughs, rising from his seat and theatrically swiping at a holographic cloud, causing it to shimmer and distort. Gasps of surprise ripple through the room.

Inspired by his action, everyone reaches for the heavens. When I catch a star between my fingers, our eyes lock. Mimicking the release of a dandelion seed, I blow the star toward him, and Arthur's grin widens.

As the meal transitions from entrée to dessert, a waiter circulates, placing a small box beside each of us.

Elodie is the first to investigate, her expression a mix of curiosity and bewilderment at the sight of what appears to be a pair of transparent contact lenses.

"They're for augmented reality," Arthur announces, clearly pleased with himself.

As we fit the lenses into our eyes, the room instantly fills with audible cries of delight. The already vivid holographic imagery around us intensifies, drawing us even deeper into Van Gogh's star-studded vision. This dinner becomes not just a meal, but an unforgettable journey through art and illusion.

"Take them with you," Arthur says. "Think of it as a souvenir, allowing you to relive this moment at will. And for now, I bid you good night."

I watch Arthur leave, then, turning to Braxton, I say, "To the Autumn Room?" Figuring we should probably go through the motions and take part in the usual after-dinner routine.

With a wry grin, Braxton grasps my hand and says, "I have something much better in mind."

22

The journey down the hall unfolds in a riot of color.

Our vision awash with the vibrant hues of brilliant golden sunflowers—thousands of them, their brown hearts surrounded by bright yellow petals—scaling the walls and sprouting a pathway along the floor that leads all the way to Braxton's door.

Apparently, these augmented reality lenses Arthur gave us aren't just limited to the world of *Starry Night*. They plunge us into the very essence of Van Gogh's most celebrated works.

The moment we step inside his room, our bodies instantly collide. Our kisses frantic and fevered, all crushing lips and swirling tongues, we hastily kick off our shoes as our fingers claw at each other, desperate to rid ourselves of our clothes.

I peel off his jacket, unfasten the long row of buttons lining the front of his shirt, while Braxton locates the zipper on the side of my dress, pulling it down, down, down, until it falls into a heap on the floor. That's when he discovers I'm not wearing a bra.

With his gaze fixed on my breasts, he releases a low, primal growl. Unfastening his belt, he shakes off his boxers and pants in one fluid move, while I rid myself of my skimpy lace thong.

Then, with our clothes discarded at our feet, we stand bared, revealing ourselves to each other. The mere sight of him makes my heart flutter as a slow, simmering heat builds deep in my core. My gaze roams the length of him, blazing a greedy trail over the smooth, muscled expanse of his chest, down past his finely honed abs, and then lower still.

A small noise of desire escapes my lips, and when my eyes return to his, I find him regarding me with a look so smoldering with intent, I can track its heat as it moves along my contours and curves.

"My God," he whispers. "You're the most beautiful thing I've ever seen. I feel like I'm caught in a dream."

"You're still wearing Arthur's contacts," I jokingly remind him.

But Braxton dismisses it with a shake of his head. "Believe me," he says, voice thick with need, "it's not that."

Clasping my hand in his, he leads me through a lively field of vibrant swaying sunflowers, and gently lays me down on the bed. As we sink onto the mattress, it instantly transforms into a soft, golden field I immediately recognize as the lush, textured landscape of *Wheat Field with Cypresses*. The sunflowers that surround us morph into the rich purple hues of Van Gogh's *Irises*, encapsulating us in a vision as opulent as it is iconic.

Above us, the old velvet canopy becomes an infinite swirling cloud-streaked sky, wrapping us in a serene veil of beauty that elevates the moment from the magical to the truly inspired.

In the midst of this stunning tableau, I find myself caught in an internal battle between all that needs to be said, the plans we still need to make, and my more immediate need to finally gratify this hunger we share. But when Braxton's lips find mine once again, a tranquil hush instantly dispels all my doubts, rendering them into dim, distant memories, until I can no longer recall what I was once so worried about.

Within the sanctuary of his embrace, time ceases to exist. The world beyond these walls, with all its trials and uncertainties, fades into nothing. Here, in the warmth of Braxton's arms, I've found my safe haven, my welcome refuge, a warm and comforting place where our love triumphs over everything else.

Determined to hang onto this beautiful, ephemeral moment, painfully aware of how easily it could vanish like sand slipping through the narrow waist of an hourglass, I empty my mind of everything but the feel of his body, his flesh upon mine.

"Tasha," he breathes against my skin, his voice weaving my name into a sacred vow. "It feels as though I've lived several lifetimes, just waiting for this."

He stretches his body over mine and I arch deeper into his touch, the feel of his bare skin on mine like a balm for my soul.

This kiss—this gloriously ravenous kiss with his tongue sliding in tandem with mine, feels like a declaration of our unbreakable bond, a promise that echoes through time.

His hands, tender yet fervent, explore the angles of my face, the curve of my neck, the swell of my breasts, as if charting the path of our shared destiny, a roadmap of devotion and desire unchecked.

He kisses me again, harder this time, our lips pressing, crushing, desperate in our mutual longing for each other. I reach a hand between us, shameless in my need to feel him against my palm, feel him everywhere I possibly can. I slide my fingers down the length of our bellies until I find him, curl around him, and stroke him until a low moan emanates from somewhere deep in his throat.

"Tasha," he pants, eyes glazed, voice gruff with urgency. "My darling, do you have any idea what you're doing to me? And what I plan to do to you in return?"

I pull my hand away, and with a fiery challenge in my gaze, I tilt my head back, and say, "Show me."

Braxton is quick to obey.

Dipping his head to my breasts, he claims me with his lips. His teeth teasing, tongue expertly flicking, until I'm driven so mad with it, I find myself lifting my hips, practically begging for more, desperate for whatever he's willing to give.

After so many false starts, I don't want to wait another second before joining with him.

"Braxton," I whisper, my fingers spiking into his silky brown hair, carefully avoiding the bandages he wears.

He taps a finger to the talisman still fastened at my neck, then dips his head lower, then lower still, his lips pressing a tantalizing trail down the length of my body, causing a deliciously unbearable heat to flood into my center.

"Please," I say, my gaze burning into his. "I need you now. I don't want to wait."

I grind against his mouth, sure I'm about to break, when he suddenly stops, lifts his head, and with a wry grin, says, "Tell me what you really want."

My breath is coming so fast, I can hardly form words. "You," I manage to huff. "I want all of you. Now."

His head dips again, blessing me with one long, tormenting stroke of his tongue. Then he dips once more, sanctifying me with another.

"Do you know how much I've missed you—missed this?" His tongue relentlessly lashes me like a famished wanderer finally offered a feast.

But as much as I love this, as much as I crave every brush of his lips on my flesh, there's something else I want even more.

"Do you have a condom?" I ask.

His gaze locks on mine and he rises onto his knees. Framed by a meadow of purple irises swaying and shivering at his back, Braxton is more magnificent than I've ever seen him.

"You know there's no rush," he says, tenderly cupping a palm to my heat. He begins teasing me with the tip of his finger, rubbing and pressing against just the right spot.

My head falls back against the pile of pillows, lost in this glorious sensation. And yet, my need for him is so immediate and raw, I won't take the chance of Arthur interfering.

"I can't wait." My voice is a rasp, torn between wanting him to continue what he started and my insatiable craving for more, more, more. "I need to be with you—no more delays."

Suddenly, his hand moves away, and I find myself aching for the warmth I just lost.

In one fluid move, he reaches for the nightstand, rips open the small package he grabbed from the drawer, then expertly rolls a condom onto himself.

His gaze, deep as the ocean and just as vast, locks onto mine. Pulling back slightly, he centers his hips, rears back his head, and says, "This is just the beginning."

My heart resonates with the truth of his words. Instinctively, I nod, understanding fully. We stand on the cusp of something new, something deeper—a transformation into who we were always destined to become.

Then, with a quick intake of breath, and a single hard thrust, he is settled inside me, and the world around us unfurls, blooming into a kaleidoscope of color and light. Van Gogh's flowers no longer relegated to the background, they shimmer and multiply until we are seamlessly woven into the fabric of the artwork.

Braxton's eyes spark and glow like stars, as brilliant, amethyst-colored irises trail down the length of my body.

"Tasha," he gasps as I hook my legs tightly around him, my hands gripping the muscles of his back, pulling him closer, deeper than I ever thought he could be. And all the while our flesh swirls like clouds as our hips continue to grind and drag, desperate for all this and more.

Together we move, our bodies rocking, hips bucking, as Braxton slides and slams into me over and over and over again.

Beneath the veil of a whirling night sky and the soft, golden wheat field yielding beneath us, we soar, piercing through constellations, bursting through stars. The two of us fused, joined, we spiral as one, until lightning cleaves the heavens, and we break, plummeting back toward earth with a gasp, a shout, a strangled cry of each other's name on our lips.

When it's over, Braxton lies by my side, gently sweeping a stray lock of hair behind my ear, as I rest a hand on his chest, soothed by the steady rhythm of his heart.

"Are you okay?" he asks, his voice brimming with reverence and adoration that mirrors the depth of his gaze.

"No," I tell him, my mouth pulling into a theatrical frown.

At first, Braxton rears back in alarm. But then catching the playful glint in my eye, he visibly relaxes.

"I'm afraid you've altered me forever," I say, my fingers skipping from his heart to his navel. "From this point forward, I'll never be the same." My fingers slink lower. "I'm going to need to repeat that experience at least once every day. But honestly, probably even more. At a minimum, twice." My fingers slip lower still, delighted to discover he's as ready for me as I am for him.

Braxton's smile widens. "I think we can arrange that," he says.

As he draws closer, his lips inching toward mine, instead of eyes that shine like stars and a face that glows with the warmth of Van Gogh's sun, his features grotesquely transform into the haunting image of one of the artist's lesser known, earlier works, *Skull of a Skeleton with Burning Cigarette*.

My breath catches.

My heart hammers hard against my chest.

As my fight-or-flight impulse kicks in, urging me to run as fast as I can.

"Tasha—you all right?" Braxton's voice, laced with worry, cuts through my panic.

In the blink of an eye, the ghastly apparition dissolves, and

Braxton's familiar features return, calming the storm of fear in my heart.

It was just a glitch. Surely, Arthur didn't intend that.

Or did he?

Braxton traces a finger along my jaw, then trails a path down my neck, over my shoulder, and along my arm to where a third golden ring has appeared.

His deep blue gaze fixing on mine, he says, "You sure you're okay?"

I push the thought away and press my lips to his, seeking refuge in his kiss.

"Always," I manage to whisper. "Always when I'm with you."

23

I wake before dawn.

The augmented reality lenses, now abandoned on the nightstand, have taken with them the vivid sunflowers and irises, the golden wheat fields, and Van Gogh's swirling, star-filled skies.

Gone, too, is the fleeting, horrific vision of the hollow-eyed skull that momentarily replaced Braxton's face.

In their absence, the room reverts to Braxton's signature moody aesthetic: walls painted a deep charcoal, aged leather couch, and a collection of dark themed art, including Caravaggio's *Narcissus* and Henry Fuseli's *The Nightmare*—each piece casting its own display of shadow and intrigue.

Stepping quietly from the bed, I leave Braxton to his dreams and make for the shower.

The warm water cascading over me is exactly the balm I need after a night that transcended all expectations. Our connection, so deep and full, has rendered me tender in the very best way. Though it wasn't my first time, last night opened a whole new realm of experience, infusing me with an overwhelming sense of love and belonging. Just thinking about those intimate moments makes my heart overflow, leaving no doubt that Braxton is my everything, as I am his.

Another flash of that pale-boned skull flits across the canvas of my mind—a harsh and brutal reminder that last night is gone. Now it's time for Braxton and me to talk, to come up with a strategy so we can plot our next moves before Arthur sends me out to locate the Star, with either Elodie or Killian riding shotgun.

With a towel draped around me, I wander into Braxton's large walk-in closet. Unwilling to face the prospect of slipping back into last night's dress, I search through stacks of the most high-end loungewear money can buy, looking for an old pair of sweatpants and a T-shirt I can borrow. Just as I find what I'm looking for, Braxton comes up from behind me.

Encircling his arms at my waist, he presses a single, sweet, tantalizing kiss to the side of my neck. "Come back to bed," he coaxes, his body enticingly warm, his voice an invitation, hinting at all the possibilities awaiting my consent.

I pause, tempted to follow him anywhere. Then turning to face him, I trace the tip of my finger along that perfectly imperfect bend in his nose. "Wish I could," I say.

"No need for wishes," he counters, sealing his words with a soft kiss on my forehead. "Here, in our sanctuary, there is literally no one to stop us from doing what we want. Inside this room, we make our own rules."

If only that were true.

"No one to stop us except Arthur," I say. "Oh, and Elodie, of course. And let's not forget Killian, who's somehow managed to make a miracle of a return." I sigh, the weight of those names dragging me back into a reality far removed from the blissful escape of last night.

The light in Braxton's eyes instantly fades, casting a dim gray pall that reminds me of turbulent, storm-tossed waters roiling beneath an unsettled sky. He runs a hand through his hair, his voice tinged with resignation. "How about this?" he says. "You get the coffee going, I'll take a quick shower, and then we'll sit down and figure things out."

After I've relayed an abbreviated version of everything that transpired when we were apart—the time spent with my dad, reuniting with Song, my brief glimpse into Arthur's plans for remaking the world—Braxton fixes me with a look, and says, "You should meet up with Killian." His words are so unexpected, I nearly spit out my coffee.

"You can't be serious?" I sink deeper into the soft, worn leather of his couch, disbelief etching my tone. "After everything I just said—that's what you choose to focus on?"

A shadow of deep discomfort crosses Braxton's face as he shifts uneasily in his seat. "Look," he says, "I'm glad Song and Anjou are safe. I'm glad your time with your dad was well spent. As for Arthur's plans, while it's certainly alarming to know he's going to eliminate large groups of people and erase entire timelines, it's not one bit surprising. Arthur curates. It's what he's always done. But now, it's up to us to find a way to stop him. And while I'm not at all thrilled by the idea of you meeting with Killian, he does work closely with Arthur, so who knows what you might learn? Also, there is wisdom in the adage about knowing your enemy."

"That's from Sun Tzu's *The Art of War*," I find myself saying, the words pulled from the secret well of knowledge hidden inside me. *"Know your enemy and know yourself and you can fight a hundred battles without disaster."* The familiarity of the quote surprises me as much as it does Braxton. "I don't know how I know that. It just came to me."

Braxton gives me a look that straddles the line between admiration and concern. "Seems like the visit with your dad really did make an impact."

I trace the rim of my coffee mug with my finger before taking a sip. "Yeah, but so far, it's mostly just quotes and random facts about art, nothing that feels like it'll be of much help. Though my dad did say I need to trust that it's there and that it'll come to me when I need it the most."

Braxton sighs. "Well, at least there's some thread of hope. I'm still kicking myself for wasting so much time with my grandfather—questioning the true nature of destiny and time."

"Did you learn anything?"

He rakes a hand through his hair, his eyes locking onto mine with a mix of revelation and frustration. "I learned that Arthur is responsible for my grandfather's death, as well as my father's." His jaw clenches with anger, eyes darkening with the weight of his past.

"And what became of your mother?" I ask, realizing I don't really know much about Braxton's history.

He scrubs a hand over his face, sighing deeply before taking a sip of his coffee. "After my father passed, we moved to Boston, where she had some distant relations. It was not an easy life, and it's there that Arthur found me. I made the same deal as you. I agreed to go with him, if he looked after her."

"Did you ever go back, to check on her?"

"Once," he says, his voice strained, eyes clouding over with a memory. "From what I could see, he kept his word. But what I don't understand is why he wants two Timekeepers under his roof."

"I'm guessing it's like the royal tradition of having an heir and a spare. Now that he knows he needs us to not only find the Antikythera's missing pieces, but to bring them back safely, he wants a backup in case something should happen to one of us. It probably explains why he never lets us Trip together."

"Makes sense." Braxton nods, the tension in his shoulders easing a bit.

"Did you manage to speak with your grandfather again?" I

ask. "You know, after Arthur left?"

"Complete silence," he says, his lips twisting in frustration. "For some reason, the watch wouldn't summon him."

I release a defeated exhale. "Okay, so what now?" I ask. "My dad says we should figure out why Arthur is doing all this. What's driving his need to go to these lengths to rule over time?"

"Because he's the ultimate control freak?" Braxton suggests.

"That's definitely part of it," I agree. "But there's got to be more to it. Maybe something from his past that continues to haunt him. If we can figure out his weakness, we might find a way to stop him. I mean, do we even know the true story of how Arthur became who he is?"

"Probably not." Braxton frowns. "But digging into Arthur's past isn't easy. I'm sure I've read every article and interview ever written about him, and it's always the same story. He's meticulous about sticking to the script."

"Which means he's hiding something."

"In this world where we see only what he wants us to, discovering the truth won't be easy."

We fall into a contemplative silence. Finally Braxton speaks up. "You've seen the Mechanism. Exactly how many pieces are left?"

I lift my gaze to the ceiling, calling up a mental image of the last time Arthur showed it to me. "There are loads of pieces still out there," I say. "More planets to find, not to mention all the gears and dials and the protective case. At this rate, it's at least a year or two away, maybe more."

A year or two of living in luxury, traveling through time, honing my skills, maybe sneaking in another visit or two to my dad, and all the while I get to love Braxton. There are worse ways to pass the time.

"In the meantime," Braxton says, drawing me back to the present, "we should start putting out feelers, see who might be willing to help us."

"There's not a single instructor we can count on," I say. "Keane, Hawke, and Roxane—their livelihoods depend on Arthur. As for the support staff..." I briefly consider Freya, who cleans my room; Charlotte, who outfits me for my Trips; and even Killian's friend Maisie, who works as a barmaid at the Hideaway Tavern. But I quickly rule them out. "Pretty much all of them have access to the book. They can come and go as they please. And yet..."

Braxton steadily sips from his coffee, waiting for me to finish my thought.

"We can definitely count on Mason," I say, confident he won't need much convincing to join us.

Braxton rests his mug against his chin, and even though I can see only the top half of his face, his skepticism is plain. "You sure about that?" He lifts a quizzical brow. "Because from what I saw last night, he made Blue." Braxton leans forward, setting his coffee on the table before us. "And I got the impression that he's very excited by the prospect. Not to mention he doesn't much like me."

"He doesn't need to like you," I say, confident that Mason is the one person, besides Braxton, that I can fully rely on. "Don't forget," I remind him, "Mason and I share a long history. And unlike the rest of us here, he came from a nurturing home, raised by a grandmother who loved him and looked after him. He had ambitions, goals he was actively working toward. He was on his way to achieving those dreams, when unfortunately, Arthur intervened."

"Or, more accurately, Arthur made me intervene." Braxton's face is glum, his voice carrying a note of bitterness.

I edge closer, place a hand on his thigh, and give it a reassuring squeeze. "You know I don't blame you for that," I say. "And neither does Mason. He's moved past it."

Braxton leans his head back, casting a gaze to the coffered ceiling above. "All right, so that makes you, me, and Mason. That's our lineup. Not exactly a formidable team."

"But it's a start," I insist, determined to stay positive. "As for everyone else…" I pause, biting my lower lip. "Oliver and Finn might be willing to help."

Braxton shoots me another skeptical look. "They had their chance to leave when they got hold of the book. Yet they chose to stay put."

"I think they got scared," I say. "In their defense, the magick is unstable, and…" My voice fades. There's no point in continuing when I can see from Braxton's frown that he's not buying a word of it.

"And what makes you think they won't be scared to partake in whatever plan we manage to hatch?" he asks.

Though I must admit there's logic to what he just said, I'm not quite willing to give up on the idea. "What about Jago?" I prompt.

Braxton dismiss the notion with a wave of his hand. "Jago's living it up—totally embracing everything Gray Wolf Academy has to offer. Have you ever Tripped with that guy?"

I nod that I have, reminding him how I was paired with him and Elodie on my first Trip to 1745 Versailles.

"He's in his element," Braxton goes on, shaking his head. "Loves every bit of it. And, I must admit, he's a natural. Both women and men practically throw themselves at him, eagerly offering up all their art and jewels in the hope he'll agree to grace their beds. Besides, isn't he still involved with Elodie?"

Catching Braxton's eye, memories of his own history with Elodie flood my mind, causing a sharp stab of jealousy that instantly reopens the wound I was sure I'd already healed. It's a feeling I despise in myself. It makes me feel petty, silly, and small. Leaving me to wonder if I'll ever fully reconcile the fact that Braxton, much like me, was once vulnerable enough, lonely enough, and desperate enough to be seduced by Elodie's glittering facade.

Sensing the sudden shift in my mood, Braxton tips a finger to the underside of my chin. "Hey there," he says, voice soft with concern. "What just happened? What is this?"

He tilts my face until I'm looking at him, and in this awkward, embarrassing moment, I'm painfully aware that my eyes shine too brightly, my cheeks burn too hot, betraying my inner turmoil, the shame my pathetic jealousy has unleashed.

How can I still be feeling this way—reacting this way—when I'm supposedly deemed powerful enough, enlightened enough, to take down the great Arthur Blackstone?

Clearly, my father must be mistaken, seeing as how nothing has changed. I'm still the same old, grudging—

Braxton leans in, pulls me close to his chest, and presses a gentle kiss to my lips. The gesture so kind, so full of empathy and understanding, my self-incriminating thoughts instantly disappear as I melt deeper into his arms.

It's in this instant, while I'm enveloped in his warmth, that I remember how I did something much worse to him.

How just a few days ago, back in Renaissance Italy, I abandoned Braxton, leaving him wounded, bleeding, and alone, so I could run off with Killian, the golden-haired liar.

"I'm sorry," I say, finding his gaze. Though I've already apologized, confessed all my sins, was it really enough? Could it ever erase what I've done?

"Don't," Braxton whispers, soothing my brow with a caring sweep of his lips. "We can't continue to beat ourselves up for what's already past. All we can do now is move forward. You and me, together."

This time when we collide, there's a tender fragility to our union that was absent last night. Instead of our bodies crushing and crashing and devouring as though we could never quite taste enough, feel enough, get deep enough, this time we meld into each other in a slow, languorous burn.

"I love you," he whispers, maneuvering me until I'm settled astride him.

I gaze down at his beautiful face, my heart bursting with affection for him; I grip his shoulders and slowly lower myself.

"Tasha—" he groans, my name fading into a long, tortured sigh.

I press a finger to his lips, quieting him, before leaning in to replace it with a deep, stirring kiss.

"And I love you," I say, searing the words into his mouth, into his soul, as the two of us become one with each other.

Battle not with monsters, lest ye become a monster, and if you gaze into the abyss, the abyss gazes also into you.
- Nietzsche

24

As I head to my room, I send a quick message to Killian.

Me: Wondering if you're free to meet up sometime today?

I stare at the words on the screen, feeling my stomach churn with disgust. I can hardly believe I'm actually arranging a meeting with the person who murdered my father.

And yet, there's no denying Braxton is right. For some reason, Killian is reaching out, and I'm in no position to ignore him.

Though I don't fool myself into thinking I can trust anything he tells me, maybe I can at least gain some useful insights.

His response comes swiftly.

Killian: Hideaway Tavern. One hour. You still know the way?

Me: See you there.

One hour to change out of Braxton's sweats and mentally prepare myself to face Killian. It should be more than enough.

Let him lead, Braxton advised, echoing his earlier guidance regarding my meeting with Arthur, and I intend to heed that advice. I'll focus solely on listening and watching, keeping a vigilant lookout for his tell—the habitual swipe through his hair as he rubs his lips together—a sure sign that he's lying.

I quickly change into a pair of black leggings, white sneakers, and a freshly laundered blue Gray Wolf Academy sweatshirt. As

I tug the top over my head, I'm a bit disappointed to see a fourth golden circle has yet to appear.

Once I'm dressed, I scrape my hair back from my face, securing it into a practical ponytail. Then I dab on a touch of clear lip balm, ensuring my appearance makes it clear that no special effort was made for this meeting. I want Killian to know, beyond a doubt, that I have zero interest in gaining his approval.

Flicking the switch on the wall, I stand before the hearth as a blaze awakens with a soft, purring *whoosh*. As I watch the fire dance, tongues of orange and yellow twisting and turning, it's as though these flames hold secrets of their own, stories from ancient times that transcend the simple pleasures of warmth.

I flick the switch again and watch them swiftly diminish and fade — a mesmerizing cycle of life, death, and renewal, unfolding right before my eyes.

You have been here before. Done this before. The words come out of nowhere, insistent and unbidden, echoing in my mind.

Well, yeah. I pretty much stand before this hearth on a regular basis.

And yet, I know it's not quite as simple as that. There's something more — something buried deep in my subconscious that's trying to claw its way to the surface.

The window.

Perplexed, I turn toward the picture window across the room. Driven by an inexplicable urge, I find my feet moving, crossing the expanse of the soft, woven rug, and stopping just shy of the glass where I raise my hand to its surface, just like I did on my first morning at Gray Wolf.

And, just like before, I'm immediately met by a sharp, icy chill that bleeds through the pane, though it no longer takes me by surprise. This rock, this isolated stretch of island, surrounded by an endlessly wind-whipped sea, is no stranger to the harsh, biting cold of an infinite winter.

Pushing onto my toes, I lean forward to peer several stories down to gaze upon Arthur's version of the Tarot Garden—a nearly exact replica of the visionary garden that artist Niki de Saint Phalle created in Italy.

Normally, the first thing I would see is the gleaming silver head of *The Magician*—a card that represents the great trickster, the creator of the universe. It's the card I always associate with Arthur, the creator of our own Gray Wolf universe.

Just beneath *The Magician* is the deep, enigmatic blue of *The High Priestess*—a force of intuition and feminine power that always reminds me of Elodie.

And, of course, it all culminates in *The Wheel of Fortune*— the card that represents cycles of change and destiny's unpredictable nature. It's the card that most resonates with me. The card that marked the beginning of the journey that landed me here.

Only today, the tarot garden is gone, replaced by a grand maze of towering, intricately carved hedges with a radiant crystal orb at its center that shimmers with an otherworldly light.

A maze that belongs to Gray Wolf's past, having no place in its present.

The place where the very first time portal was discovered.

According to Elodie, the energy was too unstable, and Arthur, not wanting to risk anyone else getting lost, decided to tear it down and had the garden built in its place, convinced that no one would go crawling around a piece of treasured art. And yet, plenty still did.

The will is a hard thing to contain, even for a man like Arthur Blackstone.

My breath catches, suspended on a thread of realization. The voice in my head had spoken the truth—I have seen this, done this before.

That's when I notice that the lights are all winking and the ground beneath me is twitching with an unsteady vibration.

As the elegant green paneling and the ornate ceiling begin to disintegrate into nothing, my feet are inexplicably rooted to the spot, rendering me a mere spectator as the world around me dissolves.

Stranded on a dwindling island of wooden floor, accompanied only by the erratic symphony of my heartbeat, I suddenly realize the Unraveling has found me.

Yet this time, the script has been flipped.

Remembering what my dad taught me, I'm no longer its victim, no longer some poor, helpless prey caught in its inexorable web.

A newfound strength surges within, and as I find my balance on this small patch of wood, I speak to whatever unseen force is driving this vision.

"Show me," I say. "Show me what I most need to see."

In less than a blink, the Unraveling obeys.

A flash of vivid red streaks across my vision, and I lean closer, palms pressed firmly to the window. I strain to discern all the details I missed the last time I saw this. I watch closely, following the twisting path, as a cloaked figure moves through the labyrinth of hedges toward the glimmering crystal sphere that sits at its heart.

Peering intently, I struggle for a clearer view as the red-cloaked figure reaches the center of the maze, touches the glimmering sphere, and then disappears as if into thin air.

Moments later, the figure reemerges, now holding a small brown object clutched in their hand—an object that wasn't present before, which I now recognize as the leather-bound book Elodie and I just used for time travel, identifiable by the rose encased in an infinity symbol on its front cover.

The very book that's now in my possession.

This is where the vision ended last time, when Braxton appeared in my room and grabbed hold of my arm.

But this time, determined to watch through to the end, I silently ask for guidance from whatever unseen force may oversee this thing.

I need the whole story. Don't hold back. Show me everything!

My wish is granted when the cloaked figure reaches up, fingers grasping the edge of the hood that conceals their identity.

As the fabric cascades down their back, my breath freezes when I take in a tumble of long, dark waves that mirror my own.

In this unfathomable moment, time itself grinds to a stop. My heart stalls, and a numbing chill spreads across my fingers and palms.

Trapped in an inescapable web of shock and disbelief, I watch as the girl lifts her head, then slowly, deliberately, looks directly toward the place where I stand at my window, revealing herself to be none other than me.

25

Impossible.

This cannot be happening.

And yet, as I watch this red-cloaked girl—the mirror image of me—now racing toward a destination I can no longer see, I'm overcome by the chilling realization that I might've just witnessed some sort of inexplicable manifestation of myself, perhaps from a past life or a long-forgotten dream.

Time is a flat circle.

The phrase spins through my head, reminding me of the conversation I had with my dad.

The illusion shatters when my slab emits a loud, piercing ping. Just like that, reality snaps back into place—the voice in my head falls silent, the room reassembles, and the labyrinth returns to the comforting familiarity of the tarot garden.

My heartbeat slows to a more regular rhythm as I go in search of the purse from last night. Finding it, I retrieve my slab and squint at the screen to find Arthur's inspirational quote of the day:

The eternal hourglass of existence is turned upside down again and again, and you with it, speck of dust! –Friedrich Nietzsche

It's a deeply unsettling choice, especially considering the bizarre Unraveling I just witnessed. It leaves me to wonder if Arthur might be monitoring us more closely than I initially thought.

A knock sounds at the door, and I race toward it, thinking it could be Braxton and eager to tell him everything I just saw. My shoulders sink with disappointment upon finding Freya standing in the hall.

At first, I assume she's here to clean my room, and I'm about to ask for a few more minutes before I go. But then it strikes me—she's not wearing her usual uniform, and there's no sign of her cleaning cart.

"Can I help you?" I ask, taking in her wild mane of bright coppery curls now freed from their usual bun, remembering the story Killian told me—how he went back in time and rescued her from a witch trial by water, a test from which virtually no one survived.

"Natasha," she says, her green eyes flashing on mine. "I have come for the book. I assume you still have it?"

"Oh, of course," I say, slightly taken aback.

Waving her into my room, I search for the backpack I brought to New York. Inside, I find a small square of paper and wonder if my dad might've put it there. Running a finger along the crease, I'm eager to read it. But knowing it'll have to wait, I set it aside and return to Freya, who waits by the hearth, and hand her the book.

"Thank you," I say. "You know, for lending it to me." I watch as she tucks it into the cloth tote bag that hangs from her shoulder, feeling torn between whether I should find a way to subtly approach her, or just let the whole matter rest until Braxton and I have had a chance to further discuss it and actually come up with a viable plan.

I mean, yes, she has access to the book, which lets her travel at will. But how does she actually feel about Arthur? Does his allowing her to live here and escape certain death make her loyal to him?

"You have something else you need to say?" Freya asks, responding to the uncertain look on my face, the way I rock back on my heels, shifting my weight between my feet.

Deciding against it, I shake my head and watch her go. Then, just as she reaches the door, I find myself saying, "Freya—"

She turns to face me.

"You do know that Elodie is behind all that." I gesture toward the bag where the book now resides.

Freya shoots me a quizzical look as though she doesn't quite follow what I'm trying to say.

"Elodie started The Way of the Rose," I tell her, hoping I don't live to regret this. But I need to start somewhere, and this seems like a good way to determine her loyalties. "She's the mastermind behind all of it."

"Is this what she told you?" Freya asks, carefully masking her feelings, giving me no hint as to what she might really be thinking.

I nod, but the way Freya regards me, her gaze vaguely hinting at a multitude of stories, leaves me unsure.

Has Elodie played me for a fool? Again?

Freya falls silent for a long, uncomfortable beat as though there's some internal choice she's struggling to make. Seeming to come to a decision, she says, "Natasha, while it is true that Elodie is the person behind the perfume, the note, and her silly secret society riddles, she is not behind the book. Or rather, she is not the book's author."

I stand before her, weighing how to respond. Though I already know Elodie didn't write it, I still ask, "Then who did create it—you?" Figuring that if she really is a witch, she probably knows her way around a grimoire or spell book.

Freya laughs, displaying the slight gap between her front teeth. There's something so enchanting about that simple imperfection, something delightfully human amid this perfectly curated, finely honed world Arthur's created. I find myself warming to it, and to her, much like my fondness for the slight bend in Braxton's nose.

But clearly, with Freya, that was a mistake. A moment later, her gaze darkens, her grin quickly fades, and for a fleeting moment, she appears hollow-eyed and bone white, reminding me of Van Gogh's skull from last night.

Then just as quickly, she's back to her copper-haired, green-eyed, lightly freckled self.

"I am not the creator," she says, her voice slightly defensive. "But if you have curiosity regarding the book's author, then you should look no further than Arthur."

I shake my head, sure that I somehow misheard. But Freya remains standing before me, not a trace of mirth on her face.

"But why would Arthur—" My voice fades, as a startling truth barrels right into me. "Because Arthur is not of this time," I say, breathless as I search Freya's face for confirmation or denial but finding none. "And yet," I continue, fitting the pieces together out loud, "somehow, maybe by using the book, he found his way here, to the future, and…" My throat goes dry, as I try to reconcile everything I once thought I knew with this new revelation storming my mind. "And he saw what was possible— what technology could one day do—which eventually allowed him to make enough money to…" *Oh my God, can it possibly be true?* I focus back on Freya, and say, "Make enough money to finance all this."

Freya regards me with a sobering look. "So," she says, "now that you know, what will you do?"

I want to tell her that I have no idea what I'll do, but that I have to do something. It's like my dad said, my only job is to stop Arthur. It's the single most important thing I can do.

To Freya, I say, "Did—did you know him before? I mean, back in…whatever time you originally came from?"

Freya shakes her head, refusing to share any details. "Natasha," she says. "I very much need to go soon. So, I give you one more question." Her eyes lock on mine. "Make it a good one, because after this, I am gone."

Something about the way she just said *gone* gives me pause. "You mean like, gone for good?" I ask.

Freya tilts her head to the side, sending a cascade of coppery curls spilling over her shoulder. "Is this really the question you want to ask?"

I shake my head, worried I might've blown it. I steal a moment to decide on the one thing that matters the most as Freya stands impatiently before me.

Finally deciding, I say, "What is Arthur's weakness? What's his Achilles's heel, so to speak? What's the one thing that's driving him to create all this, do all this? Because I know it's not just an extreme love of beauty and art. It's something else, something deeper that I can't quite grasp." Finally, I breathe, worried that I've rambled too much.

Freya fixes me with an unbending stare. Lifting her shoulders, she says, "What is it that drives anyone?" A brief silence settles between us. "Love, power, and money." She nods, and I watch her curls bounce. "And, since Arthur has more power and money than he knows what to do with, what does that leave?"

"Love?" I hear myself say. "But love of what? Art? No, he already has all the art in the world. Love of a person?" I look at her, truly perplexed. In all the time I've been here, every article and interview I've read, I've never once seen Arthur refer to a significant partner in his life. Because of this, I always assumed he was beyond all of that, that he saw that sort of primal, human, biological drive as somehow beneath him.

When I glance at Freya again, I see she's already halfway out the door.

"Who is it?" I ask, voice straining in the most pathetic

way, hoping that even if she doesn't want to give me the name, she can at least provide some kind of hint. "Who does Arthur Blackstone pine for? Who is this one person he can't claim or control or—"

Freya steps into the hall. Turning to face me, she says, "You ask too many questions. But you are a smart and clever girl, Natasha. In time, I am sure you will figure it out."

26

I desperately need to speak to Braxton, to share everything that's unfolded in the short span since I last saw him. But with my meeting with Killian imminent, I don't have time to stop by his room. So, I jot off a quick message instead.

Me: The Moon Garden in an hour?

I stare at my slab, waiting for a response that doesn't arrive. *Shit.*

Anxiety bubbles within me, my leg restless and bouncing, fingers twitching. I sift through Freya's words, dissecting everything that was said and everything that was deliberately left unsaid.

Who the hell does Arthur Blackstone love so much that he's resorted to this?

Is it some sort of Gatsby-esque attempt to dazzle and impress? But no, nothing about that feels right. There's a deeper motive at play, something more that I'm unable to grasp.

I glance at my slab once again—still no reply. Then, remembering the note from my dad is still waiting to be read, I retrieve it from the backpack. With a slight quiver in my hands, I gently unfold the paper, eager to read the message he penned.

Dearest Natasha,

I pause on my name, lightly tracing my index finger over the letters. Just the sight of his familiar scrawl has me completely choked up.

In case you're wondering, I'm writing this while you're experiencing an Unraveling. I hope that will explain why my words may come off as rushed. Though my hope is, that even when my words somehow fail me, you will still find in this letter all the love and support I intended.

To say your visit caught me by surprise isn't entirely accurate. The truth is, some deeper part of me recognized you from the moment I saw you. Like I said, something about your presence felt eerily familiar and right. Almost as though we'd met like that before. And who knows, maybe we have?

While I'm sorry that our time together always seems to be cut tragically short, I want you to know that I'm thankful for every last second I got to spend with you. Because you, Natasha Antoinette Clarke, are the sole source of my pride, my greatest accomplishment, the thing I'm most proud of in this life I've been given.

To put it more succinctly, I am exceedingly proud to call you my daughter.

Although there is still so much more I want to tell you, share with you, I will leave you with this quote from the poem "Eternity" by William Blake:

He who binds himself to a joy
Does the winged life destroy
But he who kisses the joy as it flies
Lives in eternity's sun rise

I will cherish this time that we've shared, knowing that whatever challenges you may face along the way, you will find the strength and wisdom within you to rise up and vanquish them all.

With all my love,

Dad

Tears stream down my face as I reach the end, silent sobs wracking my shoulders and burning my throat. In this moment, a seed has been planted—a fierce determination begins to take root.

Why should I worry about altering the course of personal events, when Arthur aims to remake the world?

Why shouldn't I at least try to do whatever is in my power to spare my dad from such a cruel fate?

With newfound resolve, I quickly dry my tears and tuck my dad's letter away with the one from my mom. Then, casting a final, steadying glance at my reflection, I pull my Gray Wolf tote bag onto my shoulder and head out the door, on my way to meet Killian at the Hideaway Tavern.

I breeze down the grand stairway, no longer paying any notice to the collection of priceless artworks lining Gray Wolf's walls. This place, for all its beauty and opulence, doesn't hold quite the same appeal it once did.

At the landing, I find Mason about to make his way up. Wearing a blue Gray Wolf Academy sweatshirt that matches my own, I take it as a significant, albeit silent, acknowledgment of this path we both share. Now I can only hope he's willing to walk this next path as well.

"Congratulations on making Blue." I gesture toward his sweatshirt, adorned with the Gray Wolf logo.

Mason briefly looks down, then meets my gaze again with a mixture of pride and gratification.

"When did this happen?" I ask, figuring it must've been recently, since, unlike me, he's not wearing the gold AAD signet ring that usually accompanies the achievement.

"I got the news yesterday," he says. "Just before dinner. I'd just returned from Versailles where I was actually in the same room as King Louis the Fourteenth." His excitement is palpable, his dark eyes shining with the thrill of his close brush with French royalty. "I managed to bring back a pile of jewels, which, I guess, impressed Arthur enough to grant me this." He tugs at the front of his sweatshirt, an accomplished smile playing at his lips.

While it's nice to see him so happy, something about his enthusiasm fills me with alarm. It seems the glamorous life at Gray Wolf has clearly gotten to him. Then I remember the rush of exhilaration I felt after my first successful solo Trip, and I realize it was inevitable.

"So, I guess you've adapted," I say, hoping he didn't notice the slight catch in my voice, the ring of disappointment over how quickly he caved. "Seems like you're really starting to enjoy your time here," I add, trying to gauge the depth of his contentment within the academy's walls.

He lifts his broad shoulders in a casual shrug, his lips pinching into a smirk. "Let's just say the curriculum here beats any history class back at our old school."

A shared laugh bridges the gap between us, a brief reminder of the simpler times we couldn't wait to escape. And look where it got us.

"And the compensation," he continues, his voice tinged with amusement, "is a significant upgrade from those measly tips we got at the vegan café." Running a hand over his shaved head, he bends his neck in a way that catches the light, showcasing a dazzling pair of sparkling diamond earrings that contrast beautifully against his dark skin.

"A definite upgrade from those silver studs you used to wear. Arthur's reward, I take it?" I ask, recalling how he always lets us choose a piece from the loot we brought back.

Mason nods.

"Guess that also means you'll be visiting the Vault soon," I say, quickly adding, "I mean, if you haven't already."

"Hopefully soon." Mason grins in a way that lights up his whole face. "I can't wait to get in there and choose a piece for my room. Those empty walls are really starting to drag me down."

"Which piece do you think you'll choose?" I ask, startled to find myself acting like Arthur, trying to glean some small insight into his current state, based on the artwork that most calls his name.

Mason shrugs. "Guess that all depends what's on offer."

"Everything is on offer." I sigh. "The world's most vaunted pieces, the greatest treasures, exist right here at Gray Wolf," I tell him. "All those museum pieces around the globe—they're all fakes."

Mason gives a casual nod as though he's already made peace with all that, perfectly okay with the fact that Arthur has deprived the world of genuine artifacts.

And for me, I guess that's what lies at the crux of all this— it's what stands in the way of my ability to gather a team of allies to stand alongside me. Everyone here has found a way to work around all the moral grayness in order to continue living the sort of elevated life they'd never have access to otherwise.

Hell, it wasn't so long ago when I felt the same way. I remember how I scoffed when Braxton tried to warn me of the damaging effects that Gray Wolf can have on your moral center and psyche. How once you Trip, you can never go back to the person you once were.

It was the same thing Killian said about killing when he stopped me from slaying the duke back in Versailles.

Seeing Mason now, more vibrant, radiant, and alive than I ever remember, his excitement about his new status practically crackling in the air around him, leaves me completely deflated. No longer so sure I can count on his help.

How can I ever compete with all the glamorous things that Arthur provides?

Then, almost as an afterthought, he says, "Oh, and speaking of things worth looking forward to, I trust I'll see you in the Autumn Room after dinner tonight?"

A sharp bite of discomfort lodges high in my throat, delaying my response. "Um, sure," I manage to squeeze out, my voice more strained than I intend. I'd hoped for a moment alone so we could talk privately, but it's clear he's fully immersed himself in the social life here. He's found his place, his friends, he's content. And while I'm happy for him, the timing couldn't be worse. "At least I'll try," I add, trying to mask my disappointment.

"Great." Mason leans in, pressing a quick air-kiss to either side of my cheek—an action that takes me by surprise. It's precisely the sort of performative gesture we used to mock in our old life back home. "Gotta run," he says, stepping back.

"Yeah, I…me too," I stammer, but Mason's already gone.

27

As I close the small blue gate behind me, I find Killian standing on the opposite side of the cobblestone street, casually leaning against the wall outside the Hideaway Tavern.

Objectively, with his tousled blond hair, swimming-pool gaze, and the sort of bluntly defined bone structure reminiscent of vintage Roman coins, there's no denying he's easy on the eyes.

Though for me, his natural good looks and charm have lost their allure, making it hard to believe there was a time, not so long ago, when I was swept up in all that—when I foolishly convinced myself he was a better option than Braxton.

I also thought he was perfectly suited to this strange, hidden corner of Gray Wolf, this simple, tucked-away world where most of the support staff reside.

But now that I know what lies beneath his shallow, golden-boy facade, seeing him here, standing among the thatched roofs and brightly painted shutters of this quaint, storybook village, is like stumbling upon the big bad wolf within a real-life fairy tale.

"Hello, Shiv," he says, blue eyes narrowed, steadily taking me in.

I fume under my breath, still questioning my decision to go through with this.

"After you." He holds the door open with a hint of a challenge in his gaze. "Oh, and, by the way," he whispers, as I step past him. "Nice try."

He's baiting me. Killian practically lives for mind games like this. And though I know I'm better off ignoring his remark, given this is likely the last time we'll ever speak, I can't help but bite.

"What, Killian?" My voice leaps way past annoyance, landing squarely in the realm of full exasperation. "Nice try—*what*? Just say it already. Because honestly, I have zero patience for riddles and games."

"Understood," he says. Then, as we make our way to a secluded table, he can't resist adding, "I was just making an observation on your attempt to downplay your beauty by dressing so plainly. Shame it didn't work."

I fix him with the most unimpressed look I can muster. "Are we done here? Have you said everything you need to—gotten that all out of your system?"

He lifts his broad shoulders in a noncommittal shrug. "Sure hope so," he says. "Then again, with me, you never know."

"What do you want, Killian?" I say, eager to cut through the nonsense. "Let's hear it already."

As he signals for Maisie, the waitress, he turns back to me, a smirk playing at the corners of his lips. "Not until we've ordered at least. Something to eat, and something to wash it down with. The usual for you?"

The usual. There is no usual. I've been here one time, and—

I stop the thought in its tracks. He's getting to me, and I cannot afford that.

"Whatever," I say, folding my arms. If he thinks he can read body language, this should give him something to ponder.

"Hey, Killian." Maisie leans a hip against his side of the table, the corseted top of her bar wench uniform dipping so low her prominent cleavage is at risk of spilling out.

The memory of my previous pangs of jealousy as I watched their flirtatious exchange now seems so distant, like it happened to somebody else in another time and place.

Now, as I watch her twirl her hair around her finger and flash her eyes, I find myself feeling sorry for her. She has no idea that Killian is far from the hero they've all mistaken him for. He acts solely in his own self-interest and nothing more.

Barely acknowledging me, she offers a halfhearted, "Natasha."

I give a terse nod in return, eager to move past all this and get the meeting over and done with.

"All right…" Killian begins, adopting a tone of false consideration, "Shiv here…oh, well, apologies. I guess that's Natasha to you, since Shiv is more like a private joke between the two of us."

"No, it's not," I cut in. "Not private, and definitely not a joke."

Killian's grin widens. "As you wish," he concedes. Then, turning to Maisie, "Natasha is dying for a slice of your shepherd's pie. And I'll have the same."

The only thing I'm dying for is to get the hell out of here, yet I offer a weak smile in response. No need to drag Maisie into all that.

"And to drink?" Maisie asks, her attention never straying from Killian.

"I'll have a pint," he decides, then glances my way. "Two?"

I shake my head. Not a chance. I need to remain as sober as possible with this guy. "Just water," I say, which, for whatever reason, makes them both laugh.

As Maisie walks away, I center my focus on Killian. "You asked for this meet-up, so get to it already. What do you want?"

He leans back in his seat and surveys me with a leisurely gaze. "Actually, Shiv," he says with a smirk, "'twas yourself, darlin', who reached out to me. And I 'ave ter say, I was rather surprised by your text. Delighted, fer sher, but definitely a wee bit taken aback."

I shut my eyes for a moment and take a deep, cleansing breath, trying to steel my resolve. Somewhere inside me is a bubbling cauldron of knowledge and wisdom, but when it comes to dealing with this clown and his bullshit fake accents—my last nerve is stretched to the breaking point.

Setting my focus on Killian again, I say, "Not how I remember it. But if that's the story you need to tell yourself, fine, be my guest."

Killian smirks. "Your concession is noted. It's so generous of you to acknowledge your role in putting this whole thing into play."

I'm about to unleash, but luckily, I'm saved by Maisie, who arrives with Killian's pint, though my water seems to have slipped her mind.

"So sorry," Maisie says. "I guess I forgot about you—erm, the water, that is."

When she's gone, I turn back to Killian. "You might want to reassure her that I pose absolutely no threat to whatever it is you two have."

Killian raises a brow, takes a slow sip of his beer. "And why would I say something like that?" He returns his pint to the table. "Why would you ask me to lie to the poor lass?"

Silently, I count to three. When that doesn't work, I do it again. When my composure is somewhat intact, I say, "Here's what I know. One—you killed my dad. Two—there is zero chance of anything happening between us—never, ever, ever, forever—because of the first reason. The sooner you make peace with that, the better for everyone."

Killian leans way back in his chair, tipping it on its two hind legs. "I wouldn't be too certain of that," he says.

"Well, then you grossly overestimate your powers of charisma," I snap.

Killian offers a sardonic grin. "I seem to remember you

threatening to go back in time so you could kill me and save your father," he says. "And yet, I'm still here." He rights his seat and spreads his arms wide, presumably so I can marvel at his impressive wingspan. "Which leads me to believe that you rather enjoy having me around. If nothing else, I'm witty, amusing, and as many will vouch, devastatingly handsome as well."

"Or maybe," I say, a sharp edge to my voice, "and far more likely, I just haven't gotten around to it yet."

"But you did Trip, Shiv, didn't you?" he prods, looking at me with an all-knowing gaze.

I refuse to confirm or deny.

"Because when I returned to Gray Wolf, I found you and your pal Elodie notably absent. Of course, I covered for you, and told Arthur you were feeling unwell. Which, by the way, you still haven't acknowledged."

"I'll be sure to pop a thank-you card into the mail." A smirk tugs at my lips. "Tell me, Killian," I say, "were you worried? Were you checking every five minutes to see if you still exist?"

He hesitates, giving Maisie the opportunity to set down our shepherd's pies without having to listen to this. Of course, my water is conspicuously absent.

"Maisie, darling," he says. "Aren't you forgetting something?"

Maisie casts a wary look my way before departing.

"So, Shiv, where were we?" Killian asks, refocusing on me.

"You were worried I might actually follow through on my threats against you."

"Right." He nods. "That." Attacking his plate with the vigor of one who hasn't eaten for a week, he glances at my own untouched meal. "Aren't you at least going to take a bite?" He gestures with his fork toward my plate.

I shake my head and slide the pie across the table toward him. "Look," I say, "let's cut through this charade. We both know you're the one who asked to meet when I saw you in Arthur's office. So can we please just skip this unbearable back and forth and just tell me what this is really about?"

He chuckles, pausing mid-bite, fork hovering before him. "Boy, you really have quite the aversion to the small pleasantries in life, don't you?"

I roll my eyes, seconds from walking away if he insists on continuing with this.

"All right," he concedes, "here's the bottom line…" He pauses, drawing out the moment in a clear display of dominance that annoys me to no end.

Still, I sit here and watch as he leisurely forks a piece of shepherd's pie into his mouth, deliberately taking his time to chew. After swallowing, he sets his fork down and indulges in a lengthy sip of beer. Then, with exaggerated precision, he grabs a napkin and dabs at the corners of his mouth.

While I'm sure there's someone out there who would really get off watching a man as objectively handsome as Killian eat with such gusto, for me, this absurd display is totally nauseating.

Finally, when it's over, he motions me closer, another obvious power play, but I remain right where I am, refusing to yield to him.

"Suit yourself." With a casual shrug, he takes another quick swig of his beer, pushing me *this* close to walking out. Finally, he says, "Simply put—you need to know that I can't, and won't, allow you to go through with your plan."

At first, I honestly have no idea what he's talking about.

"Arthur," he clarifies. "I know you're planning something, and I'm telling you right now, I will not let it happen."

"Is that it?" I say, confused by his need to announce this. I always assumed he'd try to stand in my way.

He nods. "Pretty much, yes."

I scoff. "You do know you could've just put that in a text—saved us both from having to do this?"

"But then I wouldn't get to see you," he says.

That's it. I'm sick of him thinking he can talk to me like this—like I'm no different from Maisie, or anyone else he can easily manipulate.

"I'm out," I say, patience frayed to its very last thread.

"And if I'm not finished talking?" he challenges.

"I'm not sure I care," I snap.

"I'm sure you don't," he says. "But that's only because you don't know what I'm about to propose."

"Still not sure I care," I say, and yet, I'm pretty sure he can see the way my resolve falters just enough for him to continue.

"Imagine," he leans in, lowering his voice, "if there was a way to have the best of both worlds."

"Meaning?" I ask, struggling to keep my curiosity from seeping into my voice.

"What would you say"—he pauses for effect—"if I told you I've figured out a way to undo what happened to your dad?"

28

I'm speechless.

Stunned.

It was pretty much the last thing I expected to hear. Especially coming from him. The shock of his words pins me in place.

Narrowing my gaze on Killian, I say, "You mean what *you did to* my dad?"

Killian's response is soft, almost remorseful. "Yes, what I did, Shiv," he says, and for once, his face is an open book. No sign of his usual tells, no swipe of his hair, no pressing of lips. And the fake accent is notably gone. "I want you to know I've never forgiven myself," he continues, and though his admission strikes a chord, it's not nearly enough to douse the anger burning brightly inside me.

"Oh really?" I say, my skepticism palpable, voice laced with bitterness. "Have you forgotten that I watched the whole scene unfold? That I saw how you casually flicked your cigarette ash onto his face, while you gloated over..." My voice fades, my anger cresting to such great heights that words temporarily escape me. "Gloated over all the vile and disgusting things that you'd one day do to me." I practically spit.

"And have you forgotten that I was only fourteen at the time? That I was young, and stupid, and full of reckless, unearned bravado? Look, I admit, I was a little piece of shit. I was naive, thought I was invincible — a complete and total asshole. But did it ever occur to you that I'm no longer that guy?"

Tossing my head back, I let out a sharp, bitter laugh. "Are you joking? Killian, you are exactly that guy," I say, my gaze like a blade. "In fact, you're the scorpion, right? Isn't that what you told me, when you recited your little scorpion and frog story back in Renaissance Italy?"

I watch as he drops his head into his hands, acting the part of a man caught in a flood of emotional distress. But I'm not buying it, not for a second. When it comes to Killian, my skepticism remains completely unshakable.

"You know, there's a quote by Maya Angelou," I say. "When someone shows you who they are, believe them the first time."

Raising his head, Killian locks eyes with me, and I know he's searching for an inroad, a crack in my resolve that doesn't exist.

"Well, unfortunately," I continue, "I didn't believe you the first time. But I do believe the last face you showed me, when you held a knife to Braxton's throat, forcing me to choose between his life and the Moon."

He sits with that for a moment, staring into his beer. "And clever girl that you are," he says, his voice so quiet I can just barely make out the words, "you found a way around that predicament, didn't you?" His expression falls flat, the spark in his eyes nearly doused, his usually full lips reduced to a thin, grim line. A weighted silence falls between us, and I'm thinking it's time to bid him goodbye, when he adds, "Perhaps I'm unaccustomed to not having my desires met."

My eyes widen. *Can he even hear himself?*

"Seriously?" I say. "What are you, a toddler?" I shake my head, unable to hide my disdain. "Are you going to throw a tantrum every time you butt heads with the world? Because all I can say to that is, Killian de Luce, you've got some serious growing up to do."

He concedes with a shrug. "Maybe you're right. And yet, you can't deny what existed between us. We had something, Shiv. Something genuine, real—something bigger than both of us. I felt the way you returned my kiss. Felt the way your hands—"

"Enough!" I cut him off, the memory of that moment filling me with a deep seething anger and regret, not just at him, but also that sad, desperate girl I so recently was. "What we had, if you can even call it that, was a mistake. A moment of weakness on my part. Nothing more."

Killian leans back, his expression hardening. "You're really going to look me in the face and tell me it meant nothing?"

"Yes," I say nodding firmly. "Because it did. Not in the way that you think."

He studies me for a moment, then sighs. "I suppose there's no convincing you otherwise."

"Don't waste your time," I tell him, my resolve steeling. "Because you and I will never happen. That's not a threat, it's a promise I plan to keep forever."

"Forever is a long time, Shiv." His voice is so quiet it's nearly inaudible.

"In this case, not nearly long enough." I shake my head, eager to be done with him. "You have an alarming sense of entitlement, you know that?"

Pushing his half-eaten pie aside, he rests his hands on the table, staring at his open palms as though the secrets of the universe were etched in those lines. "Love makes a person do crazy things," he says, as though that's somehow supposed to excuse his actions and charm the pants off me.

And yet, as annoying as I find his response, my feelings for him suddenly shift from a deep, seething anger to sheer, unadulterated pity.

Killian de Luce has no idea what love really is. And I suppose, back when I was crushing on him, neither did I.

But now that I do, now that I know what it's like to love so deeply and completely it's woven into the very fabric of my being, I can't fathom what I ever found appealing in him. Good looks and banter—it's a greeting card, a Christmas movie, a swipe of red lipstick on a pig—it's all surface, no substance.

"You're wrong about love," I say, my voice softer, hoping maybe it will help him to truly hear. "Love doesn't make you crazy. It's not drama and chaos and insecurity. Not when it's real. Love is grounding, healing, the most stabilizing force in the world."

"I want that," he says, his voice almost childlike in its yearning. "And I want it with you."

Frowning, I stand, my chair scraping softly. "But that's something you'll never have with me," I say. "My heart is already claimed."

Killian's eyes well with something that's much closer to rage than tears. "Fucking Braxton," he mutters under his breath. Then, looking at me as though he's just noticed I'm no longer sitting, he adds, "Are you leaving?"

"I am," I tell him, without a trace of hesitation.

"But I haven't even told you about my idea on how to save your father."

I pause for a moment to consider. And though there's still no sign of a tell, I don't need Killian de Luce to save my dad, not when I plan to do it myself.

"I'm afraid you're going to have to come up with another way to redeem yourself," I say, and anchoring my bag on my shoulder, I circle the table to make my departure.

"But you're not going back, are you?" he says, voice spiked with panic. "Back to 1741, I mean?"

Though I could answer, set his mind at ease, what would be the point?

I've nearly reached the door when his voice cuts through

the air. "What does fucking Braxton Huntley have that I don't?" he shouts.

Figuring that's worth a response, I turn to face him. His eyes blaze with desperation, frustration, as his cheeks flush splotchy and red.

"Braxton," I say, voice steady, "is a grown-up who understands what it means to truly love someone."

Leaving him with that, I don't allow myself so much as a backward glance. With my heart racing, I step through the door and onto the cobblestone street.

Though a part of me hopes this is the last time I'll ever have to lay eyes on Killian, another, more intuitive part, whispers that our paths are surely bound to cross once again before this is over.

29

By the time I return to my room, there's still no response from Braxton. So I send him another message, thinking he might've overlooked the first one.

Me: Back in my room. Meet me here?

Once again, I'm greeted by an extended silence that's really starting to weigh on me.

A few moments later, there's a knock at my door. Thinking it's him, I rush to open it, only to find Roxane standing outside.

"Expecting someone else?" she says, reading the flash of disappointment in my eyes.

"Thought maybe it was Braxton," I admit.

She gives me a quick, assessing once-over. "Haven't seen him," she says, her tone as crisp and formal as ever. After an awkward pause, she adds, "May I come in? Arthur wanted you to have this. He says you'll know what it's for."

I notice the sizable package on the wheeled cart beside her. Given its shape, I guess it's the engraving of *Melencolia I* that Arthur promised to send to my room.

After moving the package to lean against the plush velvet settee, Roxane reaches into her Gray Wolf tote bag and retrieves an envelope, handing it to me. It's probably a few carefully selected tarot cards and a copy of Christopher Columbus's map—more clues Arthur expects me to decipher so I can bring him the Star he so desperately wants.

Once the handover is complete, I walk Roxane back to the door, eager to be alone so I can try to reach Braxton again. But she stops in the threshold and says, "And now I'll need you to come with me."

"Where?" My response is sharper than intended, but I chalk it up to that ridiculous meeting with Killian combined with my concern over Braxton's whereabouts. Arthur wouldn't send him out on a Trip, would he? Not when he's still recovering from a head injury.

"Well," Roxane says, her chirp of a voice snapping me back to the present. "It's supposed to be a surprise. But, since you're clearly experiencing some sort of trust issues, I'll just go ahead and tell you that Arthur would like to see you in the Vault."

"Now?" The word escapes me in a rush of alarm. Arthur mentioned a trip to the Vault when he called me to his office, but my last two visits were after dinner. I was expecting the same this time.

Roxane's features harden. Or maybe they don't—her default expression is stern, making it hard to get an accurate read on her. But then, just as soon as I've thought it, I'm overcome with guilt for making snap judgments. It's not her fault that her rigid posture, severe blond bob, and thin strip of a mouth give the impression of someone with a penchant for enforcing harsh rules and doling out criticism.

"Yes," she says, voice clipped. "Right now. Arthur is waiting. So, hurry up, get moving, chop-chop."

I remain rooted in place, blinking at her incredulously.

Did she actually just say that to me?

There was a time, not so long ago, when I'd have meekly nodded and hurried along. But those days are long gone. I'm no longer some scared little newbie, fearfully bending to her authoritative commands. I know my worth here, and I refuse to be diminished by anyone.

Besides, here in the hierarchy of Arthur's world, I'm far more important than her.

I'm the one he's counting on to make his biggest dream come true.

"Please don't talk to me like that," I say firmly. "Not only is it unnecessary, but it's completely disrespectful and very unkind."

Roxane blinks, but otherwise remains silent, which spurs me to add, "When I first arrived here, I looked up to you. You seemed so strong and capable, like you really had it together. But I guess I was wrong. Because truly confident people don't treat others like that. I expected better from you."

Roxane stares at me for a long, tense moment—a silent standoff I'm more than equipped to handle. Just when I'm expecting her to retaliate, she surprises me by saying, "Noted." Then, "So, ready to go?"

Am I ready? Technically, yes.

Do I actually want to go to the Vault? Not really. I'd much rather stay here and try to figure out what the hell happened to Braxton.

But realizing I've pushed my limit, I plaster a smile onto my face, and say, "Sure. Let's do this."

With Roxane behind the wheel of an electric cart, we traverse the complex series of hallways in silence until we reach the elevator bank where Arthur is waiting.

"Enjoy!" Roxane says, giving me a quick wave as her cart speeds off.

"Natasha." Arthur grins. "You're looking well. I trust you've caught up on your rest?"

I nod and follow him into the elevator. We quickly descend into the depths of the academy. When the doors slide open, we head down a short, dimly lit hall. At the end, just like the previous times, he pauses before a brushed metal door and asks, "Ready?"

I nod, trying to muster excitement I don't currently feel.

"Welcome to the Vault!" he says, ushering me through the thick steel door.

Despite my familiarity with this place, my apathy vanishes as I take in the marvels inside, struck with awe so profound my jaw drops.

"It never gets old, does it?" Arthur laughs, guiding me deeper inside the massive, climate-controlled storeroom filled with the most important works of art known to man.

It's the ultimate museum—a lavish repository for the world's most treasured artifacts, collected through the years by Trippers like me, who've exchanged these priceless originals for meticulously crafted replicas.

I remember what Arthur said to me during my initial visit: modern society, with its preference for the mundane over true artistry, doesn't deserve these great works. He argued that when art's value is reduced to a social media checkmark, society forfeits its right to direct access. The profound act of experiencing Leonardo da Vinci's masterpieces is cheapened by the eagerness to boast about visiting the Louvre rather than genuinely connect with the artwork.

But what resonated with me the most was when he said: *Leonardo created because it allowed him to touch the divine, and when we view his works properly, we get a glimpse of that, too.*

Having met Leonardo, I can attest to its truth.

By the time Arthur fell silent, his eyes were misted with tears, and he made no move to hide it. In that moment, I understood that Arthur had a passion for beauty like I'd never seen.

But now, after my conversation with Freya, I have an entirely new understanding. Arthur's passion extends far beyond mere appreciation—there's someone out there—someone he's so desperate to reconnect with, he's determined to take control over time and curate the world for this person.

But who is this person—and what might've happened between them?

"Go on," Arthur says, jolting me back to the present. "Have a look, wander. You brought me the Moon, and now it's time for you to choose a reward. Whatever you want, it's yours for the taking."

As I walk these aisles, a silent battle rages inside me. I want to be jaded, to not care about any of this, but much like Arthur, I've always been a sucker for beautiful objects.

The cut and shine of a jewel makes my heart sing.

The play of light and shadow in a painting or photograph can reduce me to tears.

The intricate design of a perfectly tailored dress and the architectural curve of a pair of high heels have the power to transport me to another world.

I wander past masters like Picasso, Botticelli, Kahlo, Monet, O'Keefe, Rembrandt, Goya, Velázquez, Kandinsky, Klimt, Michelangelo, Caravaggio, Raphael, Vermeer, and more—circling display cases filled with the crown jewels from just about every reign throughout history. My pulse races at the idea that any of these pieces could be mine for the taking.

It's a heady feeling, making it impossible not to get caught up in the thrill of walking among such a mesmerizing collection. And I remind myself that, as morally gray as this may appear, Arthur isn't driven by greed.

While he hoards these great works of art, the small trinkets we bring back—the gems stolen from unsuspecting aristocracy— are returned to their timelines to be reallocated among those who need them the most.

I remember my surprise when he revealed how much he

enjoys redistributing wealth. In a moment of shock, I called him Robin Hood, which made him toss his head back and howl with laughter.

Arthur is not entirely bad.

He has many admirable qualities.

And, as I told my dad, he truly has been a mentor to me.

Which makes what I'm destined to do even more difficult.

Arthur trails several feet behind me, allowing me space to meander and dream.

"When you manage to unravel the mystery of the *Melencolia I*," he says, "and decipher the clues hidden in the tarot cards and Christopher Columbus's map, it should lead you directly to the Star."

I give a vague nod, wondering why he feels the need to tell me what I already know.

"And once you bring it to me, the rest of the pieces will be rendered unnecessary."

I freeze, unsure if I heard him correctly.

I whirl to face him, my hands beginning to shake so badly I hide them in the folds of my sweatshirt. "Excuse me?" I manage to say, my voice betraying my tension.

Arthur's gaze, as deep and dark as a moonless night, pins me in place. "With the Sun and the Moon now in my possession, the Star remains the last essential item. The rest is merely decoration—a sort of window dressing, if you will."

The revelation slams into me like a physical blow, forcing the air from my lungs and rendering my knees barely able to hold me.

No.

No-no-no-no-no!

"I probably should've mentioned it before," he says, a hint of apology in his tone. "But seeing how much you enjoy the challenge, I didn't want to deprive you of the pleasure of the hunt."

Pleasure of the hunt?

This game has stakes far beyond what I ever imagined.

"So, it seems the time has come," he says, hands rubbing together. "Time for you to deliver the Star, which will, in turn, allow me to fulfill my intention."

"And that intention," I echo, an icy shiver snaking its way down my spine, "is to remake the world?"

"Precisely," he confirms.

30

I stand before Arthur, my body trembling, my mouth as dry as bone, grappling with the horrifying truth of his words.

I thought I had time—a year, maybe two. But Arthur has discovered a shortcut, and now there's not enough time to devise a plan to stop him!

"I can see your disappointment," he says, gaze sharp and unwavering. "Though you've greatly enjoyed these little excursions through time, I presumed you'd feel some sense of achievement on my behalf. After all, I never could've done this without you."

With glazed eyes, I nod dutifully, my mind spinning with everything he's said and all it implies. Arthur is ten steps ahead of me in this game, and I fear I may never catch up.

"Before you came to Gray Wolf, I was at a bit of a loss," he continues. "My dream was stalled. But now, thanks to you, eternity is well within my grasp. And once you've secured the Star, you'll be free of those damn misguided Timekeepers."

I search Arthur's face for any hint of recognition that I'm one of those *damn Timekeepers*, but his expression remains impassive, unreadable—a facade I've never been able to penetrate.

And yet, clearly, he knows what I am. It's the sole reason he brought me here. Still, the question remains: *Does he realize I've discovered my destiny? That I'm no longer the same clueless girl who first arrived on this rock?*

The three golden circles beneath my sleeve begin to throb in an unbearable itch, and it's all I can do to maintain my composure, to stand steady and firm, despite the turmoil brewing within.

Arthur stands before me, exuding the aura of a man on the cusp of achieving a long-cherished dream. For him, this moment is triumphant, but for me the revelation lands with a daunting gravity. Time is slipping through my grasp faster than I ever imagined, and I have no idea how to stop it.

"Natasha, are you all right?" Arthur's tone softens, a hint of concern threading through his words.

Drawing in a deep breath, I try to wade through the storm of my thoughts. "I'm just surprised," I say, my voice steadier than I feel. "I though you wanted to fully restore the Antikythera Mechanism—see it in its entirety, with all its original pieces and components intact, including the original box it was encased in. There are still so many pieces left to be found, but now it seems—"

Arthur, his patience evidently worn thin, sharply interrupts. "You've been aware of my true intentions from the start," he says, his intense gaze locking onto mine.

I swallow past the bile rising in my throat, silently urging my stomach not to betray me. The air between us is charged with a palpable tension, but I know I can't afford to let Arthur see my uncertainty.

"And exactly how do you plan to remake the world, once I bring you the Star?" I ask, meeting the challenge in his gaze. I remind myself that I have every right to ask. He can achieve his dream only if I'm willing to cooperate.

After an agonizingly long stretch of silence, he says, "It will be a place of great beauty." As though that were somehow enough. As though his version of beauty is one-size-fits-all.

Though, having caught a glimpse of his remade world, I can at least confirm he's telling his version of the truth.

"Now," he says, directing me back to the task at hand. "Once you've made your selection, you may leave. But a word of advice: Use your time wisely, study the engraving, and ensure you're well-rested. Your next Trip will demand your best."

"You mean my next Trip to locate the Star?" I ask, needing confirmation.

Arthur gives a sharp, decisive nod.

"And have you decided who will join me on this Trip?" I watch his face closely. Last time we met, he was debating between the equally unpleasant candidates of either Elodie or Killian, so I float another name for him to consider. "Because I'm not sure if you realize this, but I've Tripped with everyone here, except Braxton."

My gaze locks on his, and though I want to remind him of the broken promise that Braxton and I would Trip to Renaissance Italy together, only for him to send Killian in his place, I refrain. We both know that, in Arthur's view, there's no debt to be settled with me.

Arthur, a master at the poker face, gives nothing away. Though I detect a slight edge to his voice, a hint of irritation, when he says, "As mentioned, I will inform you once I've made my decision."

Knowing I've broached the topic as far as I can, I navigate through rows of masterpieces under Arthur's keen surveillance. Making a beeline for Caravaggio's depiction of David slaying Goliath, I feel his piercing gaze tracking my every step.

Though I've always admired Caravaggio's work—he's a master of chiaroscuro, the use of strong contrasts between light and dark—unlike Braxton, it's not the kind of art I ever thought I could live with. It always seemed too heavy and brooding.

But now, as I stand before *David with the Head of Goliath*,

I'm swept away by its power. The work is raw, dynamic, and dramatic, depicting David in the aftermath of his victory, holding Goliath's severed head by the hair. The expert brushwork draws me in, and I feel an immediate kinship with this journey, especially the way David is portrayed in his victory.

Instead of gloating, David exhibits a sense of introspection, pondering the cost of his conquest. The face of Goliath, said to be a self-portrait of Caravaggio, hints at the toll on both the beast and the artist. If I do manage to outmaneuver Arthur, I imagine my emotions will mirror that sentiment. Such a win, while gratifying, will undoubtedly carry a tinge of bitterness.

Knowing how Arthur likes to psychoanalyze our artistic preferences, I wonder what conclusions he might be drawing as he watches me grasp the edge of the frame, ready to stake my claim. But just as I'm about to commit, another work catches my eye, and I find myself rushing toward it.

My heart skips a beat as I gaze at the scene unfolding on the canvas before me. I've always had an enormous fondness for this piece and the artist who painted it. I can hardly believe I didn't think of it before, when all this time, it's been sitting right here, mine for the taking.

Judith Slaying Holofernes, by Artemisia Gentileschi, is an absolute wonder, as is the artist herself—a young woman whose personal story is as profound as the works she created. This piece, depicting the biblical story of Judith, reflected the artist's own personal struggles and triumph over adversity.

Standing before it, I realize it resonates with me just as much, if not more, than the Caravaggio. Born to a well-established artist, Artemisia's early life was marked by trauma when she was raped by the painter Agostino Tassi, a colleague of her father. She chose to prosecute and go to trial, which was pretty much unheard of at the time. Despite being subjected to torture to verify her testimony, she prevailed. Tassi was convicted, and

Artemisia gained respect and patronage in a male-dominated field—a rarity in her time. She even became the first woman accepted into the Accademia delle Arti del Disegno and enjoyed the patronage of the Medici family and Charles I of England, among others.

Her work, somewhat forgotten after her death, was rediscovered in the twentieth century, and she's now celebrated as a pioneering figure in the history of women in the arts. She's also one of my personal heroes, and, as it happens, her painting sends a powerful message to Arthur.

"Interesting choice," Arthur says. Though I don't turn to look, I feel his gaze burning into the back of my skull.

In this powerful painting, Judith, assisted by her maidservant, executes Holofernes. The way Judith grasps his hair, pressing down on his forehead with one hand while drawing the sword across his neck with the other, is so vivid and real, I can feel the muscles straining in her arms, feel her determination to get the job done. The maidservant holding Holofernes down only adds to the sense of violence and realness.

Like Caravaggio, Artemisia used the chiaroscuro technique, intensifying the drama and highlighting the resolve on Judith's face, as well as the horror and desperation on Holofernes's as he comes to terms with his fate.

It's a painting celebrated not only for its technical skill but for its depiction of female power and resilience. Which makes it the perfect, if not only, choice I can make.

Grasping the corner of the frame, I turn to Arthur and say, "It is an interesting piece, I agree. I'll take it."

There's a challenge in my eyes. But Arthur, his own gaze on lockdown, merely nods and says, "I'll see that it's delivered to your room."

31

The second I leave Arthur's office, I fire off another message to Braxton.

Me: Need to see you – sooner = better.

Heart pounding, I rush down the hall, eyes glued to the slab, waiting for his reply. But nothing comes.

Dammit. Braxton, where are you?

Frustrated, I turn back to my room, thinking I might summon an Unraveling to see if I can locate him. But then I remember something Elodie once said about Arthur's archive — records of every change he's made since taking control of the rock. She was surprised I hadn't explored them, given all the time I've spent in the library.

Was Elodie nudging me toward the very answers I've been seeking all along?

Curiosity piqued, I change course and head to the library. As I step inside, I'm enveloped by its old-world charm. Polished dark wood walls and towering shelves of rare, first-edition books stretch up to the high, coffered ceiling. The faint scent of aged paper and leather fills the air, adding to the library's timeless allure. A quick look around confirms I'm alone.

My footsteps are muffled by the thick, green carpet as I navigate to the back and push open a heavy oak door. The air inside is markedly cooler, the silence almost reverent.

Soft, golden light filters through stained-glass windows,

casting a kaleidoscope of colors across rows of towering shelves filled with neatly organized boxes and binders, labeled by project, not year.

My fingers twitch with anticipation as I approach the nearest shelf, eyes scanning for anything that might reveal what truly drives Arthur—why he's so determined to remake the world.

With only one piece left to complete his dream, uncovering his motives has never been more urgent. Sure, I can pretend I can't find the Star, but how long can I keep up the charade? Especially with him insisting either Elodie or Killian accompany me.

If I'm going to stop him, I need to understand his true motivation, which will point me to his weakness.

Freya claims Arthur is driven by love.

But love for whom?

Is there a picture hidden among these records of someone Arthur is so desperate to reunite with that he's willing to reshape the entire world?

Figuring I should start at the beginning, I reach for a binder labeled THE LIGHTHOUSE and a box marked THE TAROT GARDEN, and set them on the large, ornately carved wooden table that sits at the center of the room.

Slipping on a pair of fresh cotton gloves, I begin flipping through old documents and newspaper clippings about the missing lighthouse keepers. The stories are interesting, and if I had more time, I might linger. But, since I'm on a bit of a time crunch and they're not of much use, I quickly move on to the box labeled THE TAROT GARDEN.

Impatient, I dump the contents onto the table and quickly sort through them. Drawings spill out—renditions sketched by the artist of the original Tarot Garden in Italy, Niki de Saint Phalle. There is a treasure trove of Gray Wolf history in these archives. But fascinating as it is, this isn't what I'm looking for.

As I return the box and binder to their places, another label catches my eye: THE GARDEN OF MONSTERS.

A shiver runs down my spine. Is there a Garden of Monsters here? And if so, how have I never seen it?

Unlike most Renaissance gardens, known for their beauty and symmetry, the Garden of Monsters—or Parco dei Mostri, as it's known in Italy—is filled with an astonishing array of grotesque sculptures. In a place like Gray Wolf—a place that's devoted to beauty—why would Arthur go to such lengths to replicate such a place unless it held a significant, hidden purpose?

I mean, it's so out of place, there must be a deeper meaning behind it.

Could this be a clue to Arthur's true motives?

My mind races as I try to piece it together. The Garden of Monsters is a labyrinth of horrors, each sculpture designed to provoke and disturb. Is Arthur's version meant to hide something, or perhaps reveal the darker side of his intentions?

One thing's for sure, I need to find this garden. It could be the key to understanding Arthur's true motivations, which in turn, just might give me the advantage I need to stop him.

As I'm reaching for the box, my slab chimes. Finally, a message from Braxton.

Braxton: Where are you?

Me: Library.

Braxton: I'm close. See you soon.

Heart thundering, I grab the box and dump the contents onto the table. More sketches, documents, and photos depicting a garden filled with bizarre statues—each meticulously crafted to mirror its Italian counterparts.

My gaze lingers on a photo of the statue of Orcus, also known as the Mouth of Hell. My skin prickles with chills as I study the image. The sculpture is of an enormous, formidable head with a gaping mouth forming an archway large enough to walk through, symbolizing the entrance to the underworld.

Orcus's eyes are hollow and deep. The broad, flat nose and furrowed forehead make for a haunting, ominous look. But it's the mouth—a massive black void with jagged teeth lining the entrance—that is the most striking feature.

A shiver of apprehension shoots through me, and I know in my bones that I'm on to something—that I need to find this place whatever it takes.

I've never used psychometry on a photo before, but I close my eyes and try to immerse myself in the energy this old slip of paper might hold.

I focus, feeling the texture beneath my fingers, trying to draw out any lingering impressions. I'm so engrossed in the process, I jump when the door bangs open and Braxton bursts in.

"Have you seen this place?" I ask, thrusting the photo toward him.

He glances at the picture, his eyes widening. "No," he says cautiously. "What's this about?"

"This," I say, my voice trembling with excitement, "is so strange, so out of context, it just might be the key to defeating Arthur."

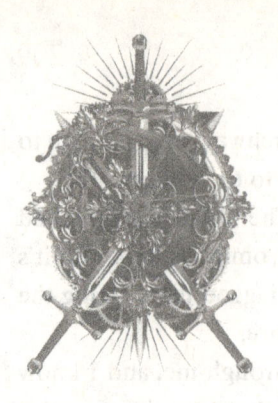

32

We leave our slabs in the library, ensuring Arthur can't track us. Arm in arm, Braxton and I quickly move down the hall, reminding me of the early days when Jago insisted we walk together like this.

Back then, I resisted, refusing to partake in what I saw as a dumb, outdated ritual. I vowed to reject all of Arthur's antiquated rules, until Jago said: *if you're smart, you'll choose your battles wisely, because there's no use fighting a match that's completely rigged against you.*

He also said to think of Arthur as a curator of the past, picking what he wants and discarding the rest.

It's almost like he was hinting at what I'm just now confirming as true. Combined with what he told me about time back in Versailles—that every moment has already been lived and continues to be lived—I wonder just how much Jago might know.

"Where are we going?" Braxton asks, snapping me back to the present.

"Following a hunch," I whisper.

As we reach the front entry, I notice it's pouring outside. Grabbing two rain slickers and an oversized umbrella from the bin beside the door, Braxton ushers me out into the biting cold.

Beneath the canopy of the umbrella, which admittedly isn't doing much good, we turn toward the Tarot Garden. My gaze instantly finds *The Magician*, *The High Priestess* beneath it, and *The Wheel of Fortune* where it all culminates.

A fleeting image of the girl in the red cape, a mirror image of myself, flashes through my mind. With my hood drawn over my head much like hers, I'm briefly overcome by the unnerving sensation that I truly have been here and done this before.

With the rain pounding overhead, I turn to Braxton and say, "Do you ever get the feeling that you've already lived this?"

"You mean like, déjà vu?" He wipes raindrops from his cheek.

"More like déjà vécu," I say. "The sensation that you've not just seen it, but actually lived it."

He shakes his head slowly, though his gaze sparks with curiosity.

"Ever since I met up with my dad, I've had this unshakable feeling that I've already lived this. Then today, in the middle of an Unraveling, I swear I saw myself—or at least, a girl who looked just like me—racing through the old labyrinth beneath my window."

We walk together in a contemplative silence. After a while, Braxton asks, "Are you familiar with the Coffer Illusion?"

I glance up at him, shaking my head.

"It's a visual phenomenon created by Anthony Norcia, a psychologist and vision scientist. The image is composed of shades of black, white, and gray, creating the illusion of a series of rectangles. At first glance, all you see are straight lines, angles, and rectangles. But, if you look closely, you'll notice there are actually sixteen circles hidden within the pattern. Once your brain finally adapts, you can't unsee it."

"Meaning?"

"The illusion illustrates how we tend to perceive certain aspects of sensory data, while ignoring others, based on expectations or familiarity."

I take a moment to absorb that.

"I guess what I'm trying to say," he continues, "is that we expect time to be linear, so we perceive it as linear. But what if it's not?"

"So, you think it's possible that I really have lived this before? Like Arthur might have me trapped in some sort of loop without my even realizing it?"

Braxton shrugs. "Considering everything I've seen here at Gray Wolf, I'd say just about anything is possible. Sometimes it feels like time doesn't move quite the same way here."

We continue beyond the gardens. When we reach a place where a narrow path cuts through the rock, I squint through the wind and rain at the barren expanse of nothingness.

"Are you sure this is the right way?" Braxton asks.

I shake my head. "I'm not sure of anything," I admit. "I just desperately hope that I'm right."

Ducking our heads, we continue our battle against the onslaught of wind and rain. Just when my leggings are soaked from my ankles to my knees, just when I'm beginning to question my sanity, we turn a bend, and I let out an involuntary gasp.

How on earth could I have possibly missed this?

Then again, Gray Wolf is brimming with so many secrets and mysteries—so many spaces and rooms I've yet to explore.

I run a sweeping gaze over the collection of monstrous sculptures, as intrigued as I am horrified. This eerie, disturbing place was a source of inspiration for two of my favorite artists, both Salvador Dalí and Nikki de Saint Phalle.

"The real one is in Northern Italy," I say. The story of this place rises to the surface of my consciousness, begging to be told. "It was created during the sixteenth century. Commissioned by Pier Francesco Orsini, to express his grief over the death of his wife, Giulia Farnese." When I hear myself utter that name, I abruptly stop.

Wait—Giulia Farnese?

A surprising link begins to form in my mind. This Giulia Farnese is a relation of the Giulia Farnese, known as La Bella, who was the mistress of the Borgia Pope. And strangely enough, I recently dined with the Pope's son Cesare in Renaissance Italy.

Everything is connected, my dad's words echo in my head.

Passing several sculptures and temples representing enormous mythological creatures, monstrous animals, mythical subjects, and enigmatic figures, all carved from bedrock, we pause before the most famous of them all: the gaping mouth of the Orcus, bearing the inscription: OGNI PENSIERO VOLA, which translates to: Every Thought Flies.

It reminds me a lot of the inscription on the plaque fronting Gray Wolf: PANTA RHEI, or Everything Flows.

As I stand before it, chills prickle my skin, though the weather is only partly to blame. This park, with its remarkable collection of statues, was designed to astound—and it definitely succeeds. The creased brow, vacant hollow eyes, and gaping mouth of the Orcus is the perfect expression of grief.

As my gaze wanders, taking in the wide assortment of statues from the mythical to the mystical, it becomes clear each one carries its own message.

The Orcus Mouth, also known as The Mouth of Hell, represents the Roman god of the underworld.

The Tortoise with a Winged Woman contrasts the slow march of time against the fleeting passage of life.

The Dragon Fighting with Lions symbolizes the eternal battle between good and evil.

The Leaning House with its deliberate tilt serves as a metaphor for the disorienting impact of grief.

And on it goes, encompassing over twenty sculptures in all.

In Italy, the statues are embedded in a lush, natural landscape. But here on this barren island, they seem to emerge seamlessly from the rock, as if sprung from nature itself.

"I know it's not the real one," I say, "but that doesn't make it any less powerful." My eyes sting, and my cheeks are flushed and wet, though it's not entirely due to the rain.

In the midst of this garden, it suddenly becomes clear Freya was right—Arthur Blackstone did love someone, and according to this place, he must've lost them as well.

It's a grief that feels hauntingly familiar, mirroring the heartache I bear for my father's death—a loss that can be traced straight back to Arthur.

How many others will suffer because Arthur has yet to find a healthier way to deal with his anguish?

Turning to Braxton, I'm overcome with the sudden urge to kiss him. Not like the first time, because while that was nice, wonderful even, it was a bit too tentative for what I have in mind. No, this time when I kiss Braxton, it's like the second time, the third time, and all the other glorious kisses we've shared combined into one. Drawing away, I peer into his bottomless blue gaze.

"What brought that on?" he asks, his hand gently caressing my rain-soaked cheek. "Not that I mind, of course. Just wondering."

"I'm not sure," I admit, still a little breathless from the kiss. "Part of it's this place—this monument to grief. And part of it's because I was worried when you didn't reply to my text."

"Sorry," he says. "I left my slab back in my room when I met with Oliver, Finn, and Keane. Looks like we have a team, by the way." He grins. Then, directing his gaze back to the statues, he adds, "So tell me, why are we here?"

"This place," I say, voice holding a gravity that claims his full attention, "is going to lead us straight to Arthur's weakness."

33

We take cover beneath the colossal, gaping jaws of the Orcus.

Wringing the water from my hair, I move to the center of what I now see as the physical manifestation of both Orsini's historic sorrow and Arthur's enduring grief.

"Arthur is a collector, a curator," I begin, struggling to put my intuition into words. "But despite all his money and power, there's one thing he can never buy—" I turn to face Braxton. "Love. He can't buy love," I repeat. "Or at least not the real kind. That's what the Monster Garden is about—a grand ode to a great love once found and then tragically lost."

Braxton nods, encouraging me to continue.

"But it goes even deeper," I say. "Arthur isn't merely a collector. He's a true connoisseur. His pursuit of beauty isn't just a passion—it's an obsession. He's poured all his money and energy into constructing this world where he's surrounded by it, immersed in it, like a balm for his deep-seated heartache. But while Arthur may be a world-class collector. He's not a creator. He can't paint like da Vinci, can't sculpt like Michelangelo, can't compose like Beethoven or Mozart. Despite his so-called unsurpassed vision, he lacks the talent to create on the level of the masters he reveres. Can you imagine how badly that must sting for someone like him—someone who's never satisfied with anything short of perfection?"

Braxton's eyes widen, caught up in the story I weave.

"To him, society is a herd of lemmings, hurtling toward mediocrity, content to feast on the mundane. After ushering life-changing technology into the world, believing it would expand our horizons, he's left to watch in dismay as it becomes a tool of isolation and division. It spreads harmful images and fills our heads with so much false and conflicting information, we can no longer distinguish truths from lies. Despite his impact, he's haunted by the world's inevitable sorrows—tragedy, death, and grief—all things he can neither control nor change. But, by restoring the Antikythera Mechanism, he believes he's found a way to rectify these wrongs. He's disillusioned with the divine—convinced that God, the universe, whoever's in charge, has let humanity down. In Arthur's mind, he possesses a superior understanding of what humankind truly needs. The mural over his desk makes it clear he thinks he can do better."

Braxton's gaze holds steady on mine. "*The Creation of Adam*," he whispers, affirming the gravity of our conversation.

"By restoring the Antikythera Mechanism," I continue, "Arthur believes he can rewrite his life's script, give himself a better, more Hollywood ending."

"Luckily for us," Braxton says, a hint of resolve in his voice, "we still have years to sort this all out. Like you said, there are loads of pieces left to uncover."

Regrettably, I have to dash his hope. "Except that's no longer true." I watch Braxton's face closely as I relay everything that's happened, all that I've learned since I last saw him.

"So, he's discovered a shortcut," Braxton repeats, eyes wide with realization.

"And any day now," I continue, "he's going to send me out to fetch him the Star."

The spark in Braxton's eyes fades as he processes everything I just said.

"And when he does," I continue, "I'm going to be ready for it."

"But how?" he asks, his brow furrowing, jaw clenching.

I break away from him and turn to the wall, tracing my fingers along the cool, damp interior of the Orcus's mouth. When I come to a spot that seems to vibrate under my touch, I flatten my palm to the rock wall. Remembering what my dad taught me, I close my eyes, take a few deep, cleansing breaths, and try to merge with its energy.

A burst of excitement shoots through me as the wall begins to shake.

Let go of whatever it is you hope to see, my father said. *Let the vision unfold on its own.*

Only this time, there's no vision. The wall continues to quiver and quake, seeming to give way beneath my weight.

"Tasha," Braxton says, "look!"

I open my eyes to find this seemingly immovable slab of stone yielding under my hand. Mirroring the hidden mechanism in my dad's New York City apartment, the stone instantly shifts, revealing a doorway to an entirely new realm.

Together, Braxton and I step over the threshold into a breathtaking space.

The moment we cross deeper into the room, the hidden door seals shut, plunging us into a world of darkness.

34

In a panic, I reach for Braxton's hand, only to find he's no longer beside me. A chill courses through me as I call out his name, my voice echoing off the cavernous walls.

A moment later, the rasp of a match striking pierces the silence, and a flickering candle's light bathes the space in a warm, unsteady glow.

"Here." Braxton steps into view, handing me a lit candle before lighting another for himself.

With my candle held high, I survey the space. The ceiling and walls are adorned with breathtaking murals, painted by some of the world's most illustrious artists. The turbulent brushwork of Van Gogh, the dramatic play of light and shadow of Caravaggio, Michelangelo's deeply devoted brushstrokes, and the insightful genius of da Vinci are all represented here.

These walls are a treasure that would easily move an art historian to tears. Yet tragically, they are destined to remain unseen by the outside world.

"Why would he keep this hidden?" Braxton's voice breaks the heavy silence, echoing my own thoughts.

"It's a gallery of grief," I whisper. "A private sanctuary for his pain. This must be where he comes to confront his demons, to bask in the beauty he can never fully possess."

In the dim glow of candlelight, Braxton's eyes meet mine, filled with wonder and sadness. "It's incredible and tragic at the same time."

I nod, my heart heavy with the weight of our discovery. "Arthur's collected the world's beauty to surround himself with what he cannot create or control. It's his way of coping with the loss he can never truly overcome."

You've been here before, done this before, a voice insistently whispers in my head.

"In Roman mythology," Braxton says, "Orcus is a god of the underworld, tasked with punishing those who break their oaths. The Romans believed that breaking a sacred promise invited Orcus's wrath—a sort of divine justice for failing to honor one's word."

The words settle over me as I stop before what looks to be an altar, carved from a massive slab of rose quartz, a stone renowned for its associations with love. Its soft pink hue glows in the candlelight, casting an ethereal light around the room, adding to the solemn, almost sacred atmosphere.

Meticulously arranged across the top is an otherworldly display of white flowers—their beauty so exquisite they seem to almost transcend this physical world. Held aloft by nearly invisible stems, they appear to levitate far above the altar, creating a spectral ambiance in the dimly lit room.

The painstaking care Arthur has taken in this arrangement, the sadness and beauty interwoven in this private shrine, speaks of such profound loss that for a fleeting moment, I find my heart breaking on Arthur's behalf.

"Ah, the Ghost Orchid," Braxton says, coming to stand beside me. "It's exceedingly rare, endangered, in fact. One of the most intriguing and sought-after orchids in the world."

"Which seems only fitting that Arthur would have so many of them," I say, trying to imagine him coming here, making a daily pilgrimage to partake in a solitary ritual of remembrance. It's a scene that's nearly impossible to fathom.

"They're typically found in swampier climates like Florida and Cuba. But of course, Arthur has found a way to cultivate them here. He has an entire greenhouse filled with them."

"So, you've seen them?" I ask, transfixed by the sight.

"I have," Braxton says, his voice so low it's almost as though he's talking to himself. "Before today, I never understood what they meant. But now, it's all starting to make sense."

I turn to him, eager to hear his perspective. "So, the Orcus, the ghost orchids—how exactly does this connect to Arthur? What do you think it means?"

Braxton takes a deep breath. "It's a bit unimaginative, but bear with me."

I give a half grin and nod for him to continue.

"I think Arthur broke some sort of oath, and he blames himself for whatever punishment or loss followed. So he comes here to appeal to Orcus, hoping for forgiveness and a chance to right his wrongs."

It's definitely obvious, yet it all seems to make sense. Sometimes the simplest explanation is the one that sits directly in front of you.

"Take a closer look at these murals." Braxton gestures toward the collection of cherubic-faced angels and horn-headed beasts, the vividly blooming flowers, and dead, barren trees. "See this one here?"

I stand beside him, captivated by the face of a woman whose beauty seems otherworldly. Her hair, a cascade of golden waves, drapes elegantly over her shoulders, discreetly veiling her form. Her eyes, a striking shade of azure, hold a depth of serenity, while her pale white skin glows with a soft, inner luminescence.

There's a tranquil confidence in her expression, her gaze subtly averted, embodying a purity and grace that seems divinely sculpted. She stands against a backdrop of calm seas and unblemished sky, her very presence a timeless ode to an idealized beauty that seems to elevate her far above this mortal plane.

"She reminds me of Botticelli's Venus," I say, breathless from the depth of care and love that went into creating her.

"Well, I'm pretty sure Botticelli painted this one, too." Braxton turns, giving me a significant look.

"Do you think that's her?" Directing my flame toward the mural, I lean in for a closer look. "Do you think this is the mystery woman Arthur is willing to remake the world for?"

A wry grin plays at his lips. "Most likely," he says. "But who does she remind you of?"

I study the mural again. My gaze inching over the beautiful woman's face…as an impossible recognition begins to nudge at my brain.

"My God," I gasp, as my whole body involuntarily shivers. "It's—"

With my heart practically pounding its way out of my chest, I glance between Braxton and the exalted face of the woman in the painting before me.

Then, I watch as he directs his candle to the place just below it, to where a young girl with the face of an angel gazes toward an unknown horizon.

"I—" My tongue is frozen, incapable of forming actual words. I'm left only to stare, as my mind spins with the undeniable truth now laid bare.

"You see it, too?" Braxton glances between the image of the young girl and me. "I haven't lost my mind?"

"N—no," I stammer. "It seems so impossible to believe and yet, it makes perfect sense. Elodie really is—"

I turn back to the painting, eyes wide with disbelief. But before I can put a voice to this startling revelation, the hidden rock door begins to creak open, and I look to Braxton in a panic, unsure what to do.

Someone is here.

And we're surrounded by walls, with nowhere to run.

Reaching for my candle, Braxton quickly extinguishes the flame. Then grasping hold of my hand, he pulls me behind the altar where we cower together.

When he snuffs his candle as well, we're engulfed in darkness, left with the foreboding sounds of our own frantic heartbeats and the soft echo of footsteps that can belong only to Arthur.

35

I n the heart of this hidden room, the air is heavy, charged with an energy that speaks of centuries-old secrets and a grief so profound, it seems to seep from the ceiling, the floor, the frescoed walls, and the very altar, we use to shield ourselves.

Huddled beside Braxton, barely daring to breathe, I hear the gruff rasp of a match. Within seconds, the room is illuminated with softly glowing light. Peering around the side of the rose quartz slab, I watch as Arthur busies himself lighting the rest of the candles.

With a solemnity that verges on ceremonial, he sets a single candle on the floor, followed by another, then another. Arranging them into a careful circle, he positions himself at the center.

When he turns his back toward us, the haunting melody of *Moonlight Sonata* suddenly blares through the chamber, catching me completely off guard.

It's the same piece he played on repeat during our Van Gogh—themed dinner, a selection I naively assumed was chosen because it paired well with the food and the melancholic atmosphere of *Starry Night*.

I should've known then that nothing Arthur does is ever by chance.

Slowly, Arthur begins to undress, and my immediate reaction is to look away, grant him privacy for this ritual that feels as sacred as time itself.

I bow my head, desperately trying to hide my face, but the movement causes the slick material of my jacket to emit a loud, crinkling noise. In my panic, my grip falters, and my umbrella slips from my grasp, crashing to the floor with a resounding crack that reverberates like a thunderclap, shaking me to my core.

Arthur freezes, his back still toward us, as he jerks his head in our direction.

The tension in the room thickens, my pulse quickening as seconds stretch into what feels like an eternity. His narrowed eyes scan the dimly lit room, the flickering candlelight casting eerie shadows across his face.

I hold my breath, heart pounding in my ears, as Braxton squeezes my hand, his grip tense.

Finally, after what feels like an infinite wait, Arthur resumes his ritual, seemingly dismissing the noise. For a man who prides himself on not missing a thing, this strikes me as alarmingly strange.

But maybe that's just the power of his own bottomless grief. Like the leaning house sculpture outside, it can easily distort your reality.

Or maybe Arthur knows we're here and wants us to see this.

Maybe our viewing this performance of grief only adds to the punishment he so obviously seeks.

With the gentle, rolling strains of *Moonlight Sonata* playing in the background, Arthur continues to disrobe until each piece of clothing has fallen to the floor. Then, lowering himself to his knees, he presses his forehead briefly to the ground, before laying his body flat against the chilled stone beneath him.

With his arms stretched out to his sides, he releases a single, soul-shaking wail that resonates deep in my bones. Seeing him in this act of prostration, I sense it's less an homage to the divine, and more a profound gesture of penance for perceived wrongdoings.

When Arthur finally rises and turns toward us, Braxton and I watch in horror as the candlelight illuminates a sight so grotesque it defies belief, straining every nerve in my body to stifle a scream.

Beside me, Braxton lets out a small, involuntary gasp, and I shudder to think what must be going through his mind at the terrible sight before us.

There, emblazoned across the center of Arthur's chest, is a swath of skin that is jarringly, shockingly alien.

It's a piece of flesh that categorically should not exist in that space.

As we watch Arthur step forward, the light casts an even harsher truth, exposing a reality too grim to deny.

The tattoo once marking Braxton's grandfather's chest—a Flower of Life symbol that, according to him, Arthur had cruelly excised—now grotesquely adorns Arthur's own skin.

The fusion of flesh and ink stands as a testament to something beyond obsession, as astonishing as it is macabre and revolting.

Arthur approaches the mural, commanding the space with a presence that's both haunted and yearning. He stands before the image of the golden-haired woman, her beauty rendered with such vibrancy, she seems on the verge of breaking free from her painted confines. Speaking to her as though she can hear him, Arthur's voice is a fervent whisper, a desperate plea.

"Soon, my love, we will be together," he says. "As soon as Natasha brings me the Star, everything will align once more. Our world, our lives, the errors of my past—all will be rectified. And we shall begin anew—our perfect love reborn, our cherished family restored—as if we were granted a second dawn. And you, my love, deserve nothing less. This time, I promise you, I will not fail you."

Then, with the same solemn reverence in which the ritual began, we watch as Arthur methodically dresses, extinguishes the candles, and puts them back in their place.

As the final flame dies, Beethoven's opus comes to an end, and darkness envelops the room once again.

36

"We should go," I say, emerging from our hiding spot behind the altar. I hold my freshly lit candle aloft, its light casting flickering shadows on the cavernous walls, as Braxton paces the room, a storm of emotions visible in his every step.

"He's not coming back," Braxton says, his voice echoing through the space. "Besides, if I run into him on the way back, I can't promise I won't kill him with my bare hands."

"No, you won't," I respond softly, wishing I could calm his frantic movements, hold him tightly to my chest, and soothe away all his anguish and fury. But I know he needs this moment to vent, so I stand back, giving him space to process his feelings.

"He's a monster," Braxton says, and I'm instantly struck by the word.

Arthur has indeed become a monster. Yet I can't help but reflect on the man he might've once been—a man who experienced love and loss so profoundly that he lost his way amid his overwhelming grief.

The Garden of Monsters, the grafted tattoo—these are but external symbols of how Arthur perceives himself, a physical manifestation of his internal torment.

Arthur embodies the tragic outcome of a man so consumed by grief, he's trapped in a vicious cycle of guilt and self-blame. It would be so easy to feel sorry for him if it weren't for his resolve to control time and remake the world.

But now, having seen the depths of his despair and the extremes he's willing to endure to recapture all that he's lost, I'm left with a clear understanding of the motivation behind all of this. And because of it, I'm significantly closer to thwarting his plans.

Now that I'm armed with the why and the what, all that remains to uncover is how.

Turning to Braxton, I ask, "She never said anything? Back when you were together, Elodie never mentioned Arthur being her actual father, not just a father figure?"

Braxton pauses, looking at me with a distant gaze before shaking his head as if to clear it of the tormenting thoughts surrounding his grandfather. "No. Never." He runs a hand through his hair, casting a glance around the strange, haunting space. Returning his focus to me, he says, "Elodie's never been one for sharing much of herself. It was mostly just—" He stops abruptly, his sentence trailing off with a dismissive wave.

"Mostly just what—physical?" I say, relieved to find the sting of jealousy that always reared its ugly head at any mention of their past is now gone.

I love Braxton. He loves me. And anything that happened before, with either of us, only served to steer us toward the path that led to each other.

But Braxton is unaware of my new sense of security. "Um, yeah," he says. "I guess, that's one way to put it." He shifts uneasily, gives an uncomfortable shrug. "Honestly, what sticks with me most is the never-ending head games. I don't know how Jago can stand it. It was way too much drama and chaos for me."

"I'm not sure Jago's all that invested," I share, remembering their casual relationship status. "It seems more like a convenient fling—a bit of fun between Trips. As for Elodie…" I pause, glancing at Braxton, debating whether to divulge what I know.

"She appears quite taken with someone named Nash."

Braxton's expression shifts to one of mild curiosity.

Then, remembering Nash is from Regency England, I say, "Do you know him? You might've been quite young, just a child, but I met him during that Trip where I…well, when I met your father."

Or more accurately, when I engaged in a sword fight with your father, leaving him maimed and bleeding on the floor.

Braxton, seemingly uninterested in delving deeper into Elodie's love life, dismisses the topic with a noncommittal, "Yeah, maybe. Regardless, I think it's clear we can't consider her an ally. Her loyalty to Arthur—whether she knows he's her real father or not—is too strong. I can't see her siding with us."

I breathe a heavy sigh and nod in agreement.

"And Killian?" Braxton says. "You sure you don't want to take him up on his offer to save your dad?"

I look at him like he's suddenly sprouted an additional head. "Absolutely not," I say, a shiver of repulsion coursing through me. "It's completely out of the question."

Braxton regards me with a cool, unwavering look. "Is it pride that's guiding your decision—or is there something else at play here?"

His question catches me off guard. "What exactly are you implying?" I ask, surprised and slightly irked that he'd even entertain such an idea.

Braxton's response is measured. "Consider this," he says, "if Killian is genuinely seeking redemption, perhaps it's worth exploring his offer. Particularly if it could lead to achieving something you deeply want."

The words linger between us. "It's not about pride," I insist. "It's about not being able to trust him. And you shouldn't, either."

Braxton meets my gaze with unwavering seriousness. "Make no mistake," he says. "I have no illusions about Killian de Luce.

I was there in that French crypt, witnessing his actions firsthand."

As the words settle, I'm struck by how what once felt like a devastating, life-altering revelation is now just another unfortunate event in a long string of them. Time and clarity have a way of softening the hard edges.

"Here's the thing," I say, "Killian might spin tales of seeking redemption, but aligning with him comes with a risk. He might promise to spare my dad, presenting it as a victory, only to turn around and target you, under the guise of liberating me for himself. And when I react with fury, he'd simply shrug and remind me: *I'm the scorpion, remember? It's in my nature. What else did you expect?*"

Braxton nods, scrubbing a hand along his jaw. "You're right. I guess I didn't want to close off any options. But facing what we now know, how do we go about stopping Arthur?"

I take a deep breath and turn my attention to the murals once more. "Arthur commissioned these pieces from some of the art world's most renowned artists," I say, directing my candle toward the scene that's closest to the hidden door. "Just like the mural over his desk, he did so with intention. There's a story here; it's coded, of course, but I'm determined to decipher its meaning."

"Go on," Braxton says, glancing between the mural and me.

"At first glance, it looks haphazard, random. But I'm sensing there's a pattern. Think of it like a graphic novel without the speech bubbles."

Braxton grins, his blue eyes reflecting the flickering candlelight.

"I think the journey starts here." Gently, I tap a finger to the wall. "And I'm thinking maybe we can gain deeper insight if we place our hands on it, together."

Braxton's gaze is as deep as the sea, and when he places his hand over mine, a surge of electricity shoots through my veins.

"Now, focus on your breathing and clear your thoughts," I say, repeating the steps my dad taught me. "As you merge with the mural's energy, let your mind be a blank canvas, open to whatever impressions may come."

Together, Braxton and I follow the mural in quiet contemplation, absorbing the tale of a boy born into scant means, a world where ascending beyond one's initial circumstances seemed a distant dream.

Yet, Arthur was exceptional—naturally industrious, and remarkably insightful for his age. His most defining attribute, however, was his foresight, a vision not just for personal advancement but for societal betterment.

When he first saw the beautiful young kitchen maid at the household where he worked, Arthur was determined to transcend their shared lowly status. His brilliance and indomitable spirit, coupled with a burgeoning grasp of alchemy, allowed him to rise above his station. Together, they fell in love, wed, and built a modest yet joy-filled life with their daughter.

But tragedy struck when his wife became gravely ill. Desperate to save her, Arthur discovered a time portal, a gateway to different eras where he hoped to find a cure. Promising a swift return, he left his family, only to become ensnared in the labyrinth of time, unable to find his way back.

By the time he finally did return, years had passed. His wife was gone, and their daughter, Elodie, had been abandoned to the harsh realities of a Dickensian orphanage. Each attempt to rewrite this fate saw him clashing with time itself, always with the same heartbreaking outcome.

"My God," Braxton says, once we near the end of the mural. "Arthur's not just fighting against the random injustices of the world, but against time itself. No wonder he's so obsessed with controlling it. It makes perfect sense." He looks at me, his eyes wide with realization. "Well, in his twisted mind, anyway."

When we reach the penultimate scene in the mural, we remove our hands from the wall and I say, "And here's how his preferred story ends." I gesture toward an image of a girl with flowing brown hair and green eyes—a girl who is unmistakably me. In this part of the mural, I am kneeling before Arthur, the Star cupped in my hands, presenting him with the final piece he needs to amend his past tragedies.

The image that follows depicts Arthur in a vision of sheer joy, his family restored, ensconced in a realm of splendor and radiance, a utopia free of all darkness.

Arthur envisions a perfect world, and it's not that I don't dream of such a place for myself. But I can't overlook the countless lives sacrificed for him to achieve this goal—my father, Braxton's father and grandfather, numerous Timekeepers across the ages, and all those lost in his early time travel experiments. And those of us here at Gray Wolf, taken from their homes, whisked away from our families and friends, the lives we'd been living, just so Arthur could edge closer to his dream.

We are all casualties of Arthur's refusal to confront a universal inevitability—the pain of losing a loved one.

Arthur Blackstone is grieving, and though I empathize with the gravity of his loss, he has no right to dictate our choices or manipulate time for his personal benefit.

This struggle Braxton and I now face goes far beyond safeguarding time—it's about ensuring society retains its freedom of choice.

Beneath my sleeve, the skin on my arm begins to itch. I lift it to find another golden circle has appeared. Looking to Braxton, I say, "I know exactly how we're going to succeed."

37

We are gathered—Braxton, Finn, Oliver, Keane, and I. These are our allies. This is our team.

A knock sounds at the door, and Braxton's head snaps up, a flicker of apprehension in his eyes. As the door swings open to reveal Mason waiting on the other side, Braxton looks even less certain.

It's not like I'm brimming with confidence, either. My heart beats unsteadily, grappling with the enormity of the responsibility we face. Mason is here at Gray Wolf because of me, because of a foolish mistake I made. And so, despite my uncertainty, including him in our plans is a risk I felt compelled to make.

If we're going to succeed and put an end to this madness, it's only fair Mason is given the chance to decide his own future and choose where he'll go next. Home seems like the most obvious choice, but in this place, it's as viable as opting for a life in eighteenth-century France.

As I look around at these faces, my thoughts drift to those who are absent from this gathering. Elodie, Killian, Jago, Roxane, Hawke, Freya, Charlotte, Maisie—their futures hang in the balance as much as ours.

Elodie, of course, will be reunited with her family, but what of the others? The countless unseen faces that populate the corridors of this academy, each with their own stories and dreams—what will become of them in the wake of our actions?

If I fail and Arthur's plan comes to fruition, it's hard to imagine him maintaining Gray Wolf in its current form. The entire foundation of this academy was built on his quest to reunite with his lost love. Once that objective is achieved, what purpose does this place serve? Where does that leave everyone who once called it home?

On the other hand, if I succeed, the future remains uncertain. While I have no intention of doing Arthur any physical harm, the reality is that anything could happen that might force my hand in ways I can't currently foresee.

Hell, the very act of withholding the Star from him could trigger a confrontation I must be prepared for, with outcomes that could reshape our reality.

The only certainty I cling to amid all this vagueness is my resolve to leave Gray Wolf behind. Though I have definite plans to visit my mom, I won't stay for long. The town that once contained my whole world now feels way too constricting. When it comes to making a fresh start, New York seems like a much better fit.

Besides, I have a key to my dad's apartment, along with a sum of money securely hidden in a safe behind Salvador Dalí's *The Persistence of Memory*. And of course, I fully expect Braxton to join me, so together, we'll start a new life.

Yet, woven through my thoughts of new beginnings is the enduring dream of rescuing my dad and mending the holes in my own family tapestry. Still, it's not without risk. The complexities of altering history, of navigating the treacherous waters of paradoxes and unintended consequences, loom large. And then, there's Nietzsche's cautionary note about battling monsters, reminding me of the fine line between changing the past and being irrevocably changed by it.

Will my inability to let go of my father turn me into a monster like Arthur?

"So," Mason begins, standing at the threshold of Braxton's

room, eyes scanning those of us gathered, "what's this about?"

The room falls silent as everyone shifts toward me, their expressions a mix of curiosity and caution at Mason's presence. Motioning for him to join me on the well-worn leather couch, I clutch Braxton's Union Jack needlepoint pillow a bit too tightly, seeking comfort and courage from its familiar texture.

"Hypothetically," I say, trying to sound casual yet meaningful, "if you had the chance to leave here and could choose any destination, any era, where would it be?"

Mason's posture stiffens, his defenses practically electrifying the air between us. "Cut to the chase, Nat," he says, his fingers absently tracing the golden crown ring I gave him to wear both as a talisman and a symbol of our deep-rooted connection. "Is this some sort of escape plan? Because I can't help but notice not everyone's here."

Despite knowing him as well as I do, his directness catches me completely off guard. Still, it serves as a stark reminder that Mason and I share too much history for this sort of evasiveness. He deserves nothing short of the truth.

"Told you this was a bad idea," Oliver mutters under his breath.

Though Mason doesn't miss a beat, I can tell by the pinch of his lips that Oliver's comment didn't go unnoticed. "Home," he states simply, catching us all off guard with the straightforwardness of his wish.

Keane, ever the facilitator, leans forward. "Remember, you can go anywhere. Your options are limitless. Any timeline, any destination you desire, it's well within reach. I can make it happen."

The offer is enticing, opening an entire world of possibilities, but Mason remains steadfast in his resolve. "Just get me off this rock," he says. "I'll handle the rest from there." His gaze shifts to me, reading the look of surprise etched across my face and those of everyone else in the room. "Seems like you all expected something different." He smirks. "Thought I'd settled in, maybe?" His voice trails off, leaving the questions hanging.

"I guess I thought you were really starting to like it here," I say. "You had that—"

"That new Blue glow." Braxton finishes the thought for me.

Curious, I turn to him, unfamiliar with the term. Which leaves me to wonder if that's how they saw me after my first Trip, when I was completely caught up in the wonders of this place.

"Honestly," Mason says, "I won't lie—it's incredible here. I mean, where else could someone like me experience all this?" He makes a wide, but vague, gesture around the room. "The way we get to dress, the food we get to eat, all this art and luxury, not to mention attending elaborate parties at Versailles thrown by King Louis XIV—it's intoxicating, to say the least."

He's not wrong. The allure of Gray Wolf is undeniable, and I'd be lying if I said there weren't plenty of things that I'm going to miss about the life I've lived here. The mundane reality that awaits us once we're off this rock seems lackluster in comparison.

But even if I chose to stay, how long could I really time travel like this? Keane, Hawke, Roxane once roamed through time as we do, yet now find themselves anchored in administrative roles, a path I've never aspired to follow.

"But eventually," Mason continues, breaking into my thoughts, "I need to start looking forward, and home is where my future lies. Plus, I really do miss my grandma."

In that moment, I lean in and hug him. Though we've been best friends for what feels like forever, such open displays of affection have been rare between us. Which is why I find myself caught by surprise when he returns the hug with equal warmth.

"All right, all right, break it up already," Oliver says. "We've got plans to make."

Pulling back, I grab my water and take a long, steady sip.

Then, meeting each of their eyes in turn, I say, "First, a little context…"

After explaining the Antikythera Mechanism's significance and Arthur's intentions once I secure the Star, I add, "I'm going to get Arthur his Star, but there's a twist. Braxton will also Trip, but he's going to Antikythera Island in Greece, in the year 1901. He'll be there just when the original Antikythera is found, so he can switch it out with a replica."

I can't help but grin. It feels like the ultimate countermove against Arthur, beating him at his own game by swapping a genuine piece of history with a fake. It's also satisfying to know that my father's contributions as a Timekeeper weren't in vain.

"I'll ensure Braxton gets there on time," Keane says, voice brimming with confidence. "I'm familiar with all the intricacies of working the control room." Turning to Mason, he continues, "You, along with Oliver and Finn, need to head to the dock. I'll secure the car keys for you, but from there, you'll have to navigate your way forward on your own."

"I can handle it," Finn says, as Oliver and Mason both nod.

Mason turns to me, brow furrowed in confusion. "And you? I don't understand. You give Arthur the Star, but it doesn't work because the Antikythera he has is now suddenly a fake?"

"Something like that," I reply, my voice betraying more uncertainty than I'd like. I'm not entirely sure how it'll work.

The situation feels as precarious as the moment I etched my name into that prison cell wall back in 1745 Versailles. If I went back now, in the present day, would my name still be there, declaring myself a member of the AAD?

"Or," Finn interjects, his tone balancing between joking and serious, "we could clear everyone out and blow the place up."

"No!" My response is so immediate and intense, it startles everyone. "We can't do that," I continue, striving to soften my tone but failing to hide my agitation. "Think of all the masterpieces here. The idea of losing them is too heartbreaking to contemplate."

Their gazes fix on me, and a sobering realization dawns: I might be more like Arthur than I ever wanted to admit. The mere thought of destroying these treasures, erasing them from existence, strikes a chord so profound, I find myself completely choked up.

Finn raises his hands in a gesture of compliance. "All right," he says, with a nod. "We'll stick with your plan. And Godspeed to us all."

Oliver is the first to extend his hand. We join ours atop his, forming a united front. Our gold signet AAD rings catch the light, and for the first time in ages, a surge of genuine optimism courses through me. Maybe, just maybe, we stand a good chance.

At the very least, it's heartening to know we're not alone in our willingness to take a stand and do what's right.

Amid our newfound resolve, the sudden, sharp peal of six slabs chiming at once blares through the room, jarring us all.

"Seriously?" Oliver sighs in frustration, as we each break away to check our devices.

Braxton gets to his first, so I edge closer, resting against his shoulder to peer at the screen.

Your Presence is requested!

Braxton looks at me, confusion creasing his brow. "What the hell?"

I understand his concern. It's reminiscent of the invitations we receive for Trips. Worried, we continue to read.

When: Tonight, 8:00 pm
Where: Halcyon
What: Saturnalia Gala
Why: A celebration to honor all your hard work

"Damn," Braxton mutters under his breath. "Looks like Arthur's accelerating his plans."

Mason looks puzzled. "I don't get it," he says. "What's a Saturnalia?"

Just moments before, I didn't know, either. But now, the explanation rolls off my tongue as if I've known all along.

"It's a tradition from ancient Rome," I explain. "A festival to honor Saturn. During Saturnalia, societal norms were flipped upside down—slaves were served by their masters, laws were relaxed, and everyone embraced freedom and festivity. It was a time of chaos and celebration. I'm sure Arthur has plans to turbocharge this event, turning it into one last blowout party to celebrate all he's achieved and the utopia he believes he's about to usher in."

Mason's hand sweeps through the air, encompassing the room. "So, this is it. Whether we choose to leave, or Arthur forces us out, he's gearing up for the finale, the end of Gray Wolf Academy as we know it."

I nod, concern threading through my voice. "You okay with this?"

Without hesitation, Mason says, "Yeah, I'm ready."

Turning to Braxton, Keane says, "Looks like you're Tripping tonight. Think you can manage that?"

The mere thought sets my stomach roiling. In theory, it all seemed so feasible. In practice, the stakes have never been higher.

What if Braxton can't find his way back?

And even if he does, what will he be coming back to?

He certainly can't return here.

I glance at Keane, panic spreading across my face. He reads my expression and quickly reassures me. "I'll make sure he's not left behind. He'll get to where he needs to be, on both ends of his Trip. Trust me."

"You're really willing to risk that?" I ask, my voice wavering.

"What risk?" Keane says firmly. "I'm as much a part of this as anyone. I've helped Arthur chase this dream. The weight of what's happening isn't just on your shoulders. Many of us have played our parts in this, so don't think I'm stepping back now. I deserve a chance at redemption as much as anyone."

Redemption—the thing Killian also claims to desire. Well, for their sakes, I hope they both find it.

Oliver stands, with Finn rising beside him. "We've got a Saturnalia party to prepare for. And I, for one, intend to dress the part."

Braxton and I also rise, watching as our friends leave the room. Once we're alone and the door closes behind them, Braxton turns to me with a serious look and says, "I have something for you."

38

Braxton presents me with a small package, elegantly wrapped and tied with a blue velvet ribbon. His expression, tinged with apprehension, takes me back to the night he gifted me the talisman for my eighteenth birthday.

Cradling the box in my hands, I tease, "Is there a special occasion I forgot about?"

He shifts nervously, a rare sight. "Well," he begins, "not that I planned it this way, but I guess it marks the end of everything we know, and the start of everything that's yet to unfold."

Inside the box, I find a beautiful golden bangle bracelet. Engraved within its curve, hidden from view, is the inscription: THE LOVE THAT MOVES THE SUN AND OTHER STARS.

As our eyes meet, Braxton's grin widens. "I wish I could claim the words as my own," he says, "but alas, Dante Alighieri got there first. But what it's meant to say is that my love for you, much like this circle, has no beginning and no end. It just simply exists, timeless and eternal."

Carefully lifting the bracelet from its velvet cradle, he gently guides it onto my wrist. And, once again, I'm left with the uncanny feeling that I've seen this before, lived this before. As if this moment has already been written in the stars, a loop in the fabric of time where past and future collide.

Time is a flat circle...

The thought dissolves when Braxton's hand finds its way to

my cheek. Drawing me closer, our lips meet in a kiss that speaks of endless cycles of love transcending the bounds of time itself.

It's a kiss loaded with the weight of moments that might never come again, charged with a silent acknowledgment of the precarious ledge on which we now stand.

It's a kiss of every word never spoken, every wish yet to unfold, a lifetime lived in the span of a heartbeat.

Our embrace deepens, a mingling of breath and being, as if trying to memorize the feel of each other, to carry this moment through whatever fate we may meet.

We draw apart, our foreheads resting together, knowing that soon, we must each walk a path that could divide or unite us across the endless spiral of time.

But for now, this fleeting moment is the only certainty we possess.

Our bodies collide once again, mutual longing igniting in a frenzied urgency, compelling us to shed our clothing with reckless abandon. Braxton's sweater is hastily removed, sailing high over his head, while my leggings split at the seams as I struggle to free myself of them.

With the remnants of our haste scattered around us, Braxton clasps my hand in his and guides me toward the sanctuary of his bed. His voice, a whisper laden with wonder, breaks the charged silence. "If I were an artist," he muses, as he arranges me amid the plush sea of blankets and sheets, "I'd capture your beauty on canvas." His index finger dances across my skin, tracing a series of intoxicating spirals that send shivers racing down my spine. "And if I were a composer," he adds, his grin spreading, "I'd compose a melody as enchanting as you."

Gently lowering himself, he seals his vow with a kiss, an intimate whisper against my skin.

The world beyond the confines of Braxton's bedroom instantly fades, leaving nothing but this electric charge strumming between us. Every touch, every breath shared, sparks a deeper connection, an unspoken understanding that transcends mere words.

As Braxton's gaze finds mine, I feel truly seen, known to my core, as if he's peering into the depths of my soul, acknowledging every shadow and light, and loving me anyway.

His body stretches over mine, and I arch against him as he presses into me. Together, we create a new space where time folds into itself, where we are both lost and found. Our souls, like our bodies, entwine in a bond as ancient as time and as new as the dawn.

When it's over, as we tumble through a sky full of stars, the outside world cruelly intrudes. The warmth of Braxton's body sprawled alongside mine, the steady rhythm of his breath, stands in stark contrast to the turmoil brewing within my heart.

Lingering together, reluctant to let go of the magical bond we just shared, I grapple with a multitude of questions now swirling through my head.

How do we hold onto this moment, this connection, when time itself could be our greatest adversary?

"What is it?" Braxton asks, turning onto his side, as he tips a finger to my chin and angles my face toward him.

I hook a leg around his hip, edging him closer. "Sometimes I wonder," I start, loathing myself for spoiling the moment by bringing this up, yet pressing on, "if maybe there's a better way…" My voice trails off, uncertain I should continue, but Braxton's encouraging nod urges me on. "I mean, what if instead of Tripping to Greece, you went back to the time before Gray Wolf Academy was built, maybe even back to when Arthur was a kid, and…I don't know, stop him somehow?"

Braxton's gaze is tender as he looks at me and says, "Tasha, darling, you do realize that if we stop Gray Wolf from being built, then you and I never meet."

A sobering silence descends upon the room. I hadn't thought of that.

"Listen." He leans in, pressing a kiss to my forehead and cupping my cheek with a loving hand. "If we're truly fated, which I have no doubt we are, our plan will work. Simply because it has to."

"I'm just so afraid of losing you," I admit.

"You won't," he assures me, pulling me deeper into his arms. "I will find you, no matter what it takes."

"How can you be so sure?" I ask, my words a whisper pressed to the soft hollow at the base of his throat.

"Because it's our destiny," he says, pressing his lips to my nose. "And our fate." The tip of his tongue traces an enticing path down my neck. "And all we can do now is trust and believe."

He lowers his head to claim my lips, and together, we love each other again.

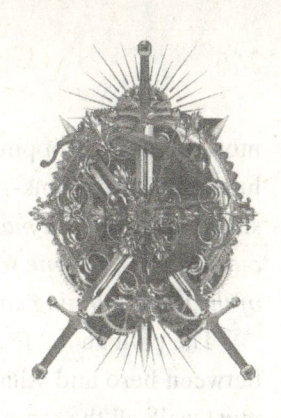

39

First thing I see when I return to my room is that Arthur has made good on his word.

Positioned with deliberate care is Artemisia Gentileschi's iconic piece, *Judith Slaying Holofernes*—my reward for procuring the Moon.

Resting just beside it is Albrecht Dürer's *Melencolia I*, the intricate engraving Arthur wants me to decipher to locate the Star.

These two pieces, each a masterpiece in its own right, serve as a visual representation of our conflicting ambitions, the monumental task I'm preparing to face.

Artemisia's painting, with its vivid depiction of determination and courage, symbolizes the daunting challenge of confronting a man like Arthur whose ambition is boundless.

On the other side, *Melencolia I*, with all its layered symbols, mirrors the complex puzzle I still need to solve to locate the Star.

As I stand before them, my shoulders slump under the weight of the responsibility I'll soon have to face.

Arthur, with his dream of remolding reality, views these two artifacts as mere steppingstones toward achieving his goal.

For me, they serve as stark reminders of the delicate balance between creation and destruction, a balance I'm sworn to protect.

Though I'm quick to remind myself that this battle is about

more than just stopping Arthur's plans—it's about protecting humanity's freedoms—a question remains that I can't seem to shake: *if we're both making choices for others, at what point do our destinies become so entangled that we are merely two sides of the same spinning coin?*

The path ahead feels like a twisted odyssey, where the line between hero and villain is beginning to blur. Yet it's a path I must walk all the same.

Reaching for the envelope Roxane left earlier, I lift the flap, and three tarot cards slide onto my palm: the Star, Strength, and the World. Each card, part of the Major Arcana, feels weighted with significance, their vibrant images resonating with a silent call to be deciphered, understood.

It's also interesting to note that these tarot cards are not from the Visconti-Sforza tarrocchi deck that Arthur usually favors. Instead, they're taken from the Rider-Waite deck, a product of a more contemporary era.

Could this selection of modern cards signify Arthur's vision for a new world?

Alongside the cards, folded with care is a copy of the map Christopher Columbus used to navigate the Atlantic. In its margins are hand-sketched symbols that correspond with the imagery found on the tarot cards. Among the engraving, the map, and these cards lies a complex puzzle—an enigmatic blend of history, art, and mysticism—that forms a cryptic guide leading directly to the Star.

Having already interpreted the engraving, I settle onto the velvet settee and arrange the cards and map on the table before me. Beginning with the Star, I try to recall what I know.

As the seventeenth card of the Major Arcana, The Star symbolizes a guiding light of hope. By adding its digits—one plus seven—it shares a numerological link with Strength, the eighth card in the deck. Though the challenge lies in determining how these cards work together.

Let's see, let's see… The Star's astrological link is Aquarius, its element is Air, while the Strength card's element is Fire, and its astrological link is Leo.

Okay, so what does that mean and how does it help me?

Usually, I have a little more time to figure this out, but with Arthur likely to dispatch me tomorrow, with either Elodie or Killian overseeing my actions, I need to unravel these mysteries sooner, rather than later. Time is a luxury I no longer possess.

Lifting the Star card to examine it more closely, I focus on the golden-haired maiden gracefully pouring water from two urns—one onto the land and the other into a natural pool. A distant memory resurfaces: my father's voice explaining that this imagery represents the healing of both present and past.

Well, that certainly tracks. It's pretty much what Arthur intends, but what else?

The maiden's nudity stands as a testament to her purity, underscored by the celestial canopy above, where a constellation of stars, one pictured in a radiant yellow, shines with exceptional brilliance and is said to be a golden beacon that guides her.

But while all of this is rich in meaning, it's starting to seem more like an esoteric collection of details rather than the clear guide I need. My frustration mounting, I tap a finger against that bright yellow star, and within seconds, a torrent of insight floods into my mind with such velocity, I scramble to grasp the enormity of it all.

As the deluge of knowledge ebbs, a singular revelation remains: the Star is not just a symbol, but rather a confluence of energies, merging the luminance of the Sun with the reflective glow of the Moon to forge a new earth.

The revelation hits like a punch to the gut. No wonder Arthur never sent me in search of any of the other planets. He must've known about this shortcut all along. Having already claimed the Sun and the Moon, the Star was always going to be the last step.

All this time it's felt like Arthur is forever ten steps ahead. But now, thanks to my dad, I'm more confident than ever that I can finally catch up.

Or at least I sincerely hope that's the case. Because if I'm wrong, the consequences will be dire for everyone.

As my fingers graze the infinity symbol on the Strength card, a cascade of insights flood my mind. Among these revelations, one stands out: the infinity symbol over the maiden's head recurs across the deck, appearing also on the Magician card—the one I associate with Arthur—and the Wheel of Fortune—the card that led both Braxton and me to Gray Wolf.

The symbol also repeats on the World card—a card that symbolizes both the end of the Major Arcana journey and, according to this, the end of my time here at Gray Wolf.

It's as if the fates have bound us all together, and now it's my job to break free.

Turning my focus to the World card, I remember that its element is earth and it's ruled by Saturn—possibly a nod to Arthur's Saturnalia party? Either way, the card represents completion, achievement, the interconnection of all things, and the joy of a seeing a long-held dream come to fruition.

But exactly whose dream will that be?

Arthur with his grandiose designs?

Or mine, with the hope of saving humanity?

The World card's two infinity symbols wrapped around both the top and bottom of the wreath can be viewed in two ways—either as the perpetual cycle of our challenges or the opportunity to redefine our fate.

As I shift my focus to the map and the symbols sketched in its margins—symbols that mirror the imagery found on the tarot cards, such as an urn, a wreath, and the face of a lion—I notice something extraordinary. The longer I gaze at them, the more they seem to animate.

Rising from the paper, they dance before my eyes like celestial guides, charting a course not only across the vast expanse of oceans, but also through the very fabric of time.

As the vision fades and the symbols fall back into place, I'm certain it's the lion that's truly guiding the way. Since the lion is featured prominently on the English royal arms, I'm pretty sure Arthur is sending me right back to where it's been all along.

Combining the two urns of the Star card, the lion depicted on the Strength card, and the Earth element of the World card, I've got a pretty good idea of exactly where I might find it.

With the final piece of this intricate puzzle now snapped into place, I leave these items as they are and head into my closet to ready myself for Arthur's Saturnalia gala.

As I sift through my wardrobe, I'm greeted by a vast collection of gowns, each a silent witness to the stories that have unfolded inside these walls.

There's the dress I wore to my first fancy dinner in the Winter Room, its fabric intertwined with memories of insecurity, anger, naivety, and wonder.

There's the one I wore on the day Braxton was tasked with teaching me swordcraft—a lesson that culminated not in mastery of the blade, but in a kiss that echoed through the very core of my being.

Tonight's selection carries a weight far beyond the aesthetics of fabric and hue—it's about making a statement, a bold declaration in Arthur's intricate game of shadows and schemes.

The dress I choose must do more than merely whisper my presence. It must send a clear, undeniable message of defiance, an unequivocal challenge to the rules of Arthur's game.

Channeling the elegance and poise of the dancer immortalized on the World card, I wrap myself in a gown of ethereal, purple silk—a silent pledge that I, too, hold a vision for the future, one starkly at odds with Arthur's darker designs.

I stand before the mirror, admiring the way the fabric swirls around me, seeming to whisper secrets of rebellion within every fold. After sliding into a pair of strappy gold heels, I adorn myself with all the treasures Braxton has gifted me—the emerald earrings, the talisman that rests against my heart, and the latest addition, a golden bracelet with its secret inscription meant only for me.

Given it's a Saturnalia celebration, some bits of gold leaf in my hair would seem fitting. Yet, lacking anything suitable, I let my hair fall in loose waves and focus on enhancing my eyes with a subtle touch of liner, hoping to highlight the defiance in my gaze.

As I pause before the full-length mirror, I remember how this all began with a makeover courtesy of Elodie. A transformation that never quite fit, leaving me feeling like I was cloaked in some other girl's skin. Yet, the person who returns my gaze now is worlds away from that scared, angry girl who first arrived on this rock. The trials I've faced, the obstacles I've overcome, and the love I've discovered have molded me into someone new—a phoenix reborn from its ashes, just like the vision I saw at my dad's.

Though Braxton will be here soon, I cross the room and stand before the window, wondering if I might catch another glimpse of the girl in the red cape—the one who looks just like me.

Outside, a winter storm rages, but the girl remains elusive. There's no lost labyrinth, and all the statues are here. *The Magician*, *The High Priestess*, and *The Wheel of Fortune*—three silent guardians shining under the silvery glow of the moon—the embodiment of Arthur, Elodie, and me—like some kind of twisted triad, an unholy trinity, bound by fate and shrouded in secrets.

As I gaze upon them, I'm reminded of the intricate dance of destiny and free will, of the shadows that lurk behind even the most enlightened intentions.

A sudden knock sounds at my door, jolting me back to the present, and I rush across the room, eager to see him.

With one hand tucked behind his back, Braxton stands at the threshold, clad in a deep blue silk tunic, dark jeans, and polished black boots.

"You are a vision." He grins, his appreciative gaze sweeping over me. "Though it seems you've forgotten something."

Pressing a hand to the fitted bodice of my dress, I shoot him a quizzical gaze, puzzled about what he could possibly mean. That's when I notice the exquisite gold leaf crown he offers me.

"May I?" he asks, and I lower my head. When I rise, I see he's now wearing one of his own.

"When in Rome." He grins. Then linking my arm with his, we make our way toward Halcyon, ready for our last party at Gray Wolf.

40

T he swell of music greets us long before we reach Halcyon's vivid orange doors. Max Richter's upbeat remix of Vivaldi's "Spring" swirls through the air, striking a stark contrast to the winter storm raging outside.

Though for Arthur, tonight marks the beginning of his own personal spring—a time for the awakening of hope, the blossoming of long-held dreams.

As Braxton and I move through the crowd, the atmosphere feels electric, alive with conversation and loud bursts of laughter. In the true spirit of Saturnalia, all the usual social boundaries are blurred.

Tonight, the elite and the support staff mingle freely, leaving me to wonder how many truly understand what this night of untamed revelry is really about.

Within this opulent setting, this enchanting, glittering, fever dream of a room—with its inky floors and undulating walls lavishly decorated with an array of artifacts collected from myriad cultures and times—is like a treasure trove, a collector's fantasy brought to life. These objects, souvenirs from journeys undertaken by Trippers, create a vivid mosaic of human history and creativity, making the room more than just a physical space; it's a crossroads where the pathways of time intersect.

My gaze moves from an amethyst chandelier overhead to the green marble-topped bar, where Elodie once served me a strange, iridescent red drink she jokingly referred to as "Strange. Sweet." Then I take in the eerie elegance of the skeletal saint snatched from the Roman catacombs—a macabre relic that, according to Elodie, was Braxton's contribution to the décor.

Yet it's Arthur's genius that's transformed what was once an exclusive nightclub reserved for Gray Wolf's elite into an otherworldly realm transcending the bounds of time. Leveraging cutting-edge holographic technology, Halcyon is now reenvisioned as the epitome of an ancient Roman domus, embodying the lavishness and scale that once defined the homes of the empire's most distinguished figures.

Columns mirror the grandeur of Rome, and the space is filled with holographic renditions of generals and gladiators who wander about. So vivid and precise is their detail, distinguishing these ghostly apparitions from real, living guests is a formidable challenge. If I thought Arthur had outdone himself with the Van Gogh immersive dinner, what he's created here is beyond anything I ever imagined.

My gaze sweeps across the guests, each of them wearing costumes that span from historically accurate tunics, togas, and silk stolas to more fantastical ensembles featuring crowns of woven blossoms and antlers, reminding me of the torch singer back at Arcana.

The fusion of past and present, reality and illusion, creates an atmosphere of surreal enchantment, as if we've all stepped into a dream where time has lost all meaning.

As we venture deeper into the throng, Braxton leans closer, his voice carrying a hint of the old formality of when we first met. "And now," he says, "would you grant me the honor of sharing a dance?"

My gaze drifts to the dance floor, haunted by the ghost of our last encounter there, when he edged so close to declaring his love, but my fear interfered, and I purposely cut him off before he could get to the words. But now, drawing upon all the lessons in etiquette and comportment I've learned in this place, I bow my head, dip into a deep curtsy, and extend my hand for him to take.

As Braxton and I make for the dance floor, the room seems to erupt in a vibrant spectacle of color and sound. Leaving the usual decorum behind, we immerse ourselves in a wave of pure, unbridled joy alongside the crowd.

Elodie and Jago edge up beside us, their combined beauty almost too much to take in all at once. Elodie, draped in a gown of ethereal white silk that clings to her body as if woven from moonlight itself, beams at me in a smile so pure and unguarded, it occurs to me that I've never actually seen her this happy, not even with Nash back in Regency England.

Is Elodie clued in to what this night truly means?

"Shall we mix it up a bit?" Jago asks, his eyes glinting with mischief. He smoothly passes Elodie into Braxton's arms, then reaches for mine. As I watch Braxton and Elodie move across the dance floor, Jago gives me a reassuring look. "You've got nothing to worry about," he says, gesturing subtly toward Braxton and Elodie. "He's completely taken with you—told me so himself."

"I know," I say, confident that all those old insecurities are now well behind me.

Jago, dressed in a white toga the same shade of moonlight as Elodie's gown, leans closer, his deep topaz gaze latching onto mine. "Though I do find myself wondering," he says, "what makes you think you can't trust me?"

His question takes me by surprise, leaving me momentarily speechless. Yet, recognizing the honesty he's always shown me, I know I owe him nothing less than the truth in return.

"It's not you, per se…" I pause, searching for just the right words. "It's more to do with your…connection with Elodie."

A trace of amusement flickers across his ridiculously beautiful face. "My *connection*?" he teases, a playful smirk tugging at his lips. "Is that what we're calling it now?"

A rush of heat creeps into my cheeks, an embarrassing blush spreading under the weight of his gaze.

"Just because we share a bed on occasion doesn't mean we engage in pillow talk," he says.

I nod in reply, then, because I know I owe it to him, I add, "I'm sorry. Truly. You were one of the first ones here—hell, one of the only ones—who was willing to help me, tell me what's worth fighting for and what's not."

"And look at you now!" His smile broadens as he runs an admiring glace over me.

Luckily, I know all too well that Jago's flirtations are merely part of his charm and never to be taken to heart. "You must be the most charismatic individual I've ever met," I say, a playful note in my voice, "and likely ever will."

He laughs, pulling me closer, and we take another spin around the dance floor. When we're back to where we started, I ask, "So, what's next? Where will you go from here?"

Stopping abruptly, Jago grasps my hands in his and levels a look so piercing, I'm left struggling to read between the lines of the unspoken message in his eyes.

"You don't need to worry about me," he finally says. "Though I have no plans to join you on your quest, I won't be an obstacle, either."

"But Jago," I start, the weight of unspoken thoughts dying on my tongue when he silences me with a cautionary gaze.

"This is not the place for that conversation," he warns, his voice carrying a seriousness I've seldom heard from him. "But rest assured, I'm not leaving. Gray Wolf is my home, and whether you like it or not, it's yours now, too."

"So you don't think I'll succeed?" A flash of anger mixed

with panic surges inside me.

Does Jago know something I don't?

I search his face, looking for clues, but before I can ask, insist he elaborate, Killian appears by my side, saying, "May I?"

I'm on the verge of telling him no, that he absolutely may not, because this dance with Jago is far from finished.

But when I glance back to where Jago once stood, I find he's already gone, vanished into the crowd.

41

Killian stands before me, a study in casual elegance. Wearing a white linen toga that drapes over one muscular, suntanned shoulder, it leaves little to the imagination about what might—or might not—lie underneath. His golden hair is artfully tousled, and his vivid blue eyes lock onto mine with an intensity that's impossible to ignore.

Yet, despite his undeniable allure, his presence fails to stir the reaction he likely expects.

"Yeah, no thanks," I say, my attention drifting across the room to where Braxton continues his dance with Elodie. His hand poised carefully at her waist, he appears to listen intently to her every word—a sharp contrast to the disinterest I feel standing before Killian.

"What's good for the gander," Killian says, his gaze trailing mine. "Come on, Shiv. For old time's sake. How about you and I trip the light fantastic together?"

I shake my head, signaling a clear and decisive end to the conversation. As I leave the dance floor, I'm halfway to the bar when he says, "Shiv, please."

I spin around, irritation bubbling to the surface in a way that's impossible to miss.

"Just a moment of your time," he says. "Then you're free to go. I promise."

Reluctantly, I give him a nod, my hesitation made clear

in every line of my body. Yet Killian's grin widens, evidently content to accept whatever concession I'm willing to make.

"Why do I have this nagging suspicion," he says, getting right to the point, "that despite my attempts to warn you, you're concocting some sort of scheme you should absolutely steer clear of?"

Determined to keep my emotions masked, I lift my shoulders in a casual shrug. "I have no idea what you're talking about," I say.

Killian regards me for a long, sobering beat, and I'm on the verge of leaving, when he finally speaks. "For the record, I've known who—and what—you are, long before those golden rings ever appeared on your arm."

I shrug once more. "I'm well aware," I say.

"Then you may also recall that Arthur once charged me with the task of eliminating people like you."

"Kind of hard to forget," I snap. Yet, as my gaze meets his, there's a complexity in his eyes I hadn't noticed before.

"The reason I warned you," he says, "is because I hoped I'd never have to make a choice like that again."

"What is it you're saying, Killian? Because it's starting to sound a lot like a threat."

Raising his hands before him in a gesture of peace, he speaks in a voice so muted, I have to strain to hear it. "I guess what I'm saying is that I do love you, Shiv. And though I know it's too late for us, that I royally fucked my chances of you ever returning my feelings, I want you to know that I'm resigned to that fate. From here on out, I will seek my pleasures elsewhere, in the hope that, one day, my feelings for you will diminish."

I meet his confession with a steady gaze, my expression steadfastly neutral, betraying none of the inner turmoil brewing inside me.

"And so," he continues, "I will promise to honor your wishes and stop chasing after you, if—"

"If I do something for you in return," I cut in. "Am I right?"

He casts a quick glance around the room before returning to me. "Just… I want you to know that what I said earlier today, it wasn't a joke. So Shiv, please, I'm imploring you, don't force me to choose."

"Choose what?" I say, my voice, like my gaze, sharp as a blade. "Between your loyalty to Arthur and this alleged love you have for me?"

Killian nods, his unwavering gaze fixed onto mine.

"Well then," I say, the words cutting through the tension like a knife. "It seems you've already made your choice." I turn away, leaving him with a final, "Good night, Killian. And good luck."

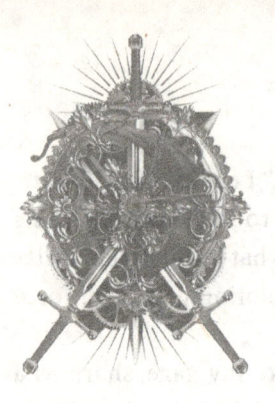

42

Braxton finds me at the bar, where I'm sipping from a glass of citrus-spiked water.

"You okay?" he asks, his expression etched with concern.

"More of the same," I say, seeing no reason to rehash what I'm sure he can guess. "And you?"

He lets out a sigh. "Elodie wanted me to know she's come to terms with us being together. Said she's happy for me, for us. Even apologized for her attempts to interfere with, her words here: *what's so clearly meant to be*."

"Do you believe her?" I ask. "Because that doesn't sound like the Elodie I know. Contrition is a foreign concept to her."

Braxton gives a noncommittal shrug, seemingly indifferent to her motives. Then, slipping an arm around my waist, he says, "Seeing as how this is our last party in this place, what do you say we make one more lap around the room before I go?"

Moving through the crowd, we skirt a holographic spectacle where gladiators battle to the death with a ferocious pride of lions, under the avid gaze of a virtual audience casting their stakes. The realism is so striking, it's easy to forget they're not real.

When we arrive at a long banquet table that practically groans under the weight of Arthur's take on an ancient Roman feast, Braxton snatches a handful of grapes and teasingly feeds them to me while playfully fanning me with his free hand. His antics spark a fit of laughter so intense, he eventually has to relent.

Drawing me closer, he whispers, "I look forward to more moments like this. Your laughter—it's a melody too seldom heard around here."

I grin, my mind filling with visions of what a normal life, in a normal place, far from the extraordinary confines of Gray Wolf, might look like.

The two of us playfully arguing over who gets to control the TV remote.

Braxton and I, wandering the aisles of a grocery store, looking for the freshest pieces of produce.

Both of us engaged in a fierce debate over the eternal question of whether toilet paper should hang over or under the roll.

The very idea of Braxton, so larger than life in so many ways, immersed in such ordinary domestic tasks, ignites another round of laugher that I find nearly impossible to control.

"What's so funny?" he asks, his lips brushing my cheek.

"Nothing," I manage to say. "Or maybe everything. I guess it depends on how you look at it, doesn't it?"

Suddenly the music stops, drawing all eyes to the stage, where Arthur stands before the mic. In a rare departure from his typical attire of understated, affluent ease, tonight he wears a costume of ancient regality, the type of which his favorite Roman emperor, Marcus Aurelius, known as the philosopher king, might've worn.

His head is encased in a gleaming bronze helmet, crowned with a black plume. His body is ensconced in armor composed of interlaced leather and metal strips. A pair of broad shoulder guards stretch down his upper arms, enhancing his formidable appearance. A purple woolen cloak, clasped at one shoulder, complements the knee-length tunic beneath, its purple hue a symbol of royalty and authority. Completing the ensemble, a pair of heavy leather sandals lends an air of authentic period detail.

Seeing him now, as he gazes among his admiring crowd, it strikes me as ironic how Arthur, who claims to have read Marcus Aurelius's *Meditations* countless times, seems to have overlooked its core message entirely.

The storied Roman emperor repeatedly cautioned against the corrupting influence of power—a pitfall Marcus Aurelius diligently worked to avoid.

And yet, Arthur Blackstone, who claims to be his greatest admirer, precisely embodies the very pitfalls the Roman emperor warned against.

Then again, it's a rare person who has a clear view of themselves.

Arthur takes the microphone in hand, his mere presence alone enough to command all our attention. "Greetings!" he calls, his voice resonating through the suddenly silent room.

Instantly, the atmosphere electrifies, the crowd erupting into enthusiastic cheers as if Arthur, standing before us in historical finery, is a rock star poised to deliver an encore performance of his biggest hit song.

It's in this moment that the depth of their affection for him becomes unmistakably clear. This room is filled with people whose loyalty to him is unwavering, their lives indelibly marked by his intervention. Rescued from the brink of guillotines, the gallows, and witch trials, they owe their very existence to Arthur's grace.

And in the midst of this new understanding, I can't help but wonder if Arthur can really turn his back on them all?

Can he really cast aside those he no longer deems necessary?

And what would they think if they were to discover his plans?

Another glance around the room tells me that their faith in him is so resolute, so unwavering, that even if I did try to convince them of what I now know, the majority wouldn't believe me.

As Arthur continues speaking, Mason quietly appears by my side. "We're about to head out," he says, subtly gesturing toward Oliver and Finn, who linger at the edge of the crowd.

"So soon?" A hint of reluctance sounds in my voice.

"Seems like the best time." He shrugs. "With everyone so distracted, we'll be able to slip away without notice."

I give a silent nod, feeling an uncomfortable knot tighten in my throat at the thought of his leaving, even though I know it's all just as we planned.

"I'm sorry," I say, the gravity of our situation adding extra weight to my words. "I never meant to drag you into all this."

"Don't." Mason shakes his head. "Don't regret a single second of it. Believe it or not, this has turned into one of the most amazing experiences of my life. It's like playing a real-life version of *Anywhere But Here*."

A laugh breaks through my tears as I remember the game we used to play back in high school, dreaming up fantastical adventures to escape the tedium of our surroundings.

"I never imagined we'd actually live out those daydreams," he says. "It's because of you that I got to experience that."

"Yeah, be careful what you wish for, right?" I try to smile, but my eyes, much like his, are brimming with tears, saying more than any words or grin ever could.

"I would hug you," Mason says, "but we can't risk drawing any unwanted attention. So, instead of goodbye, which seems way too final, I'll just say, so long. For now. We'll catch up in New York or even California, yes?"

"Definitely," I assure him.

Turning to Braxton, Mason says, "Sorry I clocked you."

Braxton rubs at the spot on his jaw where Mason's knuckles pounded his flesh in what now feels like a lifetime ago. "Wouldn't have it any other way." He grins. Then, with a nod of respect, he adds, "Good luck to you, Mason. May your journey be smooth, the seas calm, and the winds at your back."

"Highly unlikely." Mason laughs. "But thanks for the sentiment all the same."

Our farewells to Oliver and Finn are brief, and I can't help but feel a twinge of regret that I didn't get to know them as well as I might've liked.

But Gray Wolf is like that—competitive, cloaked in secrecy. A place where forming genuine connections is hindered by a constant undercurrent of doubt and suspicion.

Arthur has created this breathtaking environment and filled it with distrust, making us feel like we're always being listened to, watched, our every move monitored. It's one of my biggest grievances with him. Here, we had the potential to become a united family, all working together as one. But I guess Arthur feared that sort of unity might one day turn us against him.

My gaze shifts to the stage where Arthur continues to captivate the crowd. Then spotting Keane lingering close by, I turn to Braxton with a heavy heart. "It's time, isn't it?"

Braxton pulls me close to his chest, sealing our farewell with a kiss that resonates deep in my soul. As we part, a sea of unspoken words swirls between us. With a trembling hand, I reach up and lovingly trace the slight bend of his nose, smiling through my tears at this dashing, elegant boy who managed to claim my whole heart.

"See you in New York," I manage to whisper, struggling to hold back a sob.

"You will, indeed." He nods, his own voice equally strained but determined, his ocean blue eyes alight with an unspoken promise.

With a final, lingering glance, heavy with all the emotions we find impossible to voice, we reluctantly part.

Every step away from each other is weighted not just with the enormity of the challenge before us, but also the fervent, silent hope for the future we dream of building together.

43

As Arthur exits the stage, the room immediately bursts back to life, filled with the sounds of loud music and the lively echo of laughter.

My eyes sweep the crowd, landing on Killian and Maisie, who are tangled in each other in an intimate dance. Not far from them, Roxane moves in rhythm with Hawke, the instructor who introduced me to the concept of the fourth-dimensional road on my first day here when he set me before an Albert Einstein hologram, which painstakingly outlined a theory that, at the time, sailed right over my head.

Thinking it's probably as good a time as any to slip away, I'm edging closer to the door when my departure is stopped by a decisive hand encircling my wrist. I know without looking exactly who it is.

Elodie.

Turning, I see my guess is confirmed.

"What's the rush, Nat?" Her gaze is probing, not missing a thing.

Nat. The name I used to go by back when I was another girl, living another life. I can't help but wonder if it was an attempt to remind me of my former diminished self, or perhaps a nod to the friendship we shared long before I even knew of a mysterious academy called Gray Wolf. With Elodie, you never know.

"Just…feeling a bit tired," I say, feigning a yawn. Though the skepticism in her sharp, knowing eyes tells me she's far from convinced.

"Nonsense," she counters, reaching toward a nearby table laden with champagne flutes. She selects one for herself and hands another to me. "What shall we toast to?" She grips the stem of her glass in anticipation.

I cast a quick glance around, needing a moment to decide. Returning to her, I say, "To new adventures."

Her eyes search mine, a slight smile playing at her lips. "To new adventures with old friends," she amends, raising her glass to meet mine in a toast.

As the champagne's effervescence tickles my throat, my attention is drawn to the golden serpent pendant nestled against her chest. It strikes me as odd that I never noticed it back when she went to my school, but here, it's rare that I see her without it.

Now the serpent was more crafty than any other beast of the field...

The unexpected thought, a Bible verse, echoes through my head. As I gaze at Elodie standing before me—the human embodiment of cunning—a cold shudder travels through me.

Did she purposely sabotage my mask in an attempt to strand me in 1745 Versailles?

Is she the one who sent the diamond clip to Mason that ended up landing him here?

Did she really sleep with King Henry VIII?

Is there truth in anything she's ever told me, or is it all just an elaborate work of fiction?

This beautiful, calculating, unknowable girl has been both ally and obstacle in ways I could never have foreseen. While part of me desperately hopes this marks the end of our intertwined story, there's another, deeper layer of my being that acknowledges the void her absence will create.

Wherever we go from here, one thing is sure: I really do

hope she finds whatever it is she's looking for.

Draining my drink, I turn to her and offer a simple, "Good night, Elodie."

With her blue eyes flashing on mine, she leans in and draws me into an unexpected hug. Her voice softly whispers, "May fortune smile upon you, Natasha."

As I make my leave, I'm acutely aware of the heat of her gaze following me all the way to the door.

44

I wake before dawn.

Well before my slab sounds its chime for Arthur's daily dose of inspiration. Since this is the last of his quotes I'm ever likely to read, I give it my full attention.

What we do now, echoes in eternity. - Marcus Aurelius

I interpret it to mean the final phase of this game has now started.

By the time the notification arrives, informing me that I've been summoned to Trip, I've been prepared for what feels like a lifetime.

When the knock sounds at my door, signaling the arrival of my escort, I call out, "Just a minute!" wanting to savor a few final moments in this small, luxurious space that's served as my home.

It was here by the hearth where Braxton gave me my talisman.

It was there in that bed where we shared so many intimate moments.

On those walls is the art I was rewarded with for bringing Arthur his Gets—pieces like *Vanitas*, *The Persistence of Memory*, and, most recently, *Judith Slaying Holofernes.*

The knock sounds again, but I choose to ignore it, drawn instead to the window for a final gaze upon the tarot garden below.

I press my hands to the chilled glass, trying to summon the

vision of the labyrinth and the girl in the red cape who looked so much like me. But once again, the image eludes me.

Instead, my eyes linger on the deliberate placement of *The Magician*, *The High Priestess*, and *The Wheel of Fortune* statues, the three intertwined by the sinuous form of a serpent, a symbol of their eternal connection.

When another knock sounds, this one sharper, insistent, I turn away from the window and stride toward the door, ready to embrace my destiny with open arms and a determined heart.

Navigating a maze of corridors and passing through multiple security checkpoints, where we present our slabs and prove our identities, we finally reach the top-secret command center. It looks like it's been yanked from the faraway future and plopped down on this rock of an island.

Standing here now, I have the same feeling I did on my very first Trip—a tangled knot of anticipation roiling in my belly, growing larger by the minute.

Unlike that first time, today the pressure is immense. As my eyes settle on Arthur—the man who's orchestrated my life for longer than I can probably imagine—my heart stalls in my chest.

No longer wearing the Roman emperor armor of last night, today marks the first time I've ever seen him opting for a crisp white shirt and blazer over his usual cashmere sweater.

Arthur is dressed to reunite with his long-lost love.

And I'm here to make sure that he doesn't.

"How are you feeling?" he asks, giving me a thorough once-over. "You left quite early last night. Everything all right?"

Knowing honesty is always best, I say, "I had a feeling I'd be Tripping today, and I wanted to be well rested and ready. I know how much you have riding on this."

He surveys me with those scrutinizing obsidian eyes, not missing a thing. Once again, I wonder if he knows that Braxton and I witnessed his ritual of grief. But I quickly dismiss the thought, convinced his sorrow rendered him oblivious to everything else.

"Can you locate it?" he asks, his tone uncharacteristically hopeful.

"I'm confident I can," I assure him. "No need to worry."

"In that case," he says, his voice brisk and authoritative once more, "head over to makeup and wardrobe. Charlotte's waiting for you."

As I make my way to see Charlotte, I cross paths with Keane. Knowing it's not safe to ask, I shoot him an inquiring look. He answers with a reassuring nod that instantly fills me with relief. Then he discreetly hands me the key to my dad's New York apartment, now programmed to serve as a clicker.

Everything is unfolding according to plan. Mason, Oliver, and Finn have departed, and Braxton's journey has begun. Now I'm the final piece awaiting my turn.

Charlotte greets me with a wide grin. As I take in the warmth of her gaze and her flushed cheeks, I realize how much I'm going to miss her, and it's all I can do to fight back the tears.

Noticing the way I dab at my eyes, she says, "You are feeling all right?"

I manage a nod, fighting to regain my composure, and ease into the familiar routine of preparing for a Trip. My face is lightly powdered, my lips and cheeks tinted with rouge, and my hair is arranged in soft, face-framing curls, while the rest is swept up into an intricate bun at the back that's meticulously adorned with a scattering of pearls.

When Charlotte unexpectedly adds a dusting of gold powder as a finishing touch, I'm surprised to find that, in a certain light, I look almost blond.

"And the dress?" I say, eager to see it. Despite the weight of the challenges ahead, it's hard not to get at least a little caught up in this elaborate game of dress-up.

Charlotte responds with an enthusiastic grin, retrieving a gown from the rack. She presents it to me, and as my eyes take in the gown's delicate powder blue silk, designed with an empire waist and short, puffed sleeves, a surge of panic rises within me.

When she brings out the long white gloves and satin slippers in the same shade of blue as the gown, I can't hold it in any longer.

"This—this isn't the right timeline!" I say, my eyes wide, my voice too thin and high. "This is for Regency England, not—"

Charlotte's gaze meets mine, her expression etched with concern. "Not what?" she asks.

"I thought..." My words falter, my mouth gone suddenly dry. I silently scold myself to calm the hell down, I can't afford to raise any alarms. "I was under the impression," I say, "that I'd be Tripping to the time of King Henry VIII."

Charlotte pauses, giving me a long, perplexed look before she finally says, "This is the instruction Arthur provided. Elodie is wearing the same."

Elodie?

I shut my eyes, suppressing a sigh. So, Arthur has chosen his own daughter as my companion for the Trip.

Though I can't say I'm surprised, I do question why Arthur decided on her.

Did he think she'd pose a greater challenge than Killian?

Then again, I suppose it hardly matters. The odds of either of them helping me are slim.

As I resign myself to being fitted into a dress from an era I wasn't expecting, I wonder what additional surprises Arthur might have in store. Just when I thought I'd finally caught up, he manages to leap ahead another ten paces, leaving me scrambling to bridge the gap.

Once I'm dressed, Charlotte guides me to stand before a mirror, and my eyes fill with the sight of a me who's not really me—a girl cast in a role she never auditioned for.

Concealed beneath the long, straight column of my dress is a slender, sharp dagger I truly hope I won't need. The array of pockets hidden within the seams of the dress are filled with all the items I plan to take with me.

The thought of arriving in New York, when all is said and done, wearing a getup like this, brings a grin to my lips. If it were any other town, in any other place, it might be cause for alarm. But in a city as eclectic as New York, I doubt I'll get so much as a second glance.

"What do you think?" Charlotte asks.

After taking another good look at myself, I opt for honesty. "I'm not sure I'll ever get used to this. It feels like I'm caught in a dream."

For a fleeting moment, a shadow flits across Charlotte's gaze, hinting at something deeper I can't quite grasp. But it's gone in a blink, and she swiftly returns to her usual cheerful self.

"The gloves are fortunate to conceal your..." She gestures toward the collection of golden rings on my arm.

I give a slight nod, an unspoken understanding passing between us.

"And your talisman?" she asks.

I hesitate. Ever since the time I spent with my dad, I no longer need it to avoid falling into a Fade. Yet, not wanting to raise any suspicions, I quietly retrieve it from my pocket, watching as she takes great care securing it at my neck.

By all appearances, I'm ready. And yet, I'm not quite willing to leave just yet.

"Charlotte," I begin, my voice cautious, words measured. "If you could Trip to any era or destination, where would you go?"

I inhale a breath, waiting for her to respond.

Charlotte meets my gaze, her eyes momentarily darkening before she replies, "Gray Wolf is my home."

"But there was another place you called home once, wasn't there?" I ask, aware I'm treading on delicate ground, yet needing to know.

Charlotte clasps her hands at her waist, regarding me with an inscrutable expression. "You are familiar with the saying: *nostalgia is history stripped of its suffering*?" Her unwavering eyes hold fast to mine. "In this place, there is an absence of that pain. So this is where I choose to remain."

A silent understanding passes between us. Gently taking her hands in mine, I say, "Thank you," recalling how it was because of her that I even thought to break off a piece of my pannier to defend myself from the duke. Without her guidance, I might've never survived that night. "You've been a true friend," I add. "And I'll always be grateful for that."

Giving my hands a comforting squeeze, she says, "Good luck, Natasha. And may the fates be with you."

45

When I reach the launchpad, I see Arthur has managed to throw in yet another surprise.

Elodie is there, a vision in a pink satin dress, its cut nearly identical to mine.

But standing right beside her is Killian, his ensemble loudly declaring his allegiance.

The dark navy of his meticulously tailored tailcoat is complemented by a pink silk waistcoat that unmistakably aligns him with Elodie. Yet aside from the high-collared white shirt, intricately tied cravat, and formfitting trousers seamlessly tucked into polished Hessian boots, it's the gold pocket watch fastened at his waist that really catches my eye.

It reminds me of the timepiece I brought back from my last Trip to Regency England when I had a near-fatal run-in with Braxton's father.

Together Elodie and Killian stand like the homecoming king and queen of every high school that ever was.

I guess Arthur couldn't decide who the better chaperone for me would be, so he opted to send them both.

Awesome.

Yet, as troubled as I am by this latest development, it's Braxton's absence that hits me the most.

Soon, I tell myself. *Soon we'll be together again, and this, and all Arthur's games, will be relegated to memory.*

Killian approaches me first. "Shiv," he says, giving me a curt nod.

When I shift my attention to Elodie, her smile is strained. "I've got a bit of a champagne headache," she tells me, "so I hope you can handle whatever this is on your own."

"Of course," I reply, not buying her act for a second. Elodie is not one to overindulge. She's that odd combination of a girl who's always on the lookout for a good time while also managing to keep a tight rein on herself.

What an odd trio we make.

Killian claims to love me yet harbors a deep-seated animosity toward Elodie for reasons unknown.

While Elodie makes no secret of her disdain for Killian. And though she might play at friendship with me, I question if she truly understands what that means.

One thing is unmistakably clear: they stand united in their unwavering loyalty to Arthur.

"Ready for the big reveal?" Roxane draws an envelope from her clipboard and extends it toward me.

Big reveal, indeed. Still, I slide a finger under the red wax seal embossed with the Gray Wolf insignia, retrieving a square of paper that reads:

You are cordially invited!
When: May 16, 1814
Where: London, England
What: The May Ball
Why: To commemorate the London Season

"What the fuck?" Elodie mutters under her breath.

"Bloody hell." Killian scowls.

Though I have no idea what they're so upset about, my attention quickly shifts to the contact lenses Roxane hands to each of us.

These aren't just any lenses; they're designed to monitor time and guide us back to the portal—two things I no longer care about, since my return plans don't include Gray Wolf. Unbeknownst to them, Keane has arranged for an alternate portal in a different location to facilitate my escape.

When we're ready, Elodie, Killian, and I step onto the platform.

"You have two hours," Roxane cautions. "Should you need to leave sooner, Elodie will have the clicker."

Of course. Who else would Arthur trust more than his own daughter?

But is Elodie aware of the deeper connection they share?

Elodie wags her index finger at me, flashing the clicker that doubles as a ring. Normally, the idea of her possessing the clicker would really annoy me. Now, I truly couldn't care less.

Pressing an envelope into my hands, Roxane says, "Do not open until you arrive."

What the—?

I shoot her a questioning look, but she's already moved past it. Her gaze sweeps over each of us. "Any questions?"

In unison, we shake our heads. With a swift turn on her heel, Roxane strides toward the control room, joining Arthur, Hawke, Keane, and the rest of the team responsible for making this miracle of time travel happen.

"Ready?" Elodie asks, just as a thick glass shield rises all around us.

With one last look, I mentally bid my goodbyes. Then, grasping hold of Killian and Elodie's hands, I say, "Yeah, let's do this."

As the lights flicker and a tremor runs through the ground beneath us, I'm reminded of the peculiar similarity between the sensations of Tripping and the Unravelings I've experienced since I was a kid.

Elodie tightens her grip on my hand, and I squeeze back, feeling a surge of anticipation swelling within as a sudden gust of wind whips at our feet.

The air is now permeated with the sharp tang of sulfur; we're soon enveloped in a dense cloud of vapor that rapidly grows all around us.

A moment later, a thunderous buzz explodes through the room, and I watch in a mix of awe and apprehension as a brilliant white light streaks toward the swirling vapor, halting abruptly upon contact before transforming into a shimmering gateway.

This is it. My destiny is now moments away.

"Here we go," Elodie says, her voice brimming with an uncustomary dread.

Next thing I know, the barrier vanishes, gravity loses its grip, and we're lifted high off our feet as we're rocketed right out of this time and back into another.

Those whom the gods wish to destroy, they first make mad with power.
-Charles Caleb Colton

46

Much like the last time I was here, we arrive in the gardens of the expansive English estate. The air is filled with the scent of blooming flowers, mingling with the distant hum of polite conversation and the occasional trill of laughter.

"Well," Elodie says, smoothing her dress with a sweep of her hand, "whatever the hell this is, let's get it over with already, so I can get back to Gray Wolf." Her tone is unusually terse, her movements stiff.

Since when isn't Elodie up for a fancy party? She was practically molded and made for events like this. Not to mention that she has, as she once put it, *a serious male suitor*, who hails from this era and will most likely be here.

"Don't you want to see Nash?" I ask, remembering how excited she was last time over the prospect of reuniting with the handsome earl.

Elodie shuts her eyes, shaking her head. When she opens them, she says, "Don't you mean Nash and his new fiancée?" Her voice is thick, eyes shimmering with unshed tears. "This party is one year later, Nat. He couldn't exactly put his life on pause. I can't believe Arthur did this to me. He knows I avoid coming here in 1814 or any time after. Made that mistake once, thought I'd never have to make it again. And yet, here I am. Yay, me."

I watch as her face crumbles, and my heart swells with empathy. Which I guess explains why I find myself saying, "Okay,

Nash is engaged. So what? Last I checked, a fiancée wasn't a wife. Not yet anyway."

Elodie crosses her arms and quickly averts her gaze.

Still, I know she's listening, so I go on to say, "If what you and Nash have is real, then it's not too late. There's still time to make it work."

"I have no family here, no home, and no immediate means of support. Do you honestly think I could build a life for myself in this place?" She gestures around the expansive lawns. Her brow is furrowed, and her mouth pulled into a frown, but in her gaze, I detect a slim thread of hope, and it's just enough to pull on.

Despite the urgency of the task before me, there's an opportunity here that I don't want to miss. After everything we've been through, I really do want to see Elodie happy. She deserves a chance to finally break free of the iron grip Arthur has on her life.

"Honestly," I say, "I'm convinced you could thrive just about anywhere, especially here. I saw it with my own eyes, El; Nash is completely awed by you. Whoever this fiancée is, I'm sure she's a concession to societal pressures. Marriages here are more about alliances than affection."

"Do you really believe that?" Her eyes widen, making her look like a much younger version of herself in search of encouragement.

"I really, truly do," I tell her.

Our moment of connection is abruptly shattered by Killian's loud, obnoxious groan. "Bloody hell," he says, his English accent roaring back. But it's not like I can complain, seeing as how, for once, it's actually the appropriate time and place. "Can we dispense with the dramatics and get on with it already?"

Elodie shoots Killian a withering look. "Shut it," she snaps. "No one asked your opinion."

"Oh, honey, you haven't even begun to hear what I think

about you," Killian barks. "Is this how you—"

Leaving them locked in their mutual standoff, I dart across the gardens and step inside the grand ballroom, instantly captivated by its grandeur.

The room is vast, bathed in a soft, luminous glow, with crystal chandeliers suspended overhead, their flickering candles twinkling like distant stars. The gentle hum of an orchestra fills the air, promising a night filled with music and dance. But those pleasures are reserved for the guests; I have more pressing concerns to address.

I move through the room, immersed in the rich scent of roses and peonies, their delicate fragrances intermingling with the warm, honeyed aroma of beeswax candles in elegant silver candelabras. Though I keep to the perimeter, steering clear of the dance floor, it's hard not to get caught up in the buzz of conversation, the sudden bursts of laughter.

The atmosphere is electric, brimming with the thrill of social maneuvering and the whispers of romantic intrigue. Everyone is dressed in their Regency finery—the men in sharp coats and neatly tied cravats, the women in flowing, empire-waist gowns that mirror my own. And as I thread my way through them, it's like being immersed in a kaleidoscope—a vibrant swirl of color and movement that spins all around me.

When I sneak a glance at the dancing couples, it occurs to me that this lavish ballet of intricate social exchange is exactly the life Braxton was born into. If it weren't for Arthur's interference, he would've eventually found his way here, in search of a wife— some lucky girl from his own timeline.

It's because of Arthur that two souls born centuries apart managed to find their way to each other. And now, the responsibility falls to Braxton and me to prevent Arthur from reuniting with his beloved. A cruel irony that could easily fill me with sorrow, were it not for the grave consequences if he succeeds.

But here, in this moment, transfixed by this extravagant tableau, I feel like I walked into the pages of my favorite Jane Austen novel. Though it's not long before the brush of my gown against my skin, the heft of my hair pinned atop my head, and the subtle weight of Roxane's envelope in my grasp, anchors me to the reality of the role I must play.

Just as I start to pick up the pace, Elodie comes up from behind me and seizes my arm. "Oh, great," she mutters. "He's here, right over there."

I follow her gaze to see Nash. His dark curls, piercing green eyes, and distinctly rugged features all contribute to a charisma that's impossible to miss. Unfortunately for Elodie, he's dancing with a pretty brunette.

"I think I might throw up," she says, her grip tightening to the point where I'm sure I'll be left with bruises in the shape of her fingers.

"Listen." I turn to face her. "You are Elodie Fucking Blue. You're stunning, possibly the most beautiful girl in this room, and you're damn smart, too. Also, you've never failed to capture the heart of anyone you've ever set your sights on."

Elodie turns to me, her expression shifting, eyes clouding over. "Seems like that's not *always* the case," she says, clearly alluding to Braxton.

I study the dueling emotions playing across her face, the eternal conflict of hope and despair. This girl has played the roles of both ally and adversary in my life, but I'm done holding grudges. My only aim now is to help her get past this crisis of confidence so I can free myself to pursue my own task.

"Perhaps Braxton wasn't the right one for you," I gently suggest. "But this one, Nash, could be. So, El—I guess the only question left is: what're you going to do about it?"

To my relief, she responds to the challenge, physically transforming before me. Her spine straightens, her shoulders square, and there's a defiant tilt to her chin when she turns to Killian, who's busy cursing under his breath and rolling his eyes. Grasping his arm, she says, "Dance with me, you fucking buffoon. And make it look like you can't get enough."

Killian turns to me, his face etched with irritation and disbelief.

"One step toward redemption," I tell him, watching as he scowls but reluctantly escorts Elodie onto the dance floor.

Seizing the moment, I make my way to the study at the end of the hall, a location I've visited before. Slipping inside, I shut the door behind me and let out a sigh of relief, grateful for the moment of solitude.

The room is just as I remember it—spacious, crowned with high, vaulted ceilings, with walls bathed in a deep emerald hue. Portraits of finely dressed people are displayed all around, their gazes fixed from within elaborate gold frames.

Who might they be? The question echoes in my mind as I briefly take them in, searching for any familial resemblance to Braxton.

Is it possible the much younger version of him is here? Maybe tucked away somewhere with a governess?

Crossing the thick woven rug, I navigate past an inviting array of plush sofas and armchairs to stand before a window that offers a commanding view of the lush gardens below.

Shifting my attention to the envelope Roxane handed me, I lift the flap to find a single tarot card—the Star—waiting inside.

Only this isn't the same tarot card from before. This one is from the ancient Visconti-Sforza Tarocchi deck that Arthur usually favors.

Last time, Arthur had sent me here with only a folded bit of paper with a star etched upon it. When I failed to secure the Get, his indifference struck me as odd. *You'll have another chance soon enough*, he'd said.

In hindsight, it's clear that earlier Trip was merely a pop quiz. This one is the final exam.

Dismissing the whirlwind of thoughts clouding my mind, I set my focus on the tarot card in my hand, wondering if there's more to locating the Star than I initially thought.

In this Visconti-Sforza version, the Star features eight pointed rays and portrays a woman with blond hair, clad in a blue dress, donned with a…

A red cape…

A sudden realization tightens my chest as a rush of memories come flooding back. In my mind's eye, I can see the figure in the red cape, vanishing and reemerging inside the labyrinth that once sprawled beneath my window at Gray Wolf—a figure who bore an uncanny resemblance to me.

Does the fact that I'm dressed in blue have any relation to this?

Or perhaps this is the kind of *coincidence* that, according to my dad, doesn't exist.

Everything is connected.

When I catch my reflection in the window, I suddenly realize that, despite my hair not being blond, the gold dust Charlotte applied earlier now lends it a similar hue.

Is this tarot card meant to be a clue, or some sort of message from Arthur?

I'm so engrossed in my thoughts, I completely overlook the creak of a door opening, then shutting softly. I miss the muted footsteps that traverse the rug, crossing the room to where I now stand.

You have seen this, done this before.

This time, I know it's true.

Turning away from the window, my gaze settles on the tall, handsome man looming before me.

"Hello, Mr. Braxton," I say. "It's good to see you again."

47

Unlike our previous meeting, where this blue-eyed man feigned confusion when he came upon me, this time there's no pretense.

As our eyes connect and I take in his wavy dark hair, the precise lines of his face, and his imposing figure — a mirror image of his son — he simply says, "You. Again."

I respond with a nod, then casually drop the tarot card onto the table between us. Using the tip of my gloved finger, I slide it closer to him.

"What's the meaning of this?" His intense blue gaze darts between the card and me. "Why have you seen fit to return?"

"Because it's time to put an end to this game," I say. "Once and for all."

Under his cautious watch, I slowly roll down my glove to expose the three golden rings on my arm.

A long beat of silence stretches between us. Finally, lifting his gaze to meet mine, he says, "It's unfinished."

"Just like your son's," I retort.

"My son?" He shakes his head, lets out a gruff laugh. "My son is a child."

"Not where I come from."

His head jerks back, that sardonic laughter gone from his face. Gesturing toward my arm, he says, "And how do I know it's genuine?"

"Guess you'll just have to trust me," I say, smoothing my glove back into place.

"What is it you're after?" he asks, eyes pinching so tightly, they're just barely visible.

"I've come for the Star."

"Impossible," he seethes.

"I assure you, it's not." I struggle to keep my expression neutral, my voice firm, hoping he can't sense the unsteady thrum of my own anxious heart.

"And what of your companions?" he asks.

"They're here to stop me from what I really plan to do," I explain. "Which is precisely why I'm asking for your help—to ensure their attempts are unsuccessful."

"And what is it you plan to do?" he asks, visibly softening to the idea, but only slightly.

With my gaze fixed on his, I inhale a deep breath and divulge the whole story. Telling him about me, my connection to Braxton, the strategy we've devised together. I even confess that Braxton is now in possession of the gold pocket watch I took from him during my last visit.

"The visit where you cut me." He gives me a look I can't entirely read. *Admiration? Contempt?* It's impossible to tell.

"Your son, Braxton, taught me how to use a blade." I shrug. "Admittedly, I'd had only a few lessons. I wasn't very skilled. Hopefully, I've progressed a bit since then."

His father's eyes narrow. "It is, indeed, an interesting story you tell. One I might be tempted to believe if it weren't for one glaring detail."

I stand before him, barely able to breathe, as I wait to hear how I've failed.

"My son is not named Braxton." He folds his arms, tilts his chin high, convinced he's just caught me in an elaborate lie. "His name is—"

Before he can finish, I race to say it, so he'll know I'm legit. "His name is James," I say. "You named him after your father, his grandfather. It's only later that he decided to combine his surname with that of his mother's, which is why I know him as Braxton Huntley."

His father falls silent, surrendering the moment to the soft echoes of music wafting from beyond this room.

"So…" He gives me an inquiring look.

"Natasha," I say. "My name is Natasha Antoinette Clarke."

"So, Miss Clarke," he continues, "are you going to tell me how my son ended up living in a time several centuries from this day?"

"It's complicated." I sigh. Having already told my own father how he'll die as a result of Arthur's ambitions, I dread telling another. Though the shift in his expression tells me he already knows how his story ends.

"Arthur Blackstone," he says, catching me by surprise. I wasn't aware he was familiar with him.

"Yes," I confirm.

Seeming to take the news in stride, he says, "And so my son is a time jumper, like you?"

"He is," I reply. "But hopefully, not for much longer. We aim to end this now. And, if things go well, you can have a different ending as well."

"No." His father's response comes swift and sharp. "I'm afraid I cannot allow that."

I gape at him, perplexed. "I don't understand," I say. "Why wouldn't you at least—"

"It's a tale of hubris," he says, cutting me off.

My puzzled look deepens; now I really don't follow.

"It's the story of Macbeth," he explains.

I stand before him, waiting, unsure where he's going with this.

"Macbeth," his father continues, "much like Arthur, believed he could shape his own destiny through his actions. And his attempt to dominate his fate only made him a pawn of it, ultimately bringing about the very future he tried to escape. His tragic flaws—overweening ambition and profound arrogance—and the actions spurred by these traits led to his undoing." His intense blue eyes fix on me, a heavy silence stretching between us before he adds, "The moral of the tale is clear: humans cannot twist their destiny through misdeeds without facing grave repercussions. This is why I shall refrain from attempting to change mine."

His words leave me stunned, struggling to accept his resignation. If there's even the slightest chance to save him, why on earth would he not take it?

"Every action leads to the next," he says. "And despite the sorrow involved, I must trust that my son is precisely where he is meant to be. There's a reason two Timekeepers from different eras have been brought together."

His words settle over me, and while I won't argue with his reasoning, there's one thing I still need to make clear. "While I agree that the story of Macbeth does sound strikingly similar to Arthur Blackstone," I say, "there's one crucial difference."

Braxton's father cocks his head, his piercing gaze locked onto mine.

"Arthur doesn't aspire to be a king. Not because he lacks ambition, but because his aspirations exceed the confines of ruling a mere kingdom. Arthur seeks dominion over time itself, envisioning himself in the role of an omnipotent God, intent on remaking the world in his own image."

The response is swift, unequivocal. "Then he must be stopped."

I nod, hopeful that I've finally managed to sway him to my side.

After a brief, contemplative pause, he says, "Your companions are currently in the ballroom." He makes a vague gesture toward the door. "By all accounts, they appear to be enjoying themselves."

"They're good at pretending," I say. "It's what Arthur's trained them to do. But soon, they'll tire of all that and come looking for me. And, since you're the Timekeeper meant to stop me, here's how you can help."

48

Just as we're about to exit the study, Braxton's father retrieves a red cape casually left on a chair and offers it to me.

"Wear this," he says. "It will keep you from being easily recognized."

As I drape the cloak around my shoulders and draw the hood over my head, the significance of the moment does not escape me. Not only do I mirror the maiden depicted on the Star card from the Visconti-Sforza deck, but also the mysterious figure I spotted navigating the complex maze beneath my window at Gray Wolf.

"Do you know where we're headed?" he asks.

I nod. "The Star is hidden inside the labyrinth."

Pausing briefly before the door, he glances over his shoulder and says, "I was certain you were headed there during your last visit. I presumed that's what led you to the window. From there, looking north, it's just visible."

"Back then, I had no idea what I was doing," I admit.

As we make our way into the hall, I steal a glance at the dance floor, searching for Elodie and Killian amid the swirling throng of dancers.

"Come," Braxton's father urges, his tone insistent. "There is no time for that."

With his hand at my elbow, I duck my head and follow his lead without hesitation. To my great shame, I notice he now walks with a slight limp, courtesy of my last visit.

Making our way outside, we quicken our pace through the gardens, enveloped in a heady fragrance of jasmine and the distant strains of a string quartet, a haunting melody that seems almost in tune with our purposeful strides.

Reaching the edge of the labyrinth, Braxton's father stops. Letting go of my arm, he says, "I will remain here to keep watch." I nod, ready to dart into the maze when he adds, "May the fates be with you, Natasha."

I pause, recalling how Charlotte echoed the same sentiment. Dismissing it as a turn of phrase from another era, I venture inside.

The hedges loom high, towering far above me, their meticulously groomed branches casting shadows that dance under the moonlit sky. Drawing the cape closer, I take a moment to tap into any ancestral Timekeeper wisdom, hoping some glimmer of insight on how I might go about unlocking this maze is buried within me.

It's not long before the mark on my arm begins to thrum as my feet instinctively move. Propelled by the pull of my destiny and bolstered by the belief I can navigate it successfully, I delve deeper into the intricate twists of the labyrinth.

With each step, the feeling that time is collapsing in on itself grows stronger.

With each bend and curve the lines between past, present, and future seem to blur.

A phenomenon that only amplifies the recurring thought that once again streams through my head.

Time is a flat circle. You have been here before, done this before.

Amid this unsettling déjà vécu, my determination to shatter this endless loop has never been stronger.

I can feel it—I'm getting closer now, nearly there. The

tangible awareness of nearing my goal sends a thrill of anticipation coursing through me, vibrating deep within my bones as the rings on my arm buzz with energy, urging my legs to carry me quicker.

Rounding the final bend, I clutch the fabric of my gown, lift it past my knees, and break into a full sprint, charging toward the marble statue that looms just ahead. The guardian of eternity itself, whispering the ancient secrets ensconced within its bounds, is soon to be in my grasp.

Secure in the knowledge that the Timekeeper who would normally challenge me is now guarding the entrance to the maze, I seize the opportunity to pause before it and examine it in greater detail.

The lion, as seen on both the Strength tarot card and the World card, is a symbol of bravery and power. Like the Strength and World cards, there's also a laurel wreath, a symbol of victory and honor.

Drawn by the craftsmanship of this narrative forever captured in stone, I step closer. Noting how the lion, with its intricately carved mane and dignified stance, seems to pulsate with life, standing sentinel over the ancient treasure I believe is concealed within one of the two urns that rest atop its head.

My gaze remains fixed on those urns. On the Star tarot card, they stand as a symbol of healing the past and the present. Seeing them in this context, and knowing what's hidden inside, I'm overcome with a profound connection to history, a hallowed bond with the lineage of Timekeepers who've ventured here long before me.

How many others must've stood in this very spot, aware of the magick, the miracle, hiding inside, but chose to leave it undisturbed for the betterment of mankind?

It's a humbling reminder of the cycles of time—the rise and fall of empires, the personal quests that lead us through the complex labyrinths of our own existence.

Also not lost on me is the numerological link between the Star and Strength cards.

The Star, positioned as the seventeenth card in the Major Arcana, breaks down to eight (one plus seven) when its digits are combined and reduced, aligning it with the Strength card's placement at number eight.

In numerology, the number eight signifies power, prestige, success, and wealth—all attributes Arthur has achieved long ago.

What he seeks now is tied to another card he gave me to use as a clue. And though it took me a moment to recognize it, beyond the wreath and the lion featured prominently on it, the card offered little help in pinpointing the location of the Star, though it did convey a much deeper message.

The World card, also known as the Universe card, marks the end of the Major Arcana journey. It symbolizes completion and the joy of achieving one's highest aspiration.

The card represents the finale Arthur envisions—a future where he will rule the world and control time as he pleases.

But of course, my loyalties have shifted from serving Arthur to fulfilling my Timekeeper destiny. Which is why I must ensure his dream never comes to fruition.

For a moment, I stand in awed silence, contemplating the past and the uncertainty that lies ahead in a future unknown to me.

Then, under the lion's silent vigil, I slip off my satin shoes, and with a resolve steeled by the weight of what awaits me, I begin the climb to the top, where one of those urns hides the glimmering gem I seek.

49

I t always seems easier than it turns out to be.

What initially appeared to be a simple, straightforward climb quickly becomes a perilous challenge. My silk stockings offer little to no grip against the slick surface of the carved marble stone. Twice, I've tumbled to the ground, landing with a hard, jolting thud. But each time, I pick myself up and begin the ascent once more.

Now, with my dress badly torn and my stockings discarded below, the urns are finally well within reach.

Climbing with renewed determination, each movement cautious yet deliberate, I wrap my fingers around the cool surface of the nearest urn.

Triumph and relief tangle within me as I secure my legs around it and pull myself up inch by painstaking inch. Grasping the rim, I haul my body up the rest of the way and thrust my arm over the lip, delving a hand inside.

My fingers sweep the urn's interior, brushing against the bottom and sides. Feeling a small object, my pulse quickens, convinced I've discovered it.

Yet, as I lift it into the glow of moonlight, my spirits instantly plummet—it's merely an ordinary stone.

Still, there's one more urn left to check.

Peeling off my gloves, I let them fall to the ground. Repositioning myself before the second urn, I let my fingers glide along its interior.

Enveloped in silence, the pulsing of my heart in my ears underscores the monumental weight of this moment when the fate of the world hangs in the balance.

My fingers encounter a small, hard, smooth object, and a burst of anticipation surges through me. Instinctively, I recognize its importance, even before laying my eyes on it.

This is the moment!

Using the utmost care, I pinch the object between my forefinger and thumb, gently extracting the Star from its centuries-old hiding spot.

Even under the cover of night, the stone glimmers, radiant in its power. Despite its seemingly insignificant size, this gem holds the potential to alter destinies—to drastically change the course of the world as we know it.

For all the pride I feel in having found it, the gravity of this achievement weighs heavily. This is more than a mere triumph—it's a beacon of hope. The Star, in its luminescence, seems to whisper promises of a future yet to be told—as long as it's never, ever, able to perform the job it was made for.

Securing the stone in my pocket, I begin my descent back to the ground. My moment of victory shatters when my feet touch the earth, and the world around me fades, replaced by a swirling vortex of time and space.

I'm pulled into a vision, seeing the flickering image of a grand hall filled with ancient scholars—the air vibrating with energy as they debate the best place to hide the Star.

I watch as centuries pass in a blur. Wars rage, empires rise and fall, and the Star is moved from one hiding place to another, veiled from those who would use it for evil.

The scene suddenly shifts to a small garden at the center of a labyrinth, dominated by a large marble statue of a dignified lion with two urns on its head. A girl wearing a red cape stands there and—

What?

My heart lurches into my throat. My breath stalls in my chest, as my eyes strain to see more. But I'm yanked from the vision, only to find myself in the midst of a horrible tableau I never saw coming.

Standing before me, a dark silhouette against the moonlit garden, is Killian.

His posture is tense, and he's seized Braxton's father, holding him captive with a blade pressed sharply against his throat.

"Killian—no!" My voice quivers, failing to mask the turmoil swirling within. The Star's significance suddenly fades in the face of this more immediate danger.

Killian's gaze meets mine, desperation driving his actions. "It's over, Shiv," he growls. "At last, it's finally over. This is where the circle ends. So please, kindly give me the Star."

The circle?

My gaze darts to Braxton's father, noting his disheveled hair, torn clothing, and his knuckles now bloodied and raw. Judging by the bruises already blossoming on Killian's face, he put up a good fight before it got to this point.

But now, with Killian's blade held fast to his neck, his expression is that of a man who's resigned to his fate, ready to sacrifice himself for a much bigger cause.

When his eyes meet mine, it's with a silent plea for understanding—to do what needs to be done, to honor my role as a Timekeeper.

To spare one life for the fate of all.

With one hand clutching the blade to Braxton's father's throat, Killian extends the other toward me, demanding, "Hand it over, Shiv."

I lock eyes with him, knowing I need to tread carefully. A single misstep, a misconstrued word, could tip the scales toward an outcome from which none of us can ever return.

"You don't have to do this." I keep my voice low and steady as though trying to calm a rabid dog. "There's always another way, a better path you can choose."

"This is my path, Shiv." He shrugs. "Always has been. I thought you knew that better than anyone."

"I know a lot of things about you," I say, watching as he presses the blade deeper, causing a trickle of blood to run down Braxton's father's neck.

I inhale a sharp breath, refusing to bear witness to any more of this cruelty. The Star, now tucked within the folds of my dress, for all its symbolic hope, also serves as a stark reminder of the fine line we all walk between destiny and destruction.

"I thought you were seeking redemption," I say.

"Natasha," Braxton's father manages to say through the pain, "it was always going to end this way. And now, it's time for you to meet your destiny, too."

My eyes dart to Killian, hardly able to believe that the fate of the world teeters on the edge of this misguided boy's blade.

Beneath his unwavering gaze, I lean down and reach for the dagger strapped to my thigh.

"Nice," Killian says, his gaze lingering on my bared leg, his voice brimming with that cocky bravado I know all too well. "Though I'll admit to enjoying the show, I think we all know you won't go through with it. There's too much at stake. You won't risk it."

"Is that the story you tell yourself?" I raise a brow in challenge, as slowly, deliberately, I advance toward him. "Can you really be so certain of what I will or won't do?" I take another step. "You really think you know me that well?"

"Yeah." He nods, pushing a stray lock of golden curls from his eyes. "Actually, I do."

"You know what Jago once told me?" I muse.

"Seriously, Shiv?" Killian scoffs. "You do realize my blade is freshly sharpened, and I think you know better than anyone I'm more than willing to use it."

Ignoring him, I go on. "Jago said each choice you make causes your life to shoot off in a new direction. But at the moment of decision, all those varying choices and directions are viable—those roads are already paved."

"Yeah," Killian grunts. "Jago's a real fuckin' genius. The next Nietzsche, no doubt." He scowls, shaking his head.

"The only question now," I continue, my gaze boring into his, "is which road will I take?"

A tense silence passes between us.

"Because here's what I know for sure," I say, stepping forward once more. "You are not going to harm me."

Killian lets out a scornful laugh, increasing the pressure on his blade, deepening the wound, and causing a thicker stream of blood to gush from Braxton's father's neck. Though he barely reacts, having accepted his fate.

"I hate to break it to you, Shiv," Killian says, "but I think you might be overestimating this bond you and I share. You really think I won't harm you because I love you?" He shakes his head and frowns. "It'll pain me to watch you go. Won't lie about that. But, to my credit, I did try to warn you about making me choose between Arthur and you."

Another step forward, and I say, "The reason you won't harm me, Killian, isn't because of any feelings you may or may not harbor for me, but because, well, simply put, we both know you can't."

He shoots me a wary look, tightens his grip on the hilt of his dagger.

"You need a Timekeeper to carry the Star back to Gray Wolf. You made that mistake a few times before, didn't you? Like the time you killed my father."

I watch as his eyes narrow, his jaw clenching as his back teeth grind together. "I need only one Timekeeper," he says. "Which means one of you is expendable. Maybe I'll take this wanker here and get rid of you."

He pushes the blade harder, deeper, and I watch in horror as a torrent of blood begins to gush from the wound he made.

"Hand over the Star, Shiv," Killian barks, "and—"

Before he can finish, I spring forward.

Dagger poised well above my head, I propel myself toward him, targeting the spot where his heart might reside should he actually be in possession of one.

Startled, Killian stumbles backward as Braxton's father quickly ducks out of his hold.

"Natasha, no!" he cries out, a horrible guttural sound, but it's too late for that.

My body collides with Killian's, sending us crashing to the ground.

For a fleeting second, Killian seems to yield, his blade at his side, his swimming-pool eyes locked onto mine.

As I drive my own blade toward him, I could swear I hear him whisper, "Just do it already."

Without hesitation, I follow through, the tip of my blade sinking into his chest.

50

Killian stares at me, eyes wide with shock. "Damn, Shiv," he manages to say. "Look what you've done." His fingers fumble at his chest; when they come away, they're dripping with blood.

I lift my dagger once more. Like a replay of what happened with the duke back in 1745 Versailles, I'm more than willing to see this thing through. My resolve to finish this, finish him, is ironclad. Nothing Killian can say or do that will stop me this time.

"Natasha, don't," Braxton's father urges. "This isn't the way." He hovers close by, his neck badly bleeding; he warns me against the very deed I'm poised to commit.

"Stay out of it, old man," Killian rasps. "This here's between Shiv and me." His dagger is loosely clutched in his hand, the vibrancy fading from his eyes as blood steadily seeps from the wound in his chest. He looks at me and says, "Remember what I told you about this sort of thing?"

"Yeah," I reply, my blade steady, ready to deliver as many blows as it takes to silence him.

One for taking my father's life.

Another for attempting to end Braxton's father.

And a third for each life he's claimed over the years.

"You said I can never go back."

Killian nods, his voice a gurgling whisper, "Trust me, it's

true."

"Thing is, Killian," I say, determination hardening my tone, "I think I'm okay with that."

Overcome by a sudden surge of rage I hadn't anticipated, I drive my blade toward him, seconds away from striking once more, when a sudden cry slices through the tension.

"Dad!"

The voice is undeniably that of a child.

But how can that be? Children are never present at these parties.

Whirling around, I can't help but gasp at the sight.

There, a young boy with dark wavy hair and striking ocean-blue eyes is desperately trying to reach the man now sprawled on the ground, barely clinging to life.

Though he's so much younger than the version I know, my heart recognizes him in an instant.

A second later, my mind catches up.

Braxton!

My gaze darts from him to the person tightly grasping his arm.

This cannot be happening.

"Drop the blade, Natasha," Arthur commands.

51

Arthur looms before me, a dark figure dressed like a groom on his wedding day.

His tailcoat is perfectly tailored, crafted of the finest dove-gray wool. The white silk waistcoat beneath is richly embroidered with navy and silver threads, while his fine cotton shirt is adorned with an elaborately tied white silk cravat. His trousers are fitted, made of the softest doeskin, and tucked inside a pair of black Hessian boots, much like the ones Killian wears. But it's his lapel that tells the real story: pinned to the peak is a single ghost orchid bloom.

"Drop the blade, Natasha," he repeats, his obsidian gaze locked onto me.

Though his voice is commanding, imbued with authority, what he fails to understand is that the days of me taking orders from Arthur Blackstone are well over.

Besides, why would I willingly surrender whatever slim advantage I currently have?

My eyes dart toward Killian, only to find that amid all the confusion, he's somehow managed to edge just beyond my immediate reach. Yet the distance between us is minor, one I could easily bridge should I decide to complete what I started.

An option I've yet to rule out.

Braxton's father struggles to stand, wanting his son to think he's in better shape than he is. But the steady stream of blood seeping from the cravat he's pressed to the wound tells me he's not long for this world if he doesn't get help.

Meanwhile, young Braxton, a frightened boy of probably no more than five, struggles to free himself from Arthur's grasp, in a desperate bid to get to his father.

"Drop the blade," Arthur repeats.

"Make me," I say, with my gaze locked on his as I tighten my grip, refusing to give up or give in.

"Drop the fucking dagger, Natasha," Arthur barks, losing his cool. "Or else…" I watch in horror as he presses the sharp edge of his blade to young Braxton's throat. "Or else this little boy will never live long enough for you two to meet."

"Jesus, Arthur," Killian manages to say. "Take it easy—he's just a kid!"

If Arthur heard him, he shows no sign of it. He's a man on a mission, with a single, unwavering purpose.

I look to Braxton's father, leaving it to him to decide.

When he responds to the question in my eyes with a slight nod of his head, I turn to Arthur and say, "Please. Stop. Just… stop. It's enough already. How many lives must be forfeited for this nonsense?"

"Nonsense?" Enraged, Arthur presses the blade closer to young Braxton's neck. "You think my life's pursuit toward a better world for all of humanity is *nonsense*? Clearly, I've overestimated you."

A small trickle of blood appears on young Braxton's neck. Whimpering, he continues his struggle against Arthur, his gaze never once leaving his dad.

Only a madman would use a child as a bargaining chip. And there's no negotiating with someone who resides in a place so far beyond reason.

"Okay," I say, carefully placing the dagger on the ground near my feet. "I'm doing it, I've done it. See? I'm unarmed. Just—

leave the boy alone, please."

"You take me for a fool?" Arthur scowls. "Kick it to where you can't reach it."

Without hesitation, I do as he asks.

"Now," he commands, "kindly hand over the Star."

"I don't have it," I say, but we both know it's a lie.

Arthur practically growls. "Make no mistake," he says, "I won't hesitate to end this boy's life. He means nothing to me. The instant you set foot in Gray Wolf, Braxton became irrelevant, superfluous. The only reason I kept him around was to placate you, to ease your transition and help you come to terms with what was always destined to occur."

"Yeah, and what's that?" I ask. "What exactly is it that's destined to occur?" I keep my gaze leveled on him, less interested in hearing the answer than in keeping him talking for as long as possible.

Mainly because I have no way of knowing if Braxton has managed to switch out the genuine Antikythera Mechanism with the fake that I gave him. And if Arthur should make good on his threat, and kill the nine-year-old version of him, then the adult Braxton will cease to exist, and all of this will have been for nothing.

"I was always going to win this game," Arthur says. "I thought you were clever enough to realize that. What fun I had watching you select your rewards. The pieces you chose in an effort to send me subliminal messages." He shakes his head as though greatly amused. "That last piece, *Judith Slaying Holofernes*, was a particular favorite. I enjoyed a good laugh about that one after you left."

"Glad I was able to keep you entertained," I say, keeping a close watch on young Braxton, his father, and Killian, making sure everyone remains in place, that no one decides to make any rash moves.

"Sadly, Natasha, despite what you think, you are no Judith," Arthur informs me. "And from what I can see, you're all on your own, no maidservant to help you. Just a frightened little boy, a man not long for this life, and…" He spares a look at Killian. "Well, I think we all know where Killian's loyalties lie."

In a move I didn't anticipate, from the corner of my eye, I catch sight of Braxton's father suddenly rousing himself, making a desperate dash toward Arthur.

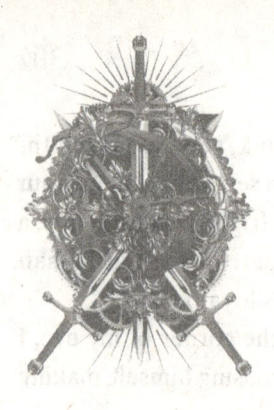

52

Arms outstretched, blood gushing from his neck, Braxton's father hurls himself at Arthur's back.

Yet before he can close the gap, Arthur swings around as though expecting the attack and aims his dagger with deadly intent.

I watch in horror as the blade traces a chilling path through the air, finding its mark in the main artery of Braxton's father's neck.

His legs buckle, and he collapses to the ground in a heavy, heart-wrenching fall, as Braxton's scream pierces the air, a harrowing cry that will haunt me forever.

"Okay," Arthur says, dismissing the life he just ended with a casual shrug. "Now there's officially no one left to help you. And don't fool yourself into thinking you can convince Killian. Thanks to you, he's not long for this world."

I glance at Killian; his normally sun-tanned face is rapidly turning the color of death.

"If he doesn't bleed out," Arthur continues, "then he runs the risk of crossing his own timeline. Either way, the odds are not in his favor."

I look to Killian who, with a slight nod, confirms that it's true.

"My God." I whirl on Arthur. "You're even worse than I thought. You don't care about any of us. We're all just disposable to you. Props you use to get what you want."

"I'll kill the kid, too," he says, further proving my point. "Really, Natasha, it's yours to decide. You want this to end? Then give me the Star."

"I will," I say, in a bid to placate him. "But, as you know, it's no good on its own. You need a Timekeeper to bring it back to Gray Wolf, and I'm your only viable choice."

Arthur laughs, and from an inside pocket of his waistcoat, he reveals the Antikythera Mechanism he normally keeps in the Vault. Unfortunately, from what I can tell, it's the real one.

Great.

As I look at Braxton, his young face streaming with tears as he stares at the crumpled form of his father, my own father's words sound in my head.

It's this damned lineage and all that comes with it... People like us don't get to move through the world with the sort of blissful ignorance everyone else gets to enjoy... A normal life is off the menu for us.

While it may be true, I refuse to give up the fight.

And yet, I cannot let young Braxton die.

Reaching into my pocket, my fingers grab hold of the Star.

Either Braxton will make it to 1901 Greece and succeed in making the switch, or we've gravely miscalculated this entire situation.

There's only one way to find out, and yet, I can't help but make one last appeal.

"Arthur," I say, "I know what this is about."

"Do you?" His gazes sweeps over me, skepticism etched in every line of his face.

"You've been grieving for so long now," I continue, "caught in an infinite cycle of sorrow and self-blame. You believe that by restoring the Antikythera Mechanism, you can undo your errors and set everything right."

A flicker of astonishment briefly illuminates Arthur's face, but it vanishes as quickly as it came.

"Hand over the Star," he demands, pressing the blade's tip into the tender wound at young Braxton's neck.

I push past the knot of fear in my throat, forcing myself to go on. "You believe you can reunite with your family and forge a utopia brimming with art, love, and beauty—a world devoid of all suffering."

Arthur presses his lips together, his attention on me unwavering. "The Star, please."

Ignoring him, I continue, "But pain is inherent to life—it's a testament to our freedom of choice. Everyone deserves a world where they can follow their passions, make their own decisions, even if you disdain those choices and consider them banal."

"This boy is ten seconds away from getting his throat cut—do you truly wish to bear that burden on your conscience?"

No. I absolutely do not. Still, I have no choice but to stall.

"Arthur," I start, my heart heavy with empathy for his pain, "you've managed to overlook one fundamental truth." I pause, gathering my thoughts in the hope of reaching him, of stopping this tragic cycle of loss. "We recognize the beauty of light only after enduring the darkness." I allow the words a moment to settle, hoping their significance can somehow take root. "And though I'm deeply sorry for all that you've lost—" My voice catches as a figure appears just beyond Arthur's shoulder. Luckily, he's too caught up in his own world to take notice. "You still have your daughter Elodie, and—"

Just then, Elodie emerges from the shadows. Taking in the alarming scene unfolding before her, she turns to Arthur and says, "What the hell is going on here?"

53

Elodie looks surprisingly disheveled. Her hair is mussed, her cheeks flushed, eyes red and swollen with tears.

"What are you doing?" Her gaze darts from Arthur, to me, then to Killian, and finally rests on Braxton's father, who lies motionless on the ground. "What's this about you being my father?"

Arthur faces her, his complexion ashen, his expression one of distress. "It was meant to be a surprise," he says, directing a sharp, accusing glance my way. "My plan was to tell you once we were all together again, reunited as a family."

"I—I'm lost." Elodie's gaze shifts between her father and me, seeking clarity amid all the chaos.

Before Arthur can explain, I seize the opportunity to unfold the entire tale. To my surprise, Arthur does not interfere.

As the truth settles, Elodie reels on Arthur, her voice loaded with accusation. "So, you never really 'rescued' me from that dreadful children's home, did you? It's your fault I ended up there in the first place. Did you ever, just once, consider what that was like for me? I was practically still a baby, and you left me alone to helplessly watch as my own mother withered and died, only to be sent to that horrible place where they—" She stops, a visible shiver coursing through her as she staggers beneath the enormity of memories too heavy to voice, the unspeakable horrors she faced in the wake of Arthur's abandonment.

"And who is this?" She turns her attention to the young boy, truly noticing him for the very first time. When a wave of recognition washes over her, she slaps a hand to her mouth. "My God!" Her eyes, wide and frantic, dart between her father and me. "He's just a child!" she cries, desperation threading through her voice when she zeroes in on the blade Arthur still holds to his throat. "This has to stop, you must—"

"I intend to," Arthur responds, his tone eerily calm. "As soon as your friend Natasha here hands over the Star, everything will be set right once more."

Elodie's gaze snaps back to me. "So do it already!" she shouts, not fully grasping the implications of her request. "To think I ended things with Nash, who was willing to leave his fiancée for me, all because I couldn't stand the thought of leaving Gray Wolf—because I was foolish enough to believe I had some kind of misguided loyalty to you." She levels a trembling finger at Arthur, the realization of her misplaced trust painfully dawning. "When all along, you—"

Arthur, losing patience, presses the edge of his blade into the delicate skin of young Braxton's neck.

"Stop!" Elodie's scream shatters the air, mirroring young Braxton's cry of distress.

Knowing I can't delay any longer, I twist the golden bracelet around my wrist, sending a silent plea to the adult Braxton who gave it to me.

Wherever he is on his journey, whatever fate awaits this younger version of him now softly whimpering before me, I silently implore that he hears this plea.

But already my desire and my will were being turned like a wheel, all at one speed, by the Love which moves the sun and other stars.

This divine love—the fabric that bonds every being, the

intricate web of interconnectedness surrounding us all—is the true ruler of eternity.

Not Arthur Blackstone, regardless of his beliefs.

Reaching into my pocket, I retrieve the Star and extend it toward Arthur. "Now, leave the boy alone," I command.

With a dismissive shove, Arthur roughly pushes the child aside, causing the young boy to stumble, fall, landing harshly on his face.

Elodie is by his side in a flash, helping him to stand. It's only then that I see the damage Arthur has done.

Young Braxton's nose is bleeding, but Arthur is oblivious to everything but the gleaming gem in my palm.

"I always knew you'd come through," Arthur says, the golden ring he always wears, that once belonged to Edward the Black Prince, glinting beneath the moon's glow.

"What will become of Gray Wolf?" I ask. "All those people who depend on you, who've remained loyal to you?"

Arthur merely shakes his head, offering an indifferent shrug. In his mind, they're already relics of the past. His aspirations for himself and the new world he dreams of do not include them.

As he steps closer, our gazes momentarily lock. His eyes, once mysterious obsidian fragments I believed concealed untold depths, now reveal an unmistakable shallowness. And while I have no way of knowing what he finds in mine, I hope he understands just how gravely he's underestimated me. Underestimated us all.

"The only thing more dangerous than ignorance is the illusion of knowledge," I whisper. It's a quote from Stephen Hawking, but Arthur is too focused on the promise of this gleaming gem to heed the warning.

With Killian and Elodie looking on, Arthur plucks the Star from my palm.

Killian inhales a sharp breath.

Elodie gasps.

As I hold my breath, hoping with everything I have that Braxton was able to make the switch.

54

Braxton
ANTIKYTHERA ISLAND
1901

Standing on the launchpad, the weight of the mission bears down on me. The fate of the world and the integrity of time itself rest heavily on my shoulders.

All around me, the intricate machinery hums with a fierce intensity, mirroring the tension coiled tightly in my gut.

My mind races as I recall every detail, every piece of information I've gathered about Antikythera Island, Greece, in the year 1901.

This is a crucial moment—the discovery of the Antikythera Mechanism, an ancient Greek analog computer that can predict astronomical events, and ultimately control time, waits to be discovered. It's up to me to switch it out with a fake.

Amid the chaos and danger, I know Tasha is out there somewhere, risking everything to see this thing through. Failure is not an option, and I can't—won't—let her down.

"Are you ready for this?" Keane's voice cuts through the wind whipping at my feet.

I take a deep breath, trying to steady myself. "As ready as I'll ever be," I reply, the words feeling heavy in my mouth.

"You have two hours," Keane reminds me. "If you overstay your visit, you're on your own."

I nod, feeling the familiar surge of adrenaline that comes with each Trip into the past. My hand tightens around the small device in my pocket—a fake Mechanism, crafted with meticulous precision and entrusted to me by Tasha herself.

Suddenly, the lights flicker as the ground beneath me begins to shake. When the air fills with choking sulfur and a thick cloud of vapor threatens to swallow me whole, I know there's no turning back. My destiny has finally arrived, and all I can do is embrace whatever fate awaits me.

This is the culmination of my entire life's journey—every single event has led to this moment.

A deafening roar shatters through the room. My body freezes in anticipation as a blinding white light explodes toward the swirling vapor, crashes into the mist, and morphs into a shimmering gateway.

Gasping for air as gravity gives out, I'm hoisted into the unknown, ultimately landing on the rocky shores of Antikythera Island.

The salty tang of the Aegean Sea assaults my senses. The waves crashing against the jagged cliffs fill the air with an ancient, primal energy. The sun beats down relentlessly, casting harsh shadows across the barren landscape, a stark reminder of the land's unforgiving nature.

I take a moment to orient myself, scanning the horizon for any sign of danger. In the distance, a group of sponge divers can be seen preparing their gear. This is it—the moment they discover the shipwreck that will lead them to the Mechanism.

I move cautiously toward them, keeping a low profile. My heart beats frantically as I approach, adrenaline coursing through my veins. I watch as they descend into the crystal-clear waters below. Time is ticking, and I need to act fast.

Ducking behind a large rock formation, I wait for the perfect moment. Minutes stretch on endlessly as I observe the divers resurfacing with fragments of bronze and marble. The excitement in the air is palpable—they're getting closer.

Finally, one of them emerges from the depths, holding a corroded piece of metal—an integral part of the Antikythera Mechanism. The moment has arrived, and all I can think about is Tasha's safety and my hopes that our joined efforts won't be in vain.

Determination propelling me forward, I stride confidently toward the group, my hand gripping tightly to the fake Mechanism hidden in my pocket. Ignoring their bewildered stares, I greet them in the bit of Greek I've carefully practiced.

The divers exchange curious glances but ultimately nod, too engrossed in their discovery to question me further. As they gather their artifacts, I edge closer, my heart racing with a mix of anxiety and excitement. Tasha's trusting gaze flashes through my mind, spurring me toward our objective.

Time dilates, stretching into an agonizing eternity as I maneuver into position. My heart pounds, each beat reverberating through my body like a drum. The fake Mechanism burns like a branding iron against my skin.

Just as I reach the edge of the rocky outcrop, the ground beneath me crumbles away. I lurch forward, grasping for anything to hold on to, but it's too late. The Mechanism slips from my grasp and tumbles into the abyss.

Panic surges through me, fear clawing at my throat as I scramble to retrieve it. Dirt and rocks cling to my fingers like leeches, hindering my movements. But I can't give up now.

Finally righting myself, I move toward the edge, eyes straining to see where it fell. There, a glint of metal catches the light. It's precariously balanced on a narrow ledge just within reach.

With renewed determination, I inch forward, lowering myself carefully down the rocky slope. The jagged edges cut into my palms, but I push through the pain.

Finally, my fingers brush against the Mechanism and I grab it, clutching it tightly as I haul myself back up.

Standing once more on solid ground, I begin to make the switch, my trembling hands barely able to hold steady. Adrenaline courses through me, sharpening my senses and drowning out all sound.

I take one last glance around to ensure no one is watching. The divers continue their work, oblivious to my actions. Every second feels like an eternity as I brush my fingers against the fake mechanism one final time, its cold surface a stark contrast to the heat of my skin.

But just as I'm about to make the exchange, a looming shadow falls over me.

My blood runs cold. I've been caught in the act.

The air thickens with tension, every sound amplified as I try to think of a way out.

But there is none.

I'm trapped, exposed, consumed by shame as I'm forced to come face-to-face with my failure.

With a heavy heart, I send a silent apology to Tasha for letting her down, hoping she can find a way to finish what we started before it's too late.

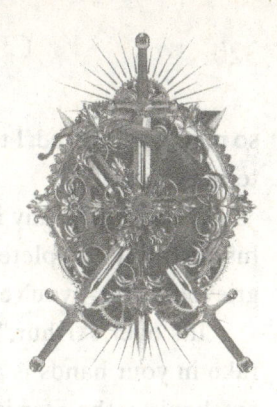

55

Arthur beams with unbridled joy—a vision of a man on the cusp of realizing a long-held dream.

Grasping the Star in one hand, he waves the Antikythera Mechanism before me with the other.

My heart skips a beat, my breath refuses to come, as I watch him position the Star into its destined slot. The fate of the world rests on this moment.

An uneasy hush falls upon us. Something is off.

I watch as Arthur's triumphant smile falters as he struggles to fit the Star into the mechanism.

He frowns, forcing it again, but the piece won't align.

"What is this?" His voice wavers, eyes narrowing as he inspects the mechanism more closely. Panic creeps into his features. He twists and turns it, desperately trying to make the piece fit, but it's useless.

His eyes dart wildly between the fake mechanism in his hands and me, disbelief swiftly morphing into rage. "What've you done?" he demands, his gaze feverish, accusing. "What the hell have you done with it? This...this is a fake!"

"I haven't touched it," I respond calmly. "I've been right here with you. For this twist, you can thank Braxton."

Arthur's gaze snaps to the young boy, quietly attempting to wake his father from an eternal slumber.

"The other Braxton," I clarify. "The adult one. The one you

so readily dismissed. I think *irrelevant and superfluous* were the terms you used?"

"Do you have any idea what you've done?" Arthur shouts, his restraint completely shattered. "You've made a terrible, grievous error—you've—"

"It's over, Arthur," I say. "Braxton has destroyed it. That fake in your hands is all that remains. Without the authentic mechanism, the Star is useless. It's time for you to stop. You will forever remain the Magician, the first card in the deck. The World was never yours to claim."

With unseeing eyes, he stares at the counterfeit mechanism in his hand, as if hoping to undo our actions through sheer determination alone.

Then suddenly, consumed by an uncontrollable rage, Arthur flings the fake Antikythera aside and charges at me with a surge of unbridled fury, his dagger menacingly poised for attack.

Without any means to defend myself, I try to sidestep, making a frantic effort to evade his strike.

"Arthur, please—" Elodie shouts, her words rushed, edged with panic. "Don't do this. It won't change anything. It's already done."

Arthur continues to advance.

In a desperate bid to dodge the lethal point of his dagger, I dart to the right. But my bare foot strikes a rock, my ankle painfully twists, and I crash toward the ground, staring in shock as the earth rushes up to greet my fall.

I land with a jolt, knowing it truly is over, done.

I have no allies here, no one willing to help.

This is how I disappear from the world.

In this pivotal moment, time seems malleable, as though it were within my power to mold. My thoughts drift back to the day Braxton and I first met, standing before a tombstone inscribed with my name.

At the time, the significance eluded me, yet the angel that rose from the headstone bore a striking resemblance to the angel depicted on *Melencolia I*.

There she sat perched at the top, one of her hands holding a pocket watch much like the one belonging to Braxton's father, while the other hand pointed toward the sky, the place where our deepest dreams reside.

Engraved on the stone beneath was my full name, my birthdate, and the date of my death, which happened to be that exact day.

Looking back, I saw it as the day when the old me died and the new one was born.

But now, what I mostly remember is how I laughed at the sight.

A laughter so unexpected, it prompted Braxton to deviate from the script, drawn to the girl who defied expectations.

It was the moment that, unbeknownst to us, first linked our fates.

And now, as Arthur expects me to shrink away from his advancing blade, I scramble to stand, determined to confront him head-on.

Just as I start to rise, his eyes appear to meet mine, though I know it's not me he sees. His vision is filled with the debris of dying dreams, the hope of ever reuniting with his wife now gone up in flames.

Arthur is reduced to the very essence of what's been driving him all along—and all that pain, all that self-blame, is now directed solely at me.

In a bone-chilling howl of despair and a quick flash of silver, my life is soon to be over. But despite being unarmed, I won't go down without a fight.

I plant my feet firmly, resolve hardening within me as I

prepare to face him, determined to end this once and for all.

Then, to my bewilderment, just as I've accepted my fate, Arthur stops, the dagger drops from his hand, and the next thing I know, his body collapses onto mine and together we crash to the ground.

It's only then, when Arthur is sprawled across me, that I notice the hilt of Killian's dagger protruding from his back.

"How's that for redemption?" Killian says, glancing between Arthur and me, the light in his eyes beginning to fade. "Looks like I chose you after all, Shiv."

At the sight of her father's crumpled body, Elodie's screams carve up the night. Rushing to Arthur's side, she drags him off me and quickly assesses his condition. Realizing he's gravely injured, but possibly not beyond saving if he receives prompt attention, she turns to us and says, "Just go, already! Both of you—now!"

I look between her and Arthur, wondering which bears the heavier burden—Arthur's palpable sense of defeat or the physical toll of his injury.

"And what about the portal, and Braxton?" I ask, gesturing toward the young boy.

"I'll handle it," Elodie says. "All of it. I promise."

I promise.

The words linger between us, leaving me to question the true value of a promise made by Elodie Blue.

My gaze is drawn to the golden serpent pendant adorning her neck, a potent symbol of fertility, protection, wisdom, healing, temptation, evil, rebirth, and immortality. I can't help but wonder which of these things might've resonated with her enough to choose it as her talisman.

There was a time when I would've believed that a promise from Elodie was worth very little, if anything at all. But the Elodie now tending to her father, despite the way he abandoned her, is not the girl I once knew.

This Trip has changed her, changed all of us, in ways we may never fully understand.

"Do you need the clicker?" she asks, blinking through tears.

I hesitate, though I'm not sure why. All our old secrets, it seems, are now out in the open. "No," I tell her. "I have my own."

She fixes me with her wide blue gaze. "Of course you do," she says, shaking her head and rolling her eyes just like the old Elodie that I knew back in school. "And what the hell is that on your arm?"

I follow her gaze to see the completed Flower of Life now marking my flesh—a symbol that my journey as a Timekeeper has come to an end.

Returning my focus to her, I ask, "How will you get back?" worried about the all-too-real possibility of her getting stranded in time.

"Who said I'm going back?" She offers a tearful grin. "Like you said, I never fail to capture the heart of anyone I set my sights on. I'm sure Nash will be more than happy to take me back. And, if not, there's always someone else, in some other place and time. Do you think you can find it within you to help Killian reach the portal?"

I turn to Killian. Considering how he spared me from the brunt of Arthur's blade, I guess I owe him that much. "Yeah," I say. "I can do that."

"Then you better hurry," Elodie warns, "because he's moments away from crossing his own timeline."

"Don't fucking tempt her," Killian mutters.

Removing the red cape Braxton's father gave me, I retrieve my dagger and use it to slice off a long strip of fabric. I carefully wrap it around the wound at Killian's chest, hoping it might help stanch the bleeding.

You have been here before. Done this before. Time is a flat circle looping back on itself.

"Lucky for you," Killian says, jolting me back to the present, "you missed my heart by an inch."

"Lucky for you," I say, tying off the makeshift bandage, "I've discovered you actually have one. Which is the only reason I'm helping you escape. Now come."

With Killian leaning on me, we start to make our way out. But not before I take a moment to kneel beside this young version of Braxton.

Offering him a piece of the red cape I cut just for him, I gently clean the blood from his nose. Then, pressing the fabric into his palm, I whisper, "I'm deeply sorry for what you're going through. Please know that your father loved you. He was immensely proud of you. And as hard as this is, you will persevere and find your way through. This, I assure you. For now, Elodie will look after you, and"—I cast a meaningful look her way—"you can trust her."

For a fleeting moment, Braxton's ocean-blue eyes meet mine, and a profound realization resonates deep in my soul. This is the reason I felt that unmistakable jolt of recognition when Elodie first showed me his photo.

As Braxton turns away, immersed in his grief, Killian and I step around Arthur, who, now lying on his side, fixes me with a wary look.

"It's not over, Natasha," he says, his voice strained, like it's taking a great deal of effort to properly enunciate my name. "The circle is mine to control, and there's no beginning or end. We will do this again, I assure you."

I pause, the weight of his words nagging at me. *Could it possibly be true? Has Arthur somehow trapped me in a loop?*

"What've you done?" I cry. "Arthur—"

Killian tugs on my arm. "Ignore him," he says. "He's lost his mind, and I'm on the cusp of blinking right out of this mortal plane if you and I don't get a move on."

Leaving Arthur behind, Killian and I make our way to the portal, where we clasp our hands together and soar into an unknown future.

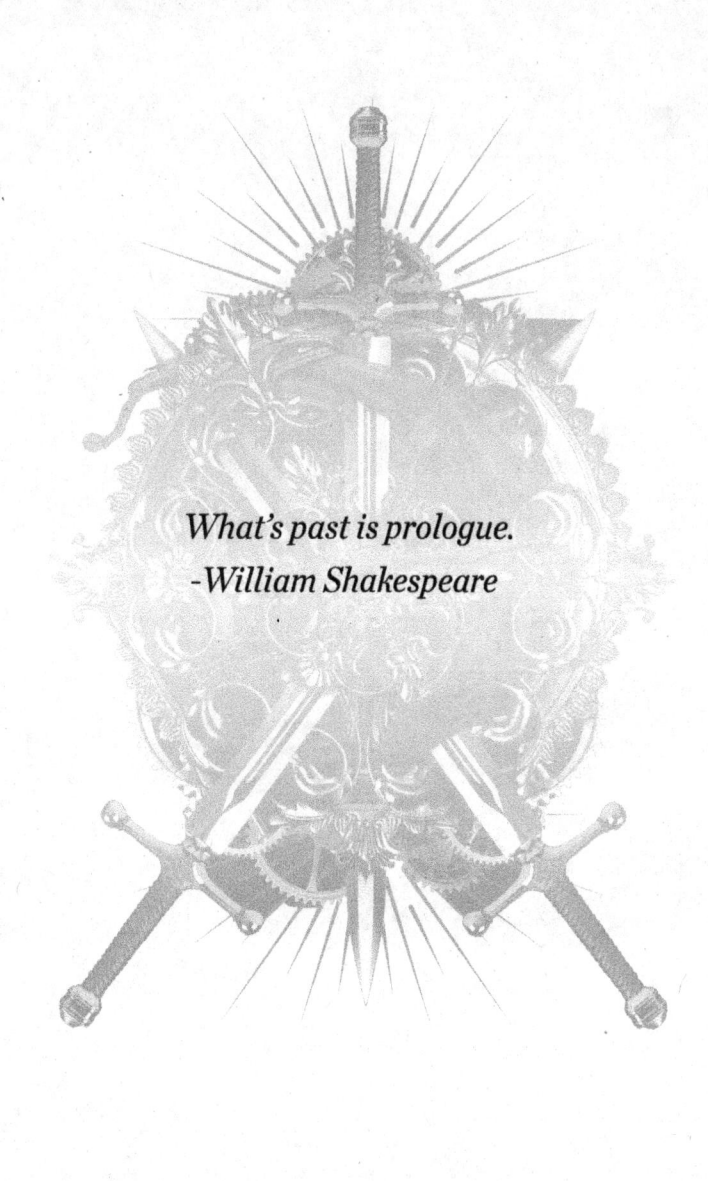

What's past is prologue.
-William Shakespeare

EPILOGUE

Natasha
New York City
Present Day

Three Months Later

I often think back to the day I first arrived in New York. How could I not?

It's the day that marked the end of what little innocence I had left and shattered my belief in my own free will.

When Killian and I arrived in Central Park, Braxton was already there, anxiously waiting for us.

"What the hell?" he said, taking in my torn dress and Killian's chest wound, slowly bleeding out.

"It's a long story," I told him. "But first, he needs help."

"I spotted a cop over there," Killian said. "But you have to pretend you don't know me, so you don't get dragged into this mess. Just tell him you found me like this."

"Yeah, except I'm covered in your blood," I reminded him. "And my clothes aren't exactly a match for this century. Pretty sure he'll put the two together."

Killian groaned in frustration. Turning to Braxton, he said,

"Be a gent, and give the lady your jacket. And Shiv," he adds, "get the hell out of here. Your boy will look out for me."

I shot Braxton a questioning look, not as convinced of his willingness to cooperate as Killian seemed to be.

"You're here because of me," Killian told him. Then, nodding toward me, he said, "A little confirmation might help."

"I'll explain later," I said, responding to Braxton's bewildered look.

"Good," Killian said. "Now that everyone's in sync, you're free to leave, Shiv."

"But what will you do?" I asked, reluctant to abandon him in a city he had no connection to. "Where will you go?"

Killian tried to grin, but his pain precluded him from getting much further than a slight tensing of lips. "I'm a survivor," he said. "Thought you knew that about me. Now, either give me a nice, long kiss goodbye, or be on your way."

"Goodbye, Killian," I said, wondering if it might be the last. "And thank you. For what you did back there. Saving me from Arthur, I mean."

Killian held my gaze, those swimming-pool eyes appearing deeper than I ever imagined they could be. Then, just as he turned away, I heard myself saying, "May the fates be with you." Then I ran like the wind.

Fleeing Belvedere Castle that day felt like escaping a diminutive version of Gray Wolf. I raced through the park, dodged pedestrians on crowded avenues, darted through traffic as I crossed city blocks, until I finally stood before my dad's building.

It looked different than it did back in 1998—it had lost some of its shine, but I knew I had the right place. And, as luck would have it, a food delivery person was exiting just as I arrived, since my dad forgot to give me the front entry key.

"Do you mind holding that?" I asked, motioning toward the door.

He gave me a skeptical look and for a handful of seconds it felt like my fate lay in the balance.

Then, with a casual shrug, he said, "Hurry up already, don't got all day." And I ran up the front steps and made my way in.

To my relief, the key to my dad's apartment still worked. As I ventured inside, I was amazed to find it looked mostly the same, with the addition of several years' worth of cobwebs and dust, of course.

I paused in the entry and bid my dad a silent thanks. "And don't worry," I added, speaking out loud, "I still intend to save you one day."

Then I froze, my own words echoing back at me and giving me pause. I recalled what Braxton's father had said about the dangers of trying to alter one's fate.

But surely my case is different, I thought. Macbeth acted from hubris, and Arthur acted from his inability to reconcile the part he played in the loss of his family.

Whereas I'd be acting from…

From love. Pain. Grief.

Just like Arthur.

Two sides of the same spinning coin.

I shook away the thought, about to make my way to the safe when the door buzzer sounded. Knowing it was Braxton, I rushed to let him in.

He must've tackled the stairs with lightning speed, because when I opened the door, he was already there, waiting for me.

In an instant, he drew me into his arms. I pressed tightly to his chest, breathing in the scent of salt air, stormy seas, and a journey still unknown to me.

"We did it," I said, loving him more than I ever thought possible. Loving him with a love that encompassed my whole heart, the entirety of my soul.

"There was a moment when I thought…" His words trailed

off as his arms tightened around me. "But yeah, we really did it," he whispered into my hair, my ear, the tender hollow at the base of my neck.

Just like the words he'd engraved on the circle of gold at my wrist, I knew we loved with an intensity that could move the sun and other stars.

This seemingly impossible bond that we share had managed to conquer the boundaries of time in order for us to find our way to each other.

Braxton is my miracle, and I am his.

As we crossed the threshold, Braxton's foot swiftly kicked the door closed, sealing us away from the world. In that sanctuary of our making, he turned to me, his gaze alight with the unspoken emotions of our separation.

Without a word, he drew me closer, his hands framing my face with a tenderness that contrasted with the urgent need in those ocean-blue eyes.

Our gazes locked, a silent conversation of longing and relief passing between us before his lips finally found mine.

The kiss was a maelstrom of feelings, deep and fervent, as if we were trying to communicate every moment of absence, every second of yearning.

Through this single connection, his lips moved against mine with an intensity that stirred my soul, igniting a fire that had lain dormant during our time apart. With each caress of his lips, each mingling of breath, we were reaffirming our bond, rediscovering the familiar yet always astonishing territory of each other's taste and touch.

The world outside faded into insignificance, time stood still, and in that moment, there was only two hearts, beating in unison—a testament to the enduring connection that distance could never undo.

When we finally withdrew, I traced a finger down the slight

bend of his nose, then along the newer, small crescent scar marking his neck. A terrible lump formed in my throat when I recalled how it got there.

"And Killian?" I asked, hoping it was the last time I ever had to say that name.

Braxton shrugged. "On his way to the hospital. Apparently, he'll live."

I nodded, surprised by my relief. As much as Killian angered me, he was right—I'm just not the killing type.

"There's so much to tell you," I said. "And I want to hear everything that happened in Greece. But first, I think we should check my dad's safe. He promised to leave a sum of money to help us start our new lives."

Together, we made our way through the hidden door, then through the secret room where I came into my power as a Timekeeper, and finally down the hall to where the Salvador Dalí reproduction still hung in its place.

"*The Persistence of Memory*," Braxton said, glancing between the print and me. "Seems like a strange coincidence, don't you think?"

There's no such thing as coincidence. Everything is connected.

My dad's words echoed in my head, but I just nodded and spun the combination lock, stopping on the numbers that equaled my birthday.

When I heard that telltale click, I looked at Braxton and said, "Ready?"

He gave a quick nod, eyes shining with anticipation.

Without further delay, I swung the door open to find a single white envelope waiting inside.

"It must be a check," I said. "Or perhaps the numbers to an offshore bank account."

With Braxton watching intently, I slid a finger beneath the envelope flap and carefully extracted the item within. My heart pounded as I stared in disbelief.

No.

No-no-no-no-no-no!

How could this be?

Once again, Arthur was ten steps ahead.

With trembling hands and a racing heart, I held it up for Braxton to see.

"My God," he said. It was all he could say.

Instead of a check or a nice wad of cash, it was a single tarot card—The Wheel of Fortune, the tenth card of the Major Arcana. The very card that started it all.

That was the moment when I realized it was true.

Time really is a flat circle.

And I am the red-cloaked girl, endlessly running through a maze with no beginning or end.

Braxton, Elodie, Killian, and I—all of us are caught in an infinite dance, and Arthur is our tireless director.

I may have won the battle, but there will always be another, and then another after that. There's no escaping this destiny, this fated role I never auditioned for.

Now, three months into our New York life, with Braxton's injuries fully healed, and our memories of Gray Wolf fading, I roll onto my side to find Braxton sleeping soundly beside me.

Rising from the bed, I drift to the window, peering into the predawn sky, my fingers instinctively seeking the small golden cage that still hangs from my neck, with its diamond star and lapis moon nestled inside. I recall a passage I once read, proclaiming that in the end, we are all woven from stardust.

That the very atoms that form us once originated from stars that shimmered in the cosmos eons ago.

For some reason I can't quite understand, I find great comfort in that.

As I lower my gaze to the expanse of apartment buildings that now serve as my view, I half expect to see the familiar arrangement of the tarot garden that sprawled before my old window at Gray Wolf—*The Magician*, *The High Priestess*, and *The Wheel of Fortune*, all melding into one another.

According to Mason, whom I saw when I flew to California to visit him and my mom, he, Oliver, and Finn all made it out, and I couldn't be happier for them. Gray Wolf was never their destiny, just an interesting experience on the path of their lives.

As for the rest of us, something tells me we'll never truly leave it behind.

Killian is recovering nicely, and to my surprise, he's decided to stay in New York. Once a week, he, Braxton, and I meet for dinner at his favorite tavern that serves a nice ale and a decent slice of shepherd's pie.

Killian claims that Elodie went back to Gray Wolf. That despite her fondness for Nash, she was never cut out to be anyone's nineteenth-century version of a wife. And though it makes sense, I'm still not entirely sure how Killian could possibly know that.

Unless, of course, he's been back there himself.

Yet another reason we're determined to keep a close eye on him. As the adage goes: *Keep your friends close and your enemies closer.*

Yes, he saved my life, but with Killian, I can never truly know why.

Was it to save me from Arthur?

Or, more likely, was it to save Arthur from committing an act that would put a permanent end to his dream?

As it turns out, my destiny as a Timekeeper didn't end with the destruction of the Antikythera Mechanism.

Apparently, Killian's blade didn't puncture as deeply as we thought. Just enough to stop Arthur, but not enough to finish him off.

And day by day this mark on my arm grows darker, more prominent, morphing into a much deeper shade of gold.

As long as Arthur Blackstone clings to the dream of reuniting his family and controlling time, it'll be up to Braxton and me to stop him.

Just the other day, an envelope appeared in the mail, bearing no return address. Though I knew right away where it came from. It had the red wax seal with the Gray Wolf insignia embossed on its front.

Inside was an article about a mysterious object known as the Roman dodecahedron. According to the piece, it's a small, hollow relic made of bronze or stone, dating back to the second and fourth centuries AD. They'd been found scattered across various parts of the Roman empire, and though their significance is unknown, some speculate...

I stopped reading there, seeing no need to go on.

Clearly, Arthur had found another way to pursue his goal, and it was just a matter of time before he'd come looking for us.

Braxton, awake now, comes up behind me. Circling his arms at my waist, he says, "My darling, are you okay?"

I lean back into his warmth, drawing strength from his steady presence, remembering Arthur's words from what now feels like a lifetime ago.

We are always writing our own stories—all day, every day. It's the ones you choose to play on repeat that determine your destiny.

"I'm more than okay. I'm happy," I say, knowing in my heart that it's true. Braxton and I are in this together, our destinies bound in a circle with no beginning or end. What's not to be happy about?

Since Arthur stole my inheritance, our lives aren't nearly

as easy as we'd hoped. But we are smart, resourceful, and we're making it work in the best way we can. Though the irony isn't lost on me that I have Gray Wolf to thank for this life we've been given.

Still, sometimes, in these early predawn hours, I wake with a start—my skin covered in a panicky sweat, my heart beating much too fast, as my mind repeatedly reminds me that Arthur is out there, safely ensconced in his luxurious fortress, still chasing eternity.

While Braxton and I bide our time here, waiting for the day when he'll snatch us off the street, put us into a hypnotic trance, and settle us back into his circular world, where all endings are nothing more than beginnings.

Someday, we'll find a way to vanquish him once and for all.

I know in my heart that it's true.

And yet, every now and then, a slim thread of doubt manages to creep its way in, just like it does now.

"What will we do?" I say, leaning deeper into Braxton's embrace.

Pressing a kiss to my cheek, then the side of my neck, Braxton replies in the same way he always does.

"We'll do the only thing we ever can do," he says. "We'll keep moving toward the light, ensuring the shadows always remain well behind us."

THE END

ACKNOWLEDGMENTS

Wow, what a journey this has been! When I first started writing this series, the pandemic was raging, and I created the world of Gray Wolf Academy to escape the uncertainty and fear of that time. Now, three books later, the story has come to an end.

I'd like to thank all the lovely readers who have joined me on this journey. Your enthusiasm and support mean the world to me.

Speaking of the world, thank you to my international publishers and translators for taking Natasha and her story to places far and wide.

I also want to extend my deepest gratitude to Elizabeth Bewley, who was with me as an editor for my very first book and now as my agent for my 30th.

And, of course, much thanks to the entire Entangled team, including but not limited to: Liz Pelletier, Stacy Abrams, Alice Jerman, Nancy Cantor, Bree Archer, Meredith Johnson, Jessica Turner, Riki Cleveland, Heather Riccio, Curtis Svehlak. It's been a pleasure working with you all.

And lastly, thanks to Sandy, my very own Renaissance man.

Chasing Eternity is the action-packed grand finale to a time-twisting young adult series that will have readers on the edge of their seats. However, the story includes elements that might not be suitable for all readers. Assault, theft, death of a parent, death of a spouse, sexual assault, physical illness, self-harm, and parental abandonment are mentioned or shown in the novel. Readers who may be sensitive to these elements, please take note.

Welcome back into the Mist...in the astonishing sequel to the instant *New York Times* bestseller *To Kill a Shadow*...

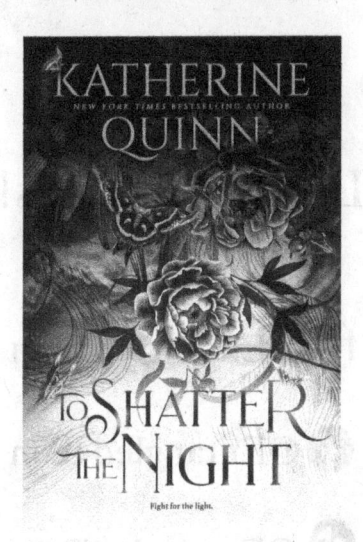

Some fear the darkness. It's the place where horror hides, concealing its rank, sharp teeth and insatiable hunger. But there is no darkness more feared than that of the mist that's overtaken the kingdom...and its brave — and ultimately doomed — soldiers.

Except for Kiara Frey.

She has nothing to fear from the night. *Not anymore.*

Driven by the fury of her splintered heart, Kiara knows that the answers — and the only possible way to a future with Jude Maddox — begin with the realm's most notorious thief, the Fox. Together, they hunt down the path to breaking Asidia's dark curse, but in the shadows, something more horrifying than the mist lies in wait. *Watching.* Willing Kiara to find the game pieces set in place long ago.

As Jude and Kiara are lured to a sacred temple — a shrine that is the home to both exquisite dreams and chilling nightmares — Kiara's newfound powers flourish but her shadows threaten to consume her.

Because here in these cursed lands, it's not the darkness that destroys the soul...*it's love.*

Let's be friends!

@EntangledTeen

@EntangledTeen

@EntangledTeen

bit.ly/TeenNewsletter

entangled teen